For Neetha

Parting Shot

LINWOOD BARCLAY

An Orion paperback

First published in Great Britain in 2017
by Orion Books
This paperback edition published in 2017
by Orion Books,
an imprint of The Orion Publishing Group Ltd,
Carmelite House, 50 Victoria Embankment
London EC4Y 0DZ

An Hachette UK company

1 3 5 7 9 10 8 6 4 2

Copyright © NJSB Entertainment Inc. 2017

A CIP catalogue record for this book
is available from the British Library.

ISBN 978 1 4091 6395 4

Typeset by Input Data Services Ltd, Somerset

Printed in Great Britain by Clays Ltd, St Ives plc

MIX
Paper from
responsible sources
FSC® C104740

www.orionbooks.co.uk

Praise for Linwood Barclay

'Nothing is more satisfying than tucking into a new Linwood Barclay novel' Shari Lapena, author of *The Couple Next Door*

'One of the best thriller writers in the world hands down' Mark Billingham

'A suspense master' Stephen King

'No one can thrill you and chill you better than Linwood Barclay' Tess Gerritsen

'Seamless, breathless and relentlessly paced, Barclay barely puts a foot wrong' *Mirror*

'Some days, all you really want is for someone to tell you a wicked-good story. Linwood Barclay answers the reader's perpetual prayer' *New York Times*

'Barclay takes the didn't-see-it-coming twist to cosmic levels' *Financial Times*

'Barclay's great talent is to infuse the most everyday things with extraordinary menace' *Daily Mail*

Linwood Barclay is the multi-million copy international bestselling author of thirteen novels, including the Richard & Judy Summer Read winner and number one bestseller, *No Time for Goodbye*. He lives near Toronto with his wife where they raised two children and is a former columnist for the *Toronto Star*.

To find out more about Linwood and his books, follow him on Twitter @linwood_barclay or Facebook f/linwoodbarclay or visit his website www.linwoodbarclay.com

By Linwood Barclay

No Time for Goodbye
Too Close to Home
Fear the Worst
Never Look Away
The Accident
Trust Your Eyes
Never Saw It Coming
A Tap on the Window
No Safe House
Broken Promise
Far From True
The Twenty-Three

THE ZACK WALKER MYSTERIES
Bad Move
Bad Guys
Bad Luck (*published in the US as* Lone Wolf)
Bad News *published in the US as* Stone Rain)

ONE

CAL WEAVER

I ran into someone on the street in Promise Falls the other day, a woman who knew me back when I was a cop here, before I left for Griffon, near Buffalo, and became a private investigator.

She said, "Oh, I didn't know you'd moved back. How's Donna? And your boy? Scott, isn't it?"

I never quite know how to answer questions like this. But I said, "I'm kind of on my own now."

She gave me a sympathetic look and nodded knowingly. "These things happen," she said. "I hope it was all amicable, that you're all still talking."

I gave her the best smile I could muster. "We talk every night," I told her.

She smiled back. "Well, that's good then, isn't it?"

TWO

Detective Barry Duckworth of the Promise Falls Police was sitting at his desk when his phone rang. He snatched up the receiver.

"Duckworth," he said.

"It's Bayliss." Trent Bayliss, the sergeant on the desk where people walked into the station.

"Yeah."

"I got a live one here." Bayliss was unable to hide the amusement in his voice.

"What're you talking about?"

"Guy got picked up wandering around downtown. Once they brought him in, he said he needed to talk to a detective. So I'm sending him your way. Says his name is Gaffney. Brian Gaffney. But he's got no ID on him."

"What's his story?" Duckworth asked.

"It's better if you hear it from him. I wouldn't want to spoil the fun." Bayliss hung up.

Wearily, Barry Duckworth cradled the receiver. Maybe Bayliss was amused, but Barry wasn't. He didn't view the job quite the way he used to. A little more than a year ago, he'd nearly died in the performance of his duties, and it had changed not only how he saw his work, but the world around him.

He liked to think he'd stopped taking things for granted. He knew it was something of a cliché, but he saw each day as a gift. Every morning, he thought back to those moments when he'd nearly had the life snuffed out of him. Took him a while to get back on his feet, too. There was a stint in the hospital, even a little plastic surgery on his face.

Perhaps the most amazing thing was, in the last year he'd actually lost some weight. He'd been about two-eighty fourteen months ago, but was now down to two hundred and thirty-three pounds. According to his calculations, that was forty-seven pounds. For a while he'd been putting new holes in his belt and just drawing his regular pants on tighter, but his wife, Maureen, said he was starting to look ridiculous. She'd dragged him to the men's shop, like he was five years old or something, and bought him some new clothes.

But he'd kept his old ones in the closet. Just in case. There might come a time when he once again found the temptations of Dunkin' Donuts too great to resist.

It had been some time since he'd had one of those.

And he wasn't going to lie. He *missed* them. But he liked being alive, and healthier, even more.

Maureen had been tremendously supportive. She'd already been trying to get him to change his eating habits. Immediately after the incident, she was so happy he wasn't dead that she spoiled him with homemade cakes and pies—no one made a lemon meringue pie like Maureen—but it was Barry who told her to stop. He'd made up his mind, he told her. He was going to take charge of his health. He was going to look after himself.

Which explained the banana sitting on his desk. The brown banana, which had been there since yesterday.

While Barry Duckworth knew what he wanted to do where his health was concerned, he was less sure about his career. It was in his role as a police detective that he had nearly died.

He wondered whether he should do something else. The trouble was, he didn't know what else to do.

He'd been a cop more than twenty years. It wasn't like he could go back to school at this stage and become a dentist. Okay, maybe not a dentist. He didn't understand why anyone would want to become a dentist. He'd rather attend a hundred murder scenes than have to stick his fingers into someone's mouth. But an accountant, now there was a nice, safe job. No one beat your face to a pulp for being an accountant.

While Duckworth coped with the fallout of nearly losing his life, the town itself was struggling to return to normal. Hundreds of Promise Falls' finest—and some not so fine—had died in a catastrophe the year before. People had never stopped talking about what happened, but now you could go an entire day, sometimes even two, without someone bringing it up.

The out-of-towners were the real problem. It was, on a much smaller scale of course, a bit like after the Twin Towers came down, when tourists wanted their picture taken at Ground Zero. This upstate New York locale had become the poster town for revenge, and almost daily someone could be spotted taking a selfie by the "Welcome to Promise Falls" sign.

Duckworth leaned back in his office chair, keeping his eye on the door to the detectives' room. It opened and a man stood there, staring in, a look of bewilderment on his face.

He probably topped out at one hundred and twenty pounds. Skinny, white, early twenties, about five feet nine inches tall. Closely cropped black hair, about three days' worth of whiskers on his face. He wore jeans and a dark blue long-sleeved shirt with a button-down collar.

He scanned the room, his eyes darting nervously. Duck-worth stood up.

"Mr. Gaffney?"

The man looked at Duckworth, blinked. "That's me."

Duckworth waved him in, pointed to the chair next to his desk. "Why don't you have a seat."

Brian Gaffney, holding his hands together in front of him, leaning over slightly, as though trying to close in on himself, sat down. He kept looking around the room, up at the ceiling, like someone entering a cave, checking for bats clinging to the roof.

"Mr. Gaffney?"

Gaffney's fearful eyes settled on Duckworth. "Yes?"

"I'm a detective." He had a pen in his hand, ready to make some notes. "Can you spell your name for me, Mr. Gaffney?"

Gaffney did so.

"And your middle name?"

"Arthur," he said. "Are we safe here?"

"I'm sorry?"

Gaffney's head movements were brief, quick twitches, like a bird taking in its surroundings. He lowered his voice to a whisper as he leaned in closer to the detective. "They might still be watching me."

Duckworth put a hand lightly on the man's arm. Gaff-ney examined it, as though not sure what it was.

"You're okay here," Duckworth assured him, think-ing, only Bayliss would see this man as a source of amusement. Whatever Gaffney was afraid of might be imaginary, but the fear Duckworth saw in the man's eyes was the real deal.

Gaffney shivered. "You need to turn the heat up."

The room was already in the high seventies. The A/C should have kicked in, but had not.

Duckworth stood, slipped off his jacket, and draped it over the man's shoulders. "How's that?"

Gaffney nodded.

"You want a coffee?" the detective asked. "That might warm you up."

Quietly, Gaffney said, "Okay."

"What do you take?'

"I . . . It doesn't matter, long as it's hot."

Duckworth crossed the room to the table where they kept the coffee machine, filled a reasonably clean mug, put in one sugar and a powdered creamer, and brought it back to the man.

Gaffney wrapped both hands around the mug, brought it to his lips and took a sip as Duckworth sat back down and picked up his pen again. "What's your date of birth, Mr. Gaffney?"

"April sixteenth, 1995." Gaffney watched as Duckworth scribbled things down. "I was born in New Haven."

"Current address?"

"They might be here," Gaffney said, lowering his voice again. "They might be cloaking themselves in human form."

Duckworth's pen stopped moving. "Who's they, Mr. Gaffney?"

Gaffney blinked and said, "I live at 87 Hunter Street. Unit 201."

Duckworth felt a touch of mental whiplash. "That's an apartment?"

"Yeah."

"You live alone, Mr. Gaffney?"

"Yes." Another nod. Gaffney's eyes were now fixed on the banana on Duckworth's desk.

"What do you do for a living?"

"Detailing. Are you going to eat that?"

Duckworth glanced at the brown piece of fruit. "Uh, you want it?"

"I don't think they fed me. I haven't eaten for a long time."

Duckworth picked up the banana and handed it to Gaffney, who took it gently in his hands, then shoved one end of it into his mouth without bothering to peel it. He bit hard so his teeth went through the skin. He chewed quickly, took another large bite, still with the peel on.

Still chewing, he said, "You know what detailing is?"

Duckworth, distracted by what he'd just seen, said, "Sorry?"

"Detailing." He swallowed the last of the banana, washed it down with some coffee. "You know what it is?"

"No."

"Like, instead of just getting your car washed, you get it detailed. Like a super- super-cleaning. I work at Albany Detailing."

"So, that's in Albany?"

The man shook his head. "No, here in Promise Falls. It's a franchise thing."

"Mr. Gaffney, the police found you wandering around downtown. When they brought you in, you said you wanted to talk to a detective."

"That's right."

"So how can I help you?"

"I made a mistake," he said.

"What do you mean?"

Gaffney surveyed the room for what had to be the tenth time, then whispered to Duckworth, "It's not your jurisdiction."

"I'm sorry."

"I mean, what can you do?" Gaffney shrugged. "Arrest them?"

"Arrest who?"

"What day is this?"

"This is Wednesday."

Gaffney gave that some thought. "So . . . two nights. I went out Monday night, and now it's Wednesday, so two nights. Unless it's, like, the *next* Wednesday, and it's been nine days."

Duckworth had put his pen down. "Two nights what?"

"That they had me." He put down the mug, ran his hand over his chin, felt stubble. "It must be just two. If they had me nine days, I'd almost have a beard by now."

Duckworth's brow wrinkled. "What do you mean, they had you?"

"I think I was abducted," Gaffney said, running his tongue over his lips. "You know about Betty and Barney Hill?"

Duckworth quickly wrote down the names. "They abducted you?"

Gaffney shook his head. "No, they were in a book. Real people. I've got an old paperback copy of it. *The Interrupted Journey*, by John G. Fuller. It happened to them, too."

"What happened, Brian?"

"They were driving at night from Niagara Falls back to their home in New Hampshire on September twentieth,

8

1961. This part of the country, you know? They'd have passed within forty miles of Promise Falls."

"Okay."

"He was black, and she was white, although that really doesn't have anything to do with what happened to them. Unless it did."

"Go on."

"So the Hills saw this bright light in the sky, and the next thing they knew, it was hours later, and they were on the road, almost home. There was all this time they couldn't account for. So they went to a hypnotist."

"What'd they think the hypnotist could do?"

"Help them remember what happened to them during those missing hours."

"And did he?"

Gaffney nodded. "They were taken aboard a ship. The aliens experimented on them, put needles and other things into them, and then made them forget it had ever happened." He shook his head slowly, wonderingly. "I never thought something like that could happen to me."

Duckworth said, "Okay. So you're saying you have two days you can't account for?"

"Yes." Gaffney trembled, as though he'd had a momentary electrical shock, and took another sip of coffee.

"What's the last thing you remember?"

"I'd gone into Knight's for a couple of drinks, like, around eight? You know Knight's?"

Ah, Duckworth thought. Knight's. One of the town's best-known bars.

"I know it," the detective said.

"I had a few beers, watched TV. It gets a little blurry after that."

"How many beers?"

9

He shrugged. "Four, five. That's, like, over an hour and a half or so."

"You're sure you didn't have more than that?"

"That's all."

"You drive yourself there?"

Strong head-shake. "Nope. I can walk to Knight's from my place. Don't want to worry about getting pulled over. Do you have another banana?"

"I don't. I'm sorry. Just a couple more questions and I'll find you something. You remember leaving Knight's?"

"Maybe. When I came out, I think someone called to me from the alley next to the bar. You can walk through there to get to a parking lot out back."

"Was this a man or a woman who called out to you?"

"A woman, I think. At least, it was in the form of a woman."

Duckworth let that go. "What did she say?"

Gaffney shook his head. "It's all pretty foggy. And then there's almost nothing for two days, until I wake up right back in the same place. I guess I stumbled out of the alley, was walking around, and that was when the cops found me. I didn't have any ID on me. My wallet's gone, and my cell phone, too."

"Is it possible you were in the alley for those two days?"

Gaffney slowly shook his head again. "People walk down there all the time. Someone would have noticed me. And they couldn't have done the experiments on me there."

His breathing became more rapid. "What if they infected me? What if they gave me some disease?" He set down the mug again, placed a palm on his chest. "What if I'm a carrier? What if I've exposed you? Jesus, oh man."

Duckworth kept his voice level. "Let's not get ahead of ourselves, Brian. We're going to get you checked out. Why would you think you'd been experimented on?"

"They . . . took me someplace. It might have been a ship, but I don't think so. There were lights, and I was lying down on a bed or something, on my stomach. I remember it smelled bad. That's where they did it."

"What did they do?"

"It felt like hundreds and hundreds of needles going into me. Probably taking samples, you know? DNA, maybe?"

His face began to crumple. He looked up, as though looking past the ceiling to the heavens above.

"Why me!" he shouted. "Why did it have to be me!"

A couple of other detectives sitting at desks across the room looked over. Duckworth put his hand back on the man's arm. "Brian, look at me. Look at me."

Gaffney lowered his gaze to look into Duckworth's eyes. "I'm sorry if coming here was the wrong thing."

"It wasn't. I'm going to try to help you. Let's get back to those needles. Why do you think that was done to you?"

"My back," Gaffney said. "It's really sore. It feels all scratchy, you know? Stings like hell."

Duckworth, with some hesitation, said, "You want me to have a look?"

Gaffney hesitated as well, as though he wasn't sure he wanted to know. After a moment, he said, "If you don't mind."

They both stood. Gaffney turned his back to Duckworth, untucked and unbuttoned his shirt, then yanked it up over his shoulders.

"How's that?" he asked.

Duckworth stared. "That'll do."

Tattooed crudely on Gaffney's back, in black letters two inches tall, was:

IM THE
SICK FUCK
WHO KILLED
SEAN

Duckworth said, "Mr. Gaffney, who's Sean?"

"Sean?" he said.

"Yeah, Sean."

Gaffney's shoulders rose and fell as he shrugged. "I don't know nobody named Sean. How come?"

THREE

CAL

I knew the name Madeline Plimpton.

She was old-stock Promise Falls. I wasn't exactly an expert on the town's history, but I knew the Plimptons were among those who'd established the town back in the 1800s. I knew they'd founded the town's first newspaper, the *Standard*, and that Madeline Plimpton had the distinct honor of presiding over its death.

I didn't know why she wanted to see me. She wouldn't say in our phone call. Clients don't usually want to talk about these things over the phone. It's hard enough doing it in person.

"It's delicate," she explained.

It usually was.

I wouldn't call her place a mansion, but it was pretty upscale for Promise Falls. A Victorian-style home built back in the twenties, probably four or five thousand square feet, set well back from the street, with a circular driveway. It was the kind of place that, at one time, would have had a black jockey lawn ornament out front. If it had ever actually had one, someone'd had the good sense to get rid of it.

I was behind the wheel of my new, aging Honda. I'd traded in my very old Accord for a merely old Accord. This one was equipped with a manual transmission, and shifting through the gears allowed me to imagine myself as someone younger and sportier. My first car, some thirty years ago, had been a Toyota Celica with a four-speed stick shift. Every car I'd had since had been automatic, until now.

I parked out front of the main double doors, my car outclassed by a black Lexus SUV, a white four-door Acura sedan, and a BMW 7 Series. The combined value of those three cars probably exceeded my total income for the last two decades.

I was half expecting a maid or butler to materialize after I pressed the bell, but it was Madeline Plimpton herself who opened the door and invited me in.

I put her at about seventy. She was a thin, nice-looking woman, bordering on regal, dressed in black slacks and a black silk top, a tasteful strand of pearls at her neck. Her well-tended silver hair came down to the base of her neck, and she eyed me through a pair of gold-rimmed glasses.

"Thank you for coming, Mr. Weaver," she said.

"My pleasure. Please call me Cal."

She did not invite me to call her Madeline.

She led me from the front hall into the dining room, where things had been set up for tea. China cups, milk and sugar cubes in silver servers.

"Can I pour you a cup of tea?" she asked.

"Thank you," I said.

She poured, then took a seat at the head of the table. I pulled up a chair near the end, to her right.

"I've heard good things about you," she said.

"I suppose, as a former newspaper publisher, you have good sources," I said, smiling.

I caught her briefly wincing and thought it was my use of the word *former*. "I do. I know just about everyone in this town. I know you used to work for the police here. That you made a mistake, moved away for a few years to Griffon, where you set yourself up as a private investigator, and then came back." She paused. "After a personal tragedy."

"Yes," I said.

"You've been back here a couple of years."

"Yes." I dropped a sugar cube into my tea. "So I guess I passed the background check. What seems to be the problem?"

Ms. Plimpton drew a long breath, then raised her cup to her lips and blew on it. The tea was hot.

"It's about my grand-nephew," she said.

"Okay."

"My niece's son. It's been quite a year for them."

I waited.

"My niece and her son live in Albany. But life for them there has become untenable."

I was pretty sure I knew what that word meant.

"And why would that be?" I asked.

Another pause. "Jeremy—that's my grand-nephew— had some issues with the courts this year that attracted an unfortunate degree of attention. It's made life very difficult for him there. Some people who don't seem to have much appreciation of the justice system have been harassing Jeremy and my niece, Gloria. Late-night phone calls, eggs thrown at the house. Someone even left a death threat in the mailbox. It was written in crayon on a piece of paper that had been smeared with excrement, if you can imagine such a thing."

"What do you mean by 'some issues,' Ms. Plimpton?"

"A traffic mishap. It got blown out of proportion. I

15

mean, I'm not suggesting it wasn't a tragedy, but the fallout has just been over the top."

"Ms. Plimpton, maybe you should start at the beginning."

Her head made a tiny side-to-side motion. "I don't see that that's necessary. I'm interested in engaging your services, and it's not important for you to know all the details. Although I can tell you that Gloria is almost more a daughter to me than a niece. She came to live with me when she was a teenager, so our relationship is . . ."

I was waiting for her to say "closer."

"Complicated," Ms. Plimpton said at last.

"I don't know what service it is you expect me to perform," I said.

"I want you to protect Jeremy."

"What do you mean, protect? You mean you want me to be his bodyguard?"

"Yes, I suppose that would be part of it. I'd want you to assess his security situation and, as you say, perform bodyguard duties."

"I'm not a bodyguard. Maybe what you need is a bouncer."

Madeline Plimpton sighed. "Well, perhaps you don't think of yourself that way, technically. But you are a former policeman. You've dealt with criminal elements. I would think that being a bodyguard really wouldn't be straying all that much from what you actually do. And I'm perfectly prepared to pay you round-the-clock for as long as your services might be required. One of the reasons I chose you was because I understand you have—I don't mean to be insensitive here, Mr. Weaver—but I understand you have no family. It wouldn't be disruptive in ways that it might be to someone else."

I wasn't sure I liked Madeline Plimpton. But then again, in my line of work, if you only worked for people you wanted to be friends with, you wouldn't eat.

"How old is Jeremy?" I asked.

"Eighteen," she said.

"And what's his last name?"

She bit her lip briefly. "Pilford," she said, almost in a whisper.

I blinked. "Jeremy Pilford? Your grand-nephew is Jeremy Pilford?"

She nodded. "I take it that you are familiar with the name."

The entire country was familiar with the name.

"The Big Baby," I said.

Madeline Plimpton winced more noticeably this time. She looked as though I'd poured my hot tea over her veined hand.

"I wish you hadn't said that. Those words were never used in his defense. That was something the prosecution came up with and the press ran with, and it was insulting. It was demeaning. Not just to Jeremy, but to Gloria, too. It reflected very badly on her."

"But it came out of the defense strategy, didn't it, Ms. Plimpton? It's basically what Jeremy's lawyer was saying. That was the argument. That Jeremy had been so pampered, so excused from ever having to do things for himself, from ever having to accept responsibility for any of his actions his entire life, that he couldn't imagine that he was doing anything wrong when he—"

"I know what he did."

"When he went out partying, got behind the wheel totally under the influence, and killed someone. With all respect, Ms. Plimpton, that's not what I would character-ize as a traffic mishap."

"Maybe you're not the right person for this job."

"Maybe I'm not," I said, setting down my cup and pushing back my chair. "Thank you for the tea."

She reached out a hand. "Wait."

I waited.

"Please," she said.

I pulled my chair back in, rested my hands on the top of the dining room table.

"I suppose it's reasonable to expect that your reaction is unlikely to be any different from that of anyone else I might approach. Jeremy has not been good at winning people over. But it was the judge's decision not to send him to jail. It was the judge who decided to put the boy on probation. It was the judge who was persuaded by Mr. Finch that—"

"Mr. Finch?"

"Jeremy's lawyer, whom you just referenced. Grant Finch. It was Mr. Finch who came up with the defense strategy, and to be honest, no one had high hopes that the judge would find it convincing. But we were ecstatic when he did. Sending Jeremy to jail would have been a terrible thing for the boy. After all, he is still a boy. He'd never have survived prison. And as horrible as the backlash to the sentence has been, it's still better than Jeremy being behind bars."

"Except now he's living in fear," I said.

Madeline Plimpton offered a small nod of acknowl-edgment. "That's true, but these things pass. Jeremy could have gone to jail for several years. Social conster-nation over his sentencing will last a few months at most, I should think. The world is always waiting for the new thing to be outraged by. A hunter who kills a prize lion in Africa. A woman who tweets a joke about AIDS. A dimwitted politician who thinks a woman's body knows how to shut down pregnancy following rape. That other judge, who gave the light sentence to the boy who raped that unconscious girl. We are so thrilled to be angered about something that we want a new target for our rage every week. Jeremy will be forgotten about, eventually, and he *will* be able to return to a normal life. But in the meantime, he needs to be safe."

I wondered about when the family of the person Jeremy had killed would get back to a normal life, but decided not to pose the question out loud.

"So yes, to your earlier comment, he was branded the Big Baby. A teenager who was coddled as though he were an infant. The prosecuting attorney mentioned it once in passing, and the media loved it. CNN turned Jeremy into a flashy logo. The Big Baby Case, with lots of jazzy graphics."

"As someone who once ran a newspaper, you must have some understanding of how those things happen."

"Indeed," she said. "But just because I owned a media outlet does not mean I approve of everything the media does."

"I really don't know that I can help you, Ms. Plimpton," I said. "But I could probably recommend some agencies to you. Ones that don't really do much in the way of investigations, as I do. They're more like tough guys for hire."

"I don't want Jeremy surrounded by a bunch of thugs."

I shrugged.

"Would you at least meet with them?" she asked. "With Jeremy and my niece? At least meet them and then make a decision about whether you want the job? I'm sure once you spoke with them, you'd realize they aren't the caricatures they've been made out to be. They're real people, Mr. Weaver. And they're frightened."

I got out my notepad and pen from the inside pocket of my sport jacket. I uncapped the pen.

"Why don't you give me their address in Albany?" I said.

"Oh, there's no need for that," Ms. Plimpton said. "They're here. They've been here for a few days now. They're out back, on the porch, waiting to talk to you."

FOUR

Barry Duckworth wanted Brian Gaffney to get checked out at the hospital, so he offered to drive him to Promise Falls General. That would also give the detective an opportunity to ask the man more questions about what might have happened to him. Any thoughts Duckworth had that Gaffney's two-day blackout was alcohol-induced vanished when he had a look at the words inked into his back.

IM THE SICK FUCK WHO KILLED SEAN did not sound like the kind of tattoo any remotely rational person—or even a blind-drunk person—would choose to have permanently etched into his skin.

If Gaffney had any notion of what was on his back, he gave no indication. So Duckworth took a photo while he still had his shirt pulled up to his neck, and showed it to him.

"Jesus," he said. "That . . . that doesn't make any sense to me."

"I think," Duckworth said gently, "this rules out your theory of what happened to you."

Gaffney had the look of a four-year-old trying to grasp a Stephen Hawking lecture. "I don't . . . That doesn't seem like the kind of thing the aliens would do."

"Yeah," Duckworth said. "We're looking for someone more earthbound here."

Gaffney, still stunned by the photo, nodded slowly. "I'm sorry."

"Sorry?"

"I must seem crazy. I'm not crazy, you know."

"Sure," Duckworth said.

"I mean, I'm a little *off*. That's what my dad says. But not crazy. You know what I mean?"

"Sure."

"I just couldn't think of any other explanation. Maybe I've been reading too many books about UFOs." He took another look at the photo on the detective's phone. "Are you sure that's a real tattoo? It's not just marker or something that'll come off?"

"I don't think so."

"It's on there *permanent*?"

"I'm no expert on tattoos," Duckworth said. "Maybe there's something you can do." But he had his doubts. "Any idea who'd do that to you?"

Gaffney looked away from the image, allowing Duckworth to put the phone into his pocket. Tears welled up in his eyes. He bit his lip. "No. I mean, the alien thing would actually have made more sense. That they'd grab some random guy and do tests on him. But this, this is totally crazy."

"Come on," Duckworth said gently. "Let's get you checked out."

On the way out to Duckworth's unmarked cruiser, the detective asked, "You got family, Brian? Parents? Brothers, sisters? A girlfriend?"

He spoke slowly and softly. "My folks live over on Montcalm. I got my own place about six months ago. They thought—my dad thought—it was time for me to try living on my own, you know? So I found a room in this two-story building downtown. I got one sister. Monica. She's nineteen. She'd like to move out but she can't afford to yet."

"How long have you been in Promise Falls?"

"Like, fifteen years. Ever since my parents moved here from Connecticut."

"Girlfriend?"

"Kinda. There's this one girl. She came in for a car wash and we kind of hit it off."

"What's her name?"

"Jesse. Like, Jessica Frommer."

"When's the last time you saw her?"

Brian pondered the question. "Maybe a week? We've been out a few times, mostly out of town or my place. I think, actually, I was supposed to call her yesterday." He looked overwhelmed. "Shit, she'll be wondering what happened to me."

"You can't think of anyone—a friend, a friend of a friend, someone in your extended family—named Sean? A man or a woman?"

"Nothing," he said. "Can I see the picture again?"

Duckworth took out his phone and brought up the photo. Gaffney stared at it and said, "I keep thinking it can't really be there. That this isn't really happening. That this isn't a picture of my back. Who could Sean be?" He returned the phone. "I've been turned into some kind of freak."

On the way to the hospital, Duckworth did a spin through a McDonald's drive-through, buying Gaffney a coffee and a biscuit stuffed with egg and sausage. The man downed it nearly as quickly as he'd consumed the ripe banana.

The Promise Falls General ER wasn't crowded. Gaffney was seen within ten minutes. Duckworth quickly briefed the doctor—a young Indian-looking man named Dr. Charles—and said he wanted to speak with him after the examination. Then the detective stepped outside where he could get a decent signal on his cell phone, and opened up a browser.

He entered the words "Sean" and "homicide" and waited. Over a million results, but the first few screens didn't turn up anything that looked relevant. Some of the hits were crime books or newspaper articles about homicides, written by someone with the first name Sean. He narrowed the search by adding the words "Promise Falls", but that produced nothing.

He went back into the ER and took a seat. A few minutes later, Brian Gaffney reappeared with Dr. Charles.

"May I discuss your particulars with the police officer?" the doctor asked.

Gaffney nodded wearily.

"Mr. Gaffney's general health seems to be okay," Dr. Charles said. "He's still a bit groggy from whatever was used to render him unconscious."

"Any idea what that might have been?"

The doctor shook his head. "But I'd like to keep him here for observation and blood tests. Do you have any idea who tattooed him? If you did, we could find out about their safety precautions, if they used proper sterilization techniques."

"We don't know," the detective said.

Dr. Charles made a clicking noise with his tongue. "Well, if the equipment used was contaminated with infected blood, Mr. Gaffney could be at risk of hepatitis B, hepatitis C or tetanus."

"Ah, man," Gaffney said.

"I'm around if you have any more questions," the doctor said, excusing himself.

Duckworth put a comforting hand on Brian's arm. "I want to take your picture," he said.

"Huh?"

"I'm going to go to Knight's, see if anyone remembers seeing you."

Gaffney nodded resignedly. Duckworth took a quick head shot with his phone, glanced at it to make sure it was acceptable. "You want me to get in touch with your parents?"

Gaffney thought about that. "I guess," he said finally.

"Why so hesitant?"

"I'm . . ."

"What is it, Brian?"

"I guess . . . I'm embarrassed. I'm ashamed of what's happened to me."

"It's not your fault," Duckworth said, although he didn't know that for certain. Maybe Brian had consumed far more alcohol than he'd let on. Maybe he'd allowed someone to do this to him, but had no memory of it. But his gut told him that wasn't the case.

Gaffney half shrugged. "I guess you should let them know."

Duckworth had him write down his parents' Montcalm Street address and phone number on his notepad. He decided he'd go there before heading to Knight's. He was just pulling out of the ER parking lot when his phone rang. It was Maureen.

"Hey," he said to her over the Bluetooth. "You at work?"

"Yeah. We've got a bit of a lull." Maureen worked at an eyeglasses shop in the Promise Falls mall. "Am I calling at a bad time?"

"It's okay."

"How are you?"

It was an innocent enough question. She'd always asked how he was when she called. But now, when she asked, he knew she was asking him something more. She was really asking how he was *doing*. She was asking how he *felt*. She was asking how he was *managing*.

Even ten months after returning to the job.

Not that he didn't ask himself every day how he was doing.

"I'm fine," he said quickly. "What's up?"

"Nothing," she said.

But he could tell from her tone that it was something, and her most frequent source of worry, after him, was their son, Trevor. Twenty-five now, back living at home with his parents, and looking for work.

He'd had a job driving a truck for Finley Springs Water. Randall Finley, the owner, had been mayor a decade ago, but was voted out after his dalliances with an underage prostitute became public. He'd made a comeback last year, though, after becoming something of a local hero, and presided over city hall once again.

Wonders never ceased. Nor, Duckworth thought, did the public's willingness to be conned.

Trevor—like his father—despised Finley and everything he stood for, and when he found another driving gig with a local lumber company, he quit the water bottling plant. But with the housing industry still taking its time to recover, and the demand for building supplies weak, he was laid off three months later. He kept his apartment another six weeks, but with money running out, he'd given his notice and moved back in with Mom and Dad while he looked for something else.

Of course, Barry and Maureen could have kept their

son in his apartment by paying his rent, but that had struck both of them as an open-ended commitment they could not afford, so they'd offered him his old room. They had mixed feelings when he took them up on it, but as it turned out, even with Trevor living under the same roof with them, they saw little of him. He was out most evenings, and returned home after Barry and Maureen had turned out their lights.

Trouble was, they often lay awake until he came home, as if he were still a teenager with a curfew. When your kids no longer lived with you, Duckworth said, you didn't care what their hours were. But when they were back sharing quarters with you, you couldn't help but wonder, and worry, what they were up to.

"Is it Trevor?" he asked now.

He heard Maureen sigh. "He doesn't seem himself these days."

"Like how?"

"You haven't noticed?"

"I don't know what you're talking about."

"Aren't cops supposed to be keen observers of human behavior?"

Duckworth wasn't sure whether she was needling him or being serious. Maybe both.

"We're distant second to mothers in that area," he said.

"Sure, patronize me," Maureen said.

"I'm not patronizing you."

"You are. You think I'm being overly concerned."

"Tell me what you've seen that I've been too dumb to notice."

"Okay, it's not anything specific. But he seems more withdrawn, more to himself."

"He's got a lot on his mind," Barry said. "He's looking

for work, and living with his parents. How much fun can that be?"

"He spends a lot of time on the computer."

"He's probably looking at job ads. It's not like you can find them in the paper any more."

"I suppose so."

They'd both wondered if Trevor needed to go back to school. Learn some kind of trade. After traveling around Europe with a girlfriend, he'd gone to Syracuse University and taken political science, and done well with it. Graduated. No one expected him to become a politician, or work for one, but they'd hoped his field of study would lead to something more challenging than driving a truck for that narcissistic asshole who was now the mayor of Promise Falls.

"I wish I had some idea where he goes off to every night," Maureen said.

"We never knew where he went at night when he didn't live with us. He's entitled to a personal life. What he does at night isn't any of our business."

"I know. I—Gotta go. Customer."

"Talk to you later," Duckworth said.

When he got to Brian Gaffney's parents' house, it was nearly five in the afternoon, and there were two cars in the driveway. It was a modest but well-maintained two-story, and the cars were mid-price GM sedans, each about five years old.

Duckworth rang the bell, and seconds later a heavyset woman in her fifties opened the door.

"Yes?"

"Ms. Gaffney?"

"That's right."

"Your first name?"

"Constance. Who're you?"

He showed her his police ID. She looked at it warily as he introduced himself. Most people, Duckworth thought, viewed his ID with some degree of alarm—cops at the door did not usually mean good news—but Constance Gaffney's reaction struck him as more cautious.

"Is your husband home?" he asked.

"What's this about?" she asked.

"If your husband is home I'd like to discuss it with both of you."

She called out over her shoulder, "Albert? Albert!"

Moments later, Albert Gaffney appeared. Balding, also heavyset, broad enough in the shoulders to obliterate his wife when he edged in front of her.

"What's going on?" he asked, loosening the tie around the collar of his white shirt. He took a quick glance at Duckworth and his ID and suddenly looked as though he had a bad taste in his mouth.

"What's this all about?"

"It's about your son," Duckworth said, adding, "Brian."

"What's happened to him?" Constance asked, stepping aside to let the detective into their home.

"He's okay," Duckworth said quickly. "He's at PFG for some tests."

"Tests?" Albert said. "What's happened?"

"He was . . . assaulted," Duckworth said. "And possibly confined for a period of time."

"What's that mean?" the man asked. "Assaulted? Was he . . . I mean, did someone . . ."

Duckworth guessed what the man was trying to ask. "He was rendered unconscious and . . ."

How did one describe what had happened to Brian?

It wasn't enough to say he'd been knocked out and tattooed. It was worse than that. One had to see him to fully comprehend the crime that had been committed against him. Duckworth supposed he could show them the photos on his phone, but somehow that didn't seem appropriate.

"The best thing to do would be to go see him," he said.

"For God's sake, Albert, get your keys," Constance Gaffney said. She shot him a stern look. "I hope you're happy."

Albert started to say something, but the look in her eyes told him to keep whatever it was to himself. Instead, he turned to Duckworth.

"Who did it?" he asked. "Who hurt my son?"

"The matter's under investigation," Duckworth said. "I have a question for you."

Albert waited.

"Do you know anyone named Sean? Someone with a possible connection to your son or your family?"

"Sean?" Brian Gaffney's father asked. "Is that who did it?"

Duckworth shook his head. "No. Does the name ring any bells?"

"No," said Albert. He glanced at his wife, then asked, "Did this happen at his apartment? At his place?"

"No," Duckworth said. "Brian says it began at a bar. At Knight's."

Albert said to Constance, with a hint of vindication in his voice, "You see? It could have happened anyway. He went there even when he still lived with us."

But something in her face said she was still blaming him for something. "I'm getting my purse," she said.

"Keys," Albert said, patting his front pockets. "Where the hell are my keys?"

While they both retreated into the house, Duckworth walked back toward his car as an old green Volkswagen Beetle—one of the originals, not the remake—came up the street and pulled over to the curb in front of the house. A young woman behind the wheel killed the engine and got out.

Duckworth remembered Brian telling him he had a sister.

"Are you Monica?" he said as she approached the house.

She eyed him warily. "Who are you?"

He told her, quickly, what he'd told her parents. Once she was over the initial shock of learning her brother was in the hospital, he asked, "When was the last time you spoke with Brian?"

"I tried to call him yesterday, but he didn't answer. I saw him last week, I guess. I popped into his work."

"Monica, do you know anyone named Sean? An acquaintance of your brother's?"

"Sean?"

"That's right."

"I don't know any Sean. A man or a woman?"

"Don't know."

"Because if he's seeing someone, I wouldn't necessarily know about it."

"This Sean might no longer be with us."

"Dead?"

Duckworth nodded. "Does that jog any memory?"

She started to shake her head, then stopped. "No, it couldn't be *that* Sean."

"What Sean?"

She tipped her head at the house across the street. "That was old lady Beecham's dog. Right after Brian got his license, he backed over him."

"He killed her dog?"

Monica nodded. "It was years ago, and even though it was her own fault for letting the dog run loose, she was pretty mad about it. But she wouldn't care now."

"Why's that?"

Monica shrugged. "Mrs. Beecham has pretty much lost her marbles."

FIVE

CAL

Ms. Plimpton led me out of the dining room, through a kitchen that was bigger than my entire apartment, and out to a screened-in porch that overlooked an expansive backyard with a working fountain. The porch was decked out with white wicker furniture decorated with plump flowered cushions. Four of the chairs were occupied.

I'd been given the impression I'd be meeting just two people, not an entourage.

I figured the woman sitting in the closest chair was Ms. Plimpton's niece, Gloria Pilford. Fortyish, decked out in white slacks, a coral-colored top and high-heeled sandals. Her blonde hair seemed to be inflated, making her head look too big for her slender body. She sprang to her feet when Ms. Plimpton and I entered the room, and those heels allowed her to look me right in the eye. When she smiled, her face wrinkled like crêpe paper, as if the muscles used to convey happiness might end up tearing her face apart.

She extended a hand and I took it.

"This is wonderful," she said. "I'm so pleased you're going to help us."

Before I could say anything, Ms. Plimpton raised a hand of caution. "He's agreed to meet you, Gloria. Nothing more than that, for now."

The smile retracted immediately, and Gloria struggled

to restore it. She turned to the three people—all male—who were still seated.

"Mr. Weaver, this is my good friend, and partner, Bob Butler."

The first man stood. Just over six feet, silver-haired, barrel-chested and strong-jawed, blue eyes. Pushing fifty, or maybe he'd recently pushed past it. Tailored slacks, open-collared white dress shirt, plaid sport jacket. He put out a hand too. The grip was firm.

"Pleased to meet you," he said. "Madeline has had good things to say about you."

"And this," Gloria Pilford said, as the second man stood, "is Grant Finch."

He was the only one in a suit, and I was betting the Rolex on his wrist was the only one in the room. He'd be the one who owned that Beemer in the driveway. He was slightly shorter than Bob Butler, but his grip was just as firm when we shook hands.

"I've also heard good things," he said, giving me a smile worthy of a game-show letter-turner. Those perfect teeth probably cost as much as his car. "I expect you already know why I'm here. I acted on Jeremy's behalf during the trial."

"Most famous lawyer in the country," I said.

He waved a hand dismissively. "Or infamous, depending on one's point of view. That'll last a week or two, then I'll be forgotten until HBO decides to make this all into a miniseries twenty years from now."

The way he said it suggested he was counting on it.

Gloria moved the two men aside so I could view the young man slouching in the wicker chair at the end of the porch. Extending her arm in a kind of *ta da!* gesture, she said, "And last but not least, my son, Jeremy."

The young man had slid so far down the chair I was worried he might hit the floor. He had the rigidity of boneless chicken. His head was inches from where the cushions met, his eyes focused on the phone he held firmly in his lap in both hands. His thumbs were moving rapidly.

His great-aunt, Ms. Plimpton, had said he was eighteen, but he could have passed for twenty or twenty-one. Short black hair, pasty complexion, as though he'd spent more time looking at video screens than running bases. It was hard to tell how tall he was, given his slithered state, but under six feet.

Without looking away from his phone, he said, "Hey."

"Jeremy, for God's sake, shake the man's hand," his mother said, like I was a puppy she wanted him to pet.

"It's okay," I said, raising a palm. "Nice to meet you, Jeremy."

Gloria smiled awkwardly at me. "Please excuse him. He's tired, and he's been under a great deal of stress."

"We all have," Bob Butler said.

Gloria had referred to Bob as her friend and partner. He wasn't the boy's father. That much seemed clear.

"Of course," I said.

"Jeremy," Gloria said, her voice struggling to stay upbeat, "can I get you anything?"

He grunted.

She turned to me for another chance at hospitality. "How about you, Mr. Weaver? A drink?"

"I'm good," I said. "Your aunt served tea."

She sighed and said quietly, "I could use something stronger. Why don't we move this conversation to the kitchen?"

Grant Finch put a friendly hand atop my shoulder as

we—all of us except Jeremy—left the sunroom. "We've all been through a lot, but at least we're coming out the other side of the nightmare," he said.

Seconds later we were standing around the kitchen island while Gloria opened the oversized stainless-steel refrigerator and took out a bottle of wine.

"Anyone?" she asked.

There were no takers.

I said, "Maybe you could tell me about the harassment you've been getting."

"It hasn't just been Jeremy," Gloria said over the pop of the cork. The bottle was already half empty. "I've been getting my fair share too. People are saying unbelievable things about me on the Internet. That I'm the worst mother in the world." Another sigh. "Maybe it's true."

"It certainly isn't," said Bob. "Gloria loves Jeremy more than anything in the world. She's a wonderful mother. I've seen that first hand."

Ms. Plimpton was stone-faced. She turned away and went to the dining room to bring in the teapot and cups.

I looked at Bob. "You and Ms. Pilford . . ." I let the sentence dangle.

Gloria moved in close to Bob and slipped her arm into his, then displayed her hand so I wouldn't miss the rock on her finger. "Bob and I are engaged. The one bright spot in my life these days." She grimaced. "No, I take that back. Jeremy not going to jail, that was a wonderful thing."

Bob smiled uncomfortably. "Gloria just needs to sort some things out before we can get married. But we've been together a few years now."

Gloria nodded. "Once I'm finally free of Jack, we can move forward. That's my ex." She rolled her eyes. "Just waiting for the divorce to go through. Bob's been so patient. He's been so good to me."

And then she dug her teeth into her lower lip.

"Well," I said. "That's great."

"And my other hero is this man right here," she said, indicating Grant Finch. "If it weren't for him, my boy'd be in jail right now." She gave Bob's arm a squeeze. "I can thank *you* for Grant."

Bob said, "Well, me and Galen."

At the mention of that name, Gloria slipped her arm out of Bob's and went back to find a glass for her wine.

Bob continued, "It was Galen who put me on to Grant. When Jeremy had his troubles, Galen immediately thought of Grant and it was a terrific recommendation."

"Galen?" I said.

Bob nodded at my puzzlement. "Sorry. Galen Broadhurst. My business associate. I'm in real estate, land development, that kind of thing."

"Is he here?" I asked.

"He actually said he might be coming up later today."

"We just couldn't have done it without you, Grant," Gloria said to Finch, pouring wine into a long-stemmed glass. Her eyes narrowed. "Even if you did make me look like a fool in the process."

It was the first thing she'd said that sounded like it was straight from the heart.

"Well," Grant said, "we all wanted the same thing. To keep Jeremy out of jail. He didn't deserve that fate."

"He certainly didn't," Gloria said evenly.

"What about Jeremy's father?" I asked. "Jack, you said?"

Gloria sipped—maybe gulped would be a better word—her first mouthful from the glass. "We split up three years ago." She shook her head. "He's not a tenth the businessman Bob is." A pause. "Not that that had anything to do with our breaking up."

"It's all very complicated," Bob said. He forced a grin. "Isn't everything?"

"No kidding," Gloria said.

"What about during the trial?" I asked. "Was Jack involved?"

"Involved how?" Gloria asked.

I shrugged. "Financially? Moral support?"

"Yeah, right," Gloria said with another eye roll.

"Maybe if you hadn't shut him out, he'd have tried harder to be there for Jeremy," Bob Butler said. He looked at me. "I paid most of Jeremy's legal costs. Grant Finch doesn't come cheap."

Finch tried to look embarrassed, but he couldn't pull it off.

Bob continued. "Galen helped with Grant's bill too. He felt something of an obligation. I mean, no offense, Gloria, but there was no way you could have afforded it."

"No," she said. "I couldn't have done it without you." It was hard to hear the gratitude in the comment.

Bob threw up his hands. "Well, anyway, I'm sure you're not interested in all this background, Mr. Weaver. I'm guessing you'd like to know more about the matter at hand."

"Tell me about that."

"Gloria," he said, "show him your phone."

She went for her purse, which was hanging on one of the chairs. She rooted around, brought out an iPhone, and started tapping away.

"Okay," she said, handing the phone to me. "That's

my Facebook page. Look at some of the things people have posted on my timeline. There were a whole bunch more but I deleted them. These have come in since breakfast."

I looked at the screen. A sampling:

You're the big baby not your son.

Worst mother in the United States of Amerika.

Kids have to know there is consequences. I feel sorry for your stupid kid having a mother like you. Your own mother must have screwed up big time to make you such an asshole.

And a simple, straightforward expression of opinion: *Eat shit.*

Gloria, who was standing close enough that she was reading them along with me, pointed to that last one and said quietly, "Let me delete that right now. I don't want Madeline to see it."

"Don't want me to see what?" Ms. Plimpton said, returning from the dining room with a tray of cups and milk and sugar.

"Nothing," Gloria said. She deleted the comment. "Okay, keep going."

I read a few more.

Youre kid should dye and so should you.

How do you sleep at night when your son is free but the girl he killed will be dead forever?

A bullet between the eyes would be too good for you.

Think you can hide from us? Wherever you go in America people will know. Everyone is watching you and your asshole kid.

The vitriol didn't surprise me. What amazed me was the fact that people left their real names attached to such venom.

I put the phone down on the counter and said to

Gloria, "Have you thought about shutting down your Facebook page? You're just giving these people a way to get in touch with you."

"I have to defend myself," Gloria said. "I can't let people get away with saying those things about me."

"You're giving them an outlet to say it," I pointed out.

She closed her eyes briefly and sighed. Clearly she'd had to explain her position on this before.

"They'd be saying it anyway. This way, I know who it is and can respond." A tear formed in the corner of her right eye. "They don't understand. They have no idea."

"How did these people become your friends in the first place?" I asked. "Don't people have to ask, and then you accept?"

Grant Finch gave me a tired look. "We've talked about this."

"I like to know who my enemies are," Gloria said defiantly.

"It's like you've opened the front door for them," I said. "What about actual phone calls? Have you been threatened that way?"

She shook her head. "Bob insisted we change our numbers, unlist them. We were getting calls every hour of the day."

Bob said, "There's more than just the Facebook stuff. Madeline, have you got your laptop handy?"

Ms. Plimpton disappeared from the kitchen and seconds later reappeared carrying one of those super-thin Macs. Bob lifted up the lid, opened a browser, and made a few lightning-quick keystrokes.

"I can't bear to look at this anymore," Ms. Plimpton said. She went to the fridge, grabbed a can of Coke. "I'll take this out to Jeremy." She exited the kitchen.

Bob turned the Mac towards me, and I read the headline across the top of the page: "Teach the Big Baby a Lesson." There was a graphic, what they called a GIF or something, of a whining infant that repeated every three or four seconds. Below that, people had commented about what they would like to do to Jeremy Pilford. Some recommended he be run over with a car, just as he'd done with his victim. Someone else called for beheading, ISIS style. Someone else liked the idea of hitting him with a car, but with a difference. They wanted him to live, as a cripple, so he could be reminded every day of what he'd done.

"This isn't the only site like this," Bob pointed out. "There's one sort of like Anonymous. You know? The network who've exposed government secrets online, who've hacked websites? Except this site, they promote a more hands-on approach. None of this social-network shaming. They advocate actual violence. There's a contest, did you know that? A 'Spot the Big Baby' contest on the site. People are invited to send in tips where Jeremy might be. The whole world's looking for him. If he goes anywhere, someone tweets about it with a hashtag of #sawthebaby or #babyspot. Some yahoos are even offering cash rewards for whoever finds him, even more money for who finds him and does something to him. For all we know, there are hacker types out there trying to figure out how to track his every move."

Something else on the page caught my eye. It was a reference to Promise Falls, but it had nothing to do with Jeremy. It was a photo of the man found responsible for the poisoned water catastrophe of a year ago. Incredibly, he'd become something of a folk hero in certain

41

communities once it became known that his monstrous crime was intended as a lesson.

The people of Promise Falls had gained a reputation for not caring when no one came to the aid of a woman being murdered in the downtown park.

Now we had a new reputation. We were the national capital for retribution.

In fact, there'd been an incident in town three months ago involving someone named Pierce. Craig, or maybe it was Greg. Something like that. Anyway, he'd been acquitted of molesting a handicapped girl, but as much as admitted later that he'd done it. The courts could no longer touch him, so someone else gave it a try.

He became a meal for a pit bull.

But what had happened to him wasn't my problem then, nor was it my problem now.

"I've seen enough," I said. Bob shut the laptop.

"Will you help us?" Gloria asked, pointing to the closed computer. "You can see that the threats are for real. My boy's a target. He's not safe." Her eyes were starting to well up.

"I can't help you find out who's making the threats," I said. "I mean, they're coming from all over the place, hundreds of them. Most of these people aren't even worried about identifying themselves. But my understanding from what your aunt said is that's not what you want, anyway."

"We just want you to protect him."

"I'm not a bodyguard. I made that clear."

"Maybe give us some tips, then," Grant Finch said. "Assess the security needs. Maybe, even just for a day or two, hang around."

He gave Gloria a look that suggested she should stay

put. Then he took me aside and said quietly, "It would give Gloria and Bob some comfort, some peace of mind. You'd be well compensated for your time. I came along today because I wanted to meet you, and I like what I see. You seem like a good man, and they could really use your help."

Ms. Plimpton returned and took a seat. She looked tired. "I gave him his Coke," she reported.

Finch broke free of me and said to everyone, "I must go. I've got a meeting back at the office in Albany in forty-five minutes and I think I can just make it."

Bob shook his hand aggressively while Gloria leaned up against the kitchen counter and drank her wine. She nodded a farewell. Madeline Plimpton, with some effort, got back to her feet to say goodbye to the lawyer.

"Goodbye, Madeline," Grant said. He took her hand in his and squeezed it as she allowed him to lean in and give her an air kiss on the side of her neck.

"Goodbye, Grant," she said. "Thank you for everything you've done."

Grant held onto her hand another second before letting go. There was some kind of history there.

As he departed, I caught Ms. Plimpton's eye and said, "Could you direct me to the facilities?"

She pointed.

I already knew where the bathroom was. I'd seen it on our way to the porch. Visiting it wasn't my true mission.

I stopped at the open doorway to the porch. Jeremy Pilford had put aside his phone. The can of Coke sat on a table in front of him.

He was staring out through the screen to the backyard. Just staring.

Moments earlier, I'd thought he could pass for twenty

or older, but now he looked no more than fourteen or fifteen.

Maybe that was what he really was. Emotionally.

He must have sensed I was standing there. He turned his head slowly and took me in. I couldn't be sure, but I thought what I saw in his eyes was hopelessness. Maybe even fear.

I nodded, stepped back, and returned to the kitchen. The three of them had been talking quietly, but went silent and focused on me.

"Okay," I said. "I'll help you."

SIX

"What do you mean, she's lost her marbles?" Barry Duckworth asked Monica Gaffney.

Looking at the house across the street, Brian Gaffney's sister said, "Mrs. Beecham is really old and I don't think she always knows what's going on. Like, one time she left her sprinkler going for five days, most of the water hitting the driveway. We've had our ups and downs with her over the years, but it got a little better after her husband died, like, ten years ago, because he was a miserable bastard, pardon my French, although she's no barrel of laughs. Why are you asking about Sean, anyway?"

"It's a name that came up," he told her.

The front door of the house opened and Brian Gaffney's parents emerged.

"Monica, Brian's in the hospital," Constance said.

She tipped her head at Duckworth. "He told me."

"Come on," Albert said, his head down as he headed for the car.

Monica broke off from Duckworth without another word and got into the back seat as Albert took up position behind the wheel and Constance settled in beside him. Duckworth watched them drive away up the street.

There was an old blue minivan parked in the driveway of the Beecham house. It was a small one-story building nearly swallowed up by untended shrubs reaching toward the eaves. The roof shingles were curling up, and a couple of cracked windows were held together with duct tape. Duckworth crossed the street, walked past the van, and rang the bell.

It was not an old woman who answered, but a thin, bald man in his forties dressed in cutoff jeans and a dark green T-shirt. He eyed Duckworth through glasses held together with a piece of tape in the middle.

"Yeah?" he said. "You here about the bedroom set?"

Duckworth shook his head. "I'm looking for Mrs. Beecham."

"What do you want?"

Duckworth dug out his ID again and held it long enough for the man to grasp what it was but not long enough to study it.

The man said, "Uh, there's no trouble here. Everything is fine."

"Are you Mrs. Beecham's son?"

"Uh, no."

"What's your name, sir?"

"Harvey."

"Harvey what?"

The man hesitated. "Don't I have the right not to tell you my name?"

"I suppose you do. You'd also be exercising your right to get on my bad side from the get-go."

"Harvey Spratt," he said.

Duckworth smiled. "That your van, Harvey?"

"It's my girlfriend's. Norma's."

"Well, Mr. Spratt, is Mrs. Beecham home?"

"Did she call you?"

"Mr. Spratt, this is the last time I ask before I start to get annoyed. Is Mrs. Beecham home?"

"Yeah."

"I'd like to speak with her."

Harvey Spratt weighed his options, decided he had few, and opened the door wide enough to admit Duck-worth. "She's downstairs watching TV," he said.

Duckworth took in the disarray as he entered the house. Cardboard boxes, piles of clothing, newspapers, paperback novels, tools, a plastic bag filled with more plastic bags, a box of souvenirs including half a dozen snow globes and an Empire State Building bank, and odd bits of furniture cluttered the living room so completely it wasn't possible to reach the sofa or easy chairs. Even if you could, they were piled with so much stuff you couldn't sit on them.

As Harvey headed for a door that led, presumably, to the basement, a woman came out of the kitchen. She was roughly the same age as Spratt, about twice his size, dirty blonde hair hanging in her eyes. Her T-shirt, done in the style of that early Barack Obama "HOPE" poster, featured an image of a man with the word TRUTH below it. It took Duckworth a moment to realize it was Edward Snowden, the former CIA employee turned whistleblower.

"What's going on?" she asked.

"Man wants to talk to Eleanor," Harvey said. "He's with the police."

"Police?" The alarm was instantaneous.

Duckworth gave her a wary smile. "Are you related to Mrs. Beecham?"

"Eleanor? No. I come in three times a week to look after her."

"You're a nurse?"

The woman shook her head. "Personal care worker. I tend to her. Take care of her, clean the house, make meals, give her a bath, that kind of thing."

Duckworth cast his eye into the kitchen. The counter was littered with dirty dishes.

"What's your name?"

"Norma."

"Last name?" What was it with these people? Duckworth wondered.

"Lastman."

"Well, Norma, it's nice to meet you. Is Mr. Spratt here helping you with your duties?"

"Harvey's my boyfriend," she said. "And yeah, he's just giving me a hand."

"With the bedroom suite that you're selling?"

She shot Harvey a look. "Actually, I'm not sure it's for sale. I have to have another chat with Eleanor."

"Which is exactly what I would like to have," Duckworth said. He tipped his head toward the door. "Down here?"

Harvey nodded.

Duckworth opened the door himself and descended the stairs into a dimly lit wood-paneled recreation room that smelled of mold and urine. Brown shag carpeting from the time of the Reagan administration covered much of the floor. The walls were adorned with cheaply framed nature scenes that looked like paint-by-number pieces. An old black-and-white movie was playing on the TV. John Wayne was riding a horse.

Eleanor Beecham was sitting on a plaid recliner, legs extended under a pink chenille blanket. She looked to be in her late eighties. Her face was pale and wrinkled, and the few gray hairs still on her head stuck out in all directions. Tucked between her thigh and the edge of the chair was a box of tissues, a remote, a checkbook, a hairbrush, and a bag of mini Mars candy bars like one would give to kids at Halloween.

"Mrs. Beecham?" Duckworth said.

The woman's head turned slowly. She focused her eyes on him and said, "Well, look who's here." There was chocolate stuck to one of her teeth.

"Have we met before?" he said.

"Don't think so."

"But you recognize me?"

"Nope."

He smiled and showed her his ID. "I'm Detective Barry Duckworth, with the Promise Falls Police." He sat down on a couch at right angles to the woman's chair.

"Nice to meet ya. You like John Wayne?"

"Sure. He was one of the great movie stars of all time."

"Whaddya mean, was? He's dead?"

Duckworth hated to be the bearer of bad news. "I'm afraid so. For a long time, now."

"Oh, that's a shame." She shook her head sadly. "Gone too soon."

"It happens. I wonder if you'd mind turning down the TV so I could ask you a couple of questions."

She hunted for the remote, pointed it to the set and muted it. "Whatcha want?"

"I wanted to ask you about your neighbors across the street."

Eleanor Beecham furrowed her brow. "What about 'em?"

"Specifically, I wanted to ask you about Brian. Brian Gaffney?"

She grimaced. "That simpleton? What's he gone and done now?"

"When's the last time you saw him?"

She struggled to remember. "The other day, I saw his

dad teaching him how to ride a bike. He caught onto it real fast."

Duckworth nodded slowly. "Right. That was probably quite a few years ago, though, when he was very young."

She studied him with glassy eyes, waiting for another question. At that moment Duckworth heard breathing behind him. He turned, spotted Norma Lastman huddling near the top of the stairs.

"This is a private conversation," he told her. He waited until the woman had retreated, and closed the door, before continuing.

"What about when he started driving a car? Do you remember that? Was there an incident with your dog?"

"With Sean?" Her face brightened.

"Yes. With Sean."

Mrs. Beecham's face appeared to melt. "He was the nicest dog. Smart, too."

"Really."

"Oh, yeah. My husband could say to him, go find my slippers, and Sean would run up the stairs and fetch them. He was a good dog. Licked himself a lot. My husband used to say he envied his flexibility."

"You remember what happened to Sean?"

"The dumb bastard squashed him," she said.

"The dumb bastard being Brian."

She pointed in the general direction of the house across the street. Even though she was in a windowless basement, she got it more or less right. "They're a bunch of bastards, them Gaffneys."

"You don't get along?"

The old woman shrugged. "They're not so bad lately, but he's a dumbass and his wife's a bitch."

"Albert and Constance," Duckworth said.

"And they got a slut daughter, too. Forget her name."

"Monica," he said.

"That's it." She glanced back at the TV. "I forgot he was dead. He would have made a great president. Better than Reagan."

"You must have been very upset when Brian ran over your dog."

"Yup. Got back at them right away."

"What did you do?"

She smiled slyly. "I can't tell you."

"Why not?"

"You might arrest me."

"Why don't you tell me anyway?" he said.

"If you arrest me, I'll deny that I told you. Do we have a deal?"

"Sure."

"I went over there late one night and slashed a few tires." She smiled proudly, showing off teeth the color of caramel.

"Well," Duckworth said. "Did the Gaffneys accuse you?"

She shook her head. "They never said nothin' to me. They wouldn't have been able to prove it, so what's the point?"

"You might be right." Duckworth leaned in a little closer. "How about more recently? Sometimes there are things that are hard to forgive, or forget, even after several years have gone by."

"That's for sure," Mrs. Beecham said.

One thing Duckworth knew for sure was that this old woman couldn't have abducted Brian Gaffney and held him captive for two days while she carved a message into his back. But that didn't mean someone couldn't have done it for her.

"Mrs. Beecham, do you have any children? Anyone else who might have been very angry with Brian about what happened to the dog?"

"Never had children." She lowered her voice to a whisper. "Mr. Beecham—that'd be Lyall—was shootin' blanks, if you get my drift."

"I see. So there was no one else who'd have been deeply troubled by what happened to Sean."

"Well, Sean wasn't too fucking happy about it," she said, and Duckworth got another look at those stained teeth as she grinned.

"Why Sean?" he asked. "It seems like an unusual name for a dog."

"We named him after my brother."

"Your brother?"

"Yeah. Sean Samuel Lastman, rest his soul. Kind of a dumb way to remember him, but what the hell. You do what you can."

"What happened to your brother?"

"He died nearly thirty years ago. Fell off a roof he was shingling."

Duckworth thought of the woman upstairs. "I just met Norma. Is there a family connection?"

Her eyes briefly sparkled. "Here's something pretty amazing. Norma came to work for me a couple of years ago. And we get talking, and I was telling her about my brother, and turns out Sean was her daddy."

"Norma's your niece?"

Mrs. Beecham nodded. "Small world, right? She didn't even know for years that he *was* her dad. Sean got some girl knocked up, never married her, and Norma was only about four years old when he died. Before Norma's mom died, she told her who her real daddy was."

"Amazing," Duckworth said. "And what about Harvey?"

Mrs. Beecham's nose wrinkled. "He's her boyfriend. He doesn't amount to much, but he helps out, too." She patted the checkbook next to her thigh. "He's getting the house all fixed up for me case I decide to put it on the market. The plumbing's got to be redone and he found something wrong with the furnace. Whatcha asking me all these questions for anyway?"

"Brian ran into some trouble," he said.

"I don't doubt it. He always was kind of a simple kid. Not downright stupid, but kinda simple." She looked back at the TV. "You about done? I'd like to see the end of this."

"Sure," Duckworth said. "Thank you for your time."

He went quietly back up the stairs. When he opened the door, he found Harvey and Norma had been huddled close to it.

"Did you catch everything?" Duckworth asked them.

"I just wanted to be sure she's okay," Norma said, wringing her hands. "What were you asking her?"

"Just a few things."

"She says a lot of crazy stuff," Norma said.

"She's pretty nuts," Harvey added.

Duckworth studied the two of them. "Either of you know Brian Gaffney?" he asked.

"Never heard of him," Harvey said.

"Nope," said Norma.

Duckworth looked at her. "Your aunt's lived here a long time. You never heard of the Gaffneys? They're right across the street."

Norma blinked. "Nope," she said. "Never."

"How about Sean?" he asked. "You know anyone by that name?"

Norma and Harvey both shook their heads.

"That's funny," Duckworth said.

"Why's it funny?" the woman asked him.

"Because that was your father's name, wasn't it?" the detective said.

Her mouth made a perfect circle. "Oh!" she said. "Yes, that's right. But I thought you meant someone we knew now."

Duckworth studied the pair for several seconds, saying nothing.

Finally, he nodded and said, "You folks have a nice day."

On the way to his car, he took a quick photo of the plate on the back bumper of the van.

SEVEN

CAL

Gloria Pilford, refilling her wine glass in the kitchen, said, "You'll help us? Really?"

"I'll have a look at your situation," I said, and then told them what it was going to cost them, per day.

Gloria looked helplessly at Bob and Madeline, no doubt wondering which of them would step up.

"It's fine," her aunt said. "I'll write you out a check for five days."

Bob said, "Madeline, I can look after this."

"No," she said in a voice that did not invite argument. "You've done enough already. Mr. Finch must have cost you a fortune."

Bob didn't disagree. Ms. Plimpton opened a drawer, found her checkbook, scribbled on one, tore it off, and handed it to me. I tucked it into my wallet without so much as a glance.

"Okay," I said. "Let's start by figuring out just what the situation *is*."

Madeline Plimpton got back on one of the island stools, next to Bob Butler. Gloria maintained her station near the fridge.

"How many people would know Jeremy's here and not at your place in Albany?"

"I haven't told a soul," Ms. Plimpton said. "Except for you."

"Neither have I," said Butler.

Gloria had busied herself putting the almost-empty wine bottle back into the fridge, her back to us.

"Ms. Pilford?" I asked.

"I'm sorry?" she said.

"Gloria, answer the man's question," Ms. Plimpton said.

Gloria closed the fridge and turned around slowly. "I haven't told anyone," she said. "Not specifically."

"What does that mean?" I asked.

Her eyes looked down, like a child who'd been caught with her hand in the cookie jar. "I might have posted something."

"Like?" I said.

"I said how good it felt to get out of Albany, to find some peace and quiet."

I nodded toward her aunt, who was closest to the laptop. I wiggled my fingers, air-typing, and she got the message, reaching for the computer and reopening it. "Could you find the page?" I asked her.

"I'll do it," Gloria said, crossing the kitchen and taking the laptop from her aunt. She made a few keystrokes. "There, I didn't really say anything."

I took the laptop from her and studied her most recent posts.

"Tell me again when you got here?"

Ms. Plimpton said, "Four nights they've been here." She made no attempt to disguise the weariness in her voice.

I scrolled down to see what Gloria had been telling the world earlier in the week. Last Friday, she'd posted: *The world is full of so many haters. People need to stop hating and start understanding.*

That morsel of wisdom had produced more than three hundred likes, and about sixty comments. Some supportive, others not so much. As I scanned through them, I guessed that about eighty per cent of them were negative. One typical reply: *And some mothers need to start teaching their kids not to run people down.*

The next day, Gloria had written: *It'll be good to get out of town. It'll be good to go where they always have to let you in.*

I was no English major, but I recognized a version of the Robert Frost line about going home.

"This one," I said, pointing, "is basically telling everyone you're going back to your home town."

Gloria became defensive. "But I don't say where it is."

I went up to search field and typed in, "Where is Gloria Pilford, the Big Baby mother, from?"

Hit *Enter.*

Up came dozens of news stories. It didn't take long to find one that mentioned that Gloria had been raised by her aunt Madeline, who lived in Promise Falls. Going back a hundred or more years, this one story went on to say, the Plimptons were among the town's founders, at one time running a tannery, and in later years starting up the town's first newspaper. Madeline Plimpton, the story said, often attended Jeremy's trial.

"There," I said. "You don't have to be Sherlock Holmes to figure out where you probably are. And no doubt Ms. Plimpton's address is easily found on the Internet."

"Oh Gloria," said Bob derisively. "You might as well have hired a skywriter to draw a big arrow pointing to the house."

Madeline Plimpton had put her head into her hands.

I said, "You're banned."

"I'm what?" Gloria said.

"If you can't stop yourself from posting, you need to stay off the computer, your phone, whatever other device you may have, altogether. You're exposing yourself. You're putting yourself in danger."

Gloria bit her lip again and turned away. "You don't understand," she said, putting both hands on the counter's edge, supporting herself. "You don't know what they've put me through."

None of us said anything.

Without turning around, she said, "I let you all make a national laughing stock out of me. I'm mocked and ridiculed. The coddling, smothering mother who kept her child from learning right from wrong. Okay, it worked. Jeremy didn't go to jail. And that's good."

Slowly, she turned around. Tears had traveled halfway down her cheeks.

"But I paid a price, too," she said. "And now you want to keep me from telling the world I'm not the person they think I am."

An unmoved Ms. Plimpton walked across the room, picked up the laptop and held it tightly under her arm.

Bob said, "Give me your phone, honey."

Gloria looked as though Bob had just asked for a kidney.

"This is humiliating," she said. "You have no right."

I said, "I can't protect Jeremy if there are leaks coming out of this very household as to his whereabouts."

"You think I'd do anything to hurt my son?" Gloria asked me.

"Not intentionally," I said. "But those postings are dangerous. Even if you don't say anything specific, people can tell where you are when you write them."

Bob said, "Come on, Gloria. Give me your phone."

Gloria wasn't ready to surrender. "I need a phone in case there's an *emergency*. You get to have your phone, Bob, so you can do all your *deals*."

"That's different," Bob said. "If I'm not making deals, then I'm not bringing in any money, and if I wasn't bringing in money, how the hell would I have paid for your son's defense?"

"I like the way you toss that in," she said. "*My* son."

"Well, he is *your* son. I think it shows how much you mean to me that I was willing to help him out despite that fact that he's not mine."

"I know, you're a hero." It was an out-and-out sneer. "You care so much about him."

"Your phone?" Bob said.

"I don't know where it is," Gloria said, with little conviction.

Bob reached behind a decorative bowl on the island. "For Christ's sake, it's right here."

She lunged for it, but she was too slow. Bob had snatched up the phone, which was in a pale pink cover with tiny white polka dots, and dropped it into the inside pocket of his sport jacket.

"That's a start," I said, although I'd have rather held onto it myself. "Now there's the business of Jeremy's phone," I said. "I'm guessing when he isn't playing games he's texting with his friends. He may also be telling people more than he should."

Gloria laughed scornfully. "Good luck taking *his* phone away."

She reopened the fridge and brought out the wine bottle.

Ms. Plimpton said, "Gloria, take it easy."

"I'm fine, *Madeline*." Gloria held up the bottle. "The only comfort I get around here is from this. None of you give a shit what I've—"

That was when we heard the crash. The sound of breaking glass.

Gloria and Ms. Plimpton let out short screams. Bob and I exchanged quick glances. The sound had come from the front of the house. I ran to the hall. Shards of glass were scattered across the marble floor, and in the midst of them, a fist-sized rock. There were narrow floor-to-ceiling windows on either side of the main door, and the rock had gone through the one on the left.

I flung open the door and saw a long-haired man— late teens, I was guessing—running flat-out to a vehicle idling at the curb. It was a blue van, the side door open.

Before the man leapt in, he glanced back and shouted, "Take that, ya fuckin' big baby!"

Then he was in the van, hauling the door shut as the tires squealed and the vehicle lurched forward.

I started to run, but there wasn't a hope of catching a look at the plate. The van was up the street and around a corner in seconds. It looked like one of those older GM vans, of which there are only about a hundred thousand in every town. And the rock-thrower was white, brown shoulder-length hair, maybe a hundred and eighty pounds. Jeans and a blue T-shirt. Not much help when it came to offering police a description.

I walked back into the house, where I found mother, aunt, and Bob Butler standing.

"Who was it?" Ms. Plimpton asked. "Did you see them?"

"A quick look is all," I said.

What struck me as alarming was not what had just

60

happened, but that all the commotion had not drawn Jeremy from the porch. Even if he'd tucked some buds into his ears, he still should have heard what had happened.

Without another word, I made my way to the back of the house again, marching straight out onto the porch. The screen door to the backyard was half open.

Jeremy was not there.

EIGHT

Barry Duckworth got back into his own vehicle and pointed it in the direction of Knight's, which was only five minutes away.

Along the way, he got stuck behind an out-of-state car that was being driven hesitantly. Brake lights coming on, then off, turn signal on, then off. The person behind the wheel of this blue Ford Explorer with Maine plates gave every indication of being lost.

When the Explorer stopped at a light, Duckworth pulled up alongside and powered down the passenger window. The driver, a man in his forties, put down his own window and looked over.

"You folks lost?" Duckworth asked.

"You know how to get to the park where the falls is?" the man asked. "Wife and I are looking for the spot where Olivia Fisher was killed."

A woman in the passenger seat leaned forward and held up what looked like a newspaper clipping. "We're checking all the spots related to the town's mass killing last year."

The man smiled. "We're true crime nuts. You know the way?"

Duckworth said, "Hang a right here, then the next right, and just keep on going."

The driver looked puzzled. "Won't that put us on the road back to Albany?"

"Yup," Duckworth said. He put the passenger window

back up, took his foot off the brake, and drove off.

He parked half a block down from Knight's. Before entering the premises, he inspected the alley next to the building. Brian Gaffney's last memory before his two-day blackout was of this location. It was no more than six feet wide, which allowed room to step around a line of trash cans. At the back end it opened out onto a small parking lot.

Duckworth walked the length of it, glancing down at the cracked and broken asphalt. Nothing caught his eye, and he didn't know what he was expecting to find. Then he cast his eyes skyward, hoping he might see a security camera mounted to the wall of the bar, or the building next to it, which was a dry-cleaning operation. No such luck.

He came back out onto the street. It was early May— nearly a year since the catastrophic events that had taken so many lives in Promise Falls—and each day seemed just a little longer than the last. The town was planning a special event later in the month to commemorate those who'd lost their lives, and Duckworth had been asked to be a guest of honor.

He wanted nothing to do with it.

He pulled on the door to Knight's and went inside. It wouldn't be fair to call this place a dive. Although a little rough around the edges, it was a decent neighborhood bar. It had the usual trappings. The neon signs for Bud Lite and Jack Daniels and Michelob. There were tables scattered about the room, booths down the right side, and the bar itself over on the left, half a dozen people perched on stools, watching a ball game playing on the TV hanging off the wall above a set of shelves stocked with liquor bottles.

The place was about half full, and Duckworth guessed it would be close to packed as more people got off work. Knight's didn't just serve booze. Four guys sitting in a booth were feasting on a plate of chicken wings. The smells of fried food and grease wafted up Duckworth's nostrils and he found himself instantly starving.

Chicken wings, he told himself, were usually served with celery and carrot sticks. That made them a balanced meal, yes? But he knew that when he got home in another couple of hours, Maureen would have pulled something together for them for dinner. Something that was not battered or deep-fried or dripping in sauce.

Be strong.

He glanced around the room and saw something that pleased him. Unlike the alley, there were security cameras in here.

A slim man about thirty years old, dressed in jeans and a checked shirt with the sleeves rolled back to his elbows, was working behind the bar, drying some mugs with a white cloth. Duckworth hauled himself up onto a stool.

"What can I get you?" the bartender asked.

Duckworth dug out his ID and displayed it for the man. "Like to ask you some questions. What's your name?"

"Axel. Axel Thurston." He squinted at the ID for a final second before Duckworth put it away. "Jesus, you're the guy."

"Sorry?"

"I know the name. You caught that guy. Jesus, you caught that guy."

Duckworth nodded.

"What are ya drinkin'?"

"Nothing, really."

"No, come on. What's your pleasure? On the house. Your money's no good here. Whaddya want? Want some Scotch? Best stuff. I got Speyburn, I got Macallan, I got Glenmorangie, I got—"

Duckworth raised a palm. "No, really. That's very kind of you. But I'm on duty, you know?"

Axel grinned. "Yeah, of course. I get that. So maybe something else?"

"Glass of water'd be nice."

Axel laughed. "Glass of water! The irony, huh?"

Duckworth didn't get it at first. Then he realized it was a reference to what had happened a year ago, when the town's water supply had been poisoned.

"Oh, yeah, right."

"Let me give you bottled," Axel said. He reached under the counter and came up with a bottle of Finley Springs. "How's this?"

"Wow," Duckworth said. "My favorite."

Axel got a glass, put some ice in it, cracked open the water and poured. "So what's up? What can I do for you?"

Duckworth brought out his phone and showed him the picture of Brian Gaffney that he had taken at the hospital.

"You recognize him?"

Axel nodded. "Sure. That's Brian."

"You know him?"

"Sure. He comes in here all the time. Brian Gaffney. Works at the car cleaning place." He grew concerned. "Shit, is he okay? Somethin' happen to him?"

Duckworth put away his phone. "Looks like somebody got the drop on him when he left here a couple of nights ago."

Axel looked puzzled. "I haven't heard anything about that? We didn't have any cops here. Nothing happened as far as I know."

Duckworth nodded understandingly. "It's complicated. Brian didn't come to our attention until today."

"Is he okay? He's a sweet guy, you know? Not the kind to ever hurt anybody. You almost feel kind of protective of him, you know?"

"What do you mean?"

Axel shrugged. "He's a bit too trusting. He could get taken in pretty easy. So's he okay?"

"Yeah. But I'd like to trace his movements over the last forty-eight hours. Were you on that night?"

Axel nodded. "Yeah. I was. Brian was sitting right where you are."

"When did he come in?"

He shrugged. "About eight? Stayed an hour or two. He comes in every couple of nights when he's done work."

"Been coming here long?"

Another nod. "He likes to talk, you know. He's interested in all sorts of weird shit. Like, conspiracy theories? Who was really behind 9/11, were the moon landings fake, did aliens build the pyramids, shit like that."

"UFOs?" Duckworth asked.

"Yeah, them. Sometimes he talked about his family, his old man."

"Albert Gaffney?"

"I don't know his name, but yeah. Brian was saying he moved out, got his own place because his dad said it was time for him to make it on his own. Thing is, I think Brian would have lived at home forever. He felt safer

66

there, I reckon. But he seemed to be doing okay on his own, far as I could tell."

"What I wondered is, did you notice anyone talking to him, taking an interest in him that night? Checking him out somehow?"

Axel shook his head slowly. "Not really. Brian usually just sits there and drinks his beer and watches the game."

Duckworth nodded in the direction of the security camera mounted on the wall close to the ceiling. "What about that?"

Axel followed his eye. "Oh, yeah."

"You got security video from that night?"

"We should. System banks it for a week or so. It's kind of good to have in case something goes down, you know. Fight breaks out, or someone thinks they got their pocket picked, stuff like that. The owner says it protects us, too, in case somebody tries to sue us for something that didn't happen."

"I'd like to see two nights ago. That be okay?"

"Sure," Axel said. "Need to go to the computer in the back. I'd check with the owner, but when I tell him it's you, fuck, he's gonna tell me to do everything I can to be accommodating. You know why?"

Duckworth waited.

Axel leaned over the bar and said softly, "His sister was one of the ones who died from the water."

"I'm sorry."

"If he was here, he'd be offering you free drinks till the end of time."

Duckworth smiled sadly. "Let's go to the instant replay."

Axel called over a waitress to watch the bar while he was gone, then led Duckworth through a back door, past the kitchen, where the smell of fries and wings made the detective light-headed, and into a wood-paneled office. The cluttered room featured a desk with a laptop.

Axel dropped into a chair and tapped away. "So two nights ago . . . and Brian came in around eight. Okay, here we are at quarter to eight."

Duckworth came around and stood at Axel's shoulder.

"Let's trade places," Axel said, offering the detective his chair. Duckworth settled in and Axel gave him instructions. "Just put the cursor there, yeah, like that, and you can go forward or backward and faster and slower, whatever you want."

Duckworth got comfortable with the controls. "Okay, I've got it." He looked at the timer in the corner that said it was 7:48 p.m. The camera captured most of the room, including the booths on the far side. Two couples were having something to eat in one, four guys were sharing a pitcher in another, and in the one next to that, a man and woman were seated side by side, the opposite bench empty. They had their heads close together, engaged in close conversation and the occasional kiss.

Axel pointed.

"Get a room, right?" he grinned.

A young man entered the scene from the right at 7:51.

"Here we go," Duckworth said. The man wandered down toward the end of the bar and perched himself on a stool, although it wasn't the same one Duckworth had just been sitting on.

"No," Axel said.

"What do you mean?"

"That's not Brian."

Duckworth put his face closer to the screen. The image wasn't crisp, but he could tell now that this man was not Brian Gaffney. But they were about the same height, had similar hair, and were both dressed in jeans and a dark shirt.

"At a glance, yeah, they look kinda the same, dressed pretty much the same," Axel commented. "Sorry about the camera. It's not exactly high-def. Look, *there's* Brian."

Axel was right. Brian Gaffney had come in, and he did place himself at the bar on the stool Duckworth had sat on minutes earlier. Gaffney raised a hand, Axel came over, chatted with him briefly, then got him a beer.

"Do you remember what you were talking about just then?"

"Just the usual shit. How was your day, how ya doin'. Nothing special."

"How'd he seem?"

"Seem?"

"Same as always? Did he seem worried about anything? Anxious at all?"

"Nope. Same old Brian."

Duckworth started fast-forwarding, but not so fast that he couldn't spot anyone paying any kind of attention to Brian. At 8:39, a short, balding man walked past and gave Brian a friendly punch to the shoulder. Brian looked up from his drink and gave the man a thumbs-up.

"Who's that?"

Axel said, "That's Ernie. Can't think of his last name. Just a regular. Sometimes they sit and have a beer together, shoot the shit."

Twice Duckworth saw Axel get Brian another beer. Axel was always on the move, tending the bar while the waitresses looked after the booths and the tables.

Axel pointed to the couple sitting together in the booth, lips now locked. "Ain't love grand?" he said.

Duckworth's eye was drawn again to the man further down the bar who bore a passing resemblance to Brian. "What was this one's name again?"

"Beats me. I only checked his ID to make sure he was old enough. But he paid in cash. Why?"

"No reason, just—Hello."

Brian was throwing some bills on the bar. Axel came over, shook the man's hand as he slid off the stool. Brian disappeared to the left.

"Where's he going?" Duckworth asked. "Is he going out a back way?"

"He's hittin' the can before he goes."

Sure enough, Brian reappeared about ninety seconds later, crossed the path of the security camera and exited to the right.

Duckworth noted the time. Brian Gaffney had left Knight's at 9:32 p.m. By then, it would have been dark outside. If someone called to him from the alley, he wouldn't have been able to see who it was.

"Well, that's it," Axel said.

Duckworth decided to watch the next few minutes of the surveillance video. Maybe Brian popped backed in briefly. Or maybe—

The two who'd been fooling around as much as talking and drinking were sliding out of the booth. The man slapped down some bills onto the check and then the two of them headed for the door, the woman first.

The camera hadn't been able to provide a very sharp image of them when they were in the booth, but as they moved out into the middle of the room, it became easier to make them out.

Duckworth clicked the pause button. He leaned in

closer and squinted, trying to get as good a look at the couple as possible.

"Something?" Axel said.

"No."

"If you're wondering who that is, I can tell you. Well, the guy anyway. The girl, I don't recognize her. But the guy, he's in here once in a while."

"Not important," Duckworth said, pushing back the chair and standing. "Thanks for all your help."

"Any time you're off duty, come on in. Drinks on the house. You like wings? We've got the best wings in town."

"They sure smell good."

"You want some to go?"

"No, that's okay, but thanks."

Duckworth left the office, walked past the kitchen and through the bar, and landed back on the sidewalk.

He wondered whether to tell Maureen that he now knew where Trevor had spent at least one of his evenings. That he seemed to have found a girlfriend.

He wondered about how much fun it was going to be sitting down with Trevor to interview him about who or what he might have seen when he walked out of that bar.

NINE

CAL

"Call Jeremy," I said, not addressing anyone in particular.

"*I* would do it," Gloria said, "but someone took my phone."

"Oh for Christ's sake," Bob said, and dug into his pocket for her cell and handed it to her.

Gloria called up her son's number and tapped the screen. She put the phone to her ear and waited.

"He's not answering," she said.

"Have you got that app that shows where his phone is?" I asked.

She shook her head.

She went to put the phone back in her pocket, but Bob held out his hand. "Gloria."

She gave him a look of exasperation and slapped the phone into his palm. Then she looked my way and said, "I wouldn't be too worried. Jeremy does this sometimes."

"Takes off?" I said.

She nodded. "He needs to get a little air, decompress, deal with the stress. When you consider what he's been through, can you blame him?"

I said, "Isn't it part of Jeremy's probation deal that he be supervised at all times? Wasn't he spared prison because you committed to always knowing his whereabouts?"

"He's been given some leeway in that regard," Bob

offered. "Because of the threats. We cleared it before we came up from Albany."

"But even if you were allowed to bring Jeremy to Promise Falls, aren't you supposed to keep close tabs on him?"

"For God's sake," Gloria said. "He's a teenager. You do the best you can, but sometimes he slips away. But he always comes back."

"Tell me you don't give him the keys to the car."

"I'm not an idiot," she said.

"Gloria," Bob said, "if the boy gets caught out on his own, they're going to throw him in jail."

"The more immediate concern," I said, "is his safety. Someone just tossed a rock through the window, and Jeremy's not here. We need to find him."

Gloria suddenly put her hand to her mouth. "Oh God," she said. "Please just make it all stop."

I pushed open the screen and walked out into Madeline Plimpton's perfectly groomed backyard. "Jeremy!" I shouted. "Jeremy!"

Gloria followed me out and shouted his name as well.

The property backed onto forest. Jeremy could easily have vanished into it. Or he might be hoofing it into downtown Promise Falls. Suddenly I wondered if he'd played us, and was actually back inside the house.

"Ms. Plimpton," I said, "check around upstairs, in case he's still here."

She vanished. We could hear her shouting the boy's name throughout her home.

I walked down to the edge of the property and scanned the woods. Somehow, I didn't see Jeremy wanting to commune with nature. Gloria was ten feet behind me, calling for her son.

"Jeremy! This isn't funny!"

"Where might he go?" I asked her, not wanting to raise the possibility that he might have left the property against his will.

She raised her hands helplessly. "I swear, I don't know. Probably someplace where there was something to do. A mall or a McDonald's or something like that. Do you think something's happened to him?" A look of panic was creeping into her face.

"There's no reason to think that," I said. "It's probably like you said. He just needed to get away from the rest of us for a while." I lightly put a hand on each shoulder. "I'm sure we'll find him."

I turned and started walking back to the house as Ms. Plimpton emerged, shaking her head. The boy was not in the house.

"Stay here," I told all of them. "I'll drive around, see if I can find him." I already had Ms. Plimpton's home number in my phone, and could call if I had any news.

I walked through the house and out the front. Ms. Plimpton, looking at the damage, said, "I'm going to call the police."

"Up to you," I said. "But it'll be a circus around here in no time if you do."

I left her considering that as I got behind the wheel of my Accord. When I got to the end of the street I had the option of going left or right. Left took me into more suburbs, but right would lead me to the downtown district. It would take someone the better part of twenty minutes to get there on foot, but this was also a bus route.

I went right.

It hadn't been ten minutes since I'd seen Jeremy on the porch, so he couldn't have gotten that far. I drove slowly, casting my eyes from one side of the road to the other. He might be staying off the sidewalk to lessen the chance of being spotted.

When I got to a cross street, I went right again. Soon I'd be reaching some strip malls and fast-food joints. I got stopped at a light and was strumming my fingers on top of the steering wheel when a faded red Miata convertible screamed through the intersection, top down.

"Son of a bitch," I said.

In the driver's seat was a young woman with long blonde hair. Next to her, waving his arms in the air above the windshield, was Jeremy Pilford.

As soon as the light changed, I made an immediate left, cutting off a pickup coming my way and earning myself a horn honk and an upraised middle finger. I could see the Miata about a hundred yards ahead. There were two cars between us, and that was fine. I didn't want to be spotted. I didn't want to initiate a chase. If the girl tried to lose me, someone could end up dead.

At least she was showing enough good sense not to drive like a maniac. She was sticking to the limit, and she needed both hands to drive. One was on the wheel, the other working the gearshift. When she changed lanes, she signalled. It was her passenger who was displaying some recklessness, continuing to wave his hands in the air, pushing himself up, his butt nearly to the headrest, poking his head above the glass.

The car moved back into the curb lane, hit the blinker, and turned in to a hamburger place. Not one of the major chains, but an independent joint called Green & Farb Burgers and Fries, named, so went the tale, after the two men who founded the place in the fifties. The locals called it Grease & Fat, which might have sounded like a negative, but sometimes that was exactly what you wanted.

By the time I reached it, they'd found a parking spot around the back of the building and were inside. I parked my Honda across the rear end of the Miata, blocking it in. It was one of the first ones, from the early nineties. The folded-down roof was faded and torn in places. I was betting the plastic rear window, once the roof was up, would be yellowed and nearly impossible to see through.

I phoned Ms. Plimpton's house. She answered on the first ring.

"Yes?"

"You can stand down."

I heard wrestling over the handset, and then Gloria came on. "Jeremy?"

"It's Cal. I found him. I'll bring him home shortly."

"Where is he? What did he—"

"I'll be back soon."

I slipped my cell back into my jacket, got out of the car, locked it, and went into the restaurant. It wasn't busy, and Jeremy and the girl were standing by the counter. It looked as though they'd already ordered. I hung back, out of sight behind a pillar, and waited until they had their food and were seated.

At that point, I went to the counter and watched as someone loaded up a wire basket with frozen fries, then lowered them into the fryer. The grease sizzled and spat. I asked the young guy at the cash for a coffee.

Jeremy and the girl were sitting on opposite sides of a table for four, leaning in close to one another, giggling and laughing.

I ambled over to their table and casually dropped into the chair beside Jeremy. They'd ordered burgers and shakes and were sharing a large order of fries. A cell phone was sitting on the table right in front of Jeremy.

"Oh, shit," Jeremy said. "You."

"Who's this?" the girl asked. She looked about the same age as Jeremy.

I smiled at her. "I'm Cal Weaver." I offered my hand. The girl, caught off guard, raised ketchup-smeared fingers. "That's okay." I said. "How's it going, Jeremy?"

"How'd you find me?" he asked.

"Honestly?" I said. "Dumb luck. Who's your friend?"

"This is Charlene," he said, rolling his eyes and slowly shaking his head.

"Who is this guy?" his girlfriend asked.

"This is my new bodyguard," he said dismissively.

"What's your last name, Charlene?" I asked.

She shrugged. "Wilson."

Jeremy said, "I've known Charlene since like third grade."

"The Miata yours, or your parents'?" I asked her.

Her tongue moved around in her mouth. "It was my mom's but she gave it to me when she got a new one."

"Correct me if I'm wrong, but isn't this a school day? Do your parents know you're here instead of in class in Albany?"

"School's over for today," Charlene said.

She had me there.

"So, you two going steady?" I asked, reaching for one of their fries and popping it into my mouth.

Jeremy rolled his eyes again. "God, what century are you from?"

I smiled. "That's what we called it back when we went to sock hops."

Jeremy blinked, as though I'd just spoken to him in Swahili.

Charlene jumped in. "We've been friends forever," she said. "Like Jeremy said, since we were just kids. I'm like the only friend he's got left. All these people who said they were his friend, once everything happened, they all abandoned him. It's like they didn't even *know* him any more. But not me."

"Yeah," Jeremy said. "It's true."

"So I came up to see him. Is that a crime?"

"It's not like *she*'s on probation," Jeremy said. "Look, she'll bring me back to Madeline's house in ten minutes."

"That's gonna be hard," I said. "I've got Charlene's car blocked in."

Jeremy wilted. "Come on, man. I just wanted to get out."

"Like the other time?"

"Huh?"

"Your mom says you've slipped out before since you got to her aunt's place."

He took a bite of his burger, looked at Charlene, as though trying to pretend I wasn't there.

"Where'd you go?" I asked.

Chewing.

"What I'm wondering is whether you were seen. Charlene here isn't the only one who knows you're staying in Promise Falls. Your entire fan base seems to have figured it out. You just missed all the fun at the house."

He stopped chewing and looked at me. "What?"

I told him about the brick through the window. He closed his eyes briefly, something that might actually have been a wince of guilt or regret.

"Is everyone okay?" he asked. "Is Madeline okay?"

"Yeah. So where else have you gone since you got to Promise Falls?"

He gave me a no-big-deal shrug. "Just around."

"Anyone recognize you?"

He looked out the window.

"Jeremy?"

"Some guys. I was walking by some assholes, one grabbed my arm, said I was the Big Baby."

"Did things get out of hand?"

He shook his head. "That was it."

"Did they follow you?"

He thought a moment. "I don't know."

I reached for another fry. I didn't see any reason why these two shouldn't finish their burgers. It'd give me time to drink my coffee.

"For someone who's supposed to be on Jeremy's side," Charlene said, "you sure seem to be picking on him."

"That so?" I said.

"All of this has been *so* unfair," she said. "Everyone thinks he's this awful kid, but he's not."

"I don't think I said he was." I was curious that she had decided to speak up. "I just want him to be safe."

"Yeah, right," she said with an eye roll. "Everyone judges. The thing is, that girl was way drunker than Jeremy and probably fell right in front of the car. Wouldn't have mattered if Jeremy was totally sober, he'd still have hit her."

Jeremy's entire body seemed to flinch as I gave the girl my full attention. "You were there?"

She shook her head quickly. "No. I mean, yes, I was at the party, but I wasn't there when it happened. But everyone knew she liked to drink. I'm just saying, that's probably what happened."

Jeremy, looking uncomfortable as he took his burger in both hands, said, "It's okay, Charlene."

"No, it's not," she said. "The whole world's been so hard on you and you don't deserve it."

Jeremy shrugged. "What are ya gonna do?" he said, and took a bite. "It's done."

"That part, maybe," I said. "But you're still dealing with the fallout. Which is why you, and your mother, need to be a lot more circumspect."

"A lot more what?" Jeremy said, the words coming out garbled between bits of meat and bun.

"Careful," Charlene told him.

I reached for the phone on the table in front of Jeremy.

"Hey!" he said, spewing a shred of lettuce.

I lit up the screen and saw an exchange of texts between Jeremy and Charlene, including instructions on where to pick him up once he'd slipped out of Ms. Plimpton's house.

I turned the phone toward him. "That's what I'm talking about."

"Give that back," he said, putting down the burger and holding out his hand.

"You and your mom really love your phones."

"She's way worse than I am. She's always texting with *Bob*."

"You don't like him?" I asked, keeping the phone out of his reach.

"He's her knight in shining armor," Jeremy said. "Her chance at the life to which she has always wanted to be accustomed."

I kept glancing at Charlene, who looked increasingly annoyed with me.

"I should get back," she said. She balled up the wrapper

her burger had come in, took a last sip of her shake. "Will you move your car?" She paused, then added, "Please?"

"Sure."

"My phone?" Jeremy said.

"Not to worry," I said, raising my hand. "It's safe with me."

We all stood. I put my coffee cup on the plastic tray. When Jeremy made no move to gather up his trash and clear the table, Charlene did it.

As the three of us were walking out, I briefly unnerved the kid taking the orders by slipping behind the counter.

"Mister?" he said.

"Just one sec."

I held Jeremy's phone an inch over the fryer, then dropped it carefully into the sizzling oil so as not to make a splash.

"What the fuck?" said Jeremy.

I slipped a ten to the kid on the till. "For your trouble. You might have to throw out that batch of fries."

TEN

Constance Gaffney had her husband drop her and Monica off at the main entrance to Promise Falls General while Albert parked the car. The couple had not said a word to each other on the drive over, and when Monica attempted to ask any questions, all either of them would say was "We'll see." Or, "I don't know."

Except once, when Constance said, to no particular question, "Your father might know that. He seems to have the answer to everything."

Albert didn't even glance in her direction.

Constance and Monica were still standing at the information desk, stuck behind an elderly couple who'd been wandering the hospital trying to find the gerontology department, when Albert Gaffney came in through the sliding glass doors.

"Where is he?" he whispered.

"We're still waiting to find out," Constance said irritably.

Albert stood silently with his wife and daughter while the older couple struggled with the directions they were being given.

"We go which way?" the woman asked. "Follow which line?"

Constance looked at Albert and tipped her head, urging him wordlessly to interrupt the two old codgers and find out where Brian was. When he didn't immediately butt in, Monica took the lead.

"Hey," she said, raising her voice and cutting in front of the couple. "My brother Brian Gaffney got brought in. Where is he?"

The woman tapped away on her computer. "Probably still in the ER," she said. "If they've moved him to a room, it hasn't shown up here yet."

"Which way?" Constance barked.

Once they'd been given directions, they made their way to the emergency department. They were told they'd find Brian in the adjoining ward in bed thirty-two. The three of them wandered in there, past beds that had been curtained off, until they reached the right one. The drape was pulled shut.

It was Monica who tentatively pulled it back to see if her brother was there.

"Hey," Brian said. "I was wondering if you guys would come." He was sitting up in bed, clad in a hospital dressing gown, covers pulled up to his waist. His clothes were piled on a nearby chair.

His sister and parents crowded around the bed. Constance leaned in to give her son a kiss first, followed by Monica. Albert stood at the foot of the bed and nodded sheepishly.

"What happened?" Constance asked. "You look okay."

"It's kind of hard to explain," Brian said. "At first I thought I'd been abducted by—Well, never mind about that. The police don't think that's what happened. But somebody kinda knocked me out and . . . did something to me."

His family members exchanged nervous looks.

"Did what?" Albert asked softly.

Brian grimaced. "It's easier to just show you. This

83

gown thing is kinda open at the back so you can see it. Just don't look at my butt, Monica." He shifted onto his side, careful to pull up the covers so as not to expose too much of himself below the waist. Monica came around from the other side of the bed, and Albert moved up from the foot.

They all saw what had been done to him at the same moment, and there was a collective gasp.

"Oh dear God," said his mother.

"What is that?" Monica asked. "Is that actually tat-tooed on there?"

"That's what they say," Brian said.

"Jesus," said Albert. He reached out tentatively and touched the words SICK FUCK.

"Why would someone do that because of a dog?" asked Monica.

"Huh?" said Brian.

"Remember Mrs. Beecham's dog?" she said.

Brian struggled to remember. "Oh, shit, yeah, the one I ran over."

"She slashed our tires," Albert recalled.

"You'd never confront her," Constance said. "You never said a word to that awful woman."

"There was no way to prove it," he said. "It wasn't like I got her on video or anything."

Brian said, "Seems like a long time to hold a grudge about running over somebody's dog."

"This would never have happened if you hadn't moved out," Constance said. "I knew that was a mistake."

"It really didn't have anything to do with that," Brian said.

Monica was still gazing at the tattoo, lightly touching the other words, just as her father had touched SICK

84

FUCK. "Who was it, Brian? Who did this? I don't think Mrs. Beecham could have done it. I mean, she's an old lady."

"I don't know. I was asleep through all of it." He rolled onto his back again. His lip started to tremble. "I'm glad you guys came."

"Of course," Constance said. "We came as soon as that police detective told us. When you get out of the hospital, you're coming back to stay with us. Your room is just sitting there."

Brian looked at his father. "I don't know. I was doing okay on my own."

"Oh, right," his mother said. "And look at you now."

Albert's neck muscles had stiffened, and his face was turning red. "You wanna move home, that's fine. But you went to Knight's all the time, right? Even before you moved out."

"Dad's right," Brian said. "This hasn't got nothing to do with my leaving home."

"What's the doctor say?" Albert asked. "Can they get that mess off you?"

Brian shook his head. "What they're worried about is, like, an infection."

"What?" said his mother.

"They gotta do tests, in case, like, I've got hepatitis or something."

"Dear Lord," Constance said.

"Shit," Monica said.

Albert slipped around to the other side of the curtain. His legs were briefly visible, and then he walked away.

"What's with him?" Brian asked.

"He feels bad, and so he should," Constance said.

Monica shook her head. "Jesus, Mom, don't lay all

85

this on Dad. He was right, wanting Brian to be on his own. It's not like he forced him to move out. He put it out there, and Brian liked the idea." She looked at her brother. "Am I right?"

"Pretty much," he said.

Monica continued. "*I* want to be on my own, soon as I can. If something happens to me, will that be Dad's fault too?"

"You always take your father's side," Constance said.

"Oh God, here we go."

"You do."

"There's no sides here," Monica said.

Brian's eyes went back and forth between them. He said, "You think you guys could take it outside?"

Constance put her hand on his. "These tests are going to turn out just fine, I know they are."

"I'm gonna find Dad," Monica said, whisking back the curtain and disappearing.

Monica returned to the ER waiting room, but he wasn't there. She wondered if he had gone back to the car. But then she spotted him down a hallway, sitting in a plastic chair, elbows propped on his knees, his head in his hands.

She strode up the hall and sat down next to him abruptly.

"Hey," she said.

When he took his hands from his face and looked at her, she saw that he had been crying.

"Maybe your mother is right," he said. "I pressured him to leave."

"Isn't that what parents are supposed to do? Make kids independent? And I just told her, you never forced him to go. You gave him the *choice* to go. He wanted to see if he could manage on his own."

Albert smiled thinly at his daughter. "I guess. But your mother didn't think he was ready."

"He'd never have been more ready," Monica said. "Yeah, maybe Brian's a bit naïve. Sometimes people take advantage of him. But he's a good soul, and it's not like you guys are going to live forever. Sooner or later he'd have to fend for himself."

"That's what I kept saying." He looked down at his hands again. "It's like he's been vandalized, you know?" The tears started to come again.

"Yeah," Monica said.

"Some fucking bastard has disfigured him for life." He paused. "I have to make this right."

"How you going to do that?"

"I don't know. I want to know who did this to him. Whoever it was, I want to look him in the eye and ask how he could do it."

"That's kinda not your thing, Dad."

"What do you mean?"

"You know. Taking people on. You're kind of—and don't get mad when I say this—but you're kind of where Brian gets it from. You don't return things to the store when they break down, you never send back your steak even when they do it wrong, you always let the other guy cut in and take the parking spot you had dibs on."

"I save my anger for the fights that matter," he said. "No sense getting killed over a parking spot."

"Oh, Dad." She leaned into him. "I mean, come on, if you were going to confront someone, you could start with Mom."

"Sometimes it's easier to go along," he said.

"You can't always do that," his daughter said.

He looked at her. "You're tough."

"You can be too," she said.

Albert paused. "I have to make it right with Brian. I have to do something."

"Yeah, well, the police are looking into it now."

Albert went very quiet. Monica slipped an arm around him, patted his far shoulder. "I love you, Dad."

He said nothing.

At the far end of the hall, Constance appeared. She walked briskly in their direction.

"There you are," she said. "I was looking all over."

"What's happening?" Monica asked.

"Nothing. I just wanted to know what happened to you two."

"We're talking," Monica said.

Constance said, "I want to speak to that policeman again. What was his name?"

"Duckworth," Monica said. "I think."

Albert stood, took a moment, then walked past his wife without looking at her.

"And just where are you going?"

"I'm going to see my son," he said without looking back.

"Yes, you should do that," she snapped.

When Albert got back to the ward attached to the ER and found his son's curtained examining room, he paused for a moment.

Steeled himself.

He whisked back the curtain.

The bed was empty. Brian's clothes, which had been on the chair, were gone.

Albert went to the nurses' station a few steps away and asked whether his son had been moved to a room or taken somewhere for tests.

"I think I just saw him walk by," the nurse said. "Far as I know, he hasn't been discharged. But come to think of it, he was all dressed."

Albert ran down to the ER, then out through the sliding glass doors to the bay where the ambulances pulled up.

There was no sign of Brian.

His son was gone.

ELEVEN

Barry Duckworth sent a text to his son Trevor: *Need to see you.*

He hit *Send* and stared at the phone for the better part of a minute, waiting to see whether Trevor would respond right away. Sometimes, when Barry sent him a message, Trevor got back immediately. But just as often, he could take an hour or two, or even into the next day, to reply. Of course, it was less of an issue now that he was living with them. Sometimes Duckworth would see his son in person and simply ask him what he wanted to know. To Trevor's credit, Duckworth thought, he was not a slave to his phone the way some people were. He often muted it and didn't check for messages of any kind until the end of the day.

After that minute, Duckworth decided not to spend any more time waiting.

He definitely wanted to talk to Trevor about being at Knight's. Was it possible he'd seen anything? He'd left the bar only a few seconds after Brian Gaffney. But in the meantime, there were other things he could do.

Phone still in hand, he looked up tattoo parlors in Promise Falls. There were three listed: Mike's Tattoos, Kinky Inky, and Dreamy Tatts.

Kinky Inky was just up the street from Knight's, so he walked it. But when he got there, he found a sign in the window that read: *Out of Bizness. Thanx for your Patronage.*

He made his hand into a visor and peered through the smudged window. The place had been cleared out. No chairs, no tables, nothing.

Hitting the other two parlors meant getting back into his car. Dreamy Tatts was seven blocks away, sharing a small plaza with a 7-Eleven and a wig shop. As he approached the door, he encountered another sign: *CLOSED*. He had missed Dreamy Tatts' business hours by ten minutes. He made a mental note that the place would reopen at noon the next day.

That only left Mike's, and Duckworth figured it might be closed too. But eight minutes later, when he rolled to a stop behind a black van out front of a shop sandwiched between a comic book shop and a lawnmower repair place, he got lucky. A neon *OPEN* sign lit up a window that was decorated with dozens of sample tattoos.

He went inside and immediately heard the high-pitched buzzing sounds of a tattoo gun. A blonde-haired woman in her mid-twenties, dressed in jeans and a red short-sleeved T-shirt, surprisingly free of any visible tattoos but with several studs in her ears, sat behind a simple desk with a computer on top of it. She was engaged in conversation with a man who was perched on the edge of the desk, pointing out something to her on the computer screen.

She eyed Duckworth with sleepy eyes and said, "Cop?"

Duckworth grinned. "Is it that obvious?"

The man turned and looked at him with sudden awareness. "Whoa, I've seen you on the news."

"Yeah, that's where I've seen you, too," the woman said.

"Ah, well, that's cheating," Duckworth said. "It's not like you've got some sort of sixth sense." He flashed his ID. "Detective Duckworth, Promise Falls Police."

The man slid his butt off the desk and grinned. "I think even if we hadn't seen you on TV, we'd know what you do for a living."

Duckworth gave him a quick look. Early thirties, two hundred pounds, short reddish hair and round cheeks. He peered at Duckworth through a pair of wire-rimmed glasses, and was dressed in tan khakis and a dark blue shirt with a button-down collar. No visible tattoos on him, either. He seemed out of place here, the detective thought. A little too clean-cut. He reminded Duckworth of Howdy Doody, that rosy-cheeked, red-haired cowboy puppet from the fifties TV show. Which was even before Duckworth's time, but some American icons had staying power.

"What gives it away that I'm a cop?" Duckworth asked.

"You just have the look," the man said.

"Come on, Cory, it's not *that* obvious," the woman said.

Cory shook his head. "First of all, you don't look like someone who's here for a tattoo."

Duckworth nodded. "You're right about that." He smiled. "And you don't look to me like a guy who'd make his living as a tattoo artist."

Cory grinned. "You got me." He stood back and crossed his arms, as though issuing a challenge. "What *do* you think I do?"

Duckworth thought a moment. "Computer programmer."

Cory's mouth dropped. "Whoa, that's not bad. I mean, that's not what I do, but I spend a lot of time on the computer."

"What *do* you do?" Duckworth asked.

"I guess I'm what you'd call a social activist," Cory said. "Causes and stuff."

"Good for you," Duckworth said.

The girl behind the desk said, "Cory, for the love of God, stop talking. Can I help you, Mr. Policeman?"

Duckworth said, "What's your name?"

"Dolores. Like from *Seinfeld*."

"Excuse me?"

"You know. The girl whose name rhymes with a female body part."

Duckworth said, "I never watched that show."

"Seriously?" said Cory.

"Seriously."

"Wow. I didn't think there was anyone who hadn't seen it," Dolores said. "I mean, I was barely born when it came on, but even I've seen all the episodes. Anyway, my friends call me Dolly."

"Hi, Dolly."

"So what can I do for you?"

Duckworth pointed up at the *Mike's Tattoos* sign. "I'd like to see Mike."

"Hang on."

She disappeared through a door into a back room where the buzzing noise was coming from. The tattoo gun ceased making a noise, and Dolly said, "Hey, Mike, there's a cop here who's never seen *Seinfeld* who wants to talk to you."

"Sure," a man said. "Send him round."

Dolly reappeared and waved Duckworth in her direction. "The doctor will see you now," she said, smirking.

Cory gave Dolly a wave and said, "See ya." Then, to Duckworth, "Good luck catching the bad guys."

Duckworth gave him an upturned thumb as Cory left

the shop, then followed Dolly into the back of the store. Mike, a thin, bearded man in his thirties wearing a pair of magnifying goggles, was hunched over a heavyset guy about twice that age sitting in what looked like a barber's chair. It was leaned back to about forty-five degrees to allow Mike to work comfortably on the man's upper arm. The tattoo was a nice rendering of a waterfall—about three inches long—and below it, the numbers 5-23-16.

Below that, the words: *I SURVIVED.*

"Hey," Mike said, not taking his eyes off his work.

Duckworth said, "Hi." Then, "That's some tattoo." There was no approval in his voice.

The man in the chair smiled. "You get it, right?"

"I get it," Duckworth said.

"May twenty-third of last year," he said. "I didn't drink the water."

"Lucky you."

Dolly pointed to the tattoo. "Jeez, Mike, shouldn't the 23 be first, and then the 5?"

"I don't think so," Mike said, suddenly looking worried. He glanced at his customer. "That's the way you wanted it, right?"

"You got it."

"Whew. You scared me for a sec, Dolly."

Mike finally looked at Duckworth. "What can I do ya for?" He moved the magnifying goggles up to his hairline.

"I want to show you something," Duckworth said, getting out his phone. He tapped the screen and brought up the picture he'd taken of Gaffney. "Do you know this man?"

Mike studied it for three seconds. "Nope."

"You're sure?"

"Pretty sure. Dolly, you recognize that dude?"

Dolores gave the picture a long look, pursed her lips, and said, "Can't say that I do."

"I have another picture," Duckworth said. He brought up the picture of Gaffney's back, then held the phone in Mike's direction.

"Jesus, what am I looking at?" He slid the magnifying glasses back down, studied the shot, then raised them again.

"What the fuck is that?" he asked.

"That's someone's idea of a tattoo," the detective said. "Recognize the handiwork?"

"Are you kidding me? That's a goddamn abortion you got there. May I?" He was asking to hold the phone to get a better look. He set the tattoo gun down and, using thumb and forefinger, blew up the image to examine the details. "Is this for real? Someone actually got this tattoo?"

"Lemme see?" said Dolly. Mike handed her the phone. "Whoa. This guy should definitely get his money back."

The guy in the chair wanted a peek, too. "Man, please don't do that to me."

Duckworth took his phone back and asked his question again, in a slightly different way. "You any idea who might have done this?"

Mike had his own question. "Why would someone get a tatt like that?"

"It wasn't voluntary," Duckworth said.

Mike's eyes went wide. "Someone did that without his permission?"

"That's fuckin' crazy," Dolly said.

"How could someone sit still that long and let someone do that to him?" Mike wanted to know.

Duckworth felt he'd told them enough already. "So you don't know whose work this might be?"

"I'd say a four-year-old did it," Mike said. "That's how bad it is. This is not the work of a professional. This is amateur night."

"Do a lot of amateurs do tattoo work?"

"They sure as hell shouldn't," Mike said.

"You ever lend out your equipment?" Duckworth asked, nodding at the tattoo gun in Mike's hand.

"God, no way. I'd never—" He stopped himself mid-sentence.

"What?"

"Dolly, when did we have that thing?"

"Thing?"

"That night someone got in here?"

Dolly thought. "That was, like, two weeks ago? I think."

"You had a break-in?" Duckworth asked.

Mike shrugged and rolled his eyes. "Not exactly. We each thought the other person had locked up, and the back door got left open one night. At first we didn't think anything had been stolen, but a couple days later I noticed one of the guns and some other stuff was missing. Figured it happened that night."

"It was my bad," Dolly said. "I shoulda checked."

"How hard would it be for someone to work out how to do what you do?"

"Well, if they got the stuff they needed, they could do it," Mike said. "They just couldn't do a very good job. I mean, I'm an artist, you know?" He nodded toward the waterfall on the man's shoulder.

"Sure."

"You wouldn't figure a guy who stole some paint

and a few brushes could turn out the *Mona Lisa*, would you?"

Duckworth took another look at the tattoo on the customer's arm. "No, I wouldn't."

"What I don't get," Dolly said, "is how you could do something like that without the guy lettin' ya."

"'Cause it hurts like a son of a bitch," offered the man in the chair.

"Did you call the police about the tattoo gun that was stolen?" Duckworth asked.

Mike made a snorting noise. "Honestly, how much effort would the Promise Falls Police have put into that?"

Duckworth nodded, taking his point. He thought about Knight's and asked, "You got cameras?"

Mike shook his head. "Hell, no. I got a lot of clientele wouldn't even come in here if they knew they were on video."

"Like bikers?"

"Bikers? No, I'm talking upstanding leaders of the community, housewives, people like that. People who think they're too respectable." He grinned. "They get tatts in some pretty interesting places. Kind of a challenge gettin' *at* some of those places, let me tell you."

Dolly smirked.

"Thanks for your time," Duckworth said.

As he was heading for the door, the guy in the chair asked, "Who's the Sean that sick fuck killed?"

"Workin' on that," the detective said.

Getting into his car, he thought it interesting that he was the only one who'd thought to ask.

Once behind the wheel, he took out his phone again and called up the picture he'd taken of the van parked in the driveway of Mrs. Beecham's house. He memorized the plate, then called in to the communications division at the station. A woman answered.

"Shirley?" Duckworth said.

"Yes, it is. That you, Barry?"

"Yeah. I need you to run a plate for me."

"Barry, when you gonna get one of those computers for your car like the real police have?"

"Are you ready?"

"Fire away."

He closed his eyes and read off the combination of letters and numbers.

"Hang on," Shirley said. He could hear her typing in the background. "Okay, got it."

"Who does it belong to?"

"Van's registered to a Norma Howton."

"Spell that last name?"

She did.

"So, not Norma Lastman," Duckworth said.

"Nope," Shirley said. "Anything else I can do for you today? Book you a cruise to Tahiti? Order you a pizza?"

"No, that'll do," Duckworth said.

TWELVE

CAL

"You're gonna have to buy me a new phone," Jeremy Pilford told me from the passenger seat.

We were pulling out of the parking lot of the burger place. I glanced in my rear-view to see Jeremy's girlfriend backing out of her spot in her red Miata, grinding the gears slightly as she did so.

"She's something," I said.

"Huh?"

"Charlene. She seems to believe in you."

"Yeah, well."

"Been friends a long time?"

"Pretty much forever, I guess."

"Girlfriend?"

He gave me a pained look. "You already asked me the going-steady question."

"Which you really didn't answer."

"You're like my mom. You're all hung up on labels. Is she a *girl*friend? She's a friend. Sometimes we're closer than at other times."

"Regardless of how close you are right now, you shouldn't have called her or let her know where you are."

"What?"

"I think the word you were looking for there is 'pardon.' Or perhaps a question, along the lines of, oh,

99

Mr. Weaver, why would you say that?"

"You think you're funny, don't you?" Jeremy asked.

I shrugged. "I don't know. I'm saving my best stuff for later. Anyway, since you're not going to ask, I'll tell you. You've got a target on your back. Now, if you want to be stupid and let the world know where you are, that's one thing. But when you invited Charlene up here to join you, you put her at risk. You want to get her killed?"

He shot me a look. "No one's going to kill me."

"Let's hope not."

"I'm not scared."

It was my turn to shoot him a look. "Then what was that I saw earlier?"

"When?"

"On the porch of Ms. Plimpton's house."

"Huh?"

"The look in your eyes. I know what I saw."

"What did you see?"

"You looked scared to me."

"Yeah, right. I'm fucking shaking in my boots."

"Fine," I said. "Look, I know the whole world's been calling you a big baby and you want to show that you're not. I get that. But the fact is, a little bit of fear is a good thing. It makes you smarter. It makes you pay attention. Now, all I'm being hired to do is have a look at your level of security, and right now I'd say it's zero. A good portion of the blame goes to you and your mother for being too free with what you say online. You might as well have put a billboard on your grandmother's front lawn advertising your arrival. Part of you wants to bust out and party, but part of you knows you may actually be in danger. That's what I saw when I looked at you on the porch."

Jeremy didn't say anything for several seconds. "Maybe. But only a little."

"Whatever. You're a soldier."

"You gonna buy me a new phone?"

"No."

He thought about that. "Bob will."

"There you go. I thought you didn't like him."

Jeremy looked out his window. "I don't know. I guess he's okay."

"What's his story?"

"He's some big real-estate guy. Has properties all over the place. He's always doing deals. Always waiting for the really, really big one, like the one he did with, you know."

"No, I don't know."

"The guy who had the party. Where it happened."

"Where the accident happened?"

"Yeah, there."

"Who's that?"

"Galen Broadhurst. He's like this mega-deal guy. But seriously, what kind of name is that? Galen Broadhurst?"

The name had come up in conversation earlier in the day, but I realized it wasn't the very first time I'd heard it. From what I'd seen on the news, it had been Broadhurst's car Jeremy had been driving when he ran down that girl. Maybe I'd know even more about him if I read the *Wall Street Journal* or the business section of the *New York Times*. So, he was a big-deal businessman. If you were born with a name like Galen Broadhurst, I suspected you were destined to be rich and powerful. You didn't meet a lot of guys at the Wendy's drive-through window with names like that.

"I watched the news about the trial," I said, "but I

don't know all the details. You want to fill me in, or is it something you'd rather not talk about?"

"I sat in court for weeks listening to all of it over and over again. You really think I want to shoot the shit with you about it?"

"What I figured," I said. I couldn't blame him.

"Anyway," Jeremy said, "Mom likes Bob because he can give her all the things my dad never could."

"What's his story?"

"Who? Bob? Or my real dad?"

"Your real dad."

"He's . . . he's kind of got his own life. He's okay. He wanted to help. You know, when I got in trouble, but my mom said no. Not that he's got lots of money or anything."

"What's he do?"

"He's a high-school teacher."

"Okay," I said. "So an expensive lawyer may be a little beyond his budget."

"Yeah, but he wanted to help other ways, like, just being supportive, you know? But Mom told him no."

"Why?"

Jeremy looked out the window. "She just did, that's all."

I decided not to push.

"And Bob?"

"He's got money. I mean, he's not super-loaded, not yet, anyway."

"What do you mean?"

"He's done a deal with Mr. Broadhurst. Bob's gonna be a multi-millionaire when it's over."

"Well," I said. "Good for him."

Jeremy shrugged. "He still seems like kind of a douche to me," he said.

"Does anyone *not* seem like a douche to you?"

Jeremy slowly turned his head my way. "It's just that I think he paid for the lawyer only because he was doing it for my mom, you know? It wasn't like he did it because he thinks I could be the world's greatest future stepson. Because, let's face it, I'll never be that."

"The fact is, he paid for your defense, regardless of his motivation."

"I guess." He watched the traffic going the other way. "So what are you going to do? Lock me up someplace to keep me safe? Because I might as well be in jail if you do."

I gave him a smile. "Tempting, but I think we'll have to come up with something else."

"Because I have rights, you know."

"Yeah," I said. "That girl you ran down had rights, too."

I regretted saying the words as soon as they were out of my mouth. As hard as this kid was to like, he'd already been judged by millions on the Internet for what he'd done. He didn't need me to chime in.

"Sorry," I said.

He looked at me, surprised.

"It's not my place to judge you. That's been done."

He was quiet for several seconds. "Thanks." After another minute, he said, "I liked her." Adding, in case I wasn't following, "The girl that, you know, got run over."

Not: *The girl I killed.*

"What was her name?" I asked.

"McFadden."

"She have a first name?"

"It's a weird name. Sounds like Sharn. Like, if you said Sharon real fast."

"What is that?" I asked.

"What *is* it?"

"I mean, is it Irish? Actually, I think it's Welsh," I said. "So you knew her?"

"Not that much. Our parents were at the party, and we ended up hanging out. I knew her a little. She lived in the neighborhood. She was sort of a friend the way Charlene is a friend, only she was kind of more of a friend that night." A pause. "The more drinks we snuck out, the drunker we got, and we started making out."

"That must have been a bit awkward."

"Why?"

"Charlene said she was at the party that night, too."

"Yeah. Her and her parents. But we were kind of avoiding her. And at that time, Charlene was mostly just a friend, not *more* of a friend." He glanced my way. "You get what I'm saying."

"I think so."

Jeremy was quiet for a moment. Then, "My mom and Bob and the lawyer, they said it wasn't my fault really. Not for the reason Charlene said. The others say they're to blame, too. And Mr. Broadhurst."

"Go on."

"I mean, first of all, Mr. Broadhurst left the keys in the car. That was a really stupid thing to do. Especially a car like that."

"Okay," I said.

"And like I said, there was all kinds of booze around, and it was easy to get. Mom and Bob should have done more to keep me from getting into it. I wasn't old enough to drink responsibly."

"I see. So you drank too much, then got in Mr. Broadhurst's car, drove off in it and ran down that girl, and they've all got to take the heat for that."

He glared at me. "I thought you said it wasn't your place to judge."

"You're making me want to reassess my position."

"God, you're just like all of them," he said sulkily.

My cell rang. I grabbed it from my pocket and put it to my ear.

"Hello."

"Bob Butler here."

"Hey, Bob."

Jeremy glanced my way.

"Is Jeremy with you?" Bob asked.

"Yeah, we're almost back to the house."

"Shit. I was thinking, if you could go the long way, that might help. You know I mentioned Galen Broadhurst might drop by?"

"I remember."

"Well, he did. But there's a bit of a wrinkle, and it might be better all round if Jeremy didn't get here until Galen's gone."

The problem was, we were already back. I'd just made the turn onto Madeline Plimpton's street. The house wasn't half a block away. There was a car parked at the curb that hadn't been there when I'd left to find Jeremy, which must have been Broadhurst's. Nice set of wheels, too.

"Oh, Jesus, I don't believe it!" Jeremy said, sitting up in his seat. "What the hell is that doing there? Why would he *do* that? Why would someone do that to me?"

"What are you talking about?" I asked, taking the phone away from my ear.

Jeremy was looking at the car. It was a red seventies-vintage Porsche 911.

"That," he said.

"What about it?"

"That's the car . . . that's the car I was driving when it happened."

THIRTEEN

Trevor Duckworth glanced down at his phone.

"Shit, my dad sent me a text like an hour ago," he told the woman sitting across from him at the round table just out front of a Promise Falls Starbucks. She was mid-twenties, green eyes, dark hair to her shoulders. She wore a black sweater, black jeans, and tan leather boots that came up to her knees.

"What's he want?"

"Says he needs to talk to me."

"What about?"

Trevor shrugged. He tapped *Im at Starbucks* and hit *Send*. He saw the dots appear, and then his father's reply: *Stay there. See you in 5.*

Trevor typed *K*, then rested his phone on the small table. "I should have told him something else."

"Why?"

"He'll be thinking, I'm out of work, and I can still afford to pay five bucks for a cup of coffee."

"Would he say that?"

"No, but he'll be thinking it. He's coming here in a couple of minutes."

"Should I go?" the woman asked. She glanced down at her latte. She'd barely started it.

Trevor hesitated. "I don't know."

"You don't know? How about, 'Please stay, I'd love him to meet you.' How about that?"

"You know it's not a good idea." Trevor thumbed his

phone to check the time. "Fine, you might as well hang in and meet him."

"He is kind of a hero," she said.

"Yeah, I know, so everyone says," Trevor said. "He's the big star."

"You two don't get along?"

Trevor sighed. "Sometimes. Sometimes not. He can be a bit of a hardass at times. Whaddya expect? He's a cop." He glanced out at the parking lot. "Shit, he was even closer than he said."

The woman followed his gaze. A heavyset man was getting out of a black four-door sedan and walking toward them.

Trevor got to his feet as his father approached. The woman smiled awkwardly. Barry Duckworth nodded briefly to his son before turning his attention to her.

"Well, hello," he said, extending a hand.

"Hi," she said.

"Dad, uh, this is Carol," Trevor said uneasily. "Carol Beakman."

"Pleased to meet you," she said. "I've heard a lot about you."

Duckworth grinned and tipped his head toward his son. "Whatever he told you, you should take it with a grain of salt."

"Is everything okay?" Trevor asked.

"Yeah, everything is fine," Duckworth said. "Just needed to talk to you."

"I'll be on my way," Carol said, reaching for her purse and putting the lid back onto her latte.

"No, please," Duckworth said quickly. "I'd like you to stay."

"I don't want to intrude, and I do have some things I have—"

"No, this may actually involve you."

Carol's eyes flashed. "I'm sorry?"

"Dad, what's this about?"

"Can we grab another chair?" Duckworth said. Trevor went to the closest table, where a woman was sitting alone. He stole the chair across from her and brought it over to their table. Duckworth took a seat.

"You want something?" Carol asked. "A cappuccino maybe?"

"No, no, that's okay. And if I go up to the counter, I won't be able to stop myself from getting a slice of that lemon cake, with the icing." He felt his mouth starting to water. "The slices aren't all that big, are they? How many calories could they be?"

"Dad," Trevor said. He said to Carol, "Dad's been trying to lose some weight."

"What do you mean, trying? I *have* lost some weight."

Carol smiled. "Congrats. It's never easy."

"Tell me about it," Duckworth said. "Okay, so . . ." He extended his arms and placed his palms flat on the small table. "I have to admit, this is slightly awkward. This sort of thing hasn't happened before."

"What sort of thing?" his son asked.

"I'll start at the beginning," Duckworth said. He told them about the police picking up Brian Gaffney, bringing him into the station. How Gaffney couldn't account for the last two days.

"What's that got to do with us?" Trevor asked.

"Well, the last thing Mr. Gaffney remembers is being at a bar."

"What bar?" Carol asked.

"Knight's," he said.

Trevor and Carol exchanged a quick look.

"When was this?" Trevor asked.

"Two nights ago. After he left the bar, he says someone called to him from the alley, and he doesn't remember anything after that."

"Wow," said Trevor.

Duckworth brought out his phone, tapped on the photo app. "Here's a picture of him. He look familiar?"

They both looked at the photo and shook their heads in unison.

"What did they do to him exactly?" Carol asked.

Duckworth hesitated. "I can show you, but it's not an easy thing to look at, I'm warning you." With that, he swiped the screen to bring up the previous photo.

"Oh my God, what is that?" Carol asked. "Someone wrote all over his back?"

"It's a tattoo. It's permanent."

"Wait, you mean, like, someone did that to him without his permission?" Carol asked.

"That's right."

"How could they do that?" she asked.

"By keeping him knocked out or sedated, it would seem," Duckworth said, and at that moment his head jerked, as though he'd just remembered something.

"What?" Trevor said.

"Craig Pierce," the detective said.

"I know that name," Carol said. "The guy who was attacked? About three months ago."

Duckworth nodded slowly, and said, more to himself than to his son and Carol, "He was sedated too. I can't believe I didn't think of that until now."

"Dad," Trevor said.

Duckworth didn't respond. He was recalling the earlier case.

"Earth to Dad, come in, please."

"Sorry," Duckworth said, as if being brought out of a trance. "There's some things I have to check out. But anyway, this guy who had his back tattooed, he—"

"That's totally sick," Trevor said.

"Yeah, it sure is." Duckworth went back to Gaffney's head shot. "Are you sure he doesn't look familiar?"

"Uh, why would you think we'd recognize him?" Trevor asked.

His father smiled sheepishly. "This is the awkward part. I went to Knight's to have a look at their surveillance footage. I focused in on the time just before Mr. Gaffney arrived, and just after he left. I thought, you know, if he'd had a run-in with someone, a fight, that'd give me an idea who might have done this to him."

Another exchange of looks between Trevor and Carol.

"What'd you see?" Trevor asked.

"Well, I didn't see anything like that. But what I did notice was that the two of you were in the bar at the time."

"Oh," said Carol, her face flushing.

"Jesus, Dad," Trevor said, shaking his head. "I never thought I'd see the day when you'd be investigating your own kid."

"It's not like that."

"It's what it sounds like to me. Just 'cause I've moved back in doesn't mean you get to stick your nose into my personal life." He looked apologetically at Carol. "I'm really sorry about this."

Carol placed a hand on Trevor's arm. "I don't think your father—"

Trevor shook her hand off. "No, this is really crossing the line."

Keeping his voice very calm, Duckworth said, "I'm only here because I thought you might be able to help me. It's not like the two of you are in any kind of trouble."

"You actually looked at us sitting there, in the bar?"

"I did."

Carol's face flushed again. "You must . . . you must have a terrible impression of me."

Duckworth smiled reassuringly. "Not at all. I was young myself once, or so I'm told. It's hard to remember back that far."

"So, basically, you watched us make out," Trevor said accusingly.

"Trevor," Duckworth said evenly, "you and Carol here are potential witnesses to a crime. You may have seen something without even realizing it. I observed the two of you in a booth, yes. Shortly after Mr. Gaffney left the bar, you left too. I'm hoping maybe one or both of you noticed something outside that might be helpful in the investigation. If you're uncomfortable being inter-viewed by me, then I can turn this over to someone else and have them do it."

Trevor was silent.

"Is that what you'd like?"

Trevor looked away. While he considered a response, Carol said, "I'm okay with talking to you. I mean, I didn't see anything, but I don't mind talking to you. Trevor, are you okay with me talking to your dad?"

"This is just weird, that's all," he said.

"I get that," Duckworth said. "I mean, it's not like I think you two tattooed this guy."

Carol laughed nervously. "Well, that's good to know!"

Trevor, however, did not look amused.

"Do you remember seeing Mr. Gaffney?"

Carol shook her head. "I don't. But," and she placed her hand gingerly over her mouth, as though she were about to tell a secret, "I wasn't really paying attention to anyone else."

"Trevor?"

"Don't remember him."

"What about when you left Knight's? You had to have come out just a few seconds after Mr. Gaffney. This would have been right around the time he met the person or persons who abducted him. Did you notice anything odd? Maybe someone hanging around outside the bar, or at the entrance to the alley? Did you hear something that sounded like a fight or a scuffle?"

"No," Trevor said quickly. "No to all of those things. We came out and went to my car and that's that." He looked at Carol. "Right?"

She studied Trevor's face for a moment before replying. "That's right. That's certainly the way I remember it."

"You didn't talk to anyone, see anyone when you came out?" Duckworth persisted.

"Didn't I just answer that?" Trevor asked before Carol could say anything.

Duckworth gave his son a slow appraisal. "Okay, then." He smiled weakly at Carol. "I thought it was worth a shot, is all." He put his phone back into his pocket and leaned back from the table.

"It's such a pleasure to have met you," he said to Carol.

"Nice to meet you too."

"What do you do, Carol?"

"I work for the town."

"That must be interesting, especially now that we have Randall Finley running things again."

"Never a dull moment," Carol said.

"And David Harwood's still his assistant, right?"

"He is. They never charged him for shooting that escaped convict."

"Lucky for Harwood. Listen, you must come by the house some time."

She forced a smile. "That'd be nice."

"I know Trevor's mother would be delighted to see you. How did you two meet?"

"Jesus, Dad," Trevor said. "This really is turning into an investigation. Does Carol have the right to call her lawyer?"

Carol forced a laugh. "Trevor, it's okay."

Duckworth raised his hands as though admitting defeat. "None of my business anyway."

He got up from the chair and gave his son one last nod. "See you later."

"Yeah, sure," Trevor said. "Can't wait."

Duckworth walked back to his car, got behind the wheel, and drove out of the Starbucks lot.

"God, I'm sorry about that," Trevor said. "I don't know what to say. I've never been so humiliated. He *watched* us."

"It's okay," Carol said quietly. "He seems like a nice guy."

Trevor said nothing.

"Do you think he could tell?" Carol asked.

"Think he could tell what?"

"That we both lied to him?"

Trevor considered that. "I hope not."

FOURTEEN

It was a long walk to Jessica Frommer's house, but Brian Gaffney wasn't troubled by that. Besides, it was closer than going back to his place and getting his car. He patted the front pocket of his jeans. At least he still had his keys. The bastard—or bastards—who'd done all this to him had stripped him of his wallet and his phone, but at least he'd be able to get into his apartment and start his car.

It sure was nice to get out of the hospital. Even though his family had come to see him, the visit had stressed him out. When his sister and mother started arguing, all he wanted was for them to leave. Once his mother left to find Monica and his dad, Brian decided he'd had enough. He wanted out of there before they returned to his room and started bickering all over again.

He felt badly for his father. It wasn't his fault that Brian had decided to move out. He'd already been thinking about doing it. He'd landed this job at the detailing shop, and while it didn't pay a fortune, it gave him enough money to rent a tiny apartment. It wasn't like rents in Promise Falls were all that high. The town had lost so many jobs in the last few years—and a year ago, so many *people*—that a lot of rental units were going empty. On top of that, a lot of people had decided to leave, move away. The town had had such a run of bad luck that many feared it was never going to end. Best to get out before things got worse.

But even though Brian believed it had ultimately been

his own decision to move out, his mother blamed his father for it. Albert had fully supported his son striking out on his own, learning to live independently. While Brian was no dummy, he was willing to concede he was no Steve Jobs or Mr. Spock or Sheldon Cooper—okay, those last two weren't real, but still—and that sometimes people could get the better of him, confuse him.

Like this whole hepatitis thing. They were going to test to see whether he was positive for it. To Brian's way of thinking, positive was good, so if he tested positive, that would mean he didn't have it. But the doctor had explained to him that a good result would be a negative result, which would mean he did *not* have hepatitis.

Fuck, who knew. Why they couldn't make things simpler, he didn't know.

His dad had told him that if he ever had a question about anything, all he had to do was phone him. But he'd be okay out in the world, Albert assured him. He'd do fine.

And Brian was doing fine. Until he wasn't.

The really good thing about being on his own, though, was privacy. Having your own place, you could come and go as you pleased. You could eat whatever you wanted. You didn't have to explain yourself.

Maybe best of all was you could have a girl over.

A girl like Jessica Frommer.

Not that she'd ever actually stayed over at his place. But he'd believed that day was imminent. All the more reason to find her now and apologize. He was supposed to have met up with her during the time he was abducted. Since he no longer had a phone, he couldn't call her, and without his wallet, he couldn't even pay for a taxi.

So he would walk.

Brian figured Jessica would be surprised to see him. Not just because he hadn't been in touch for a couple of days, but because she was unaware he knew where she lived.

One night they'd met up at the BestBet Inn, just off Route 98 on the road to Albany. Jessica never wanted to go anywhere with him in Promise Falls, and Brian wondered if that was because she thought maybe he wasn't good enough for her, that she'd run into her friends when she was with him and be embarrassed. But she'd tell him she just thought Promise Falls was boring and it didn't have any good restaurants. The BestBet, she said, had a pretty decent buffet. You could pick and choose what you wanted, and there was no limit on how much you could take.

Brian had started getting his hopes up that if Jessica wanted to meet him at a hotel, maybe she had plans that didn't end with dinner.

He turned out to be right.

So after a meal that included pasta and roast beef and chicken wings and French fries and cherry pie with ice cream and about a dozen other things, Jessica confessed to him that she had booked them a room. At some point, around the time he was loading his plate with mashed potatoes, Brian must have lost hope that it was not going to happen. Now that he knew it was on, he was sorry he'd had quite so much to eat. He felt somewhat bloated.

But whatever.

They went upstairs and their first time was fast and clumsy. But within half an hour Brian was ready to go again, and things got so hot and heavy they didn't notice that the winds outside were growing increasingly strong. Once Brian had finished, rolled off Jessica and collapsed onto his back on the bed next to her, they could hear the howling gale and the rain hitting the hotel room window. He pulled back the drapes to see a driving rain that was almost going sideways. Visibility was bad, and low spots in the road were flooding over.

Brian said they didn't have to be in any rush. The room, after all, was booked until the morning. But Jessica said she had to get back home, no matter what the roads were like. Even though they'd brought two cars, Brian offered to give her a lift. He could bring her back the following day to pick up her vehicle. But Jessica said she'd driven through some of the worst snowstorms upstate New York had ever seen, so she wasn't about to let a few puddles scare her.

Once Brian had helped her into her car, and watched her pull out of the BestBet parking lot, he ran to his own set of wheels, soaked to the skin, and took off after her. He stayed far enough back that she wouldn't see him, and besides, all he was in her rear-view mirror at this time of night was a pair of headlights.

She was right. She was a good driver. She got back to her place on Pilgrim's Way—a small one-story white house with black shutters—without incident. Brian drove right on by. He went to bed that night confident that Jessica was safely in hers.

Hey, it was just the kind of guy he was.

So, now that he was hoofing it, he knew where to go.

Along the way, he thought of all the other people he needed to get in touch with. He wondered if he still had his job at the car wash. He'd gone two days without showing up or making any calls to explain his absence.

They'd be pissed.

He figured he'd have to go to his parents' house to use

their phone to cancel his credit cards. Then there'd be the hassle of getting a new driver's license. Man, hepatitis was the least of his worries.

He reached Pilgrim's Way and strode down the sidewalk. It wasn't dark yet, so the house was not hard to find. Jessica's car, a blue compact four-door, was parked behind a Ford pickup.

Brian went up the steps to the door and rang the bell. He was thinking he'd have to show Jessica what had been done to his back, but he'd really have to work up to it. Didn't want to freak her out.

He could hear someone approaching the door. Quick, soft steps.

When the door opened, Brian had to look down. It was a girl, maybe four years old, in a pair of red pajamas. Curly blonde hair, rosy cheeks, bare feet. She looked up at Brian and grinned.

"Boo," she said.

"Uh," he said slowly, "I'm looking for Jessica?"

Could this be Jessica's little sister? She hadn't mentioned having one. If this girl was her sister, there sure was one hell of a big difference between their ages. More than twenty years, Brian figured. A visiting niece, maybe?

The little girl shouted, "Mommy!"

Brian felt a sudden queasiness in his stomach.

The child stayed by the door as Jessica shouted, "I'll be right there, Gilda!"

The girl wiggled her nose as she looked up at Brian. "What's your name?" she demanded.

Brian said, "Uh."

Suddenly Jessica was there. Her expression was one of instant panic. "Go watch TV, Gilda."

"There's nothing on."

"Go!" she said sharply.

Jessica did not invite Brian in. Instead, she closed the door partway and spoke to him through the crack. "What are you doing here? How did you find me?"

"I . . . I wanted to apologize. I was supposed to meet you and—"

"You have to leave. You have to leave *right now*."

A man's voice boomed from deeper inside the house. "Jessica!"

"Who's that?" Brian asked, starting to feel overwhelmingly confused. "Is that your dad?"

"No, it is *not* my dad," she whispered.

"Whose kid was that?" he asked. He was pretty sure he knew the answer, but he was hoping maybe, just maybe, he was wrong. Before she could answer, he said, "Aw, Jeez."

"You have to go," Jessica insisted.

"So you've got a kid?" Brian said. "And you're *married*?"

"Please," she said. "I was going to—I would have told you—"

"Ah man, I feel like such an idiot," he said. "My family's right. I really will fall for anyone's bullshit. No wonder you didn't want to be seen around here with me. I was starting to think maybe you were ashamed, but I get it now. You didn't want to be—"

A hand came around the edge of the door and opened it wider. The hand, Brian quickly saw, was connected to a thin, ropy arm. Jessica's husband was a good six feet tall, thin and wiry. His eyes were small and set deeply under his brow.

"What's goin' on?" he asked.

"Nothing," Jessica said. "Just someone . . . What is it you're selling again?"

Brian blinked. Thinking on his feet had never been an area in which he excelled. "Uh, I'm, uh . . ."

The man edged Jessica out of the way and came out onto the step. "Uh, what?"

"Ron, it's nothing," Jessica said to her husband. "He's just going door to door. Is it a charity?" She looked at Brian with wide, hopeful eyes, trying to encourage him to play along.

But he wasn't getting the message. "I just . . . I had an appointment with your wife and came by to explain why I wasn't able to make it."

"An appointment?" Ron cocked his head slightly to one side.

Brian nodded weakly. "You see, something happened to me. I was coming out of Knight's, and—"

"You should go," the man said.

"They did something to me," Brian said, talking past Ron to Jessica, his voice starting to break. "They did something awful to me. I might even have hepatitis. I don't know if I can die from that, but it could be bad. They're doing tests."

"Jesus, so you've got some sort of disease?" the man said. "Get the fuck out of here."

"No," Brian said, "it's not something you can catch. At least, I don't think so. Like I said, I . . . I was at Knight's. And when I came out, someone—it might have been more than one person, I don't know—but they grabbed me and—'

"You're some sort of fucking lunatic," Ron said. At which point he placed his palm solidly on Brian's chest and gave him a shove.

Brian was pitched off the step. He hit the lawn on his back, which briefly knocked the wind out of him. He struggled to catch his breath as he got up on his knees. But before he could stand, Jessica's husband put the toe of his boot into Brian's chest. He screamed out in pain as he hit the ground.

Ron hovered over him. "You're one of them, aren't you? You're one of the ones my wife's been whoring around with."

"I . . . I didn't know," Brian whispered.

"Just because she didn't tell you doesn't mean I won't hold a grudge."

And he kicked Brian a second time.

"You've gotten everything you got comin' to you," Ron Frommer said. "But that doesn't mean there can't be even more." He turned and went back into the house.

Before the door closed, Brian, clutching his midsection, caught one last glimpse of Jessica's fear-filled face.

FIFTEEN

Barry Duckworth drove out of the Starbucks lot after meeting with his son and his girlfriend thinking: *That could have gone better.*

What a disaster. And yet, what was he supposed to do? Ignore the possibility that his son might be able to help him with a serious investigation? He had to talk to him on the off chance Trevor had seen something that would lead Duckworth to whoever had abducted and tattooed Brian Gaffney.

Still, maybe he could have done a better job of it. Maybe he should have talked to his son separately from this new girlfriend of his, Carol Beakman. Except she was a potential witness, too. He'd needed to talk to both of them.

And *still* . . .

He should have realized that once he'd told them he'd seen them on the Knight's surveillance video, it meant that he'd seen them in an intimate moment.

Well, the hell with that, he thought. If he'd walked into Knight's, he'd have seen the same damn thing. If you were going to stick your tongue down some girl's throat while sitting in the middle of a bar, there was only so much privacy you could reasonably expect.

Maybe this would teach them to be a little more discreet, for crying out loud. Get a room.

Except, of course, Trevor's room these days was in the Duckworth home.

He let out a long sigh.

Maybe he wouldn't feel so conflicted about this if either of them had been able to tell him something useful. At least then the awkwardness would have been worth it. But as it turned out, neither Trevor nor Carol had seen a thing. They hadn't even recognized Gaffney's picture.

"Shit," he said aloud.

But the more Duckworth thought about it, the more he wondered what the big deal was. Okay, he'd seen them making out. That was unfortunate. But did it justify Trevor's hostility? Maybe he had a right to be annoyed, but why so instantly defensive?

Duckworth feared this was not the end of it. He wished now that Trevor hadn't moved in with them. If his son still had his own place, Duckworth could avoid him almost indefinitely. But at some point today, Trevor would come home. That was not an encounter Duckworth looked forward to.

Which brought up the next dilemma. How much should he tell Maureen?

Forget all the investigative implications. At a purely personal level, Duckworth was now in possession of information that Maureen, who'd expressed concern about their son within the last hour, would definitely want to know.

Duckworth now knew Trevor was seeing someone. He knew her name. He even knew where she worked. Should he let Trevor fill his mother in at some point when he felt the time was right? And if he followed that course of action, what would Maureen do to him when she eventually found out he'd had this intel all along?

What a bloody mess.

He knew he'd tell Maureen. There were some things you couldn't hold back. The trick would be trying to tell the story without making himself look like a total idiot in the way he'd handled things.

If that was even possible.

"Shit," he said again.

He kept replaying the scene at Starbucks in his head. *I embarrassed him*, he thought. Trevor had every right to be angry. The first time his father meets his girlfriend, he submits her to a police interrogation.

"I blew it. I totally blew it."

What a terrific first impression. No wonder Trevor was pissed. Duckworth decided he'd have to apologize. Tell his son he was sorry for not handling things more tactfully.

You're a cop for twenty-six years, and you still make mistakes.

God, he just wanted a donut. No, that wasn't true. He wanted half a dozen donuts.

He had to put his problem with Trevor aside for now. Duckworth had something else to think about.

Craig Pierce.

Why had it taken him this long to think about Craig Pierce?

Okay, he had to cut himself a little slack. It had only been a few hours since Brian Gaffney had been brought into the police station. Only now were some of the similarities coming into focus.

Both Gaffney and Pierce had been sedated before horrible things were done to them.

In both cases, retribution appeared to play a major role. Craig Pierce was being punished for something he'd done, and it certainly appeared Gaffney was being made to pay for what had happened to "Sean," whoever that turned out to be.

But there might come a time when Gaffney would actually consider himself lucky, at least compared to Craig Pierce.

Craig's night to remember was 3rd February. Duckworth remembered the details of his statement.

Craig awoke to the sound of falling water. Torrents of it. An unrelenting rushing.

As he began to be more fully aware of his surroundings, he noticed how cold he felt. From the waist down, anyway. It was, after all, winter. (If Craig had anything at all to be grateful for, it was that this particular February was a mild one for upstate New York.)

His buttocks and the backs of his legs were particularly cold. That, he soon realized, was because they were resting on a thin layer of snow. He was outside, flat on his back, and all evidence pointed to the fact that he was half naked.

He'd have sat up and assessed his situation, but there were some problems there. He couldn't see, for one thing. He had some kind of woolen hood on, like a ski mask, except there were no holes for eyes or nose or mouth. The damn thing was on backward.

But the more serious problem was that he could not move. His arms and legs were splayed out, like he was a starfish, and secured somehow to the ground. He could feel bindings around his wrists and ankles. He was able to brush the fingers of both hands against sticks of some kind.

No, not sticks. *Stakes*.

Craig Pierce was staked to the ground. Minus pants.

"Hello?" His voice was raspy and panicked. "Is there someone there?"

There was no light filtering through the threads of the hood. It was nighttime, no doubt about that.

"Hello?" he said again. "What's going on?"

Craig tried to control his breathing, which was becoming very rapid. He needed to concentrate on what was going on around him.

He sensed he was not alone.

Even with the background noise of the rushing water, he thought he heard people breathing. Someone—maybe more than one person—shifting weight from one foot to the other. Very, very close to him.

Whispering.

"I know you're there," he said. "What the hell is going on? What the hell is this?"

The last thing Craig could recall, before waking up staked to the snowy ground, was finishing his shift at Maria's, a pizza takeout joint. It was midnight, and he'd come out the back door. He'd walked to his Camaro, where he found a van parked so close alongside it he wasn't sure he could get the door open.

He heard someone say, "Craig Pierce?"

Then someone from behind put something over his face. A cloth. A very smelly cloth.

Nothing after that, until he heard the rushing of water.

"I can hear you!" he shouted. "I hear you talking! What the hell is this about?"

Pierce sensed movement on the ground. He believed someone was standing over him. Then he heard a voice, maybe the same one that had called out his name.

"Like you don't know."

That was when Craig Pierce had an inkling about what might be going on.

"Look, I'm sorry," he said. "Really, really sorry. I've learned my lesson."

At this point, Pierce heard other breathing, of a kind that did not sound human. More like panting, or snorting. It was the sort of sound a dog might make.

What happened next made him jump, at least as much as a man could jump while staked to the ground. Something thick and cold and wet was being poured over his body. Particularly over those parts of him that were most exposed, most vulnerable.

"Hey!" he shouted. "What are you doing? What is that?"

As if to answer his question, a few seconds later more of the substance was poured over his face. It seeped through the fabric of the hood and reached his lips and tongue, where he could not help but taste it.

It was a mixture of something. A strange combination of ingredients. Like honey, and beef. Bloody and sweet at the same time.

Then, a flash.

His picture had been taken.

Craig had the sense that whoever had done this to him—one or more, he was not sure—was walking away.

Then he heard the voice say, "Go get him, boy. Dinner is served."

The sound of something running. Something getting closer. Something panting hungrily.

Not long after that, Pierce passed out.

When the sun came up, and Craig Pierce was spotted, staked out in the middle of the park by Promise Falls, he was nearly dead.

Considering what had happened to him, Duckworth thought, he'd have been better off that way. He'd conducted interviews with Pierce in the hospital in the days following the attack.

Now he decided, three months later, that it was time for another chat with the man. He was not looking forward to it.

SIXTEEN

CAL

I put the phone back to my ear and said to Bob, "Too late. We're here."

I brought my Honda to a stop behind the red Porsche. Jeremy threw open the passenger door and ran up the driveway toward the house, careful not to look at the other car or even get near it, as though the vehicle were radioactive.

Slowly, I started toward the house. There were no police cars in the driveway, so I guessed Madeline Plimpton had decided against reporting the broken window. As Jeremy reached the front door, Gloria emerged with open arms.

"There you are," she said. "You're okay."

He avoided her welcoming hug, blasted past her and walked into the house, but not before shouting, "Not with that asshole around!"

Bob appeared, cell phone in hand. He saw me and glowered. "I told you to stall. You got here too soon!"

I stopped and waited for him to come to me.

"This is not helpful," he said, stopping six feet short of me, waving the phone in his hand.

"Like I said, we were already here."

"Where the hell was he, anyway?"

"Arranged a date with a girlfriend from Albany."

"Son of a bitch. Who?"

"Charlene Wilson."

He shook his head. "Jesus. Her."

I nodded in the direction of the sports car. "What's this? Is this really the car Jeremy was driving when he killed that girl?"

"I didn't know he was going to bring it. I swear, I don't know what the hell he was thinking."

"Galen Broadhurst?"

Bob nodded. "Yes. He needed to see me."

"And he decided to drive *this*? What did he want to do? Rub the kid's nose in it?"

Bob shook his head with frustration. "I know, I know. It was stupid. It's the first time he's even driven it since—"

"Bob!"

A man was charging out of the house. Late fifties, gray hair, about two hundred pounds, leather jacket, jeans, black lace-up boots.

"That's him," Bob said. "God, I hope he didn't run into Jeremy. This never should have happened."

"Why didn't you tell me the boy was here?" Galen Broadhurst said angrily.

"I tried," Bob said as Galen closed the distance. When the man reached us, he looked at me and said to Bob, "Who's this?"

Manners. I liked that.

"This is Cal Weaver," Bob explained. "We've brought him in to assess the risks Jeremy faces."

He eyed me up and down. "You don't look like a bodyguard to me."

I said, "Nice move, parking that car where Jeremy couldn't miss it."

"Damn it, I already explained, I didn't know the kid was here," he said. "First, the cops had the car for months, then I finally get it back and have to send it out to get it fixed. The front end was—well, hell, how do you think it was? You run someone down and that leaves some damage."

"To the car, you mean," I said. "Yeah, that's a shame."

Broadhurst pointed to the Porsche. "That's a classic vehicle that I've sunk a fortune into over the years. It's a terrible thing what happened, no doubt about it. But now that justice has been served and the trial has run its course, surely I'm entitled to get it fixed up again and move on."

"Of course," I said. "You want to get on with your life."

Galen Broadhurst gave me a long look. "You're kind of a wise guy, aren't you?"

Bob Butler made a tamping-down gesture with both hands. "Enough! Enough, for crying out loud! We're all getting off on the wrong foot here. Jesus, Galen, Mr. Weaver's already proved his value to us. Jeremy took off and Mr. Weaver here tracked him down and brought him home. Put yourself in Jeremy's shoes. Coming up the street and seeing this goddamn car. He hasn't seen it since the night everything happened."

"Fine," Galen said. "But I'm telling you, I didn't know. I got the car out of the shop this morning, wanted to give it a good run. I had papers for you to sign and your office said you were up here. So shoot me."

I was tempted. But I hadn't brought my gun with me today.

"And Mr. Weaver is not a bodyguard," Bob said. "He's a private investigator."

"Oh, are you now?" Broadhurst said. "What are you

investigating? You gonna find out who's making all these threats against Jeremy?"

"No," I said. "You'd need every police department in the country to deal with those."

"Mr. Weaver's going to keep an eye on Jeremy till things settle down," Bob said. "Just an hour ago someone went by and threw a rock through the window."

Instead of looking back at the house—Broadhurst had probably already seen the broken glass—he glanced at the Porsche, then up and down the street, probably worried about whether his recently repaired car would get caught in the crossfire of the next act of vandalism.

"That's terrible," he said. "It's terrible, and my heart goes out to you." His tone softened. "God, all the things that get triggered from one incident."

"Hardly a minor event," I said.

"True, true," Broadhurst said. "A great many lives impacted, especially the family of that poor young girl."

"If it was me," I said, "I don't know that I could ever drive that car again, knowing what happened."

"I hear what you're saying," Galen Broadhurst said. "To be honest, now that it's out of the shop and good as new, I'm thinking of selling it. It's got a tragic history, and I suspect I'll be reminded of that fact every time I get behind the wheel." He gave me a smile for the first time. "Interested?"

I shook my head, tipped my head at my aging Honda. "In my line of work, I'm better off with something that blends into the scenery."

He laughed. "Yeah, like, remember Magnum, driving around in that red Ferrari? Great car for detective work, that."

"What's a vehicle like this worth?" I asked.

"You're looking at a 1978 911 Targa, excellent condition. It'd probably run around fifty, sixty grand, maybe a little less. All depends on the market. A car's really only worth what someone will pay for it, regardless of what the book says. Am I right, Bob?"

"That's for sure, Galen," Bob said.

"I would have thought it'd be even more than sixty," I said.

"Plenty of classic Porsches out there that could run you a quarter-mill." He smiled "And I've got a couple. But I've always had a soft spot in my heart for this one."

"It was Galen's wife's car," Bob said.

"That's right," he said. "Amanda. She passed away six years ago. Big C. This was her pride and joy, and it'd be hard for me to get rid of it. I'm a sentimentalist, but sometimes you have to accept that things are the way they are and move on. Am I right, Bob?"

"You're right, Galen."

Bob seemed to have the starring role here as Galen's yes-man.

"Anyway," Broadhurst looked at me, "if you should change your mind and think you might want to buy it, or know anyone who might, here's my card."

He handed it to me. I slipped it into my front pocket.

"Well," he said, "in spite of things going a bit sour here, the documents I needed to have signed are signed, we've done our business, and I can be on my way."

"The two of you work together a lot?" I asked.

"We've done a few deals," Broadhurst said, smiling. He laid a hand on Bob's shoulder. "Just doing what I can to make Bob here a rich man. Isn't that right, Bob?"

Bob offered up a smile that looked as genuine as a spray-on tan. He said, "Last year Galen bought several blocks in downtown Albany. It's part of a proposal for some new state government offices."

"Well," I said. "I'm sure it's all over my head."

"I would imagine so," Broadhurst said. He reached out a hand to Bob for a farewell shake, but did not bother with me.

He got in behind the wheel of the Porsche, fired it up, then eased it into first and pulled away from the curb. We listened to the car work its way through the gears until it reached the end of the street, turned, and disappeared.

Bob said, "He's kind of an asshole."

"Thanks for telling me," I said.

SEVENTEEN

Duckworth did not need to look up Craig Pierce's address.

He knew where he was living, and it wasn't at his own apartment. He'd given that up after the incident, and now—like Trevor—was back living with his parents. Thank God that was the only thing about their situations that was similar.

He didn't see any point in calling ahead to ask whether this was a good time to drop by and talk to Pierce. There'd never be a good time.

Pierce's parents lived in the west end of Promise Falls on an older, tree-lined street. It was a two-story home that, while not run down, needed attention. The grass was overgrown, the shrubs crying out for a trim. The woodwork around the doors and windows could have used a coat of paint.

Duckworth parked at the curb, walked up to the door and rang the bell. It took Pierce's mother—Duckworth remembered her name was Ruth—nearly a minute to come to the door. She peered through the window first, then opened the door a crack.

"Ms. Pierce, it's Detective Duckworth."

"Oh, yes, hello," said Ruth Pierce. She opened the door far enough to admit him, as though opening it wider would allow unseen forces to invade the house. "Forgive me. You wouldn't believe the people that show up. Awful, awful people. Not quite as many as there used to be, but they still come."

"I'm sorry," Duckworth said.

"People can be so cruel. The ones that want to make fun of him, to laugh at his misfortune. They're no better than whoever did this to him."

"They can be pretty awful, it's true."

As he stepped into the house, he sniffed the air.

"That's scones," Ruth Pierce said. "They just came out of the oven. Craig loves my scones and I try to do whatever I can to make him happy. Would you like one? With some jam?"

Duckworth felt his resolve weakening, not unlike that time, on another investigation, when he arrived to question a woman just as she'd finished baking banana bread. There were some things one could not say no to.

"That sounds wonderful," he said.

"It would give us a chance to chat before you go upstairs to talk to Craig," she said. "That's what you want to do, isn't it? Talk to Craig."

"I do, yes."

"He probably knows you're here. He sits and looks out the window a lot of the day."

Her eyes drifted northward. If Craig kept an eye on the street, his bedroom had to be right above their heads. It occurred to Duckworth that there wasn't a sound coming from up there.

As if reading his mind, his mother said, "I've got the TV hooked up in there but he almost never turns it on. Mostly he's on his computer. Come to the kitchen."

Duckworth followed her, and the scent of scones. He took a seat at the kitchen table as Ruth transferred the scones from a cooking sheet to a plate. "I love them when they're still warm," she said.

"Absolutely," he said.

"You look like you've lost some weight."

"A little."

"Isn't your wife looking after you?"

Duckworth chuckled. "It's because she *is* looking after me that I've managed to lose it."

She shook her head. "That's no way to live, denying yourself the pleasures of life." She briefly froze, and then her chin began to quiver. "Oh my poor, poor boy." Her body shook with one brief sob. "There are so many pleasures he'll never know."

Duckworth contemplated whether to get up and comfort her, but she saved him the trouble, suddenly standing up straight and saying, "We have to move forward. That's all we can do."

She brought a plate with half a dozen scones to the table. "Coffee?"

"Uh—"

"You have to have some coffee. You can't have a scone without coffee. I already have some going here." She put a hand to her mouth, as though she'd just realized she'd made a terrible mistake. "I suppose what really goes with scones is tea. Would you prefer tea?"

"Coffee's perfect."

"That's good. I don't know if I even have any tea. If there are any tea bags in the back of that cupboard, they're probably ten years old. Does tea go bad?"

"I don't know." Duckworth cleared his throat, hoping to steer the conversation away from hot beverages. "How's Mr. Pierce?" he asked, meaning her husband, not her son.

Her face fell. "Oh, I guess you didn't hear."

Duckworth felt the air going out of him. "What happened, Mrs. Pierce?"

"I think it all just became too much for him. First, those horrible accusations against Craig. Brendan found that terribly difficult to deal with. Well, so did I, but he took it badly. Then the outrage that followed when the charges were dropped."

Duckworth was well aware.

It was alleged that Craig Pierce had sexually molested an eleven-year-old girl he'd encountered in a Promise Falls park. That would have been serious enough, but it was worse than that. The girl was mentally disabled, and her intellectual handicap made it easy for Craig's defense lawyer to challenge her ability to accurately identify the man who had dragged her into the bushes. The prosecutors had no DNA sample to tie Craig to the assault, and ultimately had to dismiss the charges.

Some might actually have been inclined to give Pierce the benefit of the doubt. Maybe it *had* been someone else. Perhaps the girl's confusion over identifying Pierce meant she had it wrong. But Pierce's behavior after the incident suggested guilt. He'd had hair nearly down to his shoulders, but immediately after the incident had it all cut off. When the girl was asked to pick him out of a lineup, she was looking at someone with a buzz cut.

But the clincher was what Pierce was heard to have said after the charges had been dropped. With news cameras rolling nearby, he'd been caught whispering to a buddy, "Let this be a lesson. Always pick the dumb ones."

The comment wasn't enough to re-lay the charges, but it was enough to persuade everyone Pierce was guilty, and not just folks in the Promise Falls area. The soundbite went viral. Craig Pierce became the world's most despised man on the Internet for several days. There were emailed death threats, harassing phone calls. He'd had to go into hiding until things blew over, which took the better part of a month.

Turned out not everyone had forgotten about him.

Duckworth let Ruth Pierce continue with her story.

"My husband was devastated by all of it. He was so . . . ashamed. He wanted to believe Craig was innocent, but he knew . . . we both knew he'd done what they'd said he'd done. But he had a sickness, you know? Something was wrong in his head. We were going to get treatment for him."

"About your husband," Duckworth said, steering her back.

"Then, when Craig was . . . when he was attacked, and the aftermath . . . When Craig finally came home from the hospital, Brendan couldn't even go into his room, couldn't bear to see him, the way he was. He couldn't look at him. I don't think it was shame by that point. He just couldn't bear to see his son that way. I made him . . . I made him go up."

"What do you mean?"

"Aren't you going to have a scone?" she asked.

"Of course." Duckworth reached for one, buttered it, then scooped out some strawberry jam the woman had put out and dropped it onto the scone.

Ruth smiled sadly. "I always used to love to watch a man eat."

Duckworth took a bite. "Wow. That's fanatastic. It's still hot. The butter's melting."

Her smile faded. "But it's hard to watch Craig have his dinner. I mean, there was so much damage."

They were both quiet for a moment. Duckworth waited for Ruth Pierce to finish her story.

"So I said to my husband, he's your son. You can't stay out of his room forever. He needs you, I told him. I'd made Craig some lunch. Tomato soup with crackers. He's loved tomato soup ever since he was three years old. He can make the crackers soft by putting them in the soup. That makes it easier for him. I said to Brendan, take your son his soup."

Ruth Pierce took a breath before continuing.

"And he finally said okay, he would do it. He took the tray and he went up the stairs so slow. I stood at the bottom and waited. I heard him go into Craig's room. I asked Craig later what his father said, and apparently he said nothing. Brendan came back down the stairs, and when he got to the bottom . . . he just collapsed."

Duckworth stopped chewing his scone.

"What was it?" he asked.

"They said it was a massive heart attack. They said he was gone before he hit the floor." She looked at the detective with damp eyes. "I killed him. I killed my Brendan."

"No."

"I shouldn't have made him go up. I shouldn't have let him see how bad his son looked. Not until he was ready. He needed to do it in his own time. It wasn't a heart attack, you know. It was a *broken* heart. That's what it was. His heart was so broken he couldn't continue."

Duckworth reached across the table for the woman's hand and held it. "How long ago was this?"

"Five weeks," she said.

"I'm very sorry for your loss," Duckworth said.

"Oh my gosh, I forgot your coffee."

She jumped up from the table, filled a mug, and put it on the table in front of him.

"Do you have any help?" he asked. "Other children, extended family?"

Ruth shook her head. "Just me." She wrung her hands. "I'm not quite sure what we're going to do. I've had to quit my job to look after Craig. There's some insurance money from Brendan's policy, but it won't last long. And then there's all the reconstructive surgery that Craig needs. I don't know how I'm going to manage that. He did qualify for some therapy, to help him, you know, psychologically, with what's happened to him."

She glanced at the wall clock. "In fact, she's due here pretty soon. But the surgery he needs—plastic surgery, other things—would cost a fortune. They have these things on the Internet, I think they call them crowd-funding? Where you ask people to donate a little money? And if enough do, then you can do whatever it is you need to do. But no one's going to donate to help Craig." She dug a tissue out of her sleeve and dabbed her eye. "No one cares. People think he got what he deserved."

Duckworth took a sip of his coffee and another bite of his scone.

"Are you here because you caught them?" she asked. "Did you catch the people who did this to him?"

He shook his head. "No."

Her shoulders sagged. "I figured as much. You know, I like you, Detective Duckworth, I do. I think you're a very nice man. But I can't help but think that the police really aren't trying that hard, you know? That they think Craig got what was coming to him too."

"That's not true," he said.

"Then what have you been doing? It's been three months. I heard you found out who owned that monstrous dog."

"Yes," Duckworth said. "But the dog had been stolen. We don't think the owner had anything to do with your son's assault."

"No one saw anything?"

"It was the middle of the night." Duckworth grimaced. The park next to the falls the town was named for was getting something of a reputation for horrific crimes.

"If you don't know anything, then what point is there in talking to Craig? He upsets very easily."

Duckworth hesitated. "There's been another incident."

"Oh dear me."

He raised a palm. "Not as serious as what happened to Craig. And it may not be related. But I'd like to speak with your son just the same. Maybe, since the last time we spoke, he's remembered something else."

Ruth Pierce nodded resignedly. "All right, then. If you have to do it, you have to do it."

"I want to thank you for the scone. I really shouldn't have had it, but it was irresistible. The coffee, too."

"It's nice to have someone to talk to."

"Do you get out?" he asked her.

"Oh, yes. I mean, Craig can be left home alone. And sometimes I take him for drives. He likes to go for drives. If we're out in the daytime, he'll wear something on his head, so people can't see him. He's even been going out some on his own, but only late at night, when no one can see him and he doesn't have to cover himself up. But I worry when he does that. If he has an accident or something, what will people think when they see him?

When he's with me, I can sort of run interference. You know what I mean?"

"Sure," said Duckworth.

Given that Pierce was known to be a sex offender—although not an actual convicted one—Duckworth pondered the wisdom of him going out at night on his own. Although he didn't quite pose the threat he might once have.

"The best news is, he's feeling a little more confident," Ruth said. "He's getting interested in things again, like hobbies. He's been ordering little gadgets off the Internet."

Duckworth stood and waited for Ruth to get to her feet.

"I'll try not to be too long," he said as he started to leave the kitchen.

The woman reached out and gently took his arm.

"There's something you need to know before you see him."

"What's that?"

"First of all, he's gotten a little . . . I don't want to say crazy. But considering everything, he sometimes becomes quite . . . irreverent."

"And what else?"

She let out a long breath.

"The last of the bandages have come off."

EIGHTEEN

The Gaffneys were frantic.

All evidence pointed to the fact that Brian had walked right out of the hospital. A nurse was pretty sure she had seen him pass her station in his clothes, but Albert wanted them to be sure his son had not been transferred to some other part of the building or possibly sent to a lab or something for further tests.

Hospital security guards were called, and a search of Promise Falls General was initiated.

Albert was not only hoping they'd find Brian quickly, but that they would find him before Constance came back.

Things did not work out the way he'd hoped.

When Constance returned to the ER with Monica trailing after her, she spotted her husband standing in a hallway and said, "How is he? How's Brian?"

"I don't . . . I don't know where he is right now," he admitted.

"What's going on? Have they moved him to a proper room?"

Albert shook his head.

"I don't think so. Now, I don't want you having a fit about what I'm about to say, but—"

"Good God, what's happened?" Constance asked.

"They don't know where he is."

Constance, wide-eyed, said, "They've lost Brian?"

"No, it's not that. It looks like he left."

Monica said, "Oh, shit."

Constance said, "You let him walk out of here?"

"I didn't let him walk out. When I came back, he was gone."

"We only left him for a minute," Constance said. "He must have walked right past you." She looked at the ceiling. "This is unbelievable. While you're here, you should have your eyes checked."

"Maybe," Monica said, "he went outside for some fresh air. Maybe he took a walk around the block."

"I've looked," Albert said. "I've looked all over. I think he just walked out."

"You're hopeless," Constance said.

"He can't have gotten far," Albert said, trying to put the best face on things. "He doesn't have a car, he's got no money. Unless he managed to call a friend to come and get him, he must have left on foot."

"We should split up," Monica said. "Let's go home first. We'll each take a car and see if we can find him. And who knows, maybe that's where he is."

"At least someone is thinking," Constance said.

They got in the car and went back to the house. Constance ran inside, hoping her son would be there, but he was not.

Monica said she would get in her Beetle and search the streets around the hospital. Constance would check Brian's apartment and Knight's. That left the car detailing shop to be checked by Albert.

Ten minutes later, he was there. He parked and ran inside. They knew him here. This was, not surprisingly, where he brought his pickup to have it washed. Whenever Brian was on duty, he'd hit the hot wax button without charging his dad for it.

When he entered the office, a heavyset man behind the cash looked up and said, "Hey! Where the hell's Brian been? I've been calling him for two days!"

"Hi, Len," said Albert. "Brian's in the hospital. Well, he's supposed to be in the hospital, but—"

"Oh, shit, no, what happened?"

Albert shook his head, a "don't have time" gesture. "Have you seen him? I mean, in the last hour?"

"Nope. I'd just about given up on him. Figured he didn't want the job. I didn't know he'd got hurt or anything."

"If he comes in, will you call me?"

"Yeah, sure."

Len handed Albert a used envelope so he could scribble his cell number on the back. Once he'd done that, he turned around and went back to his truck.

He debated calling his wife and daughter to see if they'd had any better luck than he'd had. But he knew Monica would call him if she found Brian. And if Constance found him, she'd probably tell Monica, who'd pass the news on to her father.

Two blocks from the detailing place, Albert spotted him.

Brian was walking slowly along the sidewalk, his back to Albert. But he knew his son, even from behind. The boy had always had a bit of a slouch. He slowed the car as he came up alongside, powered down the window, and shouted, "Brian!"

Brian stopped, turned his head slowly, as if in a daze, then bent over slightly so he could see in through the window.

"Oh, hi, Dad," he said.

He threw the car into park, got out, and ran over to

his son. When he went to hug him, Brian raised a cautious hand.

"I'm kinda hurt," he said. "My rib's really sore."

"What happened? Where did you go? You scared us all half to death."

"Sorry about that."

"Why'd you leave the hospital? What were you thinking? Why is there grass all over you?"

"I fell down." He reconsidered. "I got beat up."

"Christ, what's happened to you?"

Brian carefully pulled up his shirt to show the bruising around his ribcage. "I sort of got kicked."

"What? Who kicked you?"

"She's married," he said.

"Who's married? Brian, start at the beginning."

"She never told me she was married. I didn't have any idea."

"What are you talking about?"

"Jessica."

"Who's Jessica?"

"Can I sit down? I'm really tired."

"Come, get in the car."

Albert led him to the passenger door, opened it, got him settled. He came around the other side and got back in behind the wheel.

"You hurt bad?"

"Sorta," Brian said.

"I'm taking you back to the hospital." He moved to put the truck into drive.

"Not . . . yet. Can I sit here a minute?"

Albert turned the ignition key to the off position, killing the engine. "Sure. What happened, Brian? Talk to me."

The young man was struggling not to cry. "So I met this girl. Jessica. We went out a few times. I thought she was kind of nice."

"Okay."

"I was supposed to call her. But then this thing happened, and this shit got written on my back, and I lost the last two days, so I didn't call her."

"I'm sure she'll understand.'

"Yeah, well . . ."

"What?"

"I wanted to explain to her why I didn't call. They . . . they stole my cell phone and my wallet and everything, so I decided to walk to her house. I knew where she lived. But she didn't know that."

Albert had questions, but decided to let Brian tell the story his own way.

"A little girl answered the door. And I thought, whoa, has she got a little sister or something? And then Jessica came to the door, looking all scared shitless, you know. Telling me to go. And then this guy appears."

"Oh oh," Albert said.

"It was her husband." His eyes searched his father's. "I didn't know. Honest. I wouldn't go out with someone who was married."

"I believe you."

"You raised me better than that."

"Sure."

"I wanted to explain. But then Ron—"

"Ron?"

"That's her husband. He wouldn't let me, and then he pushed me off the front step. And then he kicked the shit out of me."

Albert felt a hot wave of rage wash over him. "No," he said.

"He said something like I deserved everything that happened to me. I think he knew that Jessica was seeing me. He called her a whore. I think . . . I think maybe she was seeing other guys, too."

Albert was replaying in his head what the man had said to his son.

"He said you deserved everything that had happened to you?"

"Something sort of like that. I got what was coming to me, I think it was. Maybe, if he knew Jessica was foolin' around on him, he'd been following her around. Maybe he saw us when we went to the BestBet."

"The hotel?" Albert said. "On the highway to Albany?"

Brian looked sheepishly at his father. "Don't be mad. I wouldn't want Mom to know I did that. Going to a hotel with a girl without, you know, being married."

"It's okay," Albert said softly, putting a hand on his son's arm.

Brian sniffed. "I liked her. I thought maybe there was something there." He bit his lip. "I'm such a dumbass. I should have known better. Maybe she thought I was good enough to cheat with, but really, why would anyone want to be with me for the long term?"

Albert squeezed his arm. "Don't say that. Don't ever say that."

Brian sniffed again. He popped open the glove box with his free hand, found a tissue, and dabbed his cheek. "I'm a nothing."

"Stop it. Stop it, Brian." Albert paused, then said,

"Tell me again about Ron, what he said and what he did. Everything you can remember."

Brian went over all of it again.

"If he knew you'd been seeing his wife," Albert said, "he'd have plenty of reason to be mad at you."

Brian blinked away some tears. "What are you saying?"

Albert hesitated. "Maybe he's the one. Maybe he's the one that did that to your back."

Brian contemplated the possibility. "I don't know. But what's the part about Sean mean?"

Albert thought about that. "I don't know. Maybe this Jessica was cheating on him with another guy with that name. And he thought you were that guy."

Brian nodded his head slowly. "I guess that's possible. I could tell that guy from the police."

"You could," Albert said. "That's a good idea. That's what we'll have to do."

"Except," Brian said, "what if it isn't?"

"What do you mean?"

"You should have seen her face."

"Whose face?"

"Jessica. After Ron kicked me, and went back in the house, she looked terrified, you know? Really scared. If the cops come by and see him, he might go crazy. He might hurt her. I mean, she really messed me up, she lied to me, but I don't want her husband to kill her or anything."

"The man attacked you," Albert reminded him. "Even if he didn't put that tattoo on you, he attacked you."

"I know, but . . . I mean, I did sleep with his wife. Like, if I was in his shoes, I might have lost it and done the same thing."

"That's no excuse," Albert said. "But maybe . . ."

"Maybe what?" Brian asked.

"Nothing," his father said, thinking. After a few seconds, he asked, "Just where does this Ron guy live?"

NINETEEN

Duckworth rapped lightly on the door to Craig Pierce's room. It was already open an inch.

"Craig, it's Detective Duckworth."

No response.

He knocked a second time, but no harder. Maybe Craig was asleep. Duckworth wasn't sure he wanted to wake him.

But this time, a voice. "Yeah, come in."

Duckworth pushed the door open. Craig, dressed in a dark blue bathrobe, was sitting in an overstuffed pink easy chair with his back to the detective. His mother was right. He'd positioned himself in front of the window with a good view of the street. The chair was a step away from the bed, which was neatly made. The walls were decorated with movie posters. *Star Wars*, *Star Trek*. There was a small flat-screen TV on top of the dresser, turned off. Next to it, a cardboard shipping parcel, opened, bubble wrap spilling out of it. There was a collection of superhero action figures on a nearby shelf, and Duckworth wondered if Craig had ordered some new ones.

Duckworth could see, even though Craig had his back to him, that the man had a laptop in front of him.

"Hey, Craig," he said.

As Craig started to turn to face Duckworth, it became clear he was in a swivel chair. He turned a full one hundred and eighty degrees.

Duckworth hoped the shock he felt didn't show on his face.

Craig Pierce was missing a significant part of his own.

His nose was gone. The cheeks were missing large chunks of flesh. Least damaged was his mouth, but his upper and lower lips were ragged.

He looked at Duckworth with only one eye. The left was mostly unscathed, but the right was closed and covered over with rough skin.

"It's okay," he said. "If you have to throw up or something, I'll understand. Bathroom's right across the hall."

"I'm fine," Duckworth said. He pointed to the bed. "Can I perch myself there?"

"Sure. Be my guest."

Look him in the face, Duckworth thought. *Don't look away.*

"I just had a chat with your mother," he said. "I didn't know your father had passed away. I'm sorry."

"Yeah. Like I said, some people just want to barf. Dad went the full Monty and had a heart attack."

Duckworth thought it looked as though Craig was trying to grin.

"He's the lucky one," Craig said. "You carry a gun?"

"I do."

"I'd ask you to shoot me, but that's probably against some kind of regulation, right?"

"Kinda," Duckworth said.

"Arrest someone?"

"No."

"Could have guessed. At least they put the dog down."

"I want to go over a couple of things again."

"Super!" Craig said. His buoyant response was jarring. "I can't imagine anything I'd like more! Which part do you want me to relive? When the pit bull was ripping my face off, or when he was making a meal out of my—"

Duckworth raised a hand. "Two days ago, someone—"

"You just don't want to hear it, do you? No one does. But I think it's even harder for guys. It all got chewed off. They didn't find anything to reattach. Maybe someone should have thought of opening up the dog and getting my bits back. How about that, huh?"

Duckworth cleared his throat. "Two days ago, someone was coming out Knight's. You know Knight's?"

"Sure. A fine drinking establishment."

"He got lured into an alley. Then he blacks out. Wakes up two days later."

"What ate him?" Craig asked. "A polar bear? A wolverine?"

"Neither. Someone did some artwork on him."

Duckworth got out his phone and showed Craig the photo he had taken of Brian Gaffney's back.

"Hmm," Craig said, nodding. "That's it? A little inspirational message?"

"It's a tattoo," Duckworth said.

"So he got off easy. What I'd give for someone to scribble shit all over my back. Throw on a shirt and off you go. No biggie."

"I take your point," Duckworth said. "But just the same, I want to find out who did this. Although what was done to him was different than what was done to you, the setup strikes me as similar."

"Who's Sean?"

"I don't know."

"Surely your victim does, though."

"He says he doesn't."

Craig's damaged mouth grinned again. "Yeah, right,

and I didn't feel up that little girl, either."

Duckworth felt any sympathy he'd had for this man slowly slipping away.

"Yes, he could be lying," he conceded.

Craig pointed to the laptop still resting on his knees. "Well, if it was the same person—or *persons*, as they say—who did it, they must be bragging about it online. Are they?"

Duckworth felt caught off guard. "I don't know."

"You don't know? And what are you again? A *detective*?"

"I hadn't gotten to that point."

Craig shook his head and made a "tsk, tsk" sound. He started tapping away on the keyboard. "If it was the same people, then they might be doing something like this."

He spun the computer around so Duckworth could view the screen. It was a website called Just Deserts. The name was plastered, newspaper-banner-style, across the top of the page. Below that, a headline that read: KID DIDDLER GETS HIS.

And a photo.

It was a picture of Craig Pierce staked to the ground, minus pants. His midsection was obscured by a dog, which was, as everyone knew by now, feasting on him.

"I've seen all this," Duckworth said. "I know about Just Deserts."

"You know they encourage this kind of thing. You know there are nutjobs out there who can't wait to be honored on their website."

"No one even knows who's behind it," Duckworth said.

"Yeah. It's like Anonymous, but with a big difference," Craig said, adopting an almost professorial tone.

"Anonymous is all about exposing government hypocrisy and making public the shit that's been kept secret. They'll even go so far as to sabotage websites and disrupt commerce and that kind of thing. And when they say they're going to expose people who belong to ISIS and fuck up their Twitter accounts or whatever, a lot of people think, hey, what the hell. We don't know who they are, but if that's what they want to do, it's okay by us. And there was that other case, the one where the hackers said they'd release all the private info on that website for people who want to have affairs. And the fuckers *did* it! *Bam.* Marriages broke up, man, it was something. But still, it's all about exposing data and secrets. Just Deserts, well, they're different. They push the envelope."

He gave Duckworth a grisly smile.

"Just Deserts likes to say that Anonymous doesn't leave any marks. When Anonymous goes after you, sure, maybe your lies have been exposed, your website hacked, but you can still get up in the morning and take a pee without blood coming out of your dick. Just Deserts likes to see bad people get physically hurt."

He leaned in close to Duckworth as if he were letting him in on a secret. "I was a bad person."

Duckworth said, "Yeah."

"So this site's inspiring vigilante nutbars all over the country." He swung the laptop back around so he could see the screen. "Like, listen to this. Sacramento, California, there was that white guy who went to a black protest rally, about all the black folk getting shot by cops? And he starts scratching under his arms and making like he's a monkey, and he gets caught on cell phone video and within a day it's being watched all over the world?"

"I remember. It was last year some time."

"Yeah, right. So the asshole gets identified, and his employer, which just happens to be the city, fires him. But that's not enough retribution for Just Deserts. So one night, the guy gets picked up right out front of his house, and he literally gets tarred and feathered."

Duckworth nodded. "I don't remember anyone getting arrested for that."

Craig shook his head in affirmation. "Nope. But they took snaps and got them to Just Deserts and up it went for all to see. Here, I can show you." He tapped out a few keystrokes, spun the laptop around again. "Check it out."

Duckworth had a look. "Yikes."

"Yeah, no shit." Craig spun the laptop back toward him. "Now we go—"

"I don't need to hear all of these," the detective said.

"—we *go to* Miami—that's in Florida, you know—where we find that dipshit Wall Street investor who bought up the pharmaceutical company and raised the price of a life-saving drug from like fifteen bucks a pill to seven hundred and thirty dollars a pill, and he's hanging out in some high-end nightclub dancing with these supermodels, and some guy comes through the crowd with a fucking syringe, right? And fucking *injects* the guy and says, 'Hope you enjoy AIDS, asswipe!' He slips away and they still don't know who it was. But it hit Just Deserts in like twenty minutes."

"Was it AIDS?"

Craig shrugged. "Who knows? I think the guy's still undergoing tests. But think how that fucked with his head, right? Then, in France, because this is not an America-only thing, you know, that woman politician who compared those millions of refugees to cockroaches—and let's face it, she was kind of onto something there—goes out to her fancy Beemer and turns the key and thousands of the little bastards start streaming out of the air vents and coming out from under the seats. And *voilà*!"

He spun the laptop around again for a shot of the woman bailing out her car, her body covered in roaches.

"Someone was waiting to take the picture, and minutes later, it was uploaded to Just Deserts. So you've got people all over the motherfucking planet inspired to exact vengeance on people who've got it coming, hoping like crazy that what they do is nasty enough to be honored on this website. And let me tell you, Promise Falls has made a name for itself in the whole getting-even department. That guy you killed last year, who poisoned half the fucking town, you know there are whole websites devoted to him?"

Every day Duckworth tried not to think about that, and every day he did. Even without reminders. He said, "Go on."

"Well, some people think he was terrific, that he made a difference. That he didn't just teach Promise Falls a lesson. The whole world took notice. They're saying, what he did, it's made people more concerned about their fellow man. Isn't that wild?"

"I sense some grudging admiration about these sites," Duckworth said. "Even after what happened to you."

Craig shrugged. "What's that phrase about an ox?"

Duckworth had to think. "It all depends on whose ox is getting gored."

Craig snapped his fingers and pointed. "That's the one. In other words, it's pretty funny until it happens to you."

"Yeah."

"So, Just Deserts has some local disciples, not

surprising, considering what went down here. More people who want to make a difference. So after they did me, they were itching for another target. Maybe that's your friend there with the Hallmark greeting on his back."

"Maybe."

"But if that's the case, they must be bragging about it, right? So what's the dude's name again?"

"I didn't say."

Craig sighed. "So say it."

"Brian Gaffney."

"Spell the last name."

Duckworth spelled it, and added that Brian was without a "y."

Craig did a few rapid keystrokes and hit *Enter*. He slowly shook his head. "Nothin's comin' up, Mr. Detective."

"Okay."

"I guess someone's got it in for wee Bri-Bri, but it's got nothin' to with Just Deserts, which would suggest to *me*, not that I am a brilliant detective such as yourself, that you're looking at someone else."

"I'll take that under advisement," Duckworth said. "To get back to why I came to see you, do you remember *anything* else about that night that you haven't already told us? Even the smallest detail? Something that might not ever have seemed all that important, but looking back, you wonder if maybe it is? Something that might be helpful in our investigation?"

"I can tell you one thing about him," Craig said.

Duckworth sat forward in his chair.

"What's that?"

"He can't spell."

"Excuse me?"

"He can't spell," Craig Pierce said. "Or at least he misspells to be clever."

"How can you know that?"

He tapped away again on the laptop. "Let's go back to the commentary he posted with the picture of me. Yeah, here we go. Have a look. And it's not just that he got my name wrong. Lots of people do that."

He spun the computer around so Duckworth could read it:

Craig Pearce gets it good. Revenj on the kiddy diddler. You can be sure he wont be mollesting anyone ever again!

Duckworth looked up. "Okay. He got your last name wrong, an extra 'l' in molesting, and there's revenj with a 'j.' That's what you're talking about."

"Right. The thing with the 'j' is deliberate, I think."

"Why?'

"Even a moron knows how to spell revenge. The other things, he's just not a good speller."

"I don't immediately see how that's helpful," Duckworth said.

"I'm sure you don't," Pierce said, shaking his head. "Just what are you people doing on the computer end of things? Going after this website to divulge the IP address that was used to post this, for starters?"

"That'd be our legal department," Duckworth said weakly. "I think they're working on that."

"You *think*?"

"I'd be happy to look into it for you, update you."

"Because," Pierce said, tossing the laptop onto the bed, "right now I feel like I'm doing that kind of work on my own. There's all kinds of signatures someone leaves when they're online. You just have to take the time to find them, correlate them, look for patterns. And seeing how I don't have much else to do . . ."

"If you've learned anything that could help us in our invest—"

"And do your work for you?" Craig settled back into his chair. His knees had been together to support the computer, and now he let them separate a good foot. The bathrobe began to part.

"Okay, there is one thing I remember, from the actual incident," he said, closing his eyes, seemingly concentrating. "Just before the dog bit down, it kind of tickled." He opened his eyes and grinned.

"It did something to you, didn't it?" Duckworth said.

"Is that a serious question?"

"I mean, you seem traumatized in a way I wouldn't have expected."

"Do you mean my cheerful demeanor?"

"I'm not sure that's what I'd call it."

Craig tipped his head. "Perhaps cheerful bordering on deranged? Did Mommy tell you my therapist is coming today? To *talk* to me? So I can share my *feelings*?"

"Thanks for your help," Duckworth said, and started to get up.

"Wait!" Craig Pierce said. "Don't go just yet."

Duckworth sat down again slowly.

"I never liked my father," Craig said. "I was never good enough for him. And then all this shit happened to me. The charges, the humiliation, the *shame* I brought down upon the family. But you know what was absolutely worst of all?"

Duckworth waited.

"It was losing my manhood. Havin' all my equipment bit clean off. That was why he couldn't come up here

162

and look at me. You believe that? He couldn't even look at me."

Duckworth could think of nothing to say.

"I've never told my mother what actually happened when my father brought me my tomato soup." Craig smiled. "She thinks good ol' Dad came up here and just got very sad, then went downstairs and had his heart attack."

Duckworth heard himself asking, "So what *did* happen?"

Another mischievous grin. "This."

Craig spread his legs further and flung back the robe to expose all that remained: ugly purple-blue bruising, jagged scars and mangled skin. Duckworth was put in mind of a blue cabbage that had been through a food processor.

"I said to Dad, 'How about them apples, or lack thereof?'"

Duckworth got up and left the room.

TWENTY

CAL

I went back into the Plimpton house with Bob Butler trailing after me. Gloria was in the kitchen, pouring herself yet another glass of wine while her aunt watched disapprovingly.

"Where's Jeremy?" I asked.

"He went upstairs," Gloria said. "He was *very* upset. Can you blame him? That asshole Galen comes by here in that car?" She shook her head. "Honest to God, I am surrounded by people who really don't have a clue. Jesus, Bob, how could you let him come up here at all, let alone in that goddamn car?"

Bob said, "I had no idea."

"Unbelievable," Gloria said to him, but now she was turning her sights on me. "Did you really throw Jeremy's phone into a fryer?"

I nodded unapologetically.

"It might keep him from making further dates with his girlfriend."

"The Wilson girl?" Gloria asked.

"Yes," I said, "Charlene."

"That little slut," Gloria said.

"For God's sake," Madeline Plimpton said. "Pot, meet kettle."

"What's that supposed to mean?" Gloria asked.

Ms. Plimpton just shook her head and left the room.

Gloria sighed and took another drink.

"Aren't you hitting that just a bit hard?" Bob asked her.

"With what I've been through, you're lucky I don't drink straight out of the bottle." She put down her glass and waved a finger at him. "I've had an idea."

"What's that?"

"Hiring Mr. Weaver here is all well and good, but maybe what we really need is one of those PR consultants."

"A what?" asked Bob.

"You know, a public relations person. Someone who could get out our side of the story. How Jeremy—and by extension, all of us—is a victim too. I mean, the judge made his ruling and that should be the end of it, but here we are being tortured on social media. Being threatened, having our reputations dragged through the mud."

Bob actually appeared intrigued. "So what would a PR person actually do?"

"She—and I would want it to be a woman, because they're *much* better at this sort of thing—would get in touch with the media and make sure some sympathetic stories are written. She'd know the right people to approach, who'd be on our side. Get them to sit down with Jeremy, interview him, see what a decent boy he actually is, not that cartoon big baby they made him out to be through the trial."

"You know anyone like that?" Bob asked her.

Gloria shook her head. "Madeline might."

I had my doubts Madeline Plimpton would be on board with this, but in the little time I had spent with these people, I supposed anything was possible.

Bob left the room, shaking his head.

Gloria put the question to me. "Do you know anyone like that, Mr. Weaver?"

"No."

She frowned. I was becoming a disappointment to her. A fried phone and now this. Here I'd been trying to persuade Jeremy's mother to stop all her interactions with the world, and now here she was trying to get her son on the *Today* show.

"Maybe it's not such a great idea after all," she said.

I decided to venture an opinion. "The more attention you bring to your situation, the longer the harassment will continue. Things'll die down eventually."

Gloria studied me. "Maybe you're right. When you're in the middle of something, you want to make it end as fast as you can, but everything you do may just prolong it."

"Something like that," I said.

"I'm sure my aunt had you all checked out, Mr. Weaver. But I don't know much about you. Are you married? Do you have children?"

"I was," I said. "And I had a son."

A glint in her eye told me she'd caught onto the past-tense phrasing, certainly where my son was concerned. "Had?" she said.

"It's a long story."

She smiled. "Have you ever heard anyone say it's a short story?"

I smiled back. "I guess not."

"I'm guessing it's not a long, *happy* story."

"You'd be right about that," I said.

"You think you're the only one with troubles," Gloria said, "and then you realize you're surrounded by everybody else's heartbreak."

For the first time, I felt myself warming to her. "I think you may be onto—"

"What the hell is this about hiring a PR consultant?" Madeline Plimpton said, striding into the room. "Bob just told me about some cockamamie idea of yours to bring someone on board to get your side of the story out? Seriously?"

"Jesus," Gloria whispered, taking another drink.

"Because a PR person is going to cost you a fortune," Ms. Plimpton said. "And I don't know where you're going to find the money for that."

"I was thinking out loud!" Gloria shot back. "Okay?"

"Doesn't sound like any thinking was going on at all," her aunt said.

I'd had enough.

As I left the kitchen, I grabbed Ms. Plimpton's laptop and took it with me to the living room. I sat down in a comfy armchair, opened up the computer and a browser, and entered "Jeremy Pilford trial" into the search field. I didn't really need a lot of background info to perform the duties I was being contracted for, but I wanted a better handle on the cast of characters, and the incident that had precipitated this shit storm.

A few hundred thousand results came back from my search, but I was quickly able to winnow those down to a handful of news accounts that summed things up pretty succinctly.

What I learned was this:

On the evening of June 15, a party was held at the Albany home of Galen Broadhurst. It was more an estate than a home. It sat on ten acres outside the city, about half of it untouched by development. Broadhurst, who had lived alone since the passing of his wife, had a seven-thousand-square-foot house to roam around in, and when he got bored with that, there was an outbuilding where he kept his stable of fancy cars. Three Porsches, one Lamborghini, an old MG, a 1969 American Motors AMX, and a new high-end Audi for daily driving.

The Porsche that I'd just seen on the street here in Promise Falls was not in the garage that night, but sitting in the driveway, right out front of the house.

The party was in celebration of a huge deal Bob Butler had done with Broadhurst, who'd acquired a tract of land in downtown Albany that would enable him to get a state contract to erect several new office buildings. The deal was worth nearly fifty million in future dollars. Butler didn't own the land, but had represented the seller, and he had been offered the opportunity to be an investor, which had the potential for a huge windfall in the coming year.

I skimmed over the details to get to what I really wanted to know about.

Butler brought Gloria and Jeremy along for the fun. Broadhurst had invited plenty of work associates, and his neighbors, including the McFaddens—Reece and Megan and their daughter Sian (pronounced, as Jeremy'd told me, "Sharn"). Gloria and Jeremy lived close enough that Jeremy and Sian attended the same high school, and knew each other.

A number of the other guests were mentioned in various articles, but the only name I recognized was Wilson. Alicia and Frank Wilson, who were, I suspected, the parents of Charlene.

Alcohol had been flowing freely at the event, and Jeremy had helped himself to several bottles of beer without anyone taking notice. It was calculated that by the time he got behind the wheel of the Porsche, he'd had ten.

Sian had made off with only one bottle, but it was wine, and the coroner's office testified that she had in all likelihood consumed all of it.

The two of them had been hanging out together out back of the property, lying on the grass, looking at the stars and continuing to drink. At some point, they got up and wandered around to the front of the house, where the Porsche caught Jeremy's attention. Jeremy'd never really been a car guy, the story said, but even someone who didn't give a shit about sports cars could appreciate that an old Porsche was a pretty neat vehicle.

He found the car unlocked, got into the driver's seat, and invited Sian to get in on the other side, which she did. He wanted her to take a picture of him behind the wheel with her phone.

Broadhurst had left the keys in the ashtray—he didn't smoke so he often tossed them there, at least when the car was right out front of the house, which was a long way in from the road. Jeremy found them, and was searching in frustration for the ignition slot. Instead of being on the steering column, as it is with most cars, including any that Jeremy had ever driven, it was to the left of the wheel, on the dash.

Before he could insert the key, Broadhurst himself came out of the house and spotted what Jeremy was up to. He came around to the driver's door, opened it, and hauled Jeremy out. Several guests who'd heard the commotion—including Bob and Gloria—had gathered around the open front door and witnessed the whole thing. Sian got out of the Porsche without being asked, and the two teenagers skulked away.

Broadhurst then did something that everyone deemed very, very stupid.

He tossed the keys back into the car's ashtray.

Even he was willing to concede that had he not been so careless, things would have turned out very differently.

About an hour later, there was a rumbling sound outside the house. No one paid much attention to it. Broadhurst's 911 was not the only sports car parked out there, and a couple of people had decided to leave early.

But a few minutes later, Broadhurst came storming into the living room and said, "Where the hell's Jeremy?" He announced that his car was missing.

The remaining guests came outside. The driveway from the Broadhurst home to the road was three fifths of a mile long, and crested a hill about a hundred yards from the house. Once a car passed that point, it was no longer visible.

But there was a reddish glow, and the sound of an idling motor, beyond the hill.

Bob and Broadhurst led the pack of people running to the scene, but everyone saw the same thing.

Sian's bloodied, twisted body lay in the grass to the left of the road. About fifty feet beyond that, on the other side of the driveway, was the Porsche, nosed into a tree, the front end crumpled. The engine continued to race.

The door swung open.

Jeremy, his forehead bloodied where it had hit the steering wheel, stumbled out of the car. Being an older-model Porsche, it was not equipped with an airbag. He looked around, dazed, blinked several times at all the people staring at him.

"What the fuck?" he said.

Reece and Megan McFadden were hovering in horror

over their daughter's body. Megan had taken the girl into her arms and was screaming. Reece looked at Jeremy and ran at him full force.

"You son of a bitch!" he cried. He threw Jeremy up against the car and started hammering him with his fists. Bob, Broadhurst and another man had to haul him off before he killed the boy. (Gloria, perhaps not surprisingly, had wanted Reece McFadden charged with assault. And equally unsurprisingly, the prosecutor had opted not to.)

Jeremy was charged with aggravated vehicular homicide. The amount of alcohol in his system constituted recklessness, and he was facing up to twenty-five years in prison.

Grant Finch, lawyer to and friend of both Galen Broadhurst and Bob Butler—and, I believed, Madeline Plimpton—was brought in. Several defense strategies were hatched. The first was to spread the blame, highlight the mitigating circumstances. There was the easy access to alcohol at the party, coupled with Galen's foolishness in leaving the keys in the car after Jeremy's first attempt to make off with it. That struck me as astonishingly stupid.

But then Grant, fearing those points would not be enough to get Jeremy off, hit upon something grander. Jeremy's mother, everyone said, had a history of micromanaging his life and making excuses for him when he did wrong. When he misbehaved at school, it was the teacher's fault. The system wasn't challenging him, so he acted out because he was bored, his mother would argue. If he got in trouble for fighting, Gloria would claim the other kid started it, even if she hadn't seen what happened. Shortly after Jeremy got his driver's license at the age of sixteen, he had backed into a lamppost and done several thousand dollars' worth of damage to his mother's car. The light on the post, she argued, was not bright enough, and she attempted to sue the town. Jeremy's behavior could always be traced by his mother to something other than her failure to make him accountable for his actions.

Grant Finch, in attempting to explain Gloria's parenting style and also garner her some sympathy, highlighted her own traumatic upbringing. She'd been raised by an emotionally abusive father after the death of her mother from cancer when Gloria was only five. By the age of eight, it was more like she was raising him. A real-estate agent with unpredictable hours, he expected Gloria to take care of the house, prepare meals and clean up after. He was relentlessly critical about everything she did, and punished her when she didn't do well in school.

I jumped to several other stories, looking to fill in the blanks. Gloria's father died in a car accident when she was eleven. Madeline Plimpton, it turned out, was Gloria's father's sister. She applied for legal custody of Gloria, and raised her from that point on.

Gloria'd always vowed that when she had children of her own, she'd never treat them the way her father treated her. All the love and attention her mother failed to share with her, she would lavish on her son. Enter the law of unintended consequence. Gloria so managed every aspect of Jeremy's life—what sports he'd play in, what clubs he'd join, what course he'd take, what friends he'd play with, even what TV shows he should watch—that he began to lose the ability to make a decision of his own. And when he attempted to, he'd get it wrong.

When he was seven years old, he nearly burned the house down while playing with matches. Gloria, so the story went, blamed the manufacturer for making matches that were too easy to light.

Finch brought in other factors that could have had an impact on Jeremy. He played video games—something he managed to do without his mother's approval—that might have made him unaware of the real consequences of reckless driving. His parents had recently split up and he was emotionally distraught. And, since they were throwing everything at the wall to see what might stick, the defense floated the idea that he had too much gluten in his diet.

The bottom line, though, was that Jeremy could not easily tell right from wrong after years of not being held responsible for his misdeeds. When he got into that car drunk, he would have had no idea that it could lead to something catastrophic.

Despite the humiliation it brought on her, Gloria Pilford went along with the defense strategy. But no one predicted how notorious it would become, or that Jeremy would end up being nicknamed the Big Baby.

Jeremy and his mother were mocked and ridiculed in TV news shows, even by the late-night comedians, as if there was anything about this story that was funny. Not that tragedy had ever stood in the way of comedy before. Back in the nineties, Jay Leno had his Judge Ito dancers during the O. J. Simpson trial, conveniently ignoring the fact that two people had been brutally murdered.

But the outrage didn't kick in big-time until the judge waived a prison sentence for Jeremy and instead placed him on four years' probation.

The fury was immeasurable. That part I was already up to speed on.

There were plenty of pictures accompanying the

articles I'd found online. The accident itself; shots of Sian McFadden, who was a beautiful young girl and would have grown up to be a lovely woman; Jeremy dressed for his court appearances in a dark blue suit that always looked too big for him, and a matching tie.

There was always that same look in his eyes. Lost, and frightened.

When I looked at the pictures, I couldn't help but be reminded of someone else. My son, Scott. Who, despite my wife Donna's and my best intentions, went off the rails. And while the drugs he experimented with weren't the reason for his death, he was headed down a road that could ultimately have killed him.

I sometimes envied my late wife, who no longer had to deal with the grief and the self-recrimination.

"A lot of it was just bullshit," said a voice behind me.

I wondered how long Gloria had been standing there, watching me read the various news stories.

"Which parts?" I asked, shifting around on the cushion.

I extended a hand to the closest chair, inviting her to sit. She took me up on it, setting her refilled wine glass on the table next to it.

"A lot of it," she said. "But there's enough of it that's true that people think the worst of me."

"News stories don't usually convey what people are like," I said. "On TV, they try to sum you up in two-minute segments. In a newspaper, your whole personality gets reduced to a couple of hundred words."

Gloria nodded. "It's true I pampered him. That I basically smothered him with too much attention. I had a horrible upbringing."

"I read about your father."

"I know I probably seem like a crazy woman to you,

but there are reasons I'm the way I am."

I said nothing.

"But some of the stories Grant told the court—they were pretty much a fiction. The playing-with-matches tale, for one. That never happened."

"It didn't?"

She shook her head. "Anything that couldn't be challenged, that supposedly happened just between me and Jeremy, where they couldn't bring in a witness to contradict my testimony . . . well, we came up with a few good tales." She smiled sadly. "It was probably like a TV series story meeting. Pitch me your most outrageous idea! You should have heard some of the ones we never used. Like where Jeremy strangled a chicken just for fun and I cooked it to get rid of the evidence."

"That didn't happen," I said.

"No," she said. "That did *not* happen. Despite what you've been led to believe, Jeremy's a wonderful boy. He really is." She grimaced. "But if I'd had to tell that story about the chicken to save him, I'd have done it."

"Sure," I said.

"Don't you think that proves I love him?" she asked.

The question seemed odd to me. "I don't think anyone ever questioned your love for Jeremy," I said. "I guess what Grant Finch was doing was showing you loved him too much."

Her eyes began to well with tears. She raised the glass to her face and tipped it to her lips, partly, I think, to keep me from seeing her cry.

"I'm the one who's always questioning it," she said, setting the glass back on the table and wiping her cheek with her sleeve. "The world says I'm a terrible mother, and maybe they're right."

We sat there a moment, not talking. Finally, I said, "Do you trust my judgment where your son is concerned?"

She looked at me with red eyes. "I suppose."

I closed the laptop and left it on the coffee table. I went up the stairs to the second floor. There were a dozen doors along the upstairs hallway, all of them open but for one. I walked past bedrooms and bathrooms until I reached the closed door at the far end.

I rapped softly on it.

No answer. Jesus, he'd taken off again.

I rapped harder.

"Yeah?" Jeremy said.

"It's Mr. Weaver."

"Yeah?"

I opened the door. He was lying on the bed, just staring at the ceiling. He turned his head slightly to take me in.

"What do you want?" he asked.

"Pack a bag," I said.

TWENTY-ONE

Barry Duckworth was pulling into his driveway when his cell phone rang. He put the car in park, turned off the engine, and dug the phone out of his pocket. The display said the call was coming from Promise Falls City Hall.

He had a bad feeling.

"Hello?" he said.

"Hey, Barry, how's it hangin'?"

"Randy," he said.

Randall Finley chortled. "Barry, aren't you supposed to call me Your Worship or Your Honor or Mr. Mayor or some shit like that?"

Duckworth thought "Some Shit Like That" did have a nice ring to it, but kept the thought to himself. "What can I do for you, Randy?"

"There's talk going around that you aren't coming to the memorial thing. Tell me that's not true."

"I'm pretty busy," Duckworth said.

"You're the fucking star of the show. You're the one that caught the guy. You have to be there."

"I'll think about it."

"Look, Barry, I'm being serious here. The town needs this. They need to honor those who died a year ago. They need to pay their respects. And everyone loves a hero. You're the hero. If you don't show up, it's like a massage without the happy ending. You gotta be there. We need something like this to counter all the shit that's been going on. You know what I saw yesterday? Go on, ask me."

"What did you see yesterday, Randy?" Duckworth asked.

"I was out by the water plant, by the tower."

It had been the deliberately contaminated water in the tower that had killed scores of Promise Falls residents.

"And there's this dumb fuck who's managed to get over the gate and gone up the stairs, and he's standing right on the top of the water tower and he's got on a cape or something like that and the words 'Captain Avenger' on his shirt. The fire department had to send a crew over to get the dumb bastard down before he killed himself. You know what, Barry? There are a lot of sick fucks out there. People who think we got what we deserved. That what happened here was justice. Can you believe that kind of thinking?"

"Anything else, Randy?" Duckworth asked.

"God, you've always been a stubborn son of a bitch. Think about it, okay? If you come, I'm gonna give you a plaque."

"I don't want a plaque."

"I've already ordered it."

"Goodbye, Mr. Mayor." Duckworth ended the call and got out of the car.

Given that his was the only vehicle in the driveway, he knew he had arrived home before Maureen or Trevor. Maureen he expected to get here at any moment. As for Trevor, who knew?

He came in the side door of the house, which led him directly into the kitchen. He took off his sport jacket, loosened his tie, rolled up his sleeves. Then he removed his weapon from his belt holster and put it in a lockbox in the laundry room, as was his usual routine.

He returned to the kitchen, opened the fridge and reached for a lite beer. He didn't know that drinking lite beer was really doing anything for him in the calorie department. Used to be he'd have only one beer when he got home, but now he often had two. He uncapped the bottle, put it to his lips, and drew on it for several seconds.

He couldn't help but feel relieved that Trevor was not home.

He opened the fridge a second time and wondered about dinner. Should he start something? Maureen usually cooked supper, but she worked all day the same as he did. But if it were up to him, they'd be eating steaks with baked potatoes smothered in butter and sour cream. He knew Maureen would have something healthier in mind. In fact, the fridge was filled with clear plastic containers of salad.

Oh joy.

He decided the best action for now was inaction. He took his beer with him to the kitchen table, sat down, and reached for Maureen's iPad, which was sitting there.

He couldn't stop thinking about Craig Pierce.

Some things, once seen, could not be unseen.

The man had suffered horrific injuries, and yet, by the end of their discussion, Duckworth was feeling no pity for him. If ever a case proved that victimization did not confer sainthood, it was Craig Pierce.

But Pierce had given Duckworth something to think about. If he and Brian Gaffney had both been set upon by the same person—or persons—why were the horrors visited upon Pierce splashed across the Internet, but not what was done to Gaffney?

Clearly someone was trying to make a point with

Gaffney. But the man with the tattooed message on his back claimed not to know what it was about. And Duckworth was finding it hard to believe that what had been done to the man had anything to do with Mrs. Beecham's dead dog. Although he had a feeling something funny *was* going on at that old lady's house that had nothing to do with Brian Gaffney.

Wait, he thought. *Maybe*—

He heard a car pulling into the driveway, the engine dying. When the door to the kitchen opened, and Maureen stepped in, Duckworth got up to greet her. He walked over, beer in hand, and gave her a peck on the cheek.

"Hey," he said. "I was going to start dinner, but I thought—"

"Oh, stop," she said.

The first thing she did, even before taking off her jacket, was kick off her shoes. "God, I've been waiting forever to do that. I know desk jobs are awful, but at least if I had one of those I wouldn't have to stand for nine hours."

"Long day?" he asked.

"Is it possible to do a twenty-hour shift in a nine-hour work day? It was like time slowed down." Maureen had worked at the eyeglass place in the mall for ten years and had never loved it. It had never been more than just a job. "What about you?"

Duckworth grimaced. "It had its moments."

"Good or bad?"

He thought before answering. "Memorable."

"Dumb question, anyway," she said, "considering what you do. Was there a high point? Or a low point that was *so low* it was a high point?"

There were a few to choose from. The tattooed man? The one who'd had his genitals bitten off? The interrogation of their son and his new girlfriend?

"Let me think about that."

"Why don't you think about it while I get changed for dinner?"

"Say what?"

"You're taking me out." She smiled and gave him a kiss. "It's so thoughtful of you."

"Do I get to pick the place?" He was already thinking ribs.

She hesitated. "Why don't we give Trevor a call and see if he wants to join us? We can let him pick the place."

When Duckworth didn't jump on the suggestion, Maureen said, "What? What's wrong, Barry?"

"I think it'd be nice, just the two of us."

"Did something happen today with Trevor?"

Duckworth was debating how much to tell her when they became aware of another car pulling into the driveway, followed seconds later by the slamming of a car door.

"Speak of the devil," he said.

The door into the kitchen opened. Trevor took one step in and froze at the sight of his parents.

"Hey, Trev," Maureen said cheerfully.

"Oh, great," he said, taking in the two of them. "I guess Dad's already filled you in."

"About?"

"Treating me and my girlfriend like a couple of suspects."

Maureen looked sharply at her husband. "What?" Then, just as quickly, back at Trevor, "Girlfriend?"

Duckworth shook his head. "It's not like that. Trevor,

you know that's not how it was."

"I never felt so embarrassed in my life," Trevor said, moving past them. "Just the way you want someone to meet your dad."

"What did you do?" Maureen asked Duckworth.

"I thought he might have been able to help me," he said. "Simple as that."

"Were you ever going to tell me about this?"

"You've been home for like two minutes," Duckworth said defensively.

"Who's this girl?" she asked Trevor.

"Carol," he said.

"Beakman," Duckworth added.

"Yeah, Dad would remember. I think he wrote it all down in his little notebook."

"Oh, for God's sake," Duckworth said. "Come on, Maureen, let's get some dinner."

"We're going out," Maureen told Trevor. "Come with us. We'll get this all sorted."

"I'll pass," Trevor said, exiting the kitchen.

"What will you eat?" Maureen asked. "I haven't made anything. There's some—"

"I'm not five, Mom," he said. "I'll figure something out." They heard him stomp up the stairs.

"It's like having a teenager all over again," Duckworth said.

"How could you do that to him?"

He raised his palms. "I'm telling you, he's overreacting. I'm sorry it happened, but he's blowing it all out of proportion. Come on, let's get something to eat."

"I don't even know if I want to go now."

"Come on. Do I still get to pick?"

She eyed him warily. "Fine. Pick."

"Let's go to Knight's."

Maureen's face fell. "You're not serious. That's not a restaurant. It's a dive."

"They have good wings," he said. "And there's something there I want to have another look at."

She shrugged. "Give me five minutes."

Maureen managed to tread more lightly going up the stairs than her son had moments earlier. It wasn't her intention to be a sneak. It was just that, in her stocking feet, she didn't make a sound when she reached the second-floor hallway and started heading to the bedroom she shared with her husband.

The door to her son's room was ajar, and she could hear him talking on his cell phone.

"I don't think it's a good idea," Trevor whispered. It sounded to Maureen like an angry whisper.

"You certainly don't have to do it on my account," he continued. "Yeah, well, maybe what we're doing *now* is the right thing."

Maureen held her position in the hall.

"I don't like being dragged into something that involves my father. Promise Falls' most famous cop. God, I thought your eyes were going to pop out of your head when you saw the picture of that dude's back."

Maureen didn't detect any admiration in his tone.

"Fine," Trevor said. "Do whatever you want . . . Yes, yes, I'm still coming. I'll meet you there."

Then, a very clipped "Bye."

Maureen continued down the hall to prepare for dinner out with her husband. But she wasn't thinking about what she would order.

What did Trevor think wasn't a good idea?

TWENTY-TWO

CAL

"Pack?" Jeremy said, sitting up on the bed.

"Yeah," I said. "I think the only way to keep you safe is to get you out of here."

He swung his feet down to the floor. "What should I pack?"

I shrugged. "Your stuff."

"My mom usually puts everything in my case when we go anywhere."

"Whatever you brought when you came from home, bring that."

"How long will we be gone?"

I hadn't really thought about that. "I don't know. Two, three days to start. Just pack whatever you've got. If you run out of stuff, we'll get more."

"Will you get me a phone?"

"No. Give me two minutes. I think your mom's okay with this, but I just want to be sure." I hesitated. "Unless you don't want to go."

He appeared dumbstruck. "Uh, I guess it's okay."

I could hear an ongoing discussion in the kitchen as I was descending the stairs. Gloria had clearly made her way back there from the living room.

"I swear, it's like you think I'm alcoholic," she said.

"I didn't use that word, you just did," Ms. Plimpton replied.

"You don't have to use it. I know it's what you mean. Let me ask you this, Madeline. Has it occurred to you that maybe I drink just a titch more than I used to? And have you asked yourself why that might be?"

"We've all been through a lot," her aunt said.

"Oh yes, what you've been through, it's just been terrible. How many times did you show up during the trial? Was it three? Four?"

"It was more than that and you know it, Gloria," Ms. Plimpton said defensively.

"And when you did come, you know what was interesting? That we had a hard time finding you at the end of the day."

"Gloria, stop."

"But one of those days, I did find you. Didn't I? But not at the *end* of the day."

"For God's sake, this has nothing to do with anything."

Bob looked at Gloria pleadingly. "Gloria."

"There you were, coming out of the hotel elevator at eight in the morning with Grant Finch."

Ms. Plimpton turned away.

"I guess the good news is women your age still like to get their motor running," Gloria said. She smiled wickedly at Bob. "That's certainly encouraging for *our* twilight years, isn't it, hon?"

Bob gave Ms. Plimpton a strained look of apology. "It's the wine."

"No, it's not," she said. "She's never appreciated a damn thing I've done for her."

Gloria waved her arms dramatically. "Oh yes, you came to my rescue after my daddy died. And I should be forever grateful."

"Can the two of you just stop this?" Bob said. "I swear

to God. Or maybe you should just fight to the death. I don't know that I even fucking care any more." He turned to leave. "I need to make a call to Galen. There's something I forgot to ask him about."

"Galen, Galen, Galen," Gloria said. "Maybe you should marry *him*."

"Damn it, would you knock it off? Galen's been a great help to us."

"Oh, I forgot," Gloria said. "He's been swell."

"He's putting a fortune into our pockets is what he's doing, letting me in on this deal," Bob said. "If you don't want us to be millionaires, just say the word."

That shut Gloria up, at least long enough for me to make my entrance.

"I have a proposal," I said. All eyes turned to me. I think they were a little stunned, and embarrassed, that I'd been a witness to their squabbling.

"What might that be?" Bob asked.

"I'll take Jeremy for a couple of days."

Gloria said, "Take him where?"

"First, away. I've got him packing his bag now. Your number-one concern is Jeremy's security. Instead of trying to make this place safe so he can stay here, it's easier to take him someplace else."

Bob was nodding. "That's not a bad idea."

"The whole country knows he's in Promise Falls. Why not let them keep thinking that? You're all big enough to look after yourselves."

Gloria looked unconvinced. "I don't know. I don't like letting him out of my sight. I didn't know this was what you were thinking."

"I'd take good care of him."

Gloria set down her wine glass. "Okay," she said. "I

guess it would be okay. I better go help him get ready."

I held up a hand. "Like I said, he's on it."

She looked hurt. "He might forget something."

"He's doing great. If we're missing something, we'll pick it up on the way."

"Where will you go?" Bob asked.

"I'm thinking about that. Maybe we'll do a road trip, keep moving." I looked at Madeline Plimpton. "You have my number if anyone needs to get in touch."

She nodded, then said to her niece, "I guess you two can go back to Albany."

"We can hang in for a few more days," Gloria said. "It's always lovely spending time with you, Madeline."

Whatever stuff Jeremy had, it all fit into his backpack. He dumped it into the trunk of my Honda, which was still parked on the street. He was about to get into the front seat when his mother came out of the house. We'd already said our goodbyes inside, but evidently it wasn't enough.

She threw her arms around him and pulled him close to her.

"You be good," she told him. Over his shoulder she said to me, "You take good care of my boy."

"You bet," I said.

Gloria put her mouth to his ear and whispered some sweet nothing. I decided to give them a moment of privacy and got into the car. Jeremy joined me in the passenger seat fifteen seconds later. His face was flushed red with what I guessed was embarrassment.

"Have to go by my place first to get a few things," I said, keying the ignition.

"Like a gun?" he asked.

"Like socks and underwear."

"Oh. Don't you carry a gun?"

"Sometimes."

"My mom got one."

"Terrific."

"She got it during the trial. Actually, Bob bought it for her. Because we were getting so many death threats."

"Did your mom take any lessons in how to use it?"

Jeremy shrugged. "Bob told her all you have to do is point it and shoot it."

"Where's that gun now?"

"When we got here, Mom was keeping it in her purse, but that freaked out my grandmother. She made her put it away. It's in the kitchen drawer right next to the knives and forks. I took it out the other night and was looking at it when they were all in the living room."

"Is it loaded?"

Jeremy nodded. "It wouldn't be much good if someone broke in and it didn't have any bullets in it."

If the car hadn't been moving, I'd have closed my eyes while I sighed. It was just as well I was getting the kid out of that house for a while.

"Where do you live?" he asked.

"Downtown."

"This town's kind of the pits, isn't it?"

"It's seen better days. Some people say it's on the comeback. We've got a new mayor. Actually, he was the mayor a long time ago, and now he's back in office. Maybe he'll make a difference."

"I heard my grandmother talking about him. She said he's got shit for brains. She said he used to hire underage hookers. Is that true?"

I nodded. These days, it didn't seem to matter what someone said or did. They'd still get elected.

We drove on in silence for another couple of miles. I glanced in my rear-view every few seconds. A black van had been riding along in my wake for the last few blocks.

"I'm just up here," I said. I pulled over to the curb in front of Naman's Books and the van continued on up the street.

"You live in a bookstore?" Jeremy asked.

"I live *over* it."

I'd had to move out for a few months, but now I was back. Naman's place had been firebombed by some racist nutcases last year when unfounded fears of a possible terrorist invasion had gripped Promise Falls. I wasn't sure Naman could make a go of it again, but he was back in business, and I had my old apartment back.

"We can leave your stuff in the car," I said, opening the door. Once Jeremy was out, I locked the Honda and led him to a door that fronted onto the sidewalk. There was a small sign on it that read: *Cal Weaver: Private Investigations.*

"Wow, just like in the movies," Jeremy said.

I unlocked the door, revealing a set of stairs going up. I extended an arm. "You first."

When we reached the top, there was a second door to unlock, and then we were in my apartment. A combined kitchen and living area, a bedroom off to the back. The whole place was smaller than his grandmother's foyer.

"Jesus, you actually live here?" Jeremy asked.

"It's not much, but it's pitiful," I conceded. I pointed to the fridge. "Help yourself to a Coke or something."

He opened it as I went into the bedroom. I kept a small travel case in the closet. I threw it onto the bed, opened up a couple of dresser drawers, and begin filling it with clothes.

"There's no Coke," Jeremy called out. "But there's beer. Can I have a beer?"

"No."

"This is going to be a real fun couple of days."

"You know what? Make us some sandwiches."

"Do what?"

"In the fridge, down below. I bought a bunch of stuff yesterday. Sliced ham, roast beef. There's a fresh loaf in the cupboard. Or if you want tuna, there's a tin in there, some mayo in the fridge. Something to eat now, and then some we can put in a cooler and take with us."

"Can't we just stop at McDonald's or Burger King when we're hungry?"

"No."

I went back into my bedroom. I finished putting in enough clothes for three or four days. Then I went to the closet, reached up to the top shelf, and brought down the case that held my gun. I wasn't that worried I was going to need it, but you never knew. Finally, I grabbed a small cooler I often used when I was on a surveillance job to keep bottled water and snacks fresh.

I zipped up the overnight bag and brought it and the cooler into the main room.

"How's it going?"

He had everything he might need to make sandwiches out on the counter. Bread, meat, butter, all spread out in no particular order. He had the look of someone who'd dumped all the pieces of a jigsaw puzzle onto the table and had only just started turning them image up. "Fine. I'm doing it. But aren't you being hired to look after me? Shouldn't you be the one to do this?"

"How can I shoot the bad guys waiting to bust in at any moment if I'm up to my elbows in mayo and mustard?"

The look he gave me suggested he couldn't tell whether I was being serious or putting him on.

I stood next to him at the counter.

"Okay, let's get a production line thing going on here. You start buttering the bread, and when you're done, move it this way."

He did as instructed. The butter was a little on the hard side, and as he attempted to spread it, it opened up holes in the bread.

I took the butter plate, put it in the microwave on medium for ten seconds, then gave it back to Jeremy.

"That's better," he said, dipping the knife into it and spreading some onto the bread. "I used to make sandwiches with my dad."

"Oh yeah?" I said. "When did your parents split up?"

He shrugged. "Long time ago. They were separated for ages, and then they finally decided to get a divorce."

"That can be tough," I said.

"Whatever," Jeremy said. He slapped some meat onto a piece of bread, lay a cheese slice on top of it, then a second piece of bread. "It's quiet here," he said.

"There's more traffic in the middle of the day," I said. "It's noisier then."

"That's not what I meant. There's not all the yelling."

"Oh, that. You live with a lot of that?"

He shrugged. "My mom and Madeline argue a lot. And then Mom and Bob, too. That's why I sneak out sometimes."

"Sure."

He slid some bread slices my way and I layered on some deli meat.

"Where are we going to go?"

"I thought we'd see all the hotspots of upper New York state."

"There are some?"

That made me laugh. "A couple. What are you interested in?"

He shrugged. "I don't know."

"You don't know what you're interested in?"

"My mom's always trying to get me interested in things I don't care anything about."

"Like?"

"I don't know. Like documentaries. The History Channel. I don't care about that stuff. I like movies. Did you see the new *Star Wars*?"

"No."

"It was okay."

"What else has she tried to get you interested in?"

He shrugged. "She likes to sign me up for sports, but I don't like sports."

"Why not?"

"Do I have to have a reason?"

"I guess not."

"There's one thing, though," Jeremy said.

"What's that?"

"You won't laugh."

"Of course not."

"I like art."

"Art? You like to paint?"

He shook his head. "I hate history, but I like reading about painters. Are there any art galleries we could go to?"

I wasn't expecting that. "Yeah, I think we could find some of those. You take art in school?"

"I was going to, but Bob told my mom that I should take something else, that I'd never get anywhere taking that. You can't get a job doing art."

"Not everything you take has to be aimed at a career."

"That's what I said, but Mom agreed with Bob."

"Would you like to be an artist? I know a little girl—well, she's not that little, she'd be twelve now, I think—named Crystal who likes to draw all the time. Those things they call graphic novels. She'd like to do those when she grows up."

"Is she good?"

"Yeah," I said. "I'm guessing she's still interested. I haven't seen her in a while. She moved out to San Francisco to be with her dad." I paused. "Her mom died."

"Graphic novels are cool, but I don't want to actually draw or anything. I'm not good at that. But I'd like to study it. Like, find out everything about great painters like Renoir and Raphael and Michelangelo and those guys. But not just classic guys. Modern stuff, too, like that dude who just threw shit all over the canvas, dribbling paint like crazy."

"You talking about Pollock?"

"That's the guy. Pollock. I'd like to get a job in a gallery or a museum or something like that. Do you think that's lame?"

"Lame? No."

"So where are we going? It's already dinner time. Are we just having a sandwich for dinner?"

"Just thinking on that," I said. "Whether to go tonight or in the morning."

The light outside was starting to fade. We could stay at my place for the night, but that would mean putting Jeremy on the couch. Still better than the jail cell he could have ended up in, but I thought maybe he deserved better than that. Jeremy's admission that he was interested in galleries had me considering a New York destination. We could be there in three or four hours. I'd have to see about a hotel reservation first.

Maybe that was why I went to the window, to see how nightfall was coming together. There weren't many cars parked along the street this time of day, now that the shops were closed, with the possible exception of Naman downstairs. He often kept his used bookstore open late because he had nothing better to do.

I guess that's why the black van on the other side of the street stood out. It was the only vehicle at the curb for half a block. I thought it might have been the same van that was riding along behind us on the way over. The windows were tinted, and I couldn't tell whether anyone was inside.

"Finish up those sandwiches," I said to Jeremy. "I gotta go down to my car for a second to get something."

"Okay," he said emptily.

I went quickly down the stairs and opened the door to the sidewalk. The van, its tail end facing me, was about five car lengths away. As I started across the street, I noticed exhaust coming out of the tailpipe. The taillights flashed on briefly, the van was shifted into drive, and it took off up the street.

Even if I'd been close enough to get a good look at the license plate, it wouldn't have done me much good. It was smeared with dirt and illegible.

When I got back up to my apartment, I said to Jeremy, "I say we go tonight."

TWENTY-THREE

Someone was rapping softly on Craig Pierce's bedroom door.

"Yeah?" he said.

The door opened. Standing there was a woman in her forties carrying a binder, a purse slung over her shoulder. Short hair, glasses, plain black skirt and off-white blouse.

"Hey," she said. "I'm sorry I'm a bit late today. I got held up with another client."

"Come on in, Ms. Sinclair," Craig said.

"Oh, how many times have I told you to call me Beverly?" she said, smiling, looking directly at his mauled, disfigured face.

Craig, standing by his dresser, broke off eye contact to examine the contents of a small shipping package.

"What do you have there?" Beverly Sinclair asked cheerfully.

"Oh, just some things I ordered," he said. He picked up one of them, something shiny and metallic and small enough to put into the palm of his hand, closed his fingers over it, and sat down in the chair by the foot of his bed.

Beverly sat in the other chair, set her purse on the floor, rested the binder atop her knees and folded her hands together. "So," she said, still smiling like someone doing a toothpaste commercial, "how are we doing today?"

"*We* are doing terrific," Craig said. His mangled lips

formed a twisted smile. "I suppose a lot of that has to do with what a good counselor you are."

"Well, thank you for that," she said, opening the binder. "But you're the one who deserves the credit. You're the one doing the work."

Craig shrugged modestly.

She consulted a page of handwritten notes on a yellow pad inside the binder. "Last time I was here we talked about you getting over your fear about going out of the house."

"Well, yes," Craig said. "But it's not so much my fear as it is other people's fear. I mean, I do look kind of scary."

"That's their problem, though, isn't it?" Beverly said. "People need to examine their own attitudes when it comes to dealing with others with disabilities or differences."

"Yeah, well, it's hard to get into a discussion about that when they're running off screaming their heads off," Craig countered.

She nodded understandingly. "Point taken. But you've been out and about more in the last week?"

"I have," he said.

"Where have you gone?"

"I've done some driving. And walking. Mostly at night."

"I think, as you regain your confidence, you'll be going out more during daylight hours," Beverly said encouragingly.

"I'm sure you're right," he said.

"And how would you describe your state of mind, say, the last week or so? Are you coming to terms with your situation?"

"My situation?" Craig asked. "That's such an interesting way to put it."

"Well, you know, I like to put things in as respectful and gentle a way as possible," she said.

"Oh, I've noticed that." Craig offered up another grisly smile. "As for my state of mind, I would say . . . it has improved."

"That's wonderful," she said.

"I've decided to try to move forward. To take control of my life rather than sit back and let it control me."

"That is very good to hear."

"I need to channel my energies, my . . . urges in a productive way," Craig said.

Beverly's smile faded. "Just what do you mean by that?" she asked.

"Which part?"

"Well," she said hesitantly, "the *urges* part."

"Oh, well—I hope you don't mind my being totally honest with you. I mean, you are my counselor and all."

"No, please, honesty is the best way to go."

"Well," and he leaned forward, almost conspiratorially, and whispered, "even though I no longer have the appliances, I've still got the owners' manuals, if you get what I'm saying."

Beverly swallowed. "I believe I do."

"So when I feel . . . aroused, in my mind, and I don't get a corresponding physical response, there's a kind of ache. Do you know what I mean? Like, you know when they talk about a phantom limb? How if your arm gets blown off in battle, you still feel the pain." He leaned in even closer. "I think what I have is a phantom hard-on."

Beverly leaned back in her chair.

"I don't really know about that," she said. "That's

something you'd have to discuss with your *physical therapist*."

Craig looked crestfallen. "Oh, I thought you were here to help me with that kind of thing, because, you know, it very much affects my self-esteem and all."

"There are . . . limits, Craig, to what I can help you with. What I am here to do is help you adjust to this new life you have, to help you understand that despite what has happened to you, this can be a new beginning."

He nodded as though he understood completely. "It's like a smile is just a frown turned upside down, right?"

Beverly Sinclair's jaw tightened. "You know, Craig, all I've ever sincerely wanted to do is help you. I know you're mocking me, but my intentions have always been genuine. You may not believe it, but I do care. I care about all my clients as if they were part of my family."

"That's nice," Craig said. "So, if you think of me as part of your extended family, maybe I could come by some time. I could meet your daughter."

Beverly's face froze.

"I think you mentioned her in passing once," Craig said. "She's fourteen, I think you said. And her name is Leanne? Do I have that right?"

Beverly said nothing.

"Maybe I should drop by," he said. "When I'm out driving at night."

Beverly found her voice. "You don't know where I live."

Craig opened his hand and studied the small metallic device he'd been holding.

"What is that?" Beverly asked.

"This," he said, picking it out of his palm with two fingers and holding it up between them, "is the niftiest little gadget. I've ordered them before, but this is a new model."

Hesitantly, as though afraid to ask, Beverly said, "What does it do?"

"It's a little tracking device. You plant it on . . . what–ever . . . and see where it goes."

Beverly closed her binder and reached down for her purse. She clutched it close to her chest. "Well, you can just hang onto it."

He gave her another hideous grin. "Who knows. Maybe I dropped one in your purse *last* week."

She put the binder on the chair so she could use both hands to open and inspect her handbag.

Craig laughed. "I'm just having some fun with you. I didn't do that."

Beverly looked at him, searched his deformed face, trying to determine the truth.

"Or did I?" he added.

Beverly snatched up the binder and opened the door. Before she slipped out into the hall she said, "I don't . . . I think I'll be assigning your case to someone else. You won't be seeing me again."

"You never know," Craig said. "We might run into each other sometime."

TWENTY-FOUR

"I hope we made the right decision," Gloria Pilford said, glass in hand. She had switched to red wine.

"Is there anything left in the cellar?" Madeline Plimpton asked, perched on a stool at the kitchen island.

"Where's Bob?" Gloria asked.

"Have you gone deaf?"

"What are you talking about?"

"You haven't heard all the racket? The power saw and the drilling."

"Oh," said Gloria. "That."

"He got a piece of plywood over where the glass was broken. Can't leave it wide open until the pane's replaced."

"No, I suppose not."

"And I think he was making some phone calls, too," Madeline said.

"Do *you* think we did the right thing? Letting Jeremy go off with a total stranger?"

"Weaver's a good man," her aunt said. "I checked him out."

"I talked to him a little, the two of us. Do you know what happened to his wife and his son?"

Madeline told her how they had both been murdered, several years ago. Gloria was quiet for several seconds, then said, "I'm sorry about earlier."

"Which part?" Madeline asked.

Gloria's eyes narrowed. "About Grant."

Madeline sighed. "It doesn't matter."

"I remember," Gloria said.

"You remember what?"

"I remember him from years ago. When he first started practicing. It was here in Promise Falls, wasn't it?"

"Yes," her aunt said.

"Was that when the affair started? Or was it before you took me in?"

Madeline glowered at her niece. "Before."

"But then at some point it ended," Gloria said.

"Grant was married. He wasn't going to leave his wife and I wasn't going to leave my husband. I was a widow a year later, but Grant had already moved on by then."

"So all those years went by and you had nothing going on?"

"That's right."

"But then you reconnected. We ended up hiring Grant to defend Jeremy."

Madeline sighed. "His wife passed away six years ago. We . . . rekindled something."

"Is it still going on?'"

"What business would it be of yours one way or another?" Madeline asked.

Gloria shrugged. "You like to know my business. I like to know yours."

"You've had too much to drink, Gloria. I'm turning in."

Bob walked into the kitchen, sport jacket on, face flushed with what looked like anger. He looked directly at Gloria.

"What?" she said, setting down her glass.

"Where is it?"

"Where is what?" she said.

"It's my own damn fault," Bob said, shaking his head. "I should have known better. I'm a goddamn idiot."

"I have no idea what you're talking about," Gloria said.

Madeline, who had put her departure on hold, looked at Bob. "What on earth *are* you talking about?"

"The phone," he said. "*Her* phone."

Madeline put eyes on her niece. "What did you do?"

"I have done *nothing*," Gloria said, raising her chin.

"The phone was in my jacket," he said. "I took it off and left it on the back of that chair this afternoon. I put it back on later, and I didn't even think about it until just now." He patted the left side of his chest. "It was in this pocket, and now it's gone."

"Maybe it slipped out when you were fixing the window," Gloria said.

"You grabbed it back," he said. "Weaver made a lot of sense when he said we should take it out of your hands. You can't be trusted not to go on there and say something stupid."

Gloria took another gulp of wine, then set the glass back down so hard the stem snapped. The glass toppled and spilled red wine across the island.

"For God's sake," Madeline said.

"You want to search me?" Gloria said, taking a step into the middle of the room, arms outstretched. "You want to frisk me? Is that what you'd like to do?"

He stood and gawked at her. "Seriously?"

"A strip search? Is that what you want? Why not? Let me oblige."

She crossed her arms, grabbed hold of the bottom of her pullover sweater with both hands, and pulled up.

"This is ridiculous," Madeline said.

Gloria's head was briefly obscured by the sweater, then it was off her body completely, leaving her standing there in a white bra and slacks.

"Gloria, stop it," Bob said.

She spun around once. "See anything? No? Okay, then." She kicked off her shoes, unzipped her slacks, and dropped them to the floor.

"It's probably in her purse," Madeline said.

Gloria pointed to the handbag sitting on the kitchen table. "Be my guest. Search all you want. Tear my room apart. I do not have that phone." Her face flushed with anger. "I will not be treated like a child."

She kicked the pants off and stood there in her underwear. "Would you like to do a body-cavity search, Bob? I bet you'd like that." She made her hands into fists and positioned them defiantly on her hips.

Bob turned and walked out of the room.

"Go on!" Gloria shouted. "I've got an idea! Why don't you phone me! See if you hear a ringing coming out of my ass!"

Madeline, evidently thinking that was a bluff that deserved to be called, went over to the landline and entered a number.

The room briefly went silent as the two women listened.

There was nothing.

"You probably have it on mute," Madeline said. "I swear, this family needs a team of therapists."

This time, she didn't stop on her way upstairs.

Gloria stood there in the kitchen, alone, in her underwear. After a minute, she found herself a new, unbroken glass, and poured herself another drink.

TWENTY-FIVE

"Isn't this a lovely place," Maureen said as she and Duckworth walked into Knight's.

"I know that tone," he said.

"What tone? I don't know what you're talking about. Would you like that booth by the arm wrestlers, or maybe next to that couple there who are trying to build a house with the sugar packets?"

"How about over here?" he suggested, locating an empty booth that wasn't close to anyone who appeared immediately objectionable.

"That looks perfect," she said. "Only three steps to the bathroom should I need it."

Within seconds of sitting down across the table from each other, a young woman came over with menus.

"Can I get you folks some drinks?" she asked.

Maureen asked for a glass of Pinot Grigio and Duckworth said some sparkling water with lime would suit him just fine.

"Is Axel here?" he asked.

The girl nodded.

"Could you ask him to drop by when he has a second?"

The girl nodded a second time and disappeared.

Maureen looked at the menu. "You're going to love this place. I don't think there's a single thing here you should be allowed to eat. Oh, wait, celery sticks come with the double-breaded jumbo wings."

"I know this isn't exactly the fanciest place in town, but what's wrong with you?"

"Nothing," Maureen said.

"You're mad at me for the Trevor thing."

"I didn't say that."

"Look, that thing with me and him, he'll get over it." His eyes darted around the bar. "It's because of this place I wanted to talk to our son."

Maureen lowered her menu. "What are you talking about?"

"Him and his new girlfriend. They were in that booth over there, checking out each other's tonsils."

"No."

"Yes."

"How'd you even know that?"

He explained how he had, by chance, come to see Trevor and Carol Beakman on the surveillance video.

"I wasn't looking for them. I was looking for something else and there they were."

She eyed him suspiciously. She was about to ask him something when Axel suddenly appeared at the table.

"Hey, Detective, how's it going?"

Duckworth introduced the man to Maureen.

"Dinner's on the house," Axel said.

Duckworth smiled. "I'm afraid I can't accept. Goes against the rules. But I do have a favor."

"Shoot."

Duckworth told him what it was. Axel said it would take him a few minutes, and would return when he had things ready.

"And I'll get some of those double-breaded jumbo wings," Duckworth said.

Axel looked at Maureen. "Garden salad," she said.

"Oil and vinegar dressing." She paused. "And an order of potato skins with extra sour cream."

Axel nodded and slipped away.

"You had me worried for a second there," Duckworth said.

"I'm having one of your wings, too."

"I'll have one of your potato skins."

"I thought I'd share my salad with you instead."

He rested his back against the seat and sighed. "Like I said, I'm sorry about earlier."

She took in a long breath through her nose.

"What? I know that look. There's something on your mind."

Maureen sighed. "I don't know how good things are between him and this Carol girl, anyway."

"Why do you say that?"

"I heard him talking to her. On the phone. When I went upstairs to get ready."

"Okay."

"He sounded angry with her. I think it may have had something to do with you, but there was something else."

"Like what?"

"Something she wanted to do, but he wasn't that keen on her doing it."

"You don't know what it was?"

She shook her head.

"So, you're an eavesdropper."

Maureen nodded.

Duckworth grinned. "Nothing wrong with that. But you know what? Whatever it is that's going on between them, it's their problem, not ours."

"I know."

"Things'll work out. I mean, I didn't even know about

her until today, so if they're on the skids, it's not like it was some long-term relationship."

"I just want him to be happy."

Axel brought their drinks. "I got it all set up for you. Your food's going to be a few more minutes, if you want to take a quick look now."

Duckworth said to Maureen, "I'll be right back."

He followed Axel to the office he'd been in earlier in the day. The bartender had brought up the security video from two nights ago on the computer screen.

"What was it you wanted to see?" Axel asked.

"The man who was already at the bar when Brian Gaffney came in. The one I thought was him."

"Oh yeah, this guy," Axel said, pointing to the screen. "The one I asked for ID."

"At a glance," Duckworth said, "you could almost mistake one for the other. I mean, they're not twins, but they're wearing much the same clothing. Same build, hair color, et cetera."

"Yup."

"Speed it up again?"

Axel advanced the video. When it reached the point where Brian Gaffney got up to leave, Duckworth had Axel slow it down.

"So there he goes." Soon after that, Trevor and Carol slid out of their booth and left too.

The man with a passing resemblance to Brian was still at the bar, looking most of the time at his phone, as though playing a game.

"Speed it up again."

The video advanced. Duckworth asked Axel to slow it down when the man got off the bar stool and started heading for the door.

He noted that the time was 9:43. Eleven minutes after Gaffney had left.

The man was passing by a table of four men sharing a pitcher when one of them suddenly grabbed his arm, pointed and said something.

"What's going on there?" Duckworth asked.

"Yeah, I remember that. They were giving him a hard time for a few seconds on his way out."

"He do something to piss them off?"

"Not that I saw. But one of these guys, he yells at him, 'Hey, you, big baby.' Or something like that."

Duckworth nodded slowly, getting as good a look as he could at the man. "I'll be damned."

"You recognize him?" Axel asked.

Duckworth just smiled. "Thanks for your help. This is better than a hundred free drinks."

He returned to the table, where Maureen was taking a sip of her wine.

"Some guy tried to pick me up while you were gone," she said as he settled back into the seat.

"You're kidding," he said.

"That's the wrong answer," she told him.

"Who was it?"

"That one over there, at the pool table, about to take a shot. Not bad looking for someone who's seeing seventy in the rear-view mirror."

"I suppose I'll have to shoot him," Duckworth said. The waitress arrived with their food. "But I'll eat first."

"Good God," Maureen said, looking at the pile of wings on her husband's plate. "I might as well just call the ambulance now."

He picked up a wing, bit into it. "I think they got the wrong guy."

"What?"

"They didn't want Brian. They wanted the Big Baby."

"I have no idea what you're talking about," Maureen said.

TWENTY-SIX

CAL

I couldn't see us making Manhattan that night. But I didn't want Jeremy to spend the night at my apartment, in case there were people who already knew we were here. The black van I'd seen out front had rattled me. It might or might not have anything to do with the brick that got thrown through the front window of Madeline Plimpton's house. It had not been a black van I'd seen speeding away from her place.

I grabbed my bag, and the cooler, which we had packed with the sandwiches and a few other snacks, and headed down to the street. I locked up my place, dumped the stuff into the car, and told Jeremy to get in. There was something else I had to do first.

I got down on my knees and, with a flashlight I took from the glove box, inspected the undercarriage of the car. Then I felt inside the wheel wells, patting my hand on the insides of the fenders. Finally, I gave the bumpers a good going-over.

"What was that about?" Jeremy asked when I got in behind the wheel.

"One time," I said, "somebody attached a tracker to my car. In fact, not one, but two."

"Whoa," Jeremy said. "Cool."

I glanced over at him. "No, it wasn't. I got someone killed."

"Oh, shit. When was this?"

"Four years ago."

"What happened?"

I ignored the question.

I got us out of Promise Falls and went south on 87 toward Albany. The plan was to get around the capital, then continue on in the same direction toward New York. We dug into the cooler and killed off all the sandwiches in the first hour. Jeremy didn't have much to say, and I didn't feel all that much like talking.

We were about to pass the exit to the Mass Pike, around Selkirk, when Jeremy suddenly said, "Can we get off at the next exit?"

"What for?"

"It's right here. Get off! Get off!"

I hit the blinker and took the exit. "What's going on?" I asked.

"When you get to the end of the ramp, take a right," he said.

"What I'm gonna do is pull over until you tell me why you made me get off the thruway."

He seemed to need a few seconds before he could work up the nerve to tell me.

"You have to promise not to tell my mom," he said.

"Come on, Jeremy, don't make me promise something I might not be able to do. You tell me, or we carry on south."

"My dad lives here," he said. "Like, close. Yeah, turn here."

I made a right where the ramp ended. "Okay," I said. "So we're going to visit your dad. That would upset your mom?"

He shrugged. "Kinda. Probably. She doesn't like him."

"That happens a lot when people split up."

"Yeah, but this is *different*," Jeremy said.

"Different how?" I glanced over, tried to read his face, but came up with nothing. "Was your father abusive to your mother?"

Gloria's own father had been abusive, and sometimes people went with what they knew, even when it was bad for them, because it was *all* they knew.

"He never hit her or anything," Jeremy said. "Nothing like that. You make a left up here."

"Didn't you say your dad's a teacher?" I asked.

"Yeah, high school."

"Why do you want to drop by?"

Jeremy gave me a look that suggested any faith he might have had that I had half a brain had been misplaced. "Because he's my dad," he said.

"Sure," I said. "Point the way."

He directed me into an old neighborhood and told me to stop out front of a modest storey-and-a-half brick house with a couple of dormer windows poking out of the roof. While the house was small and unassuming, the yard was immaculately kept, with spring flowers that looked as though they had just been planted.

"Don't freak out or anything," he said, getting out of the car before I had a chance to ask about what.

I followed him to the door. He rang the bell, and ten seconds later it was answered by a balding man in his mid-fifties wearing glasses, a pullover sweater and jeans.

"Oh my God, Jeremy," the man said with what struck me as limited enthusiasm. They faced each other awkwardly for a moment, then the man put his arms around the boy and hugged him. "What are you doing here?"

"We were just kind of in the neighborhood," Jeremy said.

The man was looking over Jeremy's shoulder at me, and his eyes narrowed with suspicion. "And this is?"

"This is my bodyguard," Jeremy said. "Dad, this is Mr. Weaver, Mr. Weaver, this is my dad."

I extended a hand. "Cal," I said.

"Jack Pilford," the man said, eyeing me suspiciously. "Bodyguard?"

"Not really," I said. I managed, in three sentences, to explain my presence.

"Okay," he said, dubiously. "Listen, Jeremy, you know I love to see you, and it's great that you've dropped by. Without, you know, calling ahead. But this is not really the best—"

The door opened wider and another man, slightly older than Jack, appeared. He looked at Jeremy, took a moment to register who he was, then said, "Oh, wow, look who's here. America's worst driver."

"Jesus, Malcolm," Jack said. "Don't be an asshole."

Malcolm set his eyes on me next. "And you must be Bob."

"No," I said. I identified myself.

"Mr. Weaver's been hired to protect Jeremy," Jack said.

"I'm not going to hurt him," Malcolm said defensively.

"Not from you." Jack shook his head. To Jeremy and me he said, "I'm sorry about this. I was trying to tell you, this isn't a very good time."

"Lovers' quarrel," Malcolm said.

"Maybe we should go," I said to Jeremy, who had the look of a kid who'd been picked last for a team.

"Why didn't you come?" Jeremy asked.

"Jeremy, we talked about this," his father said. "You know—"

"Because of your cunt mother, that's why," Malcolm said.

Jack said, "Enough." He gently pushed Malcolm back into the house. Malcolm allowed it to happen, even showing some satisfaction that his behavior had brought about that reaction. Jack closed the door and stepped outside.

"I'm sorry," he said again. "And Jeremy, you know I wanted to be at the trial, I wanted to be there for you, but Gloria, your mother—"

"You don't have to do everything she says," Jeremy interrupted.

"She said to me, and these were her exact words, 'We don't need a couple of gaylords turning the trial into a circus.' That's what she said."

"You could have ignored her."

"It wasn't just her," Jeremy's father said.

Jeremy said, "Who?"

Jack Pilford hesitated. "Madeline called me. She said she'd been talking to Grant Finch, who more or less agreed with your mother. That they had a defense worked out, that bullshit about you not understanding the consequences of your actions. They didn't want to complicate the message with stories about your father— about me—being gay. I guess Finch and Madeline thought gay was the same thing as sensitive, and if that's what I was, how come none of my influence rubbed off on you while your mother and I were still together. It was all a crock of shit, far as I was concerned, but if they had something worked out, I didn't want to mess it up. I didn't want to do anything that might work against you.

Not that the world didn't find out about me anyway."

"What are you talking about?" I asked.

Jack tipped his head back in the direction of the house. "That's what's got Malcolm riled up. I'm sure it's just a fraction of what you and your mother are dealing with, but we've been targeted, too."

"Targeted?" I said.

"Harassing phone calls, being mocked online. I'm the Big Baby's faggot father who didn't teach his kid right and wrong. How could I, half of them say, considering I'm a sick, twisted pervert."

It was like a cancer, all this social-media shaming.

"Malcolm's furious that I've had to endure this," Jack said. He smiled wearily at his son. "But I'll survive it. One day, when it all blows over, we can do something, get together. How does that sound?"

Jeremy looked at me. "I guess we should be going."

I said, "Okay."

"No, wait," Jack said. "Maybe we could go somewhere, get a cup of coffee."

"I hate coffee," Jeremy said, already walking back to the car.

We lost about half an hour detouring to Jeremy's father's house, so making it to New York tonight was no longer an option. As we neared Kingston, I felt it was time to start looking for a place to bed down. There was a Quality Inn we could see from the highway, but there were plenty of other hotels to choose from if we were willing to drive a mile or two.

I pulled up in front of the Quality Inn. "Wait here," I said to Jeremy. He'd been pretty sullen since we'd left his father's house.

I took the car key, and parked close enough that I'd be able to see my Honda from the registration desk. I wasn't convinced Jeremy wouldn't make a run for it if the mood struck him. So far, he'd seemed pretty agreeable to the whole road trip idea, although he had to be thinking dropping in on his dad had been a bad call. Then again, he could be setting me up. Maybe he'd figured out a way to get a message to his girlfriend Charlene, and she was waiting around the next bend in her Miata.

I went to the desk and asked if they had a room available with two beds. Single, double, queen, didn't matter. While the woman was scanning her computer for availability, a young couple came through the main doors.

I could hear their conversation as they walked through the lobby in the direction of the elevator.

"That was him!" the woman said.

"That was who?" the man asked.

"From the news. The Big Baby kid. That was him in the car."

"Seriously?"

They slowed, the man craning his head around to look back at my car.

I said to the woman on the desk, "Never mind."

"I've got something," she said. "Two queen beds and—"

I shook my head. "No thanks."

I got back into the car, put the key in the ignition and started the motor. I reached for the seat belt, buckled myself in.

"Full up?" Jeremy asked.

"Yup," I said.

The Hampton Inn and the Courtyard were full, but the Best Western had a spot for us. At all three places, before heading in, I made a point of not parking under any bright lights where someone might be able to spot Jeremy. Once I had us a room, I hustled him through the lobby as quickly as possible.

"They're going to think you're some sort of pervert who likes little boys," Jeremy said.

"You're not a little boy. You're eighteen."

"Oh, so it'd be legal?"

"That's not the point I was trying to make."

The room was adequate. First thing Jeremy did after tossing his bag onto one of the two beds was grab the remote and troll through all the available channels. "Wanna order a movie?" he asked.

"No."

"There's dirty ones, too."

"No."

"You think it's weird that my dad's gay?"

"No."

"That he's living with Malcolm?"

"No."

"I've never liked him."

"Malcolm?" I said.

"Yeah. Not because he's gay. Well, sort of. Because my dad fell in love with him, because they're both gay, so that meant my mom and dad split up. But mostly I don't like him because he's a dick."

"Okay," I said.

"I mean, if your dad's gonna leave, you'd like to think he had a really good reason, right? That the person he was leaving you for was going to make his life better."

"You don't think he and Malcolm are happy?"

Jeremy shrugged. "I don't even care." He propped up some pillows at his back so he could sit up on the bed.

"What are we going to do?"

"Did you bring a book to read or anything?"

He shook his head.

"I brought three," I told him. I unzipped my bag, intending to toss them out for his perusal, when my cell phone rang.

"Hello?"

"Mr. Weaver?"

"Hello, Gloria."

"Is Jeremy there?"

"Of course." I looked at him and mouthed, "It's your mom."

His head went down like a bag of sand. Blindly, he held out his hand and let me drop the phone into it.

"Hi, Mom . . . Yeah, we had some sandwiches . . . I don't know." He looked at me. "Are you going to get me a hot meal?"

"That'll be breakfast," I said.

"He says I'll get a hot meal at breakfast." He gave me a look that suggested his mother did not think that was a good enough answer. "It's okay, I'm fine. No, we drove straight here. No stops along the way. We're in Kingston now. I think we're going to New York City."

I shook my head.

"I guess I wasn't supposed to tell you that . . . Yes, I know you're my mom and you deserve to know where I am . . . Are you going to call Ms. Harding in the morning and tell her what's going on?"

I gave him a puzzled look. He whispered to me, "My probation officer."

Then, back to his mother, "Okay . . . Yes, I'll check in. Okay . . . Yes, I love you too. Goodbye."

He handed back the phone. I put it to my ear,

wondering if Gloria was still on there, wanting to give me a piece of her mind, but she'd hung up.

"She really does treat me like I'm five sometimes," he said.

"And she probably always will. Kids are kids to their parents no matter how old they are."

"She had kind of a rough time when she was little," he said.

I nodded. "I read about that."

I went back into my case and brought out three books. "I'm reading this one," I told him, holding up an old copy of John Irving's *A Prayer for Owen Meany* that I had bought at Naman's. "But you can have one of these if you want."

Onto his bed I tossed two paperbacks. *Early Autumn*, by Robert B. Parker, and *The Stand*, by Stephen King. The latter was about five times the thickness of the former. Jeremy gave them a cursory look, then picked up the remote.

"I wish I had my phone," he said.

He watched a couple of episodes of *The Big Bang Theory* while I tried to read, but I found it hard to concentrate with the background noise. Finally, I said it was time to turn in. I went into the bathroom to brush my teeth, then made way for Jeremy. He closed the door. I heard the shower running, but he was in there a long time after the water stopped.

I called out to him, "You okay in there?"

"Yeah," he said quickly. "Tummy's kind of off. I think it was one of those sandwiches. We should have gotten a pizza or Mickey D's."

The sandwiches hadn't upset my stomach.

At long last, he came out and slid under the covers of

his bed. Light from the parking lot filtered through the drapes, so we weren't in total darkness once I'd turned off the bedside lamp.

"Do you snore?" Jeremy asked.

"I've been told I do."

"Great. I heard Madeline say you aren't married or anything."

"Not any more."

"You got divorced?"

"No."

Jeremy went quiet. There was no sound from his side of the room for a long time, and I thought maybe he'd fallen asleep.

I was wrong.

"What will happen to me?" His voice came through the darkness like someone in the distance calling for help.

"What do you mean?"

"What kind of life am I going to have?" he asked. "I mean, the whole world knows who I am and hates me. What happens when I have to go back to school? What about when I want to go to college or something? If I even decide to do that. Or after that, when I want to get a job? Who's going to hire me? They'll google my name and find out who I am and what I did and they won't want to have anything to do with me. I'm like the world's biggest asshole."

"No you aren't," I said. "I think that might be Galen Broadhurst."

I heard an actual chuckle from him.

"Sorry," I said. "That was unprofessional." I shifted onto my side so that, even if Jeremy couldn't see me, my voice would project more clearly to him. "Look, I don't have all the answers. I sure can't claim to have

220

been the greatest father that ever lived."

"You've got kids?"

"I had a son."

"Oh." A pause. Then, "But not any more?"

"No."

"Oh."

"The thing is," I said, "you did what you did, and there's nothing you can do to change that. You own it. You can't hide from it. If you don't tell people up front, and they find out later, they'll think you're trying to put something over on them, even if all you're doing is what anyone else would do. Wanting people to respect their privacy."

"Yeah, sure. So I put on the top of my résumé, I'm the kid who ran over that girl?"

"No. You did something stupid. All kids, by the time they've reached your age, have done something stupid. The others are just luckier than you. Maybe they drove drunk, too, but nothing bad happened. So that's tough. But you have to accept responsibility for what you did. You can't go blaming others. You have to say, 'I did it, I own it,' and every day moving forward you have to learn from that."

Silence from the other bed.

"Does that help any?" I asked.

"Not really."

I heard him turn over and pull up the covers.

We were done.

TWENTY-SEVEN

Even with his eyes still closed, Barry Duckworth became aware that someone was in the bedroom.

He opened them, blinked a couple of times to get used to the light coming through the window, and saw his son, Trevor, standing just inside the door.

"Trev?" he said.

That prompted Maureen, under the covers next to Duckworth, to turn over, remove the eye mask that blocked out all light, and say, "What's going on, what's happening? What time is it?"

She glanced at the clock radio on her bedside table. "It's six forty. What are you doing up so early?"

Trevor was fully dressed. His hair was slightly tousled, and he didn't appear to have shaved yet this morning.

"I haven't been to bed," he said, his voice shaky. "Dad, I need help."

His father raised himself up, swung his bare feet down to the hardwood floor. "What happened, son?"

"It's Carol," he said. "Something's happened to Carol."

Duckworth dressed quickly. By the time he was down in the kitchen, Maureen had made coffee. Trevor was pacing.

"Okay, let's start from the beginning," Duckworth said, taking a mug from Maureen and standing by the counter to drink it.

"So we were going to meet up last night. After you and Mom went out for dinner."

"Where?"

"At the mall."

"Promise Falls Mall?"

"Yeah. We were going to grab a bite in the food court. They've got that movieplex there now and we were thinking we'd check out what was playing, maybe see something."

"What time were you going to meet?"

"Eight. That'd give us time to eat and see what the shows were."

"Okay."

"I got there about quarter to eight. I went to the food court first, in case she was early, but I didn't see her there, so I decided to look in a couple of stores first, and go by and see what the movies were. But I got right back to the food court for eight, and she still wasn't there."

Trevor was trembling as he spoke. Maureen put her hand on his arm as he continued talking.

"So I sat down and started thinking about what I would get to eat, but then it was five after eight, and then ten after eight, so that was when I texted her. You know, like, I'm here, where are you?"

Duckworth nodded. "Did she get back to you?"

Trevor shook his head. "Nothing. I kept looking to see if the text was delivered, and it didn't come up that it was. So then I phoned, and it went straight to message."

"She must have turned off her phone," Maureen said. "Sometimes I turn off my phone, meaning to restart it, and then I forget, and your father's trying to reach me and I've left my stupid phone off."

"Yeah, but it's more than her phone being off. She didn't show."

"What happened next?" Duckworth asked.

"I started looking around the mall, wondering if she'd gone shopping and lost track of time, always circling back to the food court to see if she was there. But she wasn't. And the whole time, I'm holding my phone, you know? In case I get a text or anything. But nothing."

"How long did you wait?"

"Except for the theaters, the mall closes up at nine. So when it got to be nine, I stood for a while where people were buying tickets, thinking maybe Carol got held up and she'd show up at the last minute, but there was no sign of her. So I left the mall, and looked around the parking lot for her car."

"What does she drive?"

"She's got a little silver Toyota. A Corolla. It's about five years old."

"Did you see it?"

Trevor shook his head. "So I decided to go by her place."

"Where does she live?"

"She's got an apartment in Waterside Towers?"

Duckworth knew it. A condo development about half a mile downstream from the falls, in the town's core.

"I drove over there, and Carol has an assigned parking space, and her car wasn't there. But then I thought, maybe she had some kind of car trouble, and came home in a taxi and—"

"Did you try her landline?" Maureen asked.

"She doesn't have one," Trevor said. "Just her cell. So anyway, I hang around in the lobby and managed to get into the building when someone else was going in, and I

224

go up to her door and bang on it, and there's no answer."

Duckworth asked, "When was the last time you tried her cell?"

"One minute before I came into your room," Trevor said. "I waited in the parking lot of her place all night. When the sun came up, I came home." He looked to be on the verge of tears. "I don't know what to do."

"Where's she work again?" his father asked.

"She works at the town hall."

"That's right."

Maureen's eyebrows went up a notch. "For Randall Finley?"

Trevor shook his head. "No, she doesn't work in the mayor's office. She's, like, in the town planning department. She's got some kind of degree in how to organize cities, that kind of thing."

"How'd you meet her?" Duckworth asked.

"Does that matter?" Trevor asked.

"Probably not," he said. "Just curious."

"I went in there to drop off a résumé, and she recognized me. We were in a couple high-school classes together. We met up later for a coffee—this was about a month ago—and we started seeing each other."

"When were you planning to bring her around her so we could meet her?" Maureen asked.

Trevor looked at her. "Seriously? That's what you're concerned about right now?"

Maureen frowned. "Sorry."

Duckworth said, "I'm sure she's fine. I'll bet there's a simple explanation. A family emergency, maybe. Something that called her out of town." He glanced at his watch. "The town hall opens up in another hour or so. We'll drop by, see if she's there."

Trevor nodded very slowly, licked his lips as though there was something he still had to say.

"There's more," he said quietly.

"What's that?" Duckworth asked.

"We weren't . . . we weren't entirely honest with you yesterday, when you talked to us at Starbucks."

Duckworth waited.

"I mean, it wasn't my place to say anything. If anyone was going to say anything, it was going to be Carol."

"Why's that?"

"She's the one who saw something."

"Saw something at Knight's? When you were leaving?"

"Not something, exactly. Just someone. And she didn't see anyone doing anything. In fact, it's probably nothing."

"I don't understand."

"Okay, so we're coming out of Knight's, and it's kind of dark, and we're heading for my car—I'd picked her up at her place that night—and she goes, 'Hey, how you doin'?' to someone."

"She saw someone she knew?"

"Yeah. This woman, standing by the alley that goes down the side of Knight's. You know where I mean?"

"I do."

"So Carol goes up to her, but I kind of hang back, because it's not anybody I know, and I feel kind of funny when she introduces me to a friend, because she's got a good job, and I'm still trying to find something, and I don't want to have to do a whole bunch of explaining."

"Sure."

"So she talks to this girl for about thirty seconds, then says goodbye, and then me and her go to my car and that's kind of it."

"Who was she?"

Trevor shrugged. "I asked her, and she said just someone she knew, no big deal, and she actually seemed a bit
pissed because this friend didn't seem to want to talk to
her anyway. Kind of gave her the bum's rush."

"That's it? That's the part you left out?"

"Okay, so, when you found me at Starbucks and started asking us about being at Knight's, that really, honestly
pissed me off, you know."

"I got that," Duckworth said.

"I mean, I was thinking of introducing her to you
guys, but before I get a chance to do that, suddenly there
you are interviewing us like we're a couple of suspects or
something. But then after you left, we were talking, and
that's when she mentioned that she had spoken to this
friend of hers. She said that even if we didn't see anything
suspicious, maybe her friend had. She wondered if she
should tell you, and then she thought maybe it would be
better to get in touch with the friend, and if she did see
anything, *she* could get in touch with you herself."

"Okay."

"Carol felt bad that the very first time she meets my
dad, she's not straight with him. She thought that if that
other woman knew anything and could help you, that'd
be a nice way to make it up to you. Not that you'd ever
have known in the first place."

Maureen said, slowly, "That's what you were talking
about."

Trevor looked at her. "What?"

"On the phone, last night. I was going past your room
and I heard you say something like you didn't think it
was a good idea."

"You were listening to me?"

"It was just something I heard when I was walking by," she said.

"Yeah, that's what we were talking about. I said she didn't have to do anything, that she didn't have to get involved just to try to make a good impression on him." He tipped his head toward his father.

"But she decided to do it."

Trevor nodded. "She said she was going to give her friend a call. That's all. Just call her up and tell her something had happened around that time at Knight's, and that if she saw anything she should get in touch with you."

"That was the last time you spoke with her?" Duckworth asked.

His son nodded.

"You remember anything at all about this woman?"

"It was dark. And like I said, I didn't go over. She was probably around our age."

"White? Black?"

"White."

"Had she been in Knight's earlier?"

"Not that we saw."

"And no name? Carol must have mentioned her name if you talked about this a few times."

"At first, when I asked who it was—you know, right after she saw her—she just said she was a friend. And it didn't really matter then. It wasn't an issue until you came and talked to us. And I said, after, what about your friend, and Carol said, maybe I should get in touch with her."

"How would she know how to contact her?"

"She said she knew her from where she worked, that she had a number for her."

Duckworth sighed. "Okay, that whole business, that's my problem. What we want to do now is confirm that Carol is okay."

"Yeah, right."

"Is it possible," Duckworth asked gently, "that maybe she thought things weren't working out? That she didn't want to see you any more, but couldn't find a way to tell you to your face? So she turned off her phone, didn't answer her door?"

Trevor looked at him with misted eyes. "I don't know. I mean, if that's what she did, I wasn't picking up the signals, you know?"

Duckworth put a hand on his shoulder. "Here's what I'm going to do. You don't want to give her the idea you're stalking her or something. So why don't I go into the town hall, down to the planning department, and see if she's there. In the meantime, you stay here, keep trying her on your phone. If you want, go back to her apartment, see if her car turns up. Does that sound like a plan?"

Trevor nodded. "I guess so."

Duckworth smiled. "Good. That's what we're going to do."

He gave his son a hug, then gave Maureen a kiss on the cheek as he headed for the door.

Duckworth phoned Trevor ninety minutes later.

"You got any news?" he asked his son.

"Nothing. I'm at her place. No sign of her car. You?"

Duckworth hesitated. "Carol Beakman didn't show up for work today. And she didn't call in sick."

TWENTY-EIGHT

CAL

Jeremy was up and dressed and ready to hit the road before I even had my clothes on. I was in the bathroom, stepping out of the shower. He knocked on the door. I wrapped the towel around me and said, "Yeah?"

He poked his head in. "I'm starving. You okay with me going down for breakfast without you?"

I hesitated. I didn't want the kid taking off on me, but if he'd wanted to disappear, it would have been easy enough to do that when I was in the shower. He hardly needed to ask. And where was he going to go? How would he make his escape? Not that I didn't trust him— well, I didn't trust him—but I had brought not only my gun into the bathroom but my car keys, too.

"I'm not gonna do a runner," he said. "I'm just really hungry."

"Fine," I said, hitting the fan in the hopes it would clear the fogged mirror.

His head withdrew. Seconds later, I heard the door to our room open and close hard. I was a little worried that maybe someone at this hotel—as had happened at the other one before I decided to bail—might recognize him. But that was going to be a potential problem wherever we went.

I quickly shaved, tossed the towel into the tub, and came back into the room. My phone was sitting on the dresser. That might have appeared foolish, leaving it there. But I had a four-digit passcode on it, so Jeremy wasn't going to be able to use it to make a call or message his friends.

I got into fresh socks and underwear, slipped on my pants and tied my shoes. As I put on my shirt and started doing up the buttons, I went to the window and looked outside. It was a little after eight in the morning, and traffic was busy as people headed to work.

I gazed down into the parking lot.

"For shit's sake," I said.

There was a red Miata convertible down there, top up. I couldn't be certain that it was Jeremy's girlfriend's car. Red Miatas were not exactly rare. But it was an early one, the color was faded, and the top torn and ragged.

I hurriedly did the last of my buttons, grabbed my jacket, gun and phone, and bolted from the room. I skipped the elevator and took the stairs, going down them two at a time, then booted it down the first-floor hallway until I'd reached the hotel's dining area. There were about thirty people there, many of them working the breakfast buffet table.

A quick scan of the room did not produce Jeremy.

In the time it had taken for me to get to the first floor, Jeremy could be in that car with Charlene Wilson and halfway to the interstate by now.

I went back to the lobby and out the main doors. I needed half a second to get my bearings. Our window hadn't faced out the front of the building. The lot where I'd seen the Miata would be around the side of the hotel.

I ran.

As the other parking lot came into view, I saw the Miata, this time with the top down. Jeremy was in the passenger seat, Charlene was behind the wheel, but they were turned toward each other, and it looked like they were kissing.

The car was not running.

As I came up to Jeremy's door, winded, he looked at me sheepishly. "I was coming right back in," he said to me. "We're not going anywhere."

I wanted to blow my stack.

"Yeah, Mr. Weaver," Charlene said. "It's just a visit. Honest. I'm not taking him anywhere."

"How?" I asked him.

"What?"

"How did you get in touch?" The first thing I thought of was the phone in the room, but I was pretty sure Jeremy had never used it.

He couldn't look me in the eye. "It's no big deal. It was only for a little while."

"What was only for a little while?"

His head dropped as if the tendons in his neck had been severed. Then, slowly, he dug into the front pocket of his jeans and drew out a cell phone.

"Jesus," I said.

It had a pale pink cover with tiny white polka dots. I recognized it instantly as Gloria's phone, the one she had surrendered to Bob. Evidently, not for long.

"How'd you get this?" I asked.

"Mom stole it back from Bob and gave it to me when we were leaving the house," he admitted. Probably, I thought, when she came running out to give him one last hug before he got in the car.

"So when your mom called last night, that was all for show?" I asked.

Jeremy nodded.

"And I guess you weren't in the bathroom forever last night because you had a stomach ache?"

Another sheepish nod. "I gave my mom another call, and got in touch with Charlene."

"I'm an idiot," I said. "I should have guessed."

"Can Charlene come in and have breakfast with us?" he asked, oblivious to the fact that I was close to a meltdown.

"You know what Bob told me," I said. "That there are all sorts of nutcases out there on the net, hoping to track you down. Maybe even get a cash reward. Every time you go on a phone—particularly one registered to you or your mom—or go on Facebook, or any of those other goddamn sites, you're just helping them. They'll find a way. For all we know, even the press is doing it. What did I say to you yesterday, about whether you liked Charlene? That if you did, you better not get in touch with her, because you're exposing her to risk. I swear, Jeremy, you just don't get it, do you?"

"I was real careful," Charlene said. "I made sure no one was following me."

I opened Jeremy's door. "Let's go," I said. "And give me that phone."

He handed it over.

"If you put that one in a fryer, my mom'll be real mad," Jeremy said.

"I'm not going to do that," I said. I dropped it onto the pavement and stomped it with the heel of my shoe. Then I bent down and picked it up to check that the screen was damaged to the point of unusable. It was.

"God, you really are an asshole," Jeremy said, getting out of the car.

"Goodbye, Charlene," I said, taking Jeremy by the

elbow and steering him back to the hotel entrance.

"This is not fun," he said.

"No shit."

I regretted my language. I was supposed to be the adult here. I hadn't been hired to turn Jeremy into a likeable kid, just keep him safe. The truth was, I wasn't making much progress on either front. I'd held out the possibility of taking him into Manhattan to explore some art galleries, but now I was reconsidering. If he got away from me there, I'd never find him.

We were nearly to the main entrance when Charlene came up alongside in the Miata, the engine revving in first as she slowed the car to a crawl.

"I'm sorry," she said. I wasn't sure which of us she was talking to. Maybe both.

I wasn't looking at her. Instead, I raised my hand and pointed a finger in the direction of the exit. Maybe, if I'd looked her way, I would have been better prepared for what happened next. I might have seen what was coming and been able to stop it, although, honestly, I don't know how. At the very least, I might have yelled at Charlene to hit the gas.

Just before the crunch of metal on metal, I heard the gunning of a car engine. Then the red Miata jumped forward.

Charlene screamed and her head snapped back and whacked the headrest. Jeremy screamed, too, and took a leap in the direction of the hotel, instinctively trying to get out of the way.

I whirled around, reaching just as instinctively for my weapon.

The sound of the crash was followed almost instantaneously by the squealing of brakes. Charlene had hit hers, and the driver of the car that had rear-ended her had also made an abrupt stop.

It took only half a second to recall the woman behind the wheel, and the man sitting next to her. It was the couple from the lobby of the first hotel the night before. The ones who'd recognized Jeremy.

Not that I had a perfect view of them. Both front air-bags had deployed. They'd deflated enough for me to see that the man had a phone in his hand, holding it in camera mode, and the woman had put her hand over her mouth in what looked like a gesture of shock and horror. I was guessing she hadn't meant to ram Charlene's car, but had gotten caught up in the moment.

The man had flung open his door and was aiming the phone at Jeremy, snapping away. But then he saw me, pointing my gun at him.

The woman behind the wheel started screaming.

"Donny!" she shouted.

Donny put his hands over his head. "Jesus! Don't shoot! Don't shoot!"

I yelled at Jeremy, "Check Charlene!"

He ran toward the Miata. I moved toward Donny, who still had his hands in the air. "Get down," I said.

He lay flat on the pavement, head down, arms out-stretched. "Please don't shoot me!" he said again.

I tucked the gun away and leaned into the car from the passenger side. "Are you hurt?" I asked the woman.

"It was an accident!" she said. "I didn't mean to hit that car! Donny said speed up, the kid was going back into the hotel!"

"Are you hurt?" I repeated.

While she'd hit the Miata hard enough to make the airbags go off, it was still a low-speed accident. Damage to the cars, I'd noticed seconds earlier, appeared minimal.

"I . . . I don't know," she said, patting her face and her chest. "I . . . I think I'm okay."

Several staff from the hotel had run outside. I shouted, "Call 911."

A couple of them nodded, as if it had already been done.

"Donny just wanted a picture," the woman said. "For the website. There's money!"

I moved away from the car and said to Donny, still splayed out on the asphalt, "Get up."

Jeremy was with Charlene. He'd opened her door and she was sitting sideways, her butt in the seat, her feet on the pavement. She had her head down and was rubbing the back of her head.

"How is she?" I asked.

Before Jeremy could speak, Charlene said, "My neck hurts."

"You're going to have to go to the hospital," I said. "We'll call your parents."

Jeremy was kneeling, trying to peer up into her face. "You're going to be okay. Everything's going to fine. It's their fault. Those idiots. They caused this."

I wanted to smack him.

"See if you can stand up," he said.

"No," I said. "Don't move, Charlene. Just stay right where you are."

Already, I thought I heard a siren in the distance. I looked in the direction of the parking lot entrance. It wasn't what I saw pulling in that caught my attention, but what was pulling out.

A black van.

236

Duckworth told Trevor to stay at Carol Beakman's building. He would come to him.

Ten minutes later, he was pulling into the lot in his black, unmarked police cruiser. Trevor was sitting on the edge of a short brick edifice that ran the length of the building, phone in hand. The moment he saw his father, he jumped to his feet. Duckworth brought the car to a stop in the no-parking zone directly out front of the building.

"Let's find the super," he said.

They went into the lobby together. Duckworth found the directory button marked "Building Superintendent" and leaned on the buzzer.

Several seconds later, a crackling female voice said, "Yeah?"

"Police."

"What?"

"Police," Duckworth repeated.

"Hang on."

Duckworth said to Trevor, "This Toyota she drives. I don't suppose you know the plate off the top of your head?"

"Jeez, no, how would I know that?"

"That's okay. Just asking." He got out his phone, entered a number. "Yeah, hi, it's Duckworth. I need you to try to track down a plate for a silver Toyota Corolla, around 2012, registered to a Carol Beakman." He gave the address. "Yeah, okay, give me a call when you know anything."

The super, a pale woman in her forties wearing a dark blue bathrobe, turned the lock on the glass door and opened it. "Can I see some ID?"

Duckworth displayed it. He asked her name, which was Gretchen Hardy.

"What's the problem?"

"We're worried about one of your tenants," he said. "She's not answering her phone or knocks to her door."

"If you've already been to her door, whaddya need me for?" Gretchen asked.

"We need you to let us into her apartment."

"Don't you have to have a warrant for something like that?"

Duckworth shook his head. "We're not searching it. We just want to see if she's there, and if she's okay."

Gretchen Hardy nodded. "Go on up to the third floor. I'll meet you there."

Going up in the elevator, Duckworth asked Trevor, "What about family?"

"Huh?"

"Remember I mentioned that maybe there was some kind of family emergency. Do Carol's parents live in Promise Falls? She got any brothers or sisters? Maybe she spent the night with one of them."

"Her parents both died a few years ago. She said something about a brother, but he lives in Toronto, I think."

The elevator opened onto the third-floor hallway. Trevor led his father down to a door with tarnished brass numbers that said 313.

Seconds later, a fire door at the end of the hall opened and Gretchen emerged. The sound of her flip-flops echoed with every step. When she reached Carol's apartment, she inserted a key into the lock.

"Hope she doesn't have the chain on. If she's got the chain on, we're not going to be able to get in."

"If she has the chain on," Duckworth said, "we'll have to kick in the door."

"Who pays for the damage? The police going to pay for that?"

It turned out not to be an issue. She turned the knob and the door opened wide.

Trevor went through first. Duckworth reached out, grabbed his arm to hold him back.

"Let me do this," he said. "You stay right here."

Trevor, with reluctance, held his position.

"You a cop too?" the superintendent asked him.

"No."

"I didn't think so. But I've seen you around here before."

"Maybe so," Trevor said.

Duckworth quickly moved through the apartment. It was a one-bedroom, decked out with inexpensive but tasteful furniture that had an IKEA look about it. Flowered throw cushions on the couch, magazines perfectly stacked on the coffee table. Trevor watched him go into the bedroom, come out, go into the bathroom, come out, then, finally, check the kitchen.

"She's not here," he said, returning to where his son stood.

"Can you tell anything?"

Duckworth sighed. "I don't see anything out of the ordinary. Everything looks fine. I saw a couple of purses in the bedroom, but most women have several. Neither of them contained a wallet or car keys."

"She had to spend the night somewhere," Trevor said.

Gretchen chortled. "Hey, women today, they don't have to come home every night."

Duckworth said, "Thanks for your help, Ms. Hardy. You can lock the place up now."

He steered his son back into the hallway and in the direction of the elevator.

"What next?" Trevor said. "If she's not here and she's not at work, then—"

Duckworth's cell rang. He dug it out of his jacket and put it to his ear.

"Duckworth here. You get a plate from that info I gave you? What?" He stopped walking. "Say that again?"

His head seemed to be dragged down by whatever he was hearing.

"What is it?" Trevor asked.

Duckworth held up a shushing hand. "Okay," he said into the phone. "Don't touch anything."

He put the phone back into his jacket and started to move toward the elevator again, but Trevor stopped him.

"What is it? What'd they say? What did you mean, don't touch anything?"

"Outside," Duckworth said.

They went down in the elevator and through the lobby in silence. Once outdoors, Duckworth stopped. "Go home," he said.

"What do you mean, go home? I'm not going home. What's going on?"

"Trevor, really. I mean it. When I know something, I'll call you."

Trevor stood up straighter, defiant. "I won't. Whatever

that call was about, wherever you're going, I'm going too."

Duckworth sighed. "They found a car."

Trevor followed his father's unmarked cruiser to an industrial district on the south side of town. Duckworth turned down Millwork Drive and drove past a storage unit operation, a cardboard manufacturer and a cement products place before hitting his blinker out front of a one-story plant that made and sold floor tiles.

A Promise Falls police cruiser, lights quietly flashing, was blocking the way in. When the uniformed cop behind the wheel spotted who it was, he pulled out of the way, allowing Duckworth, and Trevor, to drive in.

Duckworth parked in a spot near the entrance, and Trevor pulled in next to him. As Trevor got out, he called over to his father, "I don't see Carol's car."

"They say it's around back. We walk from here."

The two of them headed down the side of the building. When Trevor started to break into a trot, his father said, "With me."

Trevor held back and walked alongside his father.

As they came around the back, they encountered another police car, this one with a female officer behind the wheel. When she saw the two men approach, she got out.

Duckworth didn't need to flash his ID. Everyone on the Promise Falls force knew who he was.

"Detective Duckworth," she said.

"Officer Stiles, right?" Duckworth said.

She nodded. "Yes, sir." She cast an eye at Trevor.

"This is my son, Trevor," Duckworth said. "He's

been trying to reach Ms. Beakman since last night without success. Where's the car?"

She pointed. "Just the other side of that Dumpster."

"How did we hear about it?"

"The manager here, he spotted the car there this morning, and when he had a closer look he got concerned. He called it in about the same time as you were trying to get a plate for Ms. Beakman's car."

"What was he concerned about?" Trevor asked.

Duckworth held up a finger. Trevor went quiet.

"Let's have a look," the detective said.

Officer Stiles led them around a rusted open-topped trash container that was a good five feet tall. It had been blocking the view of a silver Toyota Corolla. The driver's door was wide open.

"That's the car," Trevor said urgently. "That's it."

"Okay, so I'll ask Trevor's question," Duckworth said to Stiles. "What was it that raised the manager's concern? Was the car like that when he found it? With the door open?"

Stiles nodded. "That's right. He thought it looked kind of odd. Plus, it was running."

"The engine was on?"

"That's right."

"It's not now."

"He says he turned it off, but left everything else as it was."

Keeping his hands inside his pockets, Duckworth walked slowly around the car, leaning in over the driver's seat, noticing that the key was still in the ignition.

"What do you see?" Trevor asked.

Another raised finger.

Duckworth reached into his pocket and pulled out

242

a pair of latex gloves. He pointed to a spot about ten feet away and said to Trevor, "I want you to stand over there."

"Why?"

"Just do it."

Trevor took five steps back. "This okay?" he asked with a hint of sarcasm.

"That's fine."

Duckworth went back to the open door and leaned down to flick the tab that opened the trunk. The lid lifted an inch.

"Why are you looking in there?" Trevor asked.

Duckworth said nothing. He came around to the back of the car and, using one gloved index finger, gently lifted the lid.

Even from where Trevor was standing, it was clear what the trunk contained.

"Oh Jesus," he said, moving forward.

Duckworth quickly turned around. "Do not take a step closer."

"It's her! Oh my God, it's her. It's Carol."

"No . . ." Duckworth said slowly.

"What?

Duckworth examined the body of the woman in the trunk of the Corolla. He needed a moment to remember where he had seen her before. Definitely not at Starbucks with his son.

Of course, she looked different now. Her face bloated, the blue strangulation marks around her neck.

But he was pretty sure this was the woman who could not believe he had never watched an episode of *Seinfield*.

It was Dolores, from the tattoo parlor.

Dolly to her friends.

THIRTY

CAL

Jeremy and I followed the ambulance carrying Charlene Wilson to a hospital that was no more than ten minutes away from the hotel. The paramedics handled her with great care, but there did not seem to be a strong indication that Charlene was seriously injured. It would probably take an X-ray before anyone knew for certain.

Charlene had given me her cell phone and brought up a number where I could reach her mother, whose name was Alicia. (So I was right about the Alicia Wilson mentioned in that story about the party at Galen Broadhurst's place.) I made the call while we were en route to the hospital.

I guess I was expecting a more frantic reaction, but Alicia Wilson was all business once I had explained who I was and why I was calling.

"Where did this happen?"

I told her.

"Which hospital are they taking her to?"

I told her.

"Will the boy be there?"

I told her he would be.

"Forty-five minutes." She hung up.

I looked over at Jeremy. "What's the story on Charlene's mother?"

"Well, aside from the fact that she hates me, I guess

she's okay," he said, trying to sink into his seat where maybe I wouldn't notice him. "She'll shit a brick when she finds out Charlene's been coming to see me."

"Something to look forward to," I said.

I found a place to park a couple of blocks from the hospital. We took two seats side by side in the ER waiting room while Charlene was being looked at. Jeremy sat with his hands clasped together down between his legs, his head bowed.

"You wanna talk?" I asked him.

"Not really," he said.

"Okay."

"Are we still going to New York?" he asked.

"I'd have to say that's kind of up in the air right now. I'm going to have to let your mom and Ms. Plimpton and Bob know what's happened."

His head seemed to droop further.

"What happened to the other two?" he asked.

"The ones who rammed Charlene's car? I don't know. The police were dealing with them. They're not my concern."

We'd been sitting there for the better part of an hour when a smartly dressed woman with auburn hair walked into the ER like she owned the place. She went straight to the admitting desk and said, "I'm Alicia Wilson. Where's my daughter? Charlene Wilson."

I got up and approached.

"Ms. Wilson," I said. "Cal Weaver. We spoke on the phone."

She eyed me the way one might examine a bug in a jar. Her eyes went to Jeremy, and the look she gave him was even more contemptuous.

"I will speak to you after I have seen Charlene."

She turned and disappeared into the rabbit's warren of examining rooms.

"She looked kinda mad," Jeremy said when I sat back down next to him.

"You don't miss much," I said.

Alicia Wilson reappeared five minutes later. We both stood as she stormed across the waiting room.

"How's your daughter?" I asked.

"They say she's fine," Alicia said. "I'm going to take her home with me. Do you know what happened to her car?"

"I don't," I said. "Couple of scratches on the bumper, but not much beyond that that I could see. I think it's at the hotel."

"Hotel?" She fixed her eyes on Jeremy. "The two of you were at a hotel?"

"No," I said quickly. "Jeremy and I were there. Charlene drove down to see Jeremy this morning."

She still had her eyes on the boy. "You are a despicable worm."

Jeremy said nothing.

"It wasn't enough that you got one girl killed. You want to go for a second?"

Even though I knew the circumstances here were very different, I didn't want to wade too far into this. Alicia had plenty of reason to be angry with Jeremy, even if her own daughter had to shoulder some of the blame.

"I didn't make her come," Jeremy said meekly. "And I didn't run that car into hers."

"Oh, don't think for a minute that Charlene isn't going to get an earful. But you—you shouldn't even be free. You should be in jail, and not for some short visit, either."

If I were Alicia Wilson, I wouldn't feel much different-ly. Charlene wouldn't be here if Jeremy hadn't told her where he was. He'd clearly done nothing to discourage her from coming to see him for the second time in two days, even after my lecture about putting her at risk.

If I were Alicia Wilson, I'd rip his face off.

There was also our chat of the night before, once the lights were off, about owning up to his actions, about taking some responsibility for them.

"You got anything you want to say, Jeremy?" I asked him.

His eyes searched mine, as though he might find the answer there.

"Like what?" he said.

Alicia laughed. "He's unbelievable." The laughter quickly faded. "Stay away from my daughter. If you ever so much as wave to her from across the street, let alone send her a text, I'll get a restraining order against you."

Jeremy looked down.

Alicia turned and walked away.

"You had a chance there," I said.

"A chance to what?"

"To do something right. To say you were sorry. To accept even some share of responsibility for what happened."

"I just . . . I didn't know what to . . . I . . ." His eyes were wet. "Do you think," he asked me tentatively, "I could just say goodbye to Charlene?"

"With her mother there? Are you serious?"

His chest collapsed, his body a balloon that had just been pricked.

"I need to call your mom. Let everyone know what's going on."

Jeremy sighed.

We exited the ER and started walking back to my Honda. I didn't want to have my chat with his mother in his presence, so I got out my keys and said, "If I give you these, you promise not to run off with the car?"

He took them. "Yeah, like I could even drive your car."

"I'm not even sure I thought to lock it," I said. When we'd arrived, we'd raced straight into the ER to see how Charlene was, and some things had probably slipped my mind.

As Jeremy walked away, I entered a number into my phone. Madeline Plimpton answered.

"Mr. Weaver?"

"Hi," I said.

"We were going to call you. Well, Bob or I were going to. Not Gloria."

"What's going on?"

"We think Gloria might have given her phone to Jeremy. She took it out of Bob's jacket and we can't find it anywhere."

"That's exactly what she did," I said.

"Oh my. I hope it hasn't caused any kind of trouble."

I filled her in on the latest developments.

"Good Lord," Ms. Plimpton said. "You just can't catch a break, can you?"

I smiled that she directed some of her sympathy to me. "I'm wondering if this changes anything. You want me to stay on the road with him, or bring him back?"

"I can discuss it with Gloria and Bob—I might even have a word with Grant about it—but honestly, I don't think coming back here is an option."

"Why's that?"

"There was a protest out front of the house last night. About a dozen people, waving signs that said things like 'Big Baby go home.' We had to call the police to have them dispersed."

"Okay," I said. "I was going to take him to New York, but I don't think that's such a good idea any more."

Madeline Plimpton said nothing.

"Hello?"

"I'm just thinking," she said. "I have a place."

"A place?"

"On the Cape. Cape Cod. My husband and I bought it years ago. I haven't been there since he passed away. I still own it, but it's in the hands of a rental agent. People book it for the summer months. But it's only May. It might not be rented."

"Would anyone be able to track us down there? Seems wherever Jeremy goes, people figure it out."

A hesitation. "I don't know. It's owned through a company, so my name's not really attached to it. I haven't been to the Cape in years. And Gloria—in case you're worried she might inadvertently let something slip—probably thinks I sold it years ago. But the good news is, it's on the beach, you've got some privacy, there won't be many people around through the week, it being so early in the season. I could make a call, see if it's available right now. It's not that far out. East Sandwich. Beautiful view of Cape Cod Bay."

I thought about it. Finding a place to hunker down seemed better than moving from hotel to hotel.

"The question is, how long do we go on like this?" I asked.

A sigh. "I know."

"Let's take it a day at a time. You find out if the

place is available and we'll go from there."

We said our goodbyes.

I found Jeremy right where he was supposed to be, sitting in the passenger seat of my Honda. He was relentlessly pounding the side of his right fist into the top of his thigh with everything he had.

THIRTY-ONE

Duckworth brought everyone in. The crime-scene unit, the coroner, extra police to cordon off the area near where Carol Beakman's car had been found and to interview possible witnesses. Dolores, also known as Dolly, had no identification on her so Duckworth had no last name or address.

But he did know where she worked.

"What about Carol?" Trevor asked. "Where the hell is she?"

That was the question.

Her car had been found with someone else's body in it. That didn't bode well for Carol, no matter how one looked at it. She could end up being a second victim, or she might have had something to do with what happened.

The first place Duckworth instructed the uniformed officers to start looking was the Dumpster that sat right next to the silver Corolla. But it was nearly empty, and it didn't take much of an examination to determine there was no body in it. There might, however, be something in there the killer, or killers, had discarded.

Everything had to be gone over with the proverbial fine-toothed comb.

Now Duckworth had to decide where to focus his attention. He had a homicide and a missing person case.

And those two events tied back, it appeared, to Brian Gaffney.

Brian Gaffney was abducted just after leaving Knight's.

Carol saw someone she knew as she and Trevor were leaving.

Carol told Trevor she was going to talk to that woman and suggest she get in touch with Duckworth if she saw anything.

Carol disappeared.

Dolores, who worked at a tattoo parlor where a tattoo gun was supposedly stolen, turned up dead in Carol's car.

And speaking of tattoos, Duckworth now thought there was a strong likelihood that Gaffney was not the intended target. He had more than a passing resemblance to someone else in that bar who Duckworth was now sure was the kid from that court case that had garnered national attention, the one who got off with probation after running a girl down with a car because he'd never been taught to appreciate the consequences of his actions.

God, what a world.

There were plenty of people, Duckworth now realized from the Craig Pierce incident, who'd like to teach that young man—Jeremy Pilford was his name—a lesson or two.

The night before, after he and Maureen returned from their dinner at Knight's—the best meal Duckworth had had in months, by the way—he went online to refresh his memory on some of the details of the Pilford case.

When he saw the name of the girl Jeremy Pilford had run down with that businessman's Porsche—Sian McFadden—it all came together for him. It was very possible that whoever had written that tattoo on Brian Gaffney's back had made a spelling error. "Sean," he was betting, was supposed to be "Sian."

As theories went, it wasn't a bad one.

It had been Duckworth's plan, until Trevor showed

up a couple of hours earlier, hovering over his bed, to start looking into the possible Pilford angle.

In fact, that wasn't the only thing he wanted to look into. Something, he thought, was fishy across the street from the Gaffney household. Mrs. Beecham's tale of learning that her caregiver was actually her niece beggared belief. And finding out that the name Norma Lastman had given Mrs. Beecham was different from her van registration also bothered Duckworth.

But those things would have to wait. Right now, Duckworth needed to find out everything he could about Dolores, and that meant a visit to her boss, Mike.

Trevor, who'd finally done as he was told and was waiting by his car, ran toward his father when he appeared.

"What do we do now?" he asked.

"*We* don't do anything," Duckworth said.

"What do you mean? We have to keep looking for Carol."

"I know. You got a picture of her?"

Trevor nodded.

"Email it to me."

Trevor got out his phone, opened up the photos, and turned the device around to show his father. "How about this?"

It was a shot of Carol seated at a restaurant table, presumably across from Trevor. The lighting was poor and half her face was in shadow.

"Any others?"

Trevor swiped his finger across the screen several times, stopping on a selfie shot of Carol and him sitting on a bench with the falls in the background. Trevor had his arm around her, his face pressed up close to hers.

"It's a good shot of Carol," Duckworth said, but his voice lacked enthusiasm.

"What?"

"Do you have another one?"

Trevor shook his head. "What's wrong with this one?"

Duckworth hesitated, then said, "No, it's fine. Email that to me."

"There's a problem. Tell me."

"It's the fact that you're in the picture."

"I can be cropped out."

"I know." Another hesitation. "Here's the thing, Trevor. I shouldn't even be talking to you about this any more."

"What do you mean?"

"Don't take this the wrong way. But this is now a homicide investigation, as well as a missing person case. You have an involvement, and I am, at least right now, the lead investigator. And you're my son. That may taint this investigation. My judgment might be called into question at a later date."

"Yeah, but that would only matter," Trevor said, "if I was guilty of something. But I didn't have anything to do with that woman in the trunk of Carol's car. And I don't have any idea what's happened to Carol."

"I know."

"You *do*, right?" Trevor pressed. "You do know I don't have anything to do with any of this?"

"Of course. But that doesn't matter. Look, just let me do what I have to do. If you hear from Carol, if you get any new ideas about where she might be, you call me. But you can't tag along. That just won't fly."

Trevor made his hands into fists, then opened them. "It's not right."

"Yes, it's right," Duckworth said. "One thing."

"What?"

"That woman in the trunk. Is she the one Carol saw outside Knight's?"

Trevor shrugged. "Like I said, I didn't get a look at her then, and I sure didn't get a look at her just now."

"Do you remember if Carol said her name was Dolores, or Dolly?"

Trevor blinked. "Maybe. Not Dolores, but she might have said Dolly. I never really picked up on it."

Duckworth laid his hand on his son's shoulder. "Okay. I have to go."

There was an awkward hesitation between them, then Trevor reached out and grasped his father's arm.

"I'm scared to death," he said. "I'm scared to death about what's happened to Carol."

"Me too," Duckworth said.

He parked out front of Mike's tattoo business, but before he got out of the car he had other matters to deal with. The first was to start distributing that picture of Carol Beakman Trevor had sent him. He forwarded it to the station, then got on the phone to provide further details. He wanted every Promise Falls police officer to be on the lookout for her. Then he asked for Shirley in communications and ordered up an immediate news release on Carol Beakman. Tweet it, post it on the department's Facebook page, get it to all the local TV news programs.

"And crop that picture," Duckworth said, "so it only shows the woman's face."

"You don't want this guy in the picture?" Shirley asked.

"No."

"He might end up being a suspect or something," she said.

"Just take him out of the shot."

"Got it. Only trying to help. He actually looks a bit like you. Only, you know, a *lot* younger."

"Thanks for that, Shirley."

"Call 'em as I see 'em."

"There's something else I need."

"Fire away, boss."

"You know that Big Baby case?"

Shirley made a snorting noise. "Who doesn't?"

"The kid's name was Jeremy Pilford. Can you google him? See if there's anything that connects him to Promise Falls? I think he might be in our neck of the woods."

"Seriously?" Shirley said.

"Yeah. I think I saw him on some surveillance video at Knight's. Is that so hard to believe?"

"You haven't listened to the news this morning?"

"What are you talking about?"

"There was a protest last night. They had to send a couple of cars out."

Duckworth pressed the phone closer to his ear. "A protest where?"

"You know Madeline Plimpton? Used to be publisher of the *Standard*?"

"Yeah, of course."

"Her place."

"Her place? Why her place?"

"The kid's been staying there. Kind of hiding out, but not very well. About a dozen or more people wandering on the street out front, waving signs, the usual."

"What's the connection? Why here?"

"Plimpton's the little bastard's great-aunt or something.

Her niece Gloria is the kid's mother. What I hear is, the kid's been getting all kinds of harassment in Albany, so they came up here. But there's a contest or game on some website inviting people to report sightings. Remember the Craig Pierce thing?"

"I do."

"Kind of like that."

"It's a strange world we live in now, Shirley."

"Hey, tell me something I don't know. You need anything else?"

"No. Catch ya later."

Duckworth ended the call. The mention of Craig Pierce prompted him to make another call.

"Chief Finderman's office," a woman said.

"It's Barry Duckworth. Chief in?"

"Hang on."

A pause, then, "Barry?"

"Rhonda," Duckworth said. The detective's working relationship with Promise Falls police chief Rhonda Finderman had had its ups and downs over the last year or two, but things had been reasonably amicable lately. "The Craig Pierce thing."

Duckworth could almost hear her wince on the other end of the line.

"Jesus, yeah," she said. "What about it?"

"Where are we on legal challenges with that?"

"Still trying to get that site—Just Deserts, I think it is?—to reveal details of the video posting that could lead us to whoever took the picture and put it up there, but it's with the lawyers. Could take forever, and we might never get the answer we want. Even though they're not, by any standard, a legitimate news organization, they're saying they have an obligation to protect their sources, that it's a freedom-of-the-press thing. It's total bullshit, is what it is."

"There might be another approach."

"Tell me."

"Well, I'm not the expert. But I was talking to Pierce today, and—"

"God, how's he doing?" Finderman asked. "I mean, he's a loathsome character, but what happened to him, no one deserves that."

"You might change your mind if you met him. Anyway, he suggested that if we were doing our job properly, we'd be going at this another way."

Finderman hesitated, then said, "Victims often feel that way."

"Thing is, I think he might be onto something. Have we got any computer experts in the department?"

"If we don't, I'll find somebody. What's the idea?"

"You look at all the postings, look for I guess you'd call them signatures. Turns of phrase, misspellings. Search the Internet for those signatures. That kind of thing."

"Sounds like it might be worth a try," Rhonda said.

"Okay. Talk later."

Duckworth slipped the phone back into his jacket and got out of the car. Mike's Tattoos was open, and he went straight inside. Mike was sitting at the main desk.

"Hey, you again," he said. "You catch who stole my tattoo gun?"

Duckworth shook his head. "Sorry."

Mike smiled. "Just kidding. I knew the police wouldn't give a shit about that. As you can see by the fact that I'm sitting here, I am a little short-handed today. Which is just as well, since I don't have any appointments in the book until later this afternoon. Unless, of course, you're here to get a tattoo of Columbo tattooed on your chest."

"No." Duckworth cocked his head to one side. "Anybody ever actually get one of those? A Columbo tattoo?"

"Nope, although one time I was in this really cool bookstore in Belfast that had a painting of him on the ceiling. Only crime fighter I've ever inked onto anybody is Batman. Done his face on a couple people, but the logo, you know, the bat with the circle around it, is more popular. Also, the big S from Superman. Had a few of those over the years. So if you haven't found my stolen equipment, what brings you back?"

"I noticed Dolores isn't here."

Mike raised his arms in a hopeless gesture. "A no-show today. Didn't even have the courtesy to phone in."

"What's Dolores's last name?"

"Guntner."

"Do you have an address for her?"

"There a problem?"

"An address would be helpful."

Mike opened a drawer in the desk and rifled through some papers. "Here we go." He grabbed a scrap of paper, scribbled on it, and handed it to Duckworth. "It's actually a farmhouse that belonged to her parents. They're in a nursing home now, I think, and she lives there by herself."

"A nursing home? In Promise Falls?"

"Yeah. Davidson House, I think."

"I know it." Duckworth glanced at the piece of paper Mike had handed him. Dolores had lived at 27 Eastern Avenue. He pocketed the paper. "Thanks."

"If you want to talk to her here, she might show up later. It's not like it's the first time she's been late. She might have partied a little too hard last night. Try after lunch. She might be in then."

"I don't think so," Duckworth said.

Mike's face darkened. "What do you mean?"

"A woman tentatively identified as Dolores was found dead this morning."

"Fuck, no," he said, standing. "What are you talking about? Dolly's dead?"

"I'd like to ask you a few questions about her."

"Hold on," Mike blustered. "What happened to her?" His mouth open, he put his hand to his forehead. "Jesus, did she kill herself?"

"Would that not surprise you?" Duckworth asked.

"Well, I mean, she's kind of a flake. *Was* kind of a flake. God, I can't believe it."

"What do you mean, a flake?"

"Just, I don't know, just different. Man, I can't believe this. First of all, the kind of people who work in a tattoo shop"—and he touched his fingers to his chest—"myself included, are not your usual type who go to work in a bank every day. I'm not saying we're all nuts and suicidal, only that we're different."

"How was Dolores different?"

"She got worked up about things. Like, she was pretty plugged into current events and shit, which I don't care anything about. She talked about all the injustice in the world, stuff like that, people who got away with doing bad things. I mean, she was pretty funny, too, not serious all the time about it, but there were things that upset her, like global warming and those fuckers on Wall Street."

"Was she always like that?"

Mike thought. "No, actually. She's been, you know, kind of radicalized in the last year, I guess. I mean, not radicalized like all that Islam ISIS stuff, but just more fired up about shit."

"How long had she worked here?"

He had to think again. "Four years?"

"Did you know her before that?"

He shook his head.

"So what happened a year ago that got her more plugged in to what was happening in the world?"

"All the shit that went down right here, for one thing," Mike said.

"The mass poisoning?"

"Yeah. She said it never would have happened if we all just cared more for our fellow man. Remember the Olivia Fisher case? When she was being murdered and screaming and nobody came? What am I saying, of course you know all about that."

Duckworth asked, "Anything else that might have had an impact on her, say, more recently? The last three or four months?"

"Maybe that guy she's been seeing."

"What guy?"

"Cory."

Duckworth recalled the young man in the khakis who was sitting on the desk the first time he was here. "I met him," he said. "You have a last name for him?"

"Calder. Cory Calder."

"An address?"

Mike frowned. "How would I know where he lives? He doesn't work for me."

"Tell me about him."

"Why are you asking? Did Dolly off herself, or did something else happen to her?"

"I don't think Dolly killed herself."

"Then what—was it a car accident or something?"

"No."

Mike pondered what must have seemed like the only other possibility. "Wait, somebody *killed* her?"

"Yes," Duckworth said evenly. "I'm sorry. I'm sure you want to know more, but right now the most important thing you can do is help me by answering my questions. Did you notice anything about her in the last few weeks or months? Anything different?"

"Uh, okay, well, I guess the answer would be yes."

"Tell me."

"She *was* more anxious. And quieter, too. She seemed to have a lot on her mind. I mean, she could put on a good front for people walking in the door, but she seemed pretty agitated a lot of the time."

"Did she talk about what might be troubling her?"

"Not much, but I had a sense it was about Cory."

"What's your take on him?"

"I don't know. Kind of a weirdo, really."

"You ever hang out?"

Mike shook his head. "No. But I'll say this about him. He's a guy who talks himself up a lot."

"What do you mean?"

"Like, he could have been Bill Gates, or Steve Jobs. In his head, he's a lot more important than he really is. Does that make sense?"

"I think so. Anything else?"

"He liked to watch, sometimes."

"Liked to watch what?"

"When I worked. How I did it."

"He watched you do tattoos?"

"Yeah. But only if it was okay with the customer."

Duckworth made some mental notes. "Back to Dolly.

Did she ever talk about Craig Pierce? Or Jeremy Pilford?"

"Who the hell are they?"

"Pierce was the guy who basically admitted he molested a mentally disabled girl, but got away with it, and Pilford was the one they called the Big Baby."

"Oh yeah. She did mention them. Asked me what I thought." He shrugged. "I hadn't actually thought a whole lot about them, except to say that people usually got what was coming to them, sooner or later."

"But she did mention them."

Mike nodded.

"What about Carol Beakman? You ever heard that name?"

"Never. That doesn't ring any bells at all. You know, there was one really funny thing she asked me one day."

"What was that?"

"She wondered if the court system was easier on women than men. Like, if a man forced a woman to do a bad thing, would they punish her for it?"

"Dolly actually asked you that?"

"Yeah. I thought it was weird, but didn't make much of it. Why would she ask that?"

"Hard to say."

"She said there was some case in Canada she read about, where this couple kidnapped and killed some girls but the woman pretty much got off because she said she was abused and forced to participate."

"I know the case," Duckworth said. "Twenty years ago or more."

"Dolly said something like, women sometimes get a pass when they don't deserve to."

"Interesting." Duckworth nodded his head in gratitude. "Thanks for all your help."

"Can I ask you something?"

"Sure."

"You said your name's Duckworth, right?"

"That's right."

"You any relation to Trevor, by any chance?"

Duckworth felt caught off guard. "Uh, yeah. He's my son."

Mike smiled. "I wondered, because, you know, it's not the most common name in the world."

"You know Trevor?"

The man shook his head. "No, no. It's just, I did a tatt for him not long ago."

"You did?"

"Yeah. Nice guy."

"When was this exactly?"

Mike thought. "Two weeks, maybe? I don't know. Around the time my tattoo gun was stolen, I think. Listen, say hi to him for me, will you?"

"Yeah," Duckworth said. "I'll be sure to do that."

THIRTY-TWO

CAL

It dawned on me that in all the morning chaos, Jeremy and I had missed breakfast. By the time we'd finished with the hospital and been chewed out by Charlene Wilson's mother, it was pushing eleven in the morning.

"You hungry?" I asked as we drove back to the hotel. We still had to grab our stuff and settle up with the front desk.

"I don't know," Jeremy said, his voice barely above a whisper.

In the twenty-four hours that I'd known this kid, this was the worst I'd seen him. The morning's events had left him shaken. Up to now, my feelings about him had been mixed. A troubled young man, for sure, but also a pain in the ass. For the first time, I actually felt worried for him.

It was seeing him pound his own leg hard enough to hurt himself that had sparked my concern. I wondered if that was a one-off, or if I needed to be worried about Jeremy doing anything else to cause himself harm.

"We'll hit the hotel and grab our bags, then figure out what to do next," I said.

Nothing.

Whatever the police had decided to do about those two clowns who'd run into the back of Charlene's car, they were no longer at the hotel. The cops, and the couple who wanted a picture of Jeremy, were gone. So was their car. But Charlene's little Miata was there, waiting to be picked up.

I didn't want to leave Jeremy alone, so I had him come back to the room with me. We quickly packed—we hardly had anything anyway—and headed back down to the lobby, where I paid our bill.

The man at the front desk said, "That sure was something."

"Huh?"

"Out front this morning," he said.

"Oh, yeah. Do you know what the cops did with those two?"

He shook his head. "Took some statements then let them go on their way, far as I could tell."

I grunted. Then I thought of something.

"Did you have anyone staying here last night with a black van?"

The man grinned. "Is that a serious question?"

"I saw one driving out of the lot about the time of the accident. I thought it might be someone I know."

"Sir, we take down car makes and license plate info, but I couldn't tell you if we had a guest with a black van."

"Sure, of course," I said. "Dumb question."

I thought about asking if they had video surveillance, and if they did, whether they would let me have a look at it. But, assuming they even allowed it, what was the point? So maybe someone else, someone with a black van, wanted to catch a picture of Jeremy out in the wild. What of it? Whoever it was, he was one of many. I couldn't be chasing them all down.

Walking to my Honda, Jeremy said, "What black van?'

"Probably nothing," I said.

We tossed our bags in the trunk and got settled in up front. "I think I saw a diner a couple of blocks from here. Sound good?"

Another whisper. "Sure."

We'd passed a Bette's Grill on the way to the hospital. I found it again and pulled into the lot. The place wasn't slammed. The breakfast crowd was done, and the lunch hour was still thirty minutes away. We were about to be shown to a table when Jeremy stopped dead in his tracks. Head down, arms hanging straight at his sides.

"Jeremy?"

His eyes were sealed shut, his lips pressed together.

"Jeremy, talk to me."

His shoulders were trembling. The kid, I believed, was on the verge of some kind of meltdown.

"Never mind," I said to the waitress.

I put an arm around Jeremy's shoulders and directed him back out of the restaurant to the parking lot. I got him as far as the car before his legs began to weaken. It was like the boy was melting. He went down to his knees, almost in slow motion. I knelt down with him, turned him so that I could rest his back against the car.

A woman walking by said, "You okay?"

I smiled and raised my hand. "We're good."

I settled down beside him. I still had my arm around his shoulders and pulled him in to me. I don't know whether that caused what happened next, or just allowed it to happen sooner.

He sobbed. He sobbed so hard his body shook.

I didn't know what else to do but hold onto him. I could have told him everything was going to be okay, but he probably wouldn't have believed it any more than I did. His life was a mess. Where to begin? He was responsible for a young woman's death, his home life was chaotic, and the entire world hated him. Even his father didn't want to spend any real time with him. The boy had been reduced online to a caricature. A whining, pampered infant.

But he was more than that.

All I could think to say was "Let it out."

He let it out.

A few more people walked by, giving us curious glances, but I waved them away with my eyes before any of them asked questions or offered help.

Jeremy mumbled something I couldn't make out.

"What was that?" I asked.

This time, I heard it, although only barely. He said, "I want to die."

I squeezed his shoulder a little harder. "No. I mean, yeah, I believe you. But no."

He cried for another couple of minutes. The front of my shirt was wet with tears and snot. He slipped from my grasp, dug into his pocket, and brought out some ragged tissues.

"I got more in the car," I said.

"It's okay."

He dabbed his eyes and blew his nose. Then he just sat there, staring straight ahead, trying to regain his composure.

"Feel good to let it out?" I asked.

"Maybe a little."

There was a muffled rumbling sound. Jeremy looked at me and said, "What was that?"

"That was my stomach," I said. "I am, not to put too fine a point on it, fucking starving."

He actually laughed, briefly. "Yeah, I guess I could eat something too. But I can't go back in there." He was looking at Bette's. "Everybody in there has seen me losing it. They'll all be staring at me. Can we go someplace else?"

"Sure."

He got up first. I extended a hand and he helped me up. He might have been the one with the emotional breakdown, but I was the one with old knees.

I unlocked the car and we got back in.

"I don't care about going to New York," he said as I keyed the ignition.

"Yeah, well, there may be a change of plan anyway," I told him.

"What?"

"I'm waiting on a call from your great-aunt. I'll let you know after she gets back to me."

He nodded complacently.

"Jeremy," I said gently, as we left the diner parking lot, "during the trial, and since—ever since all this first happened—have they gotten any help for you?"

"Help?"

"You know. A counselor? Someone you could talk to about all the shit that's happened?"

He shook his head. "Like a shrink?"

"Yeah, like a shrink, but not necessarily."

"My mom said what I needed more than anything was love."

"Yeah, well, that's nice, no doubt about it. But when you say something like what you said a few minutes ago, that tells me maybe you need somebody to talk to about those, you know, kinds of feelings."

He shrugged. "I don't know. I like talking to you."

"I'm not a professional," I told him.

"Maybe I don't need a professional," he said. "I just need someone who gives a shit."

Did I give a shit? I guessed I did, to a point.

My eyes were looking about half a mile ahead. "I think that's another diner."

"Okay. Do I have to get breakfast stuff?"

"You can get whatever you want."

My cell phone rang. I fumbled for it in my jacket, put it to my ear.

"Weaver," I said.

"It's Madeline Plimpton."

"Hi."

"The beach house is available."

"Okay."

"Let me give you the name of the real-estate agent who manages it for me."

"I'm driving. But can you tell me where the house is, roughly?" She told me, and to be sure I had it right, I repeated the house number. "And you said North Shore Boulevard in East Sandwich?"

"That's right."

"Can you send me all the other details in an email?"

"Yes," she said.

"Does anyone else know that we're going there?"

"Just the real-estate person," she replied.

"Let's keep it that way," I said, glancing occasionally in my rear-view mirror. I kept wondering if I'd see that black van again.

"Fine," she said matter-of-factly.

"How are things there?" I asked.

"What a joy to spend time with family," she said. "Keep us posted of any developments, please, Mr. Weaver."

"Sure."

She ended the call.

"What's going on?" Jeremy said.

"I don't suppose you packed a bathing suit," I said. "I know I didn't. Although, this time of year, water's probably still too cold to swim in."

"Huh?"

"We're going to Cape Cod."

"Oh," he said.

I turned in to the second restaurant, switched off the engine, and pulled up on the emergency brake, as was my habit.

A thought suddenly occurred to me. I whipped my head to the side, looked at Jeremy and snapped, "What was that you said before?"

I'd startled him. He recoiled. "What?" He was wide-eyed. "All I said was 'Oh.'"

"No, not then. Before. When we were leaving the hospital."

"I don't know what you're talking about."

"As we were leaving the hospital, you said something. Around the time I had to make a call on my cell. I sent you to the car."

He shrugged. "I don't remember."

It didn't matter. I didn't need him to remember. I knew what it was.

"Don't worry about it." I studied him for another moment, then said, "Let's get something to eat."

THIRTY-THREE

Dolores Guntner's 27 Eastern Avenue address might have sounded like a place in a residential section of Promise Falls, but it was outside the town. Eastern, as the name implied, led east out of town, and the numbers started a couple of miles outside the town limits. Out there, the houses, many of them attached to farms, were spaced far apart and back from the road.

This far out of Promise Falls, people had mailboxes erected at the end of their driveways. As Barry Duckworth drove slowly, he was looking for a mailbox name as well as a number.

He spotted a mailbox with GUNTNER written on the side in slanted peel-and-stick letters, the type you could get at Home Depot. The house was white with a black roof, a porch wrapped around two sides of the structure. About twenty yards beyond the house was a barn that, while not about to collapse, had seen better days. The once red sideboards were mostly gray, and the roof was sagging in the middle. Duckworth wondered whether it would survive a winter of heavy snow.

He parked the car close to the porch steps and mounted them to the front door. Mike had said he believed Dolores lived in the house alone, now that her parents were in a nursing home. But that didn't mean someone might not be here.

Duckworth rang the bell. When no one came after ten

seconds, he leaned on the button a second time. Again, no response.

He tried the door and found it locked. He peered through the window, saw what appeared to be a perfectly ordinary living room. Couch, comfy chairs, a television. He went down the porch steps and slowly walked down the side of the house, rounded the corner, and went up two steps to a back door. He peered through the window into a kitchen that didn't look as though it had been updated since JFK was in short pants.

He turned the doorknob, and while the place was locked, there was some play in it. He tried again, this time putting his shoulder into it, and the door swung open.

There were no beeps, so no security system.

"Hello!" he called out. "Anyone home?"

He waited a moment. Then, "This is the police! Detective Barry Duckworth with the Promise Falls Police!"

Nothing.

He went through the house slowly, starting with the first floor. He wanted to check recent incoming and outgoing calls, but while there were wall jacks, there were no phones to be found. Duckworth guessed that after her parents went into the home, Dolores Guntner, like so many of her generation, canceled the service and relied strictly on a cell phone.

The kitchen, dining and living rooms didn't turn up anything that caught his immediate attention. He went into the basement first, but like many farmhouses along this stretch of road, it was a far cry from a rec room with a pool table and a minibar. The floor was dirt, the ceiling exposed beams that he had to be careful not to bump his head on. Light was by way of a couple of exposed bulbs.

Duckworth peered behind old boxes and piles of junk and failed to spot anything that raised any alarms. He had his doubts anyone had been down here in a long time, except possibly to service the furnace.

He came back up to the first floor, then went up the stairs to the second.

There were three bedrooms, but only one that appeared to have been used for sleeping. One had been turned into a spillover room to hold boxes of files and old clothing and shoeboxes of photographs. He riffled through one of them, guessing them to be pictures Dolores' parents had collected over the last half-century or more.

The second bedroom was clearly where Dolores spent her nights. The bed was unmade and a woman's clothes were scattered on the floor.

The third bedroom also contained a bed, a single that was pushed up against the wall to allow room for a desk, a computer chair, and some bookshelves. An open laptop sat on the desk, its recharging cord attached and leading to a wall outlet off to one side. Next to the laptop was a framed picture of Dolores, looking pretty much as Duckworth remembered her from the tattoo parlor, standing between a much older couple he assumed were her mother and father.

He tapped the spacebar and the screen came to life. The background pic featured a dragon and a woman with very blonde, almost white hair. Duckworth wasn't sure, but he thought this was a scene from that *Game of Thrones* TV show.

He was worried the computer might be password-protected, but it wasn't. He pulled back the computer chair, dropped himself into it, and clicked onto the web browser. Once it had filled the screen, he clicked on the search history, crossing mental fingers that it had not been cleared.

It had not.

Dolores had traveled far and wide on the World Wide Web. Facebook pages, Twitter, local weather, celebrity gossip.

One of the sites she had been on in the last twenty-four hours had been Just Deserts. When Duckworth clicked on it, the headline that immediately popped up was "Where is the Big Baby?"

He scanned the most recent sightings of Jeremy Pilford in the Promise Falls area. Plus one out-of-focus shot in front of a hotel that was identified as being in Kingston, New York, south of Albany. That one had supposedly been taken just a few hours ago.

Duckworth said, "Hmm."

He decided to let the computer experts examine the laptop more closely. He wanted to complete his walkabout.

When he had finished his tour of the top floor, he went back down to the kitchen and exited the house the same way he'd entered it. Standing in the fresh air, his eyes settled on the barn. As he walked toward it, he didn't see anything to suggest this was still a working farm. No cows or pigs or chickens, and none of the deposits they left behind. Nor did he see any farm equipment. No tractor, not even a pickup truck. Maybe he'd find a vehicle in the barn.

There was a wood door built into the concrete foundation, which rose out of the ground a good five feet before the sideboards soared up toward the roof. Duckworth tried the door and found it unlocked.

He went inside. Where he had entered, the barn was open right to the sagging roof. Some sunlight filtered through the slits between the wallboards, dust mites dazzling in the streams. About halfway across, a lower level, with its own ceiling, had been built into the structure. An open door beckoned him forward.

He got to the door, stepped through the opening. The room was dark, and he looked for a light switch, finding one about a foot to the left of the door. He flicked it up.

It was a workshop. Along one wall, a wood bench and a set of cabinets that looked as though they had been taken from the kitchen of an old house and rehung there. Various tools were scattered across the top of the bench. The floor was dirt that had been packed down over several decades.

The room smelled of hay and mould and dirt and shit.

A few feet away, in the middle of the room, was a single bed.

It was an old, rusted metal bed that could be folded up and rolled away. Lying atop it was what Duckworth was willing to bet was the original mattress. It was uncovered, blue and white striped, with several small rips where the stuffing was attempting to escape. As he got closer, he could see that it was covered in stains that probably ranged from various bodily fluids to oil, varnish, coffee and booze.

Some of the stains looked like blood.

What particularly caught his attention were the four short lengths of rope attached to each corner of the bed.

Next to the bed, at one end, stood a red folding chair made of metal and plastic. Its newness made it stand out.

Every bit as interesting as the four lengths of rope was what Duckworth found sitting on the chair. It was a small item, with an electrical cord at one end. He noticed an extension cord on the floor that led to an outlet above the workbench.

He hadn't seen a lot of these devices in his lifetime, but he'd seen one at Mike's in the last day, so he now knew a tattoo gun when he saw one.

THIRTY-FOUR

CAL

The easiest way to get to the Cape from Kingston was to head back north toward Albany until we hit I-90, take it east all the way to 495, about half an hour this side of Boston, then work our way southeast. When I looked it up on my phone, I figured it would take us the better part of four hours.

Jeremy didn't have much to say, and I didn't try all that hard to draw him out. He seemed to be doing a lot of thinking.

At one of our pit stops along the interstate, I studied the directions to the East Sandwich beach house Madeline Plimpton had sent me in an email. I entered them into the GPS gadget that normally sat in the glove box, but which was now to take a prominent position atop the dashboard, with the aid of a suction cup device.

"You should have a nav system built right into the dash," Jeremy said, coming out of his self-imposed vow of silence.

"I don't think they knew what a nav system was when they built this car. I'm just happy it has a radio."

"How long are we going to this place for?" he asked, not for the first time.

"We're taking things a day at a time, pal," I said.

I was pretty good with my trip estimate. Three hours and fifty-eight minutes after we'd left the restaurant in

278

Kingston, we were turning off Old King's Highway, also known as 6A, onto Ploughed Neck Road, heading for North Shore Boulevard. Grey shingled beach houses dotted the horizon. We turned onto North Shore and Jeremy helped me look for the number Ms. Plimpton had given me.

"There it is," he said.

I hit the brake and cranked the wheel to turn into the driveway. The tires crunched on a mix of gravel and sea-shells. We parked at the back of a two-story house with a set of steps going up the side. I found a key under a mat where Ms. Plimpton had told me in her email the rental agent would leave it. While I opened the first-floor door, Jeremy disappeared up the outside flight of open-backed stairs.

The first floor consisted of two bedrooms, a decent-sized kitchen, a living room and a bathroom. There was the usual Cape Cod kitsch one might expect. Ship models on shelves and atop the fireplace mantel, paintings of the sea, a fisherman's net artfully hung on one wall. Bookshelves were jammed with old paperbacks and board games. There was a circular metal staircase at the other end that led up to the second floor, where I found another bedroom and a sitting area with sliding glass doors that opened onto a spacious deck.

That was where I found Jeremy. He'd accessed it from the set of steps that ran up the outside of the house.

I unlocked and slid open the doors and felt the cool breeze from Cape Cod Bay blow over my face. About sixty feet of tall grasses separated the house from the beach, and beyond that, blue water that seemed to go on forever.

"The ocean is beautiful," Jeremy said, hands on the railing taking in the view.

"Not technically the ocean," I said, "but definitely beautiful. The Atlantic's on the other side of the Cape." I made my arm into an L, like I was trying to show off my muscles. "If this is the Cape," I said, and pointed to where my arm met my shoulder, "we're about here. All this is the bay, and out here is the ocean."

He nodded. He pointed into the distance, slightly to the right. "That looks like land there."

"Yeah. Way, way up there is Provincetown. You can almost see it."

We looked up and down the beach at the neighboring houses. "Doesn't look like anybody is up," I said. "I don't think we have to worry about being spotted around here."

He nodded.

"Have a look around inside," I said. "You get first pick of bedroom. Then I think we should go into town and get a few groceries. We don't need to go out for all our meals. There's a pretty good kitchen."

"Okay."

He went inside to check the place out while I went back to the car to bring in our stuff. I made up a list of things we needed at the store, calling out to Jeremy as I wrote.

"What do you want to make for dinner?"

"Huh?" he shouted from the upper floor.

"We'll take turns making meals. I'll do tonight. You do tomorrow."

Silence. Then, "I could do hot dogs."

"Something better than that."

Another brief silence. "I guess spaghetti?"

"Great. Tomato sauce?"

"Yeah. And meatballs?"

"Got it."

I checked the cupboards to see if there were any basics left behind by previous guests. We were good for salt and pepper and sugar, and there was even some coffee for the coffee maker. I now knew we could survive anything.

Jeremy came down the spiral metal staircase to find me sitting at the kitchen table. "Can I have the upstairs bedroom?"

The first-floor bedrooms, and the kitchen, only offered a view of the grass between the house and the beach. From upstairs, you could see the bay.

"Sure," I said.

"Do you have cookies on the list?"

"No. You want some?"

"Oreos."

"Done."

I finished the list, folded it and tucked it into the front pocket of my jeans. "Let's head into town."

"Okay."

We got in the Honda and I backed us onto North Shore Boulevard. Then I put the car in neutral and applied the parking brake.

"I've got an idea," I said.

"What?"

"Why don't you drive? I've been driving all day."

"Huh?"

"Yeah. Take the wheel."

"I can't," he protested.

"Why not?"

"They took away my license for, like, forever." He

glanced down between the seats. "Anyway, I can't drive a stick."

"Okay," I said. "But some day, you'll get that license back, and you don't want to lose your skills. As for the stick, that's no big deal. I can teach you in seconds."

I could see fear in his face again.

"I don't know."

"Look," I said, pointing down the road. "It's deserted. There's no one around. It's the perfect place for a lesson."

He bit his lip, still thinking it over. "I've never really been into cars. I mean, I liked it when I could drive one, but I'm not some guy who wants to go tearing around a race track or anything."

I wasn't going to force him to do anything he didn't want to do. "Okay."

"I know what you're thinking," he said. "If I'm not into cars, why'd I want to mess around with that Porsche?"

I said nothing.

"I was just goofing around. In fact, it was Sian who said, like, wow, what a neat car. So I kind of went along, like I was interested. It's not like I'm blaming her or anything. I'm just explaining."

"Sure," I said.

I put the Honda in first and was easing off the clutch and giving it some gas when Jeremy said, "Okay."

I stopped the car. "Okay?"

He shrugged. "I guess I could give it a try."

"Great." We opened our doors. He walked around the front of the car as I walked around the back. Having traded seats, we closed our respective doors. I buckled my seat belt and waited for Jeremy to buckle his.

"Do you know the principle of driving a standard?" I asked him.

"Not really. I mean, I've watched Charlene do it. I think she's the only one I know who even knows how to drive one. She told me that in Europe and England and stuff, that's pretty much what everyone drives, but hardly anyone does here."

"Okay. First thing we do is get comfortable with the gearshift. Shove down the clutch with your left foot, yeah, that's right, and leave it there. Now, grab the gearshift, pull it ever so slightly to you and forward. Good, that's first. Straight back and toward you, that's second."

He moved the stick back and forth, getting the feel of it.

"Straight up the middle, that's third. Back is fourth, up to the right is fifth. Yeah, that's good."

"What about reverse?"

"We'll worry about reverse later. Now, how to shift gears." I raised my palms, moving them back and forth in an alternating fashion. "So my left hand, that's your left foot. All it worries about is the clutch. My right hand is your right foot, and it handles the gas and the brake."

"How do you heel-toe? I've heard about that."

"When you're ready for the Indy 500, we'll talk about heel-toe. Right now, we just want to get to the grocery store. So, to put it in gear, you push in the clutch with your left foot, and hold back with your right." I made the motions with my hands.

He still had the clutch depressed from when I showed him how to move the gearshift around. "Got it."

"Now put it in first."

He put it in first.

"Now you're going to slowly ease off the clutch at the

same time as you give the car some gas."

"Both at the same time?"

"That's how it's done. Haven't you ever watched Charlene do this in her car?"

"If I'm looking at her legs, it's not for that reason."

I grinned at him. "I hear ya. Give it a try."

Jeremy took a deep breath. He let the clutch out too quickly before giving the car some gas. It bucked and stalled.

"Oh, shit," he said.

"It's okay. So press down the clutch, turn back the key and start us up again."

He got the engine going. I told him to repeat the procedure, and again the car bucked suddenly and died.

"I can't do this," he said. "I can't."

"When my dad was teaching me stick," I said, "I nearly destroyed the car before I got it right. It's hard at first, but once you get the hang of it, you never forget."

"Like riding a bike?" he asked.

"Like that," I said.

Another deep breath. He started the car again. And again he let off the clutch too quickly and the car died.

"I'm wasting our time," he said.

"You got someplace to be?" I asked.

So he started the car again. Let out the clutch more slowly, feathered the gas. The car bucked, but it did not stall. We were moving.

"I did it!" he said.

The car, still in first, was whining loudly. It was screaming to go to the next gear.

"You did," I agreed. "Now you have to get it in second."

"Oh, fuck," Jeremy said. He looked terrified.

"It's okay. This part's easier because we're moving. Clutch in, foot off the gas." I glanced over, saw that his feet were in the right position. "Now pull the stick straight back and toward you."

He tried, but he let the clutch out too quickly and there was a horrible grinding sound.

"Jesus!" he shouted.

"It's okay, it's okay, just push the clutch back in and we'll try it again. Okay. Clutch stays in, pull the shifter straight back. That's it. Now ease out the clutch and give it some gas."

The car bucked, but less like a bronco this time. We continued to move forward. There was sweat on Jeremy's upper lip. To be honest, I was soaking under the arms. I'd never been a great passenger, even with good drivers.

"Ready for third?"

Jeremy took several short breaths. "Okay."

"Same deal. Clutch in, foot off the gas, stick straight up to the middle. Got it. Now, clutch out, give it some gas."

That time, he was pretty smooth. I looked ahead and saw that we were soon going to run out of road.

"Okay, we're going to stop. So, light on the brake with your right foot. Not hard, or we'll stall. That's it. Now clutch in all the way, harder on the brake."

The car came to a stop.

"There," I said. "Now—"

The car suddenly lurched forward, tossing my head back into the headrest. We moved ahead only a couple of feet before the car died.

"What did I do?" Jeremy asked, a look of horror on his face.

I laughed. "It's okay. You let out the clutch without putting it in neutral."

He put his head back and closed his eyes. "Shit buckets," he said. "That was torture. I can't do any more."

"Okay, that's our lesson for today. I'll drive us into town. You shouldn't be on the main road anyway, not till you have your license back. But we'll do this again tomorrow."

He shot me a look. "Are you kidding? Do we have to?"

"Why not? Something like this takes practice. Before long, you'll have the hang of it." I gave him a pat on the shoulder. "You did good, Scott."

He gave me a puzzled look. "Who's Scott?"

I felt stunned. "Sorry," I said. "My head was someplace else there for a second."

When we got to the grocery store, I gave Jeremy the list.

"What's this?"

"Grab a cart, find that stuff."

He didn't have to tell me he'd never shopped for groceries before. It showed on his face. But after surviving his driving lesson, maybe he felt this was a challenge he could handle.

"What are you going to do?" he asked.

"I want to make a phone call."

"What if someone recognizes me?"

A good point. I went to the trunk, popped it, found him a baseball cap with a Toronto Blue Jays logo on the front. "Put that on, pull it down low."

"Where did you get this?"

"Just wear it."

I sent him on his way. Once he'd freed a cart from

the string of them stored just outside the store, and gone inside, I got out my phone. I dug into my pocket for a business card I'd been given the day before, looked at the number, and entered it into my cell.

A woman answered. "Broadhurst Developments. How may I help you?"

"I need to speak with Galen," I said.

"I'm afraid he's in a meeting," the woman said.

I laughed. "That's what he tells you to say no matter what, right? Look, it's a friend of his. Tell him it's Cal Weaver. It's important."

"Hold, please."

There were several seconds of silence. Then, "Hello?"

"Galen Broadhurst?" I said.

"Yeah. This is Weaver?"

"That's right."

"The detective I met yesterday?"

"You got it."

"What's up? My secretary said this was important."

"I might have made it sound a little more urgent than it actually is. But given why I'm calling, I thought you might want to take the call."

"What?" He sounded wary.

I laughed. "It's nothing bad. It's about your car."

"What about my car?"

"You said you were thinking of selling it."

"Well, maybe."

"You said it'd probably go for around fifty thousand. I just wondered how firm you were on that."

"You're seriously interested?"

"All my life I've wanted something like that, but I've always found a way to talk myself out of it. But you said it's just had an overhaul, so I'm guessing it's in good

287

shape, although I'm sure you'd understand if I wanted to have a mechanic take a look at it."

"Yeah, of course. That's just smart."

"Can you tell me a little more about the car again?"

"Well, it's a 1978. It's got just over forty thousand original miles on it. I've got all the receipts for the work that's been done on it over the years. It's a Targa, so it's got the removable roof panels. All Porsche parts on any of the work that's been done. Tires have almost no wear on them."

"That sounds promising."

"It's immaculate. I guess I'm surprised you'd be in the market for it."

"Why's that?"

"Well," and now it was Broadhurst's turn to laugh, "that shitbox you were driving didn't exactly suggest to me that you're a car nut."

"Pretty hard to do surveillance work in a Porsche," I said. "I know a sports car isn't meant to be luxurious, but does it have air?"

"No A/C," he said. "When it's hot out, you take the roof off, turn it more or less into a convertible."

"And it's automatic transmission?" I asked.

A sharp intake of breath. "Are you kidding me? It's a stick. You don't want a car like that with an automatic."

"That's fine," I said. "Just asking. Wouldn't want it any other way. Look, let me think about it, and I'll get back to you."

"Okay. You want to take it for a spin, have some guy check it out, let me know."

"Got it. Take care."

"So long."

I ended the call and slipped the phone back into my

pocket. Stood there leaning up against the Honda, staring at the grocery store.

Thinking.

Finally, I went inside, where I found Jeremy pushing a nearly empty cart. When he saw me, he reached in, showed me the only thing he'd found so far.

"I got the Oreos," he said.

THIRTY-FIVE

Albert Gaffney lay awake most of the night wondering what he should do.

Should he call the police about Ron Frommer? It was possible Frommer was the one who'd kidnapped Brian and tattooed his back, but then again, was it likely? There was no strong evidence that he'd done it. Not that he didn't have a motive for being angry with Brian. If Frommer knew Brian had been fooling around with his wife, Jessica, well, just about anyone might lose their cool in a situation like that.

But what he'd actually done to Brian—knocking him down and kicking him in the ribs—sounded more like what a guy would do to another guy who'd slept with his wife. Pure, straightforward violence. And in a way, you could almost excuse someone for that. Albert was certainly not going to forgive the man for beating up his son, but given the circumstances, well, you could kind of understand where he was coming from.

Really, though, would Frommer abduct Brian and drug him and tattoo something that made no apparent sense onto his back? But then again, *someone* had done it. And regardless of who it turned out to be, it *still* wasn't likely to make any sense, Albert figured.

He considered his options. He could, in the morning, call that Duckworth guy and tell him what had happened to Brian when he went to visit Jessica Frommer. At least that way, Frommer would be on Duckworth's radar. Let the police figure out whether he'd had anything to do with what happened to Brian during those two lost days.

The only problem was, Brian did not want his father to do that. He was worried that Ron Frommer, who gave every indication of having a short fuse, would hurt Jessica if the police were called. Not because he'd suspect her of calling them—although he might—but because he was the kind of guy who, when upset, lashed out at whoever was close at hand.

What to do what to do what to do?

The other option, the one that had been keeping Albert awake and staring at the ceiling, was to talk to Ron Frommer himself.

Confront the man. But not, you know, in a really confrontational way. Approach him in a semi-public place, ask him flat out whether he was the one who'd done that horrible thing to his son. Of course, he'd deny it either way, but if Albert got the sense he was lying, at that point, he'd go straight to Duckworth with his suspicions.

No matter how Brian felt.

The thing was, Monica was right. Albert did not like confrontations. Wasn't that why he'd had so much trouble standing up to his own wife all these years? But this—this was different.

This was about his son.

This was about Brian.

By the time he got up the next morning, he had decided what he would do. He would, first of all, tell them he was not coming into the bank today. Albert Gaffney was the assistant manager of the Glens Falls branch of the Syracuse Savings and Loan, north of Promise Falls. An excruciatingly boring job in a mind-numbing office, it suited Albert Gaffney just fine. He went in every day, added up numbers, made sure things balanced, checked to make sure the pens at the tellers' windows had ink in them.

In the twenty-two years he had worked there, they had had not one single holdup. They had discussed firing their security guard, an elderly man who slept through most of his shift, to save some money, but when the guard got wind of it, he offered to do the job for fifty per cent less.

"It's better than sitting at home," he said.

Albert believed that his time at the bank had taught him how to read people. So if this Frommer character lied to him, Albert figured he would know.

When Constance heard her husband booking off work, she assumed it was so that he could spend the day at the hospital with Brian, who had been readmitted to finish the tests he'd walked out on the day before, and to be treated for his bruises. That was, in fact, the reason Albert had given for not coming to work. But when Constance asked what time they were going to go over, Albert said he had some errands to run first.

"What errands?" she wanted to know.

"Just errands," he said, and fled the house before a full-fledged interrogation was under way.

He drove to the address Brian had given him the day before for the Frommers. By seven thirty in the morning, he was parked on their street, a few houses down. Fifteen minutes later, a man Albert assumed was Ron Frommer came out of the house, got into a pickup truck, and backed it out of the driveway. Albert was able to make out the words "Frommer Renovations" on the door.

When the pickup moved up the street, Albert put his beige four-door sedan into drive and followed. Maybe, he thought, Frommer would stop someplace for coffee.

That would be a good place to approach him, where there were lots of other people around. Frommer wasn't going to try anything violent when there were plenty of witnesses.

Or so Albert hoped.

Albert was not what one would call skilled in self-defence. He had never taken karate or judo classes. In school, he did not go for organized sports. In college, he was not on the football team.

Sometimes he played golf.

Frommer drove past several places where he could have bought coffee. A Dunkin Donuts, a McDonald's, a couple of local diners.

So much for that idea.

His route was taking him out of town. Albert was thinking maybe he should have googled Ron Frommer before heading out this morning. Maybe he could have found out where he worked. He was starting to think maybe he hadn't thought this through as well as he could have.

About five miles out of Promise Falls, along a wooded stretch of highway, Frommer put on his blinker and turned into a driveway. As far as Albert could tell, there was nothing to turn into there.

Just woods.

The truck disappeared down a gravel road.

Albert slowed the car and pulled over to the shoulder. Where had Frommer gone? Should he follow?

He sat there, listening to the engine idle. Gripped the steering wheel tightly. Felt sweat soaking his shirt under his arms.

"All I want to do is talk to him," he said to himself. "That's all. Just a conversation."

Slowly, he turned off the road and inched his way down the driveway, tires crunching gravel along the way. A few yards and the driveway turned into a clearing in the woods. In front of him stood an A-frame chalet-style house. Set up out front of it were a couple of sawhorses and a work table.

Albert stopped the car a few feet behind the pickup. The tailgate was already down, revealing various tools and lengths of lumber. Frommer, wearing a ball cap with a long visor, was already out of the truck, strapping on a work belt. When he saw Albert's car approach, he stopped what he was doing and took off the hat.

Albert stopped the car, turned off the engine, and slowly got out.

"Hello," Frommer said.

"Um, hello, how are you?" Albert said, taking a few steps forward, near the back of the pickup.

"Can I help ya?" Frommer said, smiling.

"You . . . you're Ron? Ron Frommer?"

"I am indeed," he said.

"You do renovations?"

He nodded agreeably. "Doing some work here on the Cunninghams' place while they're in Europe. Were you looking for them, or for me?'

"I was . . . I guess I was looking for you?"

"What's the name?"

"Albert. My name is Albert."

"Pleased to meet you, Albert." Frommer extended a hand and Albert shook it. The man had a firm grip. Albert was betting his own hand felt soft in Ron's callused one. "So again, what can I do for you?"

"I'm, uh, I wanted to ask you a couple of questions."

"Shoot."

"You know . . . well, you've met my son."

Ron nodded. "Okay. What's your son's name?"

"Brian." Albert watched the man's face.

"Brian?" Ron said. "Brian who?"

"Brian Gaffney."

Ron's smile began to fade. "You say Brian Gaffney is your son?"

Albert nodded nervously. "I believe you met him yesterday."

Ron put the hat back on his head. "Mister, you should turn your car around and go."

"You . . . you hurt him pretty bad. He's back in the hospital."

"Like I said, you should go."

Albert was tempted to take a step back, but he held his ground. "I know . . . I mean, I can sort of understand why you did that. Finding out your wife, finding out that she had been seeing my son, I can see why a man might lose his temper over something like that."

Ron Frommer moved his tongue around in his mouth, poking out his left cheek, then his right.

"I'm not saying that was the right thing to do. I think you should be charged for that, I do, but all I'm saying is I understand. But that's not what I want to ask you about."

"Really. And what would you like to ask me about?"

"I want to know about the other thing you did to him. I want to know why you did *that*."

This was how Albert had practiced saying it, in his head, as he lay in bed. Act like he already knew Frommer had done it.

See if that shook him up.

He searched the man's face, looking for any clue.

Ron Frommer said, "What the fuck are you talking about?"

Albert swallowed. "I think you know."

Frommer studied him for another three seconds, then grinned. "I'll tell you what I know."

"Yes?" Albert said hopefully.

"I know that only a pussy sends his daddy to settle scores."

Albert blinked. "That's . . . that's not the issue at all. My son is not . . . he's not that. He's a good boy."

"A boy? A good *boy*?" Ron chuckled. "What is he, twelve years old?"

"Don't say that. That's uncalled for."

"So little Brian sends his daddy to have a word with me. I mean, if that doesn't prove he's a pussy, what would? Why didn't his mommy come too? Did she stay home to read him a story?"

"I'm going to tell the police about you," Albert said, his voice starting to shake.

"Make sure you call the pussy police," Frommer said. "I think they could help you. You seem pretty much like a pussy, too. Get the fuck out of here. I've got work to do."

He turned his back and started walking toward the house.

Albert stood there, feeling the shame and humiliation wash over him like hot tar.

He'd gone face to face with this man, hoping for some sort of insight, a clue that would lead him to decide, one way or another, whether this man had anything to do with what happened to Brian.

He didn't know any more now than he had before he got out of the car. At least, not about Ron Frommer.

But he believed he had gained some insight into himself.

He was a little man.

He was a small man.

He was a pussy.

Frommer reached the sawhorses, stopped. "Fuck, where's my saw?"

Albert glanced into the back of the pickup. There were two different power saws, a ladder, a crowbar, about twenty lengths of two-by-four.

Frommer was striding back toward the truck.

"You still here, Pussy Man?"

When Albert played this moment over and over in his mind later, he would recall that everything seemed to go red. It was as though blood had washed over his eyes.

But it wasn't blood. It was some rage-induced optical illusion.

He had no memory of forming intent. He didn't think to himself, "Hey, I should pick up that crowbar and swing it into that son of a bitch's head and beat the living shit out of him with it."

He didn't think that.

He just did it.

He grabbed hold of the iron bar, and as Frommer rounded the end of the pickup, Albert swung with everything he had.

Frommer only had enough time to say "What the—" before the bar connected with his temple.

There was the sound of skull cracking.

Frommer dropped instantly, but before he hit the ground, his head bounced off the edge of the tailgate.

He lay there on the gravel driveway, not moving, blood streaming from his head.

Albert began to giggle uncontrollably.

THIRTY-SIX

Barry Duckworth called the forensics team still scouring Carol Beakman's car for clues to tell them that when they were finished there, they'd have to come out to Dolores Guntner's property. You'd think, a town the size of Promise Falls, one forensics team would be enough.

In the meantime, he decided to do some more scouring of his own.

Slowly, he explored every inch of the barn out back of Dolores Guntner's house. A step-by-step search. As he began, he got out his phone and made a call.

"Dad?" said Trevor.

"Yeah. Where are you?"

"Still hanging around Carol's apartment. She hasn't shown up. Every time a taxi comes down the street, I look to see if it's her. Where are you?"

"At the home of the woman who was in the trunk of Carol's car. I found out her last name is Guntner. Heard it?"

"No, but you know when you said her name was Dolly?"

"Yeah?"

"I'm wondering if maybe I did hear that name when Carol saw the woman outside Knight's. I thought I heard her say 'Golly.' You know, like golly, there's my friend. I wonder now if she was actually saying her name."

"Huh," Duckworth said.

"What does that mean?"

"I'm just thinking."

"What?"

"Why don't you come out here?"

"Where's here?"

Duckworth gave him directions to the Guntner house.

"I thought you didn't want me hanging around while you were doing your investigating?" Trevor said.

"There's something I want to ask you."

"So ask."

"In person."

Trevor was quiet for a moment. "Okay. I'll be there in a few minutes."

Duckworth continued with his search, slowly walking through both levels of the barn, looking for anything that might catch his eye. Although the structure did look as though it was once used for the care of livestock, not much evidence of that remained beyond a few strands of hay scattered across the floor.

Once he'd finished wandering the inside of the building, he exited it. He wanted to walk the perimeter of the barn, explore the grounds around it. In one direction was a large expanse of field, and in the other, near the barn, a forested area.

First, however, he wanted that picture on the desk in the upstairs room that showed Dolores with two people Duckworth figured were her parents, now in the Davidson House nursing home. He went back inside, up the stairs, grabbed the picture, and came back down.

As he came out of the house, a car was turning in off the main road and coming up the gravel driveway, a dust stream trailing behind it. It stopped and Trevor got out.

Duckworth walked over to greet him.

"Drove by once and missed it," Trevor said. "Turned around, saw your car."

"Great."

"What did you want to talk to me about in person?"

"I guess I just want to get ahead of things," Duckworth said.

"What does that mean?"

"I don't want any surprises."

"I'm still not getting you."

"I think it's possible you knew, or might have met, the woman in that trunk."

Trevor's eyes went wide. "I knew her? This Dolores person?"

"That's right."

"I told you, I never heard that name before."

"Okay," said Duckworth. "But I'm wondering if you've met her. Let me show you something."

He held up the framed picture he'd taken from the house.

"Who's this?"

"This is Dolores Guntner. And I think these are her parents."

"Okay."

"Take a good look at her."

Trevor studied the picture. "Actually, maybe."

"Where do you think you might have seen her?"

He shook his head slowly. "I'm not sure."

"Maybe a tattoo parlor?"

Trevor's head rose sharply. He looked into his father's face. "What?"

"You might have met her at Mike's. When you were getting your tattoo."

Trevor's expression of confusion transformed into

300

contempt. "What the hell is going on here? Have you got cameras on me everywhere? In bars, in tattoo parlors, places of business all over Promise Falls? If I go into a McDonald's to take a piss, have you got pictures of me with my dick in my hand?"

"Whether you like it or not, what's going on today involves you. I'm not saying it involves you in a bad way, but you're a common thread. Your girlfriend is missing, possibly after talking to this Dolores woman, and she's someone you've come into contact with."

"This is unbelievable."

"Do you remember this woman or not?"

"Yes! I remember her!"

"What do you remember about her?"

"She took my money, okay? I paid her. I gave her my Visa card and she put it into a machine, then she gave it back. Is this about me getting a tattoo, or is it about me spending money on one when I don't even have a job?"

"I don't give a damn about that. You're old enough to make your own decisions."

"But you don't like it."

"I'm telling you I don't care about that."

"How do you even know I went to Mike's?"

Duckworth sighed. He realized he was doing it again. Maybe, when you were a cop, there was no good way to ask your son questions.

"I'd been there before, asking about tattoos. Because of that guy with the message on his back. I met Dolores. When I saw her in the trunk of Carol's car, I recognized her, went back to talk to Mike. He asked if I was related to a Trevor Duckworth." He tried to smile. "Should I have said no?"

"Jesus," was all Trevor could say.

"So I figured maybe you'd met that woman in the trunk, even if you didn't realize it. And now that you know who it is, maybe you noticed something, heard something, anything about her when you were at Mike's."

"Good story," Trevor said.

"It's the truth," Duckworth said. "I just don't want to get blindsided. Any connection you have to any of this, I have to know."

"You think I had something to do with this?"

"I'm not saying that. Of course I don't."

"You should be trying to find Carol instead of wasting time talking to me." Trevor shook his head angrily. "I never should have got it."

"What?"

"The tattoo. It was a mistake."

"Yeah, well, that's how people feel sometimes, after they get one."

"Let me show it to you," Trevor said.

"It's okay, you—"

"No, really, I want to."

Trevor unbuttoned the cuff on his left arm and started rolling up his sleeve. When he couldn't get it past his elbow, he said, "Shit."

He unbuttoned the front of his shirt halfway, far enough that he could slip it off his left shoulder.

"There, have a look," he said.

Duckworth looked. It was pretty simple, as tattoos went. Four numbers. 6201. He felt sorrow and shame pressing down on him like a weighty cloud.

"Want me to explain what it means?" Trevor asked.

There was no need. Duckworth knew his own badge number when he saw it.

THIRTY-SEVEN

CAL

When we got back to the beach house, we unpacked the groceries. I'd wanted to buy some beer, but I didn't want to have to tell Jeremy he couldn't have one, and I didn't want to drink in front of him. At eighteen, he was certainly old enough to have one, despite what the laws of New York state might say, but given his troubles, it didn't seem particularly appropriate.

But I did buy some soft drinks and a bag of ice. I took enough cubes to fill two glasses before putting the rest of it into the freezer, and poured us a couple of Cokes.

"Let's sit on the deck," Jeremy said.

"Sure."

We took our drinks, and a bag of Doritos, outside and sat on some plastic garden chairs.

"I didn't even know Madeline had this place," he said. "I guess she didn't tell my mom because then she'd have wanted to use it."

"They have a complicated relationship?" I asked.

"Oh yeah. I mean, Madeline's like my mom's mom, but not really. Because Madeline mostly raised her, but I think my mom always kind of felt that she didn't have to do what her aunt told her because she wasn't her real mom."

"Okay."

"My mom had it pretty bad, though, before she went to live with Madeline. Her dad treated her like a slave. I know she seems kind of over-the-top at times, but there's reasons why she is the way she is."

"I get that. We're all products of our upbringing."

"So who's Scott?" Jeremy asked.

The question caught me off guard. "He was my son."

"So, like, he's dead?"

"Yes."

"Sorry, man."

"Thanks."

"What happened to him?"

I didn't want to get into all of it, but I said, "He was goofing around on the roof of a building, getting high, and then someone pitched him off the side."

"Oh, man, that's brutal. And your wife?"

"She's dead, too." I looked out at the bay, tracked a passing seagull with my eye. "She was shot."

Jeremy clearly didn't know what to say to that. He took a sip of his Coke, stuffed a couple of Doritos into his mouth.

Finally he said, "Everybody's got shit to deal with, don't they?"

"Yeah."

"You think you've got it bad, and then you find out other people got it worse."

"Yup."

"How long ago did all this happen?" he asked.

"About five years."

"So, are you kind of getting over it by now?"

"No."

"At some point, don't you have to?"

I smiled at him. "I don't know that I want to. And

even if I did, they come to me. Every night."

"Like, in your dreams?"

I nodded.

Jeremy drank more Coke, ate a chip. "Where are those books you brought?" he asked.

"They're in my case. Plus there's about a thousand books on the shelves here."

"There's games, too. Do you like board games?"

"Some," I said. "After I grill some steaks, you want to play Scrabble or something?"

Jeremy considered that. "I guess. But I'm not very good at it."

"Well, neither am I. Look, I've got a call to make. I might walk down to the beach. You cool here?"

"Sure."

I got up out of the chair. I already had my phone in my pocket, so I didn't need to go back into the house. As I was heading for the stairs that led from the deck down to the beach, Jeremy said, "Mr. Weaver?"

"Yeah?"

"I'm sorry about your kid. You know, your son. And your wife. What was her name?"

"Donna."

"Yeah, and her."

"Thanks," I said.

I descended the stairs, then took the level boardwalk that traversed the grassy area. Not wanting sand in my shoes, I kicked them off, left them on the boardwalk, and strolled out onto the beach.

I looked up a number, then dialed.

"Finch, Delray and Klein," a woman said.

"Grant Finch, please."

"One moment."

A pause, and then another woman. "Grant Finch's office."

"Hi. Is Grant in?"

"Mr. Finch is in a meeting. May I help you?"

The whole world was in a fucking meeting. "My name is Cal Weaver. I'm a private investigator. It's about Jeremy Pilford. He's in my protection. I need to speak with Mr. Finch."

"Just a moment."

More dead air. Fifteen seconds later, a pickup.

"Mr. Weaver?"

"Mr. Finch, thanks for taking my call."

"Is everything okay with Jeremy? Is he all right?"

"Jeremy's fine."

"Where are you?"

I hesitated. "We're kind of on the move."

"Sure, of course. I was speaking to Madeline Plimpton. She mentioned that. No sense making it easy for the crazies. What can I do for you?"

"I'm not sure how to begin," I said. "I guess I need you to explain something for me."

"What would that be?"

"I know I've come in at the tail end of this. I wasn't around for the trial, I wasn't part of the investigation, so the point I'm about to raise may have been addressed. This may be nothing, but right now, it seems like something."

"Okay," Grant Finch said slowly.

"I let Jeremy drive my car today."

"Oh. I don't know if that was such a good idea. Operation of a motor vehicle violates the provisions of his probation. His license is suspended."

"Yeah," I said. "I figured that. But we were on a pretty

deserted road, no one around this early in the season."

"Are you in some sort of vacation area?" he asked.

I'd made a slip. "Like I said, on the move."

"Well, go on with your story, but I must caution you, Jeremy should not be driving."

"I get it. The thing is, I wanted to give him a chance to try driving a standard."

"I'm sorry, what?"

"A stick. You know. I've got a Japanese car. It's got a standard transmission."

"I know what you mean by stick, Mr. Weaver. I'm just not getting the point yet."

"He was pretty terrible at it."

"That's not at all surprising. Most cars these days are equipped with an automatic transmission. You and I may have learned that whole clutch and gas thing back in our youth, but it's not something they teach in driver's ed, far as I know. My daughter is twenty and she's never driven a car with a stick shift."

"Exactly," I said.

There was a pause at the other end. "Tell me where you're going with this."

"Jeremy wasn't just terrible at it. He stalled the car repeatedly. Just about shook my teeth loose, we did so much bucking. It was clear to me he'd never driven a stick in his life. Did this come up at all during the trial?"

"I can't say that it did."

"You know Galen Broadhurst's Porsche is a stick?" I said.

There was a pause. "I can't say that I know that one way or another."

"You and Galen are friends, right? You've known each other a long time."

"It's true that we've known each other a long time. I've acted on his behalf for years. And yes, we are friends. But that friendship is related to our business relationship."

"Had you ever had a ride in that Porsche, before the incident?"

"I . . . I can't recall."

"Well, take my word for it. The car is a stick. I saw Galen drive away in it, and I called him earlier today to confirm it."

"Mr. Weaver." Grant Finch took a deep breath. "Surely you're not going to suggest that Jeremy did not drive that car."

"I'm not quite sure what I'm suggesting. But it crossed my mind."

"That's preposterous," Finch said.

Now there was a word you didn't hear every day.

"Why is it preposterous?" I asked, watching a sailboat pass in the distance.

"As you said yourself, you haven't been in on this from the beginning," Finch said, starting to sound slightly patronizing. "Believe me, if I ever thought that was germane, this stick business, I would have raised it. But frankly, it was never even on our radar."

"So you didn't consider this in the boy's defense, not for a second."

"What did I just tell you? I formulated a defense, and it worked very well. Perhaps you've noticed that Jeremy is with you and not in prison."

"Yeah, there's that," I said.

"And Jeremy never brought this issue to my attention. You'd think if anyone was going to do it, he would have."

"I don't think Jeremy even knew. The only time he

ever got near the car, he was drunk, so he wouldn't have remembered. He never took note of it. And it's not something he would have intrinsically known. He's not a car nut. Other people, people who are into cars, you just know an old 911 is likely going to be a stick shift."

"Listen," Grant Finch said, unable to keep his impatience with me out of his voice, "if you had been there, at the trial, you would have heard testimony from several witnesses who saw what happened."

"What did they see, exactly?" I asked.

"I can't believe we're having this conversation."

"Humor me."

"At least five people from that party saw Jeremy get out from behind the wheel of that car. Blood from his forehead was on the steering wheel. There was a DNA match."

I said nothing.

"And," Finch continued, "earlier in the evening, he was seen in the Porsche, fumbling with the keys, trying to start it, before he was stopped."

"I know. The keys were left in the ashtray."

"Right."

"And even after that, Galen Broadhurst left the keys in the car."

"A decision he has to live with the rest of his life," Grant Finch said. "Don't think for a moment he isn't haunted by that every single day."

"Yeah, I met him yesterday," I said. "He seems pretty tormented."

Finch let that one go. "Despite that lapse in Galen's judgment, the real responsibility, I'm afraid, rests ultimately with Jeremy."

"You say at least five people saw him get out of the car

after Sian McFadden had been run down."

"That's right."

"How many people witnessed him getting *into* the car?"

Was that a sigh I heard? I was clearly trying the man's patience. "It would seem self-evident that if he was getting out of the car, he had, at some earlier point, gotten into it," he said. He made no effort not to be patronizing.

"That's not my point," I said.

"What is your point?"

"The point is *when* he got into it."

"I'm sorry, I'm still not getting you, Mr. Weaver."

"Did he get into the car before the crash, or after the crash?"

"What?"

"Let me ask you this. You say five people saw him getting out of the car. No one saw him getting into the car. How many people saw the actual accident? How many saw him hit Sian McFadden with the Porsche?"

"No one," Finch said without hesitation. "It doesn't matter. Mr. Weaver, let me ask you something. If someone rams your car in the parking lot, and you get out and see a driver in the other car, do you need to have seen him get *into* that car to know who hit you?"

"Why do you sound more like a prosecutor than a defense attorney?"

"I've had just about enough. I did everything I could for that boy. Jeremy is free today because of the work I did."

"Are you telling me it never occurred to you or anyone else to look at the whole stick-shift thing?"

"Even if someone had mentioned it, which they did not, it would have been a non-starter. You can't structure

310

a defense with two wildly divergent strategies. We can't suggest he was never in the car at the same time we concede he was but was not responsible for his actions."

I thought about that.

"Are you still there, Mr. Weaver?"

"I'm here."

"Look, forgive my tone. I can tell by what you're saying that you're concerned for Jeremy. Believe me, we all have been, from the very beginning. No one more than Gloria, who was willing to sacrifice her reputation, to be ridiculed, in fact, to save her son. At every step of the way we've acted in his best interest."

"Sure," I said.

"So I appreciate your bringing this to my attention, but I wouldn't worry about it."

"But how do you explain it? How do you explain the fact that Jeremy could not drive my car? At least, not without a lot of instruction. And that was sober. How did he get behind the wheel of Galen Broadhurst's car and, drunk out of his mind, instantly master the art of a manual shift?"

"The fact is, somehow he did," Finch said. "Have you considered that he was putting you on?"

"What?"

"Maybe he was having some fun with you. Maybe he *does* know how to drive a car like that, but pretended not to."

When I didn't say anything right away, Finch said, "Mr. Weaver? You there?"

"Yes," I said.

"Did you hear what I said? Maybe he was just pretending not to—"

"I heard you."

"Although I can't think of a single reason why he would do that," Finch said. "Can you?"

I was about to say no, I couldn't.

But then something occurred to me.

"Thanks for your time, Mr. Finch," I said, ending the call.

THIRTY-EIGHT

Barry Duckworth would have asked his son about why he'd tattooed his badge number onto his shoulder, but his phone rang.

"Duckworth," he said.

"Hey, it's Shirley."

"Oh, hi," Duckworth said.

"I've got that picture of Carol Beakman circulating, but now I'm doing somebody else's job. You called in wanting info on some guy named Cory Calder? They left it with me since they think I don't look busy enough."

"I'm always happy to hear from you," Duckworth said, his eyes still on his son, who was doing up the buttons on his shirt and rolling down his sleeve.

"Okay, he's thirty-one, date of birth September twentieth, 1984, he lives at 87 Marshall Way, he—"

"Hang on," he said. "You sending all this to me?'

"Of course. Nobody writes anything down any more, Barry."

"Okay. Main thing I want is an address. That a house or an apartment?"

"It's a house."

"Thanks. What about a car?"

"I'm finding a 2007 Chrysler van. Black. Plate number in the stuff I'm sending you."

"Anything else?"

"That's just official stuff. You want me to google him?"

"Would you?"

"I'll get back to you."

Duckworth put his phone back into his jacket.

"I thought I heard Carol's name," Trevor said.

"Yeah. There's nothing new. Her picture's being circulated." Duckworth rubbed his hand hard over his mouth, squeezing his lips together. He pulled it away and said, "So, tell me about that."

He was pointing at his son's shoulder.

Trevor shrugged. "I was looking for a way to honor my hero."

Duckworth closed his eyes for a second, shook his head. When he opened them, he smiled. "Gonna be hard to rub off."

"Yeah," Trevor said. "I'm thinking maybe I could add some numbers to it and try to get a cell phone to match it. Or turn it into a zip code."

Duckworth lowered his head. "I'm sorry about the last couple of days. All I'm trying to do is my job. I go where the investigation takes me."

Trevor looked away and shrugged. "I guess I'll keep looking for Carol."

"Okay. And I've got places to check out. I'd like to stay here, but I can't. Can I ask you one more question?"

"What."

"You ever heard of a guy named Cory Calder?"

"No. Who's he supposed to be?"

"Dolores Guntner's boyfriend."

Another shrug. "Nope."

"Okay."

Trevor opened his car door. Clearly this was not going to be one of those goodbyes accompanied by a hug. He settled in behind the wheel, turned the car around, and aimed it for the main road. Duckworth watched him wait for a tractor-trailer to speed by, then turn onto Eastern and head for town. The tires squealed briefly as he hit the gas.

Duckworth put the framed picture of Dolores on the front passenger seat of his car, then went to the trunk and took out a roll of yellow crime-scene tape, which he used on the two doors to the house and all accesses to the barn. Not that tape was going to keep anyone out who was intent on getting in, but it would warn anyone who might have entered innocently to stay the hell away. He then called for a patrol car to come and sit on the property until the forensic team showed up.

He couldn't spend any more time here.

He got into his car and fired up the engine. He knew Promise Falls well enough that he didn't have to look up Marshall Way. Maybe, he mused, he should quit police work and start up a taxi service. Become one of those Uber drivers. Uber was already in Promise Falls, although he'd never taken advantage of the service. And while the drivers no doubt faced the same risks as any other cab driver, Duckworth was betting none of them had been nearly beaten to death in the course of their duties, as he had.

The Calder residence was a tasteful two-story red-brick house with simple white columns flanking the front door. The yard was meticulously maintained, not a single blade of grass out of alignment where lawn met sidewalk. One of those small Lincoln SUVs, in white, sat on the jet-black driveway, which shone as though wet. It looked to have been resurfaced very recently.

Duckworth went to the door and rang the bell. Seconds later, it was opened by a slim, gray-haired man in his seventies wearing a plaid shirt with a buttoned-down collar, and perfectly creased slacks.

"Yes?" he said.

Duckworth got out his ID and allowed the man to examine it. "Detective Duckworth, Promise Falls Police."

The man's nose wrinkled. "Yes?"

"I'm looking for a Cory Calder."

"He's not here," the man said.

"Who are you, sir?"

"Alastair Calder. I'm Cory's father. Is there some kind of problem?"

"Where would I find Cory?" Duckworth asked.

"I have no idea," Alastair said.

"Does he live here?"

"He does. But I'm not his minder. He's a grown man."

"May I come in, sir? Maybe you can help me clear up a few things."

Alastair Calder hesitated, then opened the door wider. Duckworth thought he might be offered a seat in the living room, but it looked like a living room no one ever sat in. Vacuum cleaner tracks remained visible in the broadloom.

"This way," Alastair said, leading Duckworth deeper into the house. He opened an oak door to a study. A desk dominated the room. Bookshelves, completely jammed, lined two walls. One wall was mostly window that looked out onto a treed backyard, and the final wall was reserved for framed photos and diplomas and various awards. There was one chair behind the desk, and another in front of it.

"Have a seat," Alastair said. Duckworth sat. "Now what's your business with my son?"

"When did you last see Cory?"

"I asked you what your business was with him."

"And I asked you when you last saw him."

Alastair Calder pursed his lips and drew in air through his nose. "Some time yesterday, I believe. We don't check in with each other."

"But you did say he lives here."

"Yes.

"Who else lives here?"

"No one."

"Just you and your son."

"That's what I said." He sighed. "My wife died three years ago. We had two other children. They're both married. My son is in Tokyo, researching ways to turn ocean water into drinking water. My daughter is a doctor. She's in Europe, assisting in the refugee crisis, which is never-ending."

"And Cory? What does he do?"

"He lives here," Alastair said, a hint of contempt in his voice. "What do you want with him?"

"Do you know Dolores Guntner?"

His eyes widened. "Dolly?"

Duckworth smiled. "Yes."

"Yes, I know her," he said with a disapproving shake of the head. "My son is old enough to choose his own girlfriends, I am afraid."

"So Dolores, she's been seeing your son?"

"For some time, yes. Is this about Dolores? What's she done? It wouldn't surprise me in the least if she was up to no good. Do you know where she works?"

"A tattoo parlor."

"Exactly. What else do I have to say? What's she done?"

"She got herself killed, Mr. Calder."

He sat upright in his chair. "She what?"

"She's dead, sir."

His face fell. "Dear God, what on earth happened?"

"Her death is being treated as a homicide."

"You can't be serious."

"So I'm speaking with anyone who knew her. I'm told your son was her boyfriend, so he'd be at the top of the list of people I need to talk to."

"You can't think he'd have anything to do with this. He's got his flaws, but he wouldn't do anything like that."

"But he may know something that would help me in my investigation. So let me ask you again. Do you know where he is?"

"I . . . don't."

"Do you anticipate him coming back any time soon?"

"I really have no idea."

"You seemed to suggest earlier he doesn't have a job."

"Not . . . not currently."

"I need you to call him and find out where he is. He must have a cell phone."

"He does."

Duckworth sat and stared at the man. Alastair, growing increasingly uncomfortable, finally reached for the phone on his desk. He hit one button, put the phone to his ear and waited.

He grimaced. "It's gone straight to message." He waited a second, then said sternly, "Cory, it's your father. Call home immediately." He replaced the receiver.

"He's turned his phone off," Duckworth said.

"Or he's someplace he can't get a signal. I'm sure that's all it is. What happened to the girl? I demand to know."

"What do you do, Mr. Calder?" Duckworth asked.

Alastair blinked, evidently offended that his demand

was so quickly ignored. "I'm an advocate," he said.

"Uh, an advocate for what?" Duckworth asked. "Or should I ask whom?"

"Both," he said. "For decades, my wife Annette and I directed campaigns for countless individuals and agencies in areas of social justice, environmental protection, the wrongly accused and convicted, freedom-of-speech violations, the list goes on."

"I see. How would you advocate, exactly?"

"Is this really important, Detective?"

"Just getting a sense of things, Mr. Calder."

"Our company mapped out strategies, guided these organizations through courses of action. We got our start in advertising and public relations, so we were well grounded in the arts of persuasion and advocacy. We used those skills to make this a better world, rather than trying to sell things to people they probably didn't need in the first place."

"And you did all this from Promise Falls?"

"No," he said. "From New York. My wife had roots in this part of the state, and when we retired—although it's never been a complete retirement—we moved up here. That was seven years ago. But as you can see," and he waved his arm across the study, "I'm still engaged in things." He leaned forward, his arms resting on the desk. "Tell me my son is not in some kind of trouble."

"I don't know," Duckworth said. "Why don't you tell me about him?"

Another sigh. "He lives in the shadow of his brother and sister," he said. "They've gone on to do great things, to make a difference. Like their parents. Cory has struggled in that regard."

"How?"

"He . . . he looks for shortcuts. He's impatient. The road to success is not a superhighway. It has plenty of bends and detours, and sometimes the bridge gets taken out in a flood. Many of us find another route, even if it takes us hundreds of miles out of our way. Cory turns the car around and goes home." His face saddened. "Annette said I couldn't expect him to have the same drive as the others. We had to let him be who he was, whatever that turned out to be. And that's turned out to be a kid—a young man—who spends a lot of time on the computer, arguing with the world."

"He doesn't share the social conscience the rest of your family is known for?"

"I wouldn't say that," Alastair Calder said, with what sounded like just a hint of pride. "He does care about injustice. He's on the web all the time, debating it with people. I'll hear that damn tapping at three in the morning, and go into his room and tell him enough is enough. And he'll tell me he just has to make one more point with some stupid idiot in Oklahoma or Dublin or Cape Town. Like he's trying to win the planet over to his point of view. It's like that cartoon of the person on the computer saying he can't come to bed because someone is wrong on the Internet."

"What sort of issues does he get fired up about?"

Alastair frowned. "Who knows? Sometimes I think he's just *looking* for something to get riled about. He sees others jumping on some bandwagon and he has to get on too. He says this whole social-network thing is a way to get back at people."

"Get back at people?"

He shrugged. "To get revenge. To make sure people get what's coming to them. That's never what my wife and I were about. We weren't about revenge. We were always about justice."

"Can you recall any specific instances?"

Alastair had to think. "Well, take that son of a bitch who attacked that retarded—sorry, my apology, we don't say that any more, terrible word—that mentally challenged woman. He pretty much admitted he did it, but he got off. Cory thought that was pretty disgusting."

"I guess you heard what happened to that person," Duckworth said.

"Oh yeah, terrible. Even considering everything."

"What about that kid who ran down the girl?" Duckworth asked. "His defense that his mother's pampering sabotaged his ability to understand the consequences of his actions."

"The Big Baby," Calder said.

"That's the one. So you know the case. Did Cory ever mention it?"

The man's face grew concerned. "Why are you asking?"

"Did he?"

"Just the other day. How could you have guessed that?"

"Have you ever heard of a website called Just Deserts?"

"What is that? Some cooking site or something?"

"No," Duckworth said. "It's a site that encourages vigilantism. People become heroes on that site when they've taken action against a person deemed to have gotten away with something. Like the man who sexually molested that girl."

"What kind of vigilantism?" Alastair asked.

"I guess that's up to whoever is carrying it out." Duckworth frowned.

"So what the hell are you suggesting? That Cory is striving for recognition on this site?"

Duckworth shrugged. "Maybe it's the shortcut to achieving a social good like his brother and sister." He paused. "Or his mother and father."

"This is . . . no, this is ridiculous. And what does that have to do with this Dolly girlfriend of his? She never did anything wrong like that."

"Certainly not that I know of," Duckworth said. "But that's why it would be helpful to speak with your son."

"Let me try him again." Alastair snatched up the receiver and pressed that one button again. "It's still going to message."

"Maybe he's expecting you to call," Duckworth said. "And he knows it's not going to be good news."

Alastair cradled the receiver. "Jesus Christ," he said. He ran his hand over his mouth nervously. "None of this makes any sense. I know what happened to that man you referenced. Craig Pierce. He was attacked by a dog. He was disfigured."

"Yes."

"You don't think Cory had anything to do with that?"

"Mr Calder, I'd like to have a look at Cory's room. I can do it now, with your permission. Or I could see about getting a warrant."

Alastair Calder sat, Buddha-like, for several seconds, not blinking, not moving. Finally he said, "You're not going to find anything."

"Maybe not," Duckworth conceded. "But I'm guessing that right now, you're as anxious as I am to find out whether I will."

THIRTY-NINE

Albert Gaffney did not giggle for long.

After a very brief, giddy celebration of Ron Frommer's demise, he began to appreciate what he had actually done.

"Oh God," he said aloud. "Oh God oh God oh God."

He dropped the bloodied crowbar he'd used to crack Ron Frommer's skull. Blood continued to leak from Ron's temple as he lay there on the ground by the back of his pickup truck.

Albert looked around, on the off chance that someone might have seen what he'd done. But the house Frommer had been working on, in his role as a renovator, was tucked into the woods off the main road. So long as squirrels could not be called to testify, Albert was probably going to be okay.

But no, he thought. *I have to call the police. I have to tell them what I did.*

That would be the moral thing to do, right? He'd tell the police what he'd done. Okay, he might shade things slightly. Tell them that Ron Frommer was threatening him when he grabbed the crowbar. It was self-defense.

And even if Frommer hadn't actually been threatening him at the moment Albert struck him, he was probably going to. The man had attacked his son. He had a history.

"Yes," Albert said under his breath. "I had to do this. I had no choice. He was attacking me. He'd attacked my son, and now he was attacking me."

The good thing was, Ron was not going to be able to contradict his story.

They'd have to take Albert's word for it. And let's face it, he was the assistant manager of the Glens Falls Syracuse Savings and Loan. He was a respected member of the community. Ron Frommer, on the other hand, was—

"*Ohhhhh.*"

Albert's head snapped around to look at Ron Frommer. The man's eyelids were fluttering. He was trying to open his eyes.

He was alive.

"No no no no no," Albert said.

No, wait, he thought. This was good news, wasn't it? He hadn't killed the man. Frommer was alive. If Albert called 911 right now and got an ambulance out here, if they got Frommer to PFG fast enough, they might be able to save him.

Yes. That was very true.

It seemed clear what the right thing to do was.

Except if Ron Frommer lived, he'd be able to tell the police that he hadn't been threatening Albert Gaffney.

"*I was just standing there when he swung that pry bar into my fuckin' head. Who'd have thunk it, a pussy like that?*"

But maybe, Albert thought, he'd hit Frommer hard enough that he wouldn't remember what had actually happened. It was still going to be one man's word against another's.

"Fuckin' hell, what happened?" Ron Frommer said. He reached a hand up to the side of his head, felt blood, murmured something.

A voice in Albert's head said, *Finish him off.*

It would be easy enough. Ron Frommer might be

alive, but he was dazed and seriously injured. All Albert had to do was pick up the crowbar and take another whack at him. One should do it. The man wouldn't be able to offer any resistance.

He took a step over to where he'd dropped the iron bar, picked it up. He stood over Ron Frommer.

When he'd struck the man the first time, he'd been in a blind rage. He hadn't thought about what he was doing. It was an impulse. He had acted instinctively.

But this was different. He had to make a conscious decision to end this man's life.

He moved the crowbar from one hand to the other. When he'd hit him before, he had held it with one hand. The next time, he thought, if he used two, swung it almost like a golf club, he'd have more power behind it. He'd knock the bastard's head clean off.

Suddenly, he felt the urge to vomit.

He turned, ran several feet to the edge of the woods, leaned over, and threw up. Three times.

I can't do it.

He stood, took a few deep breaths, then went back to his car. He opened the trunk and dropped the crowbar in, slammed the lid. Then he went back to Frommer, got down on his knees and put his mouth up close to the man's ear.

"Just hang in there," he said. "I'm going to take you to the hospital."

Frommer said, "Rmmrr."

"Do you think you can get up?"

Frommer didn't move.

"I'm going to get you to the car," Albert said. "Okay? I'm going to get you to the car."

He moved to behind Frommer's head and got his

hands under the man's arms. Frommer was a slim build, but as a dead weight—well, almost dead—he was still a lot to carry. Albert did not have to do a lot of heavy lifting in his day job, but he managed to get a good, solid grip on the man. As he hoisted him higher, Frommer's head almost level with his own, blood smeared his shirt and jacket and neck.

He resisted the urge to vomit again.

He dragged the man toward his car. Once he had him there, he managed to free one hand to open the back door on the driver's side. Somehow he got Frommer inside, then had to push him onto his side and shove him across the seat so that he could get his legs in.

He slammed the door shut, leaned his back against the car and took a moment to catch his breath.

He knew he should have called an ambulance, but he was worried that it could take a long time to get to this location. And if they missed the driveway, it could take even longer. Albert was confident he could get Frommer to the hospital more quickly.

He eased himself off the car, turned, and was horrified to see bloody smears on the door. He rubbed at them with the sleeve of his jacket, but it only made things worse.

There was nothing he could do about it.

He got behind the wheel, switched on the engine, and turned the car around. He raced to the end of the drive-way, glanced hurriedly in both directions to make sure no one was coming, then hit the pavement with a squeal.

"Not much longer," he said, turning his head to speak to Frommer. "Ten minutes tops! Just hang in there."

Soon he was back in town. Far off in the distance, he could make out the blue H atop Promise Falls General.

And then the car turned.

Turned off the route that would have taken them to the hospital.

It was as though the vehicle had a mind of its own.

It didn't, of course.

It was Albert who had decided, at the last minute, that he was not going to take Ron Frommer to the hospital.

He was going to take him to his place.

FORTY

CAL

Jeremy and I made some more sandwiches, this time with the stuff we'd bought in town. He was actually getting into it, laying out the bread, slapping a slice of cheese on each one, putting on mounds of deli meat, squirting a dollop of mustard on each.

"Maybe I should get a job in a restaurant," he said.

"When I was a little younger than you, I had a job doing dishes in a diner."

"Just dishes? You didn't cook or anything?"

"Just dishes. My fingers would be all wrinkly at the end of my shift."

We took our food up to the deck. Far out in the bay, Jeremy spotted a massive ship.

"I saw some binoculars on the shelf," I told him.

He went back into the house and found them, then came out and stood at the deck railing, the binoculars up to his eyes. "It's one of those ones that carries cargo containers," he said. "They're all different colors. They look kinda like kids' building blocks."

I reached out a hand from where I was sitting and he handed the binoculars to me. I took a look, scanned the horizon where water met sky. If it weren't for the fact that we were here hiding from Internet nutbars who wanted to hurt Jeremy, this would be a pretty nice place to chill out.

When Jeremy had finished his second sandwich, I said, "Let's take a walk."

"Where?"

"The beach."

"Okay."

Once we'd descended the set of wooden steps that led us down to the beach, we took off our shoes and left them there where we could find them later. Jeremy ran toward the water, stood in the sand where the waves were coming in, let them wash around his ankles as they receded.

"It's freezing," he said, glancing back at me.

"Let's walk this way," I said, pointing east. We strolled just along the edge of the surf, our feet getting wet every few seconds.

"I like it here," Jeremy said. "We've almost got the beach to ourselves."

He was right, although we weren't the only ones out here. Looking both ways, I saw maybe ten or twenty people wandering more than a mile of shore. Almost no one was in a bathing suit. Most, like us, were in long pants rolled up to the knees. Some were smart enough to wear light jackets, as the breeze coming in off the bay was cool. I wished I'd brought one. But if the cold bothered Jeremy—aside from the waves that touched his feet—he gave no indication.

"I want to talk to you about something," I said.

"Yeah? What? Is this about how I should have told Charlene's mom I was sorry?"

"No, but we can come back to that later."

"I *am* sorry," he said.

I nodded, placed a hand briefly on his shoulder. "Okay. But first, I want to ask you about earlier. When you were driving my car."

He looked at me worriedly. "Shit, did I break it? I broke it, didn't I? I'm sorry. It was your idea."

I shook my head, "No, the car's okay." It occurred to me that he might actually have done some damage to the clutch, but if he had, I hadn't noticed anything on our drive back from town. "What I'm asking is, was that for show?"

"Was what for show?"

"Your ineptitude."

"My what?"

"You were totally shitty at it," I said. "Was that an act?"

"An act? What are you talking about?"

Maybe I shouldn't have come at this so directly, but there was a theory floating around in my brain. "What I'm wondering is, could you be taking the blame, willingly, for something you never did? To protect someone you care about, maybe? But now, you're wondering if that was a mistake. You want me to think it couldn't have been you so I'll point everyone in the direction of who really did it."

"I have no idea what the fuck you are talking about," he said.

If Jeremy's current confusion and his performance in the car yesterday were all part of an act, he deserved an Oscar. The theory floating around in my brain was now taking on water and sinking to the bottom.

"Really, what are you talking about?" he persisted.

I held up both hands, palms forward. "Okay, let's rewind. Forget I brought any of that up. Let me start again. But I do want to talk about the night it happened. I know that may be hard for you, having to answer questions from me when you've already had to tell a hundred people the story. But bear with me, okay?"

He eyed me apprehensively. "Okay."

"Tell me everything."

"Everything?" he said.

"Just tell me about that night. No, hang on."

An elderly couple was approaching. They each nodded and smiled. I said, "Beautiful day."

The woman said, "If it would just warm up some!"

"Soon enough," I said. "Come summer, we'll be complaining about how hot it is."

"Ain't that the truth," the man agreed. They continued walking, and seconds later had disappeared behind us.

"Okay, tell me," I said to Jeremy.

"Like, everybody was screaming and shouting and someone hauled me out of the car and Mr. Broadhurst was there and Bob was there and lots of other people and then Mr. McFadden, he started pounding on me and they had to pull him off. It was really awful."

"Go on."

"And I saw Sian lying there, and I couldn't believe I'd done that. You keep thinking, if only I could go back in time one hour and change things, you know?"

"Tell me about when you got into the car."

"I just got in it, I guess."

"Was Sian with you when you got in?"

"She couldn't have been in the car with me, because how would I have run into her?"

"Sure. But I was thinking, maybe she got in, and you drove around some, and then she got out and you were still in the car. Maybe something like that."

"I think what happened," Jeremy said, "is she went

running up the driveway and then I got in the car to catch up with her."

"Why do you say you think that's what happened?"

Jeremy shot me a look. "What does that mean?"

"It means just what I said. You say you think that's what happened."

"Yeah."

"But you don't know."

"I was kind of pissed out of my mind. You remember that part, right?"

"Okay, let's go back to earlier in the evening," I said. "When Broadhurst found you in his car, and Sian was with you. Do you remember that?"

He nodded. "Yeah. Mostly."

"So—Hang on again."

A short, stocky woman was walking purposefully our way. This wasn't a stroll. This was exercise. I was about to say hello when I noticed she had wires leading down from her ears. I gave her a friendly wave, which she ignored as she passed us.

"You're really worried about people hearing us," Jeremy said.

"Just being careful. So Broadhurst finds you in the car."

"Yeah, and he's really pissed, especially since I've got the key in my hand and I'm trying to figure out how to start it. But the place where you put the key in wasn't in the usual spot, in the steering column thingy. I'd just figured out where it was, over to the left of the wheel, when Broadhurst opens the door and tells me to get the fuck out."

"So you never got the car started."

"No."

"And you found the key in the car?"

"Yeah. It was sitting in the tray between the seats."

"That seems kind of dumb."

"Yeah, well, he did that a lot because it was his own property, and the house is a long way from the road, and he said, like, when he testified, that he was always losing keys, so if he just left it in the car, he'd find it."

"A car that nice."

Jeremy shrugged. "They asked him about that, and he said if he was going someplace, he didn't leave it. But out front of his house, yeah, sometimes."

"So he finds you in the car, with the key in your hand—is that right?"

A nod.

"So what happens to the key?"

"He takes it from me."

"And what does he do with it?"

Water rolled in, froze our ankles briefly, and slid back out.

"What's he do with it?" Jeremy repeated.

"Yeah."

"I guess he put it in his pocket."

"So he didn't put it back in that tray where you found it."

"Well, not right then. Probably later."

"Okay," I said. "But you seem to remember that incident, that confrontation, quite clearly."

"Pretty much," he said. "I wasn't so hammered then."

"So now tell me about the second time you got in the car."

"That's a lot fuzzier," he said quietly.

"Because?"

"Sian and I went back into the house and snuck out

some more to drink. So we . . . well, I was pretty shit-faced the second time I got in the car. But that time, I would have known where to put the key."

"If the key was there."

"Well, I guess it fuckin' had to be," Jeremy said. He stopped. "Is there a reason why you're goin' on about this? And I still don't get that other stuff you were asking me, about protecting someone?"

"I asked you to bear with me."

"Fine," he said, in a voice that suggested it was not fine at all.

"Do you remember Broadhurst reaching over you, before you got out of the car, to put the keys back where you found them?"

"No. But he must have done it after."

"So between the time that you and Sian got kicked out of the car, and the time you got in it again, what did you do?"

"Like I said, we went in, scored two nearly full bottles of wine that had been opened, and went back outside."

"Outside where?"

"Uh, like, outside."

"Front of the house? Back of the house?"

"We wandered up the driveway, toward the main road. There's kind of a hill there, you know?"

"I don't. I've never been there."

"Oh, right. So we were drinking straight out of the bottles. One was red, one was white, and we were sharing back and forth. We sat on the bench."

"What bench?"

"There's this fancy bench along the side of the driveway, just over the hill. We sat there and drank and looked at stars and shit."

"When did you come back and get in the car?"

He had to think about that. "Around then, I guess. Sian must have stayed by the bench while I walked back to get the car."

"You know that?"

He shrugged. "Like I said, that's when it starts getting awful fuzzy. Somewhere along the line I think I blacked out or something."

About a hundred yards ahead, a young man was standing with his feet firmly planted in the wet sand, facing out into the bay, looking contemplative. From where we were, his eyes appeared to be closed. Water rushed in around his legs and out again, but he never moved.

"So let's say," I said, "you go back to the car, start it up, then drive over the hill, and that's when Sian must have gotten off the bench and stumbled into your path, or maybe you veered toward her. Something like that."

"And hit the tree."

"How did you do it?" I asked.

"What's that supposed to mean? You mean, like, how could I do something so stupid? That's kind of what everyone's asked. And it's because I didn't understand the consequences of my actions."

He said that last sentence like he was reading it off a teleprompter.

"That was the defense strategy," I said. "But do you really believe that?"

A hesitation. "I guess."

"It's a load of shit and you know it, but it worked," I said.

"Whatever."

"But that's not what I'm asking you. How did you do it?"

"Do what?" he asked impatiently.

"Drive the car."

"Lots of people are able to drive cars when they're drunk. They just do a shitty job of it."

I put out a hand to stop him. I turned and looked at him. "The car's a stick."

"What?"

"Galen Broadhurst's car is a stick shift."

"No, it couldn't be," Jeremy said. "You're wrong."

"I'm not. I made some calls to confirm it."

"But . . . that doesn't make any sense. Maybe the shift in your car is harder to use or something."

"I don't think so. I can't see you managing a manual transmission in any make of car. No offense, but you were pretty terrible at it. A few more lessons and I think you'll be fine, but today? Not so great."

"But how . . . Maybe it's one of those shifters that can go back and forth. Like, you can shift it if you want, but you don't have to."

I put a hand on his shoulder to steer him forward, and resumed walking. "No, it's not like that. I don't get how someone who'd never driven a stick before could not only hop into that Porsche and drive it, but could do it drunk."

Jeremy didn't say anything. He kept looking down at the millions of grains of sand, as if one of them contained the answer and all we had to do was find it.

"But . . ."

"But what?" I asked.

"But that seems like a kind of obvious thing. I mean, I guess somehow I must have driven it, although I don't see how. But if the whole stick thing could raise, whaddya call it, some sort of reasonable doubt, I think Mr. Finch would have brought that up."

"You'd think so. It was never part of the defense strategy discussions?"

"I wasn't really part of those," he said.

"I talked to Grant Finch. He said if it had been an issue, you should have raised it."

"How could I raise it? I didn't know."

"How familiar were you with the car?"

Jeremy thought. "The first time I saw that car was when I got in it. When I was shitfaced. The second time I saw it was yesterday, parked out front of Madeline's house."

I'd been there. Jeremy didn't go anywhere near it, so he couldn't have looked inside it, wouldn't have noticed what was between the front seats.

"Look, Mr. Weaver, Mom and Bob and Mr. Finch and Madeline and even Mr. Broadhurst all talked about the best way to get me off, and they came up with, you know, the whole Big Baby thing. And even though I hated it, at least I'm not in jail now."

"True enough," I said. "But is it possible, Jeremy, that you didn't *want* the stick-shift thing to come up?" I was diving down for that theory, seeing if it could be brought back to the surface, given mouth-to-mouth.

"Huh?"

"Is it possible it *did* come up, and you shot it down?"

I might as well have told him the sky was green, the way he looked at me. I couldn't help but wonder if he was putting on a show. Overreacting on purpose.

"That's nuts," he said.

"Tell me about Charlene."

"What about Charlene?"

"Were things a little more serious with her that night than you've let on? Was she your girlfriend? Were you seeing her and Sian at the same time?"

"I don't know what you're getting at."

"Help me out here, Jeremy. Something about this is not right. Let me ask you again. All this time, have you been taking the blame for someone else? Willingly?"

"What?"

"I noticed Charlene knows her way around a stick shift. And she made a point yesterday of saying that Sian ran in front of the car, that anyone would have hit her, drunk or not. Why would she say that?"

"That's just her opinion." He shook his head angrily. "This is all bullshit."

I had another question, but we had almost reached our contemplative guy. He must have heard us coming, because he opened his eyes and turned to look in our direction.

"We'll talk about this later," I whispered to Jeremy.

"I don't think so," he whispered back.

The man on the beach gave us a broad smile. "Hey."

"You had a real Zen thing going on there," I said.

The man nodded. "I guess so. It's just so . . . wonderful."

"Yup," I said. I've always been a master of small talk. I glanced at Jeremy, who was looked slightly shell-shocked. His eyes weren't focused on this new guy, or anything else for that matter. He was just staring.

"Haven't seen you on the beach before," the man said.

"We just got here," I told him.

"Well, it's nice to meet you." He extended a hand and I took it. "What's your name?"

"Cal," I said.

He put out his hand to Jeremy and asked the same thing. I felt an instant sense of panic.

Don't tell him your name. Don't tell him your name.

Jeremy, almost robotically, held out his hand.

"And you are?" the man said.

I tried to catch Jeremy's eye, but he still wasn't tracking very well.

He said, "Uh, I'm Alan."

I breathed an inward sigh of relief. Even in a stunned state, he had enough good sense to give a fake name.

"Well," the man said, "nice to meet you both. Might see you again. I'm Cory, by the way."

FORTY-ONE

Alastair Calder led Duckworth up to the second floor of the house and opened the first door on the right.

"This is Cory's room," he said.

Maybe Duckworth expected all young men's rooms to look as though a bomb had just gone off in them, but Cory's world was meticulous. The bed was made, the desk uncluttered. A shelving unit was packed tightly with CDs and DVDs and books, but there was a sorting system for all of them. The disks were arranged alphabetically, the books into subcategories. Science-fiction novels were grouped, then alphabetized by author, and the same was true for non-fiction titles. Graphic novels were collected according to character, so stories featuring Batman, regardless of who wrote them, were stacked alongside each other.

"He's neat," Duckworth said.

"I'll give him that," Cory Calder's father said.

The bed, which was about a foot lower than a typical one, seemed to float in the room. Duckworth noted that the mattress sat directly on a platform, without a box spring, and the supporting legs were set back just far enough to be invisible.

He checked out the desk. There was a desktop computer with an oversized monitor not much thicker than a finger. Wireless mouse, wireless keyboard. He gave the mouse a shake and the monitor came to life, but it was password-protected.

"You know your son's password?"

Alastair shook his head. "No."

"Could you guess at it?"

"No."

Duckworth nodded. Nothing about the room was jumping out at him. He scanned the items on the shelves. The DVDs were mostly science fiction or fantasy. *Star Wars*, *Lord of the Rings*, *The Hobbit*. As he scanned the spines of the books, he was hoping for titles along the lines of *Do-It-Yourself Tattoos* or *Kidnapping 101*.

What he had not really expected to find was one called *Sedation: A Patient Handbook*.

He pulled it from the shelf and showed it to Alastair. "What do you make of that?"

"I don't know what to make of it," Alastair said.

There were also, on the same bottom shelf, a number of textbooks that Cory must have hung onto from his high-school or college days, most of them chemistry-related. It was looking to Duckworth as though Cory might have the smarts to keep someone unconscious for a couple of days.

And if the books didn't supply enough information, there was always the Internet. All you had to do was google it. Which was why Duckworth was sorry he wasn't going to be able to immediately get into Cory's computer, if at all.

He went to the closet and opened it.

"Whoa," he said.

Instead of clothes on hangers, the entire closet had been turned into shelving, but not for socks or shirts or underwear. The compartments were neatly stuffed with boxes—some empty, some not—ranging from the very small to briefcase-sized. The packaging labels indicated that most of this stuff was electronic equipment.

Alastair, standing behind Duckworth, said, "He saves the packaging for everything he gets. And all the instructions and the manuals."

Duckworth read the labels. Modems, chargers, cables. But more interesting things, too. Surveillance-type equipment. Listening devices. Microphones.

"Why would Cory have stuff like this?" he asked.

Alastair looked. "I don't know." His face grew dark.

Duckworth closed the door to the closet. He got down on his knees and lifted the bed skirt, preparing to peer beneath it. But kneeling in the closet, standing, and now getting down again had made him momentarily light-headed. He rested his elbows on the bed and took a moment to ask Cory's father another question.

"Where does he get the money?"

"Money for what?"

Duckworth tipped his head toward the closet. "All the electronic goodies."

Alastair swallowed and said, quietly, "I give it to him. I give him what you'd call an allowance, I suppose." He looked ashamed. "It's just easier sometimes to let him have what he wants."

"Sure," Duckworth said.

His head feeling back to normal, he went down on his hands and knees and peered under the bed. There was almost nothing there, not even dust. But there was something up near the head of the bed, tucked against the wall by the baseboard. Whatever it was, it seemed to reflect the tiny amount of light that was getting under there.

Duckworth shimmied his body along the floor to get closer, and reached his hand under. His arm wasn't long enough, but he was able to get a better look at the item. It was a jar. About six or seven inches tall, with a metal cap on top. It carried no label, but it appeared to be something spaghetti sauce might have come in.

"Do you have a stick or a ruler or something?" he asked Alastair Calder.

"What is it?"

"Something under here I can't quite reach."

"What does it look like?"

"A jar."

Duckworth heard Alastair opening drawers. Finally he came around the bed and handed the detective a pair of scissors.

"I couldn't find anything else," he said.

Duckworth held the scissors by the pointed end, reached under the bed, and was able to connect with the jar. He moved it slightly in his direction, noticed a shimmering, and realized it contained some kind of liquid, in addition to something else. Very carefully, so as not to knock it over, he edged it even closer with the scissors until he was able to reach it with his hand.

He passed the scissors back to Alastair, then stuck his arm back under the bed and drew the jar out. Then he got to his knees and, still holding it in his hand, rested it atop the bed.

"Sweet Jesus, what the hell is that?" Alastair asked.

Duckworth checked the lid to see that it was on tight. The liquid in the jar had a yellowish tinge. Sitting on the bottom was a wrinkled, fleshy mass about the size of two small chicken gizzards. But they did not look like gizzards to Duckworth.

"What do they look like to you?" he asked Alastair.

"They look like . . . My God, they appear to be testicles."

"That's what they look like to me," Duckworth said. "And I think I know who these just might belong to."

So maybe the dog hadn't swallowed everything after all.

FORTY-TWO

Cory Calder felt energized. A nice way to feel, after so many missteps.

He'd met Jeremy Pilford. Face to face. Shook his hand. Looked him right in the eye! Well, almost. Jeremy seemed a little preoccupied at that moment, like maybe that guy with him had told him something he didn't want to hear. Whatever. It didn't matter.

This was so different than what had happened with Craig Pierce, or even Brian Gaffney, although the less said about that one the better. Cory had to admit, he felt bad about Gaffney.

Gaffney had looked, at a glance, so much like Jeremy Pilford. He was even dressed more or less the same. Cory and Dolly had watched Jeremy go into Knight's and were waiting for him to come out. And when he did, or when someone who looked very much like him did, Dolly said, "Hey, how ya doing, can you help me out here? I dropped a contact."

The dude stepped into the alley, Cory came up behind him, chloroformed him. They dragged him to the van, which they'd left parked at the end of the alley.

Would have been so much better if it had been the right guy.

And then, to make matters worse, someone recognized Dolly as Cory was getting Gaffney tucked away. Fucking *chatted* with her.

Anyway, what was done was done. Sometimes, trying

to do the right thing, innocent people got hurt.

Tell me about it.

At least Gaffney had never seen them, never had a real look at them. Not even Dolly, who'd called him into the alley. It was dark, and they were confident he'd never be able to describe her for the cops. The whole time they had him in the barn at Dolly's place, he was out of it, but they'd kept him blindfolded, just in case. So they were able to let him go. Dumped him out of the van two days later in the same place they'd found him, and took off.

Man, they sure fucked that one up. And after all the trouble Dolly had gone to steal the necessary equipment from her boss.

The Pilford kid was still out there, with no idea how close he'd come to having to pay for what he'd done.

Cory felt committed to correcting his mistake.

They'd gotten it so right with Craig Pierce. Wow, had they ever. Man, when that dog made a meal of him, boy, *that* was something else. Dolly threw up, but Cory was blown away by what they'd accomplished. For a moment, he thought maybe they'd gone too far, that Pierce was actually dead, because that was not what he wanted. Cory believed, at least at the time, that it was better for bad people to endure their punishments.

So he chased off the dog and went back to see if Pierce had survived. The son of a bitch was still breathing, but Jesus, what a mess. And there was even a little something left behind, that must have fallen out of the dog's mouth. Cory had taken some pictures, but here was an actual souvenir. (He was proud of the fact that he'd never been a particularly squeamish kid.)

The real payoff had been the attention the deed gar-nered. Cory uploaded the pictures to Just Deserts, careful not to leave any digital trail that would lead back to him, with plenty of information about what Pierce had done. He thought very carefully about the words that would accompany the pictures, about how "revenj" had been exacted upon this disgusting pervert.

The website ran with it. Scores of other sites picked it up.

Seeing the response was without question the most exciting thing that had ever happened to Cory Calder. He sat on the website non-stop for several days, watching the fallout. First, the site tracked the number of visitors. There were thousands of them, and that didn't even count the other sites that carried the story.

And then there were the comments. Every few minutes, more people weighed in. Some thought that whoever'd done this to Craig Pierce, an act described as everything from despicable to worthy of a Nobel prize, should be prosecuted to the full extent of the law. Others lauded him, called him the best kind of vigilante, a hero who was stepping in to do what was right when the courts had failed to live up to their obligations.

One person went to so far as to compare him to Batman, even though Batman was not known particularly for using a dog to bite off a bad guy's junk.

Cory even went on the site himself and left a comment, saying that whoever this guy was, he was terrific.

When he was at home, up in his bedroom, his father down the hall, he had to keep a lid on his enthusiasm during his repeated checks of the site. But when he was at Dolly's place, he was uncontrolled in his excitement, letting out whoops of delight as he sat in front of her computer.

"Look at this!" he'd cry, calling her again and again to

look at the screen. "Look what they're saying!"

She wasn't always as excited about it as he was, and that troubled him some. But after all, he was the mastermind of this operation. It made sense that the enthusiasm levels were somewhat lopsided.

Even though his name never appeared—and a good thing too—he reveled in the attention. He wished there were some way to tell the world with impunity that he was the one responsible.

Very quickly, the online adulation became addictive. As the comments began to wane in the weeks following the attack on Craig Pierce, Cory became agitated and restless. He needed to keep the interest alive, to maintain the debate. Praise or condemnation, it didn't matter. What mattered was that the world was talking about *him*.

So he started to think about his next project.

How he wanted to rub the noses of his goddamn brother and his goddamn sister in it.

How Daddy loved them. So fucking proud.

There was Caitlin over in Europe, helping those people who'd fled Syria with little more than the clothes on their back, taking perilous boat journeys, half of them drowning. That little kid on the beach. One night, Cory and his father were watching CNN when a story came on about the refugees. They were literally walking out of the water, their boat having gone down about a hundred feet offshore, carrying babies in their arms, everyone crying and screaming. There were aid workers on the beach, waiting for them. Doctors and care workers and all that shit, and suddenly Alastair pointed to the screen and shouted, "It's Caitlin! Look, it's Caitlin! It's your sister!"

Yep. It was Caitlin. Running up to a man with a limp

little girl in his arms. She took the child away, worked frantically on her, getting air into her lungs, bringing her back to life.

His father didn't stop talking about it for days.

Then there was his brother, Miles, who at least didn't make it to CNN, but he was doing great work, oh yes he was. Big-shot scientist halfway around the world, finding ways to make seawater drinkable. Your basic save-the-world kind of thing. No biggie. Quoted in *Scientific American*, even the *New York Times* once or twice. A genius, they called him. Yeah, well, Cory could remember the time he locked the keys in his Infiniti with the engine running. Didn't seem like any great genius that day.

Well, you didn't need a medical degree or a PhD in whatever it was his brother had to make your mark in the world. There were other paths to greatness.

In many ways, Cory considered what he had been doing more noble, because it was anonymous. He wasn't on CNN. He wasn't getting quoted in the *New York Times*. He was working behind the scenes to effect change. Didn't that make it more genuine? More real?

Except there were times when he wondered, maybe he should just tell his father. "You think Miles and Caitlin are such hot shit? You see them putting themselves on the line the way I have? Running the kind of risks I'm running? I could go to *jail*. I could get sent away. You don't see them taking those kinds of chances."

So many times he'd wanted to say it. Not only so his father would stop thinking his so-called useless son wasn't so useless after all, but to see the expression on his face.

In the last twenty-four hours, Cory had had a feeling that was going to happen sooner or later. When his father came to see him at the police station with a lawyer in tow.

Cory had to admit things hadn't gone so well lately.

Not that there hadn't been some major successes. Finding Jeremy for one. He'd tracked him down, lost him, and found him again.

He'd picked him up leaving his great-aunt's house the night before, getting in that Honda with the old guy. It had been no trick figuring out he was at Madeline Plimpton's house. The whole world had worked that out. Little wonder the kid was hightailing it out of there.

Cory had followed them to some Promise Falls apartment over a bookstore. But then the old guy must have seen his van, because he came running out onto the street, heading their way.

"Oh shit, here he comes," Dolly'd said, and Cory had tromped on the accelerator.

By the time he'd come back, the Honda was gone.

Shit.

He'd lost him.

But overnight he checked the Just Deserts website, and some other similarly themed places on the Internet, and in came a reported sighting of Jeremy Pilford in Kingston, New York. Some couple had spotted him in a hotel lobby.

Once Cory had dealt with some other unexpected matters, he got in the van and drove to Kingston.

He searched the parking lot of the hotel where Pilford had been seen, but he could not find that Honda. Maybe, he thought, they'd realized they'd been spotted and gone elsewhere. He wandered the lots of other area hotels, and around five in the morning got lucky.

Now that he'd located them, what to do? Follow

them, he figured, and wait for an opportunity. But he had to admit to himself he had no plan. He was, to say the least, rattled by other events that night. In addition, he no longer had an assistant. But as he sat in that hotel parking lot, trying to formulate a strategy, something happened.

Some dumbass couple rammed a car while trying to snap a photo of Pilford. Cory knew that was going to draw the cops, so he took off. But he took a spot just down the street, and before long, an ambulance went past, followed by the Honda. The car was left a block away from the hospital, and it was at this point that Cory really caught a break.

It had been left unlocked.

This time, he'd come better prepared, and he only needed thirty seconds. He opened the driver's door, dropped down, his knees on the pavement, and reached under the front seat. Clipped the small mike and transmitter into place. Closed the door and got out of there.

All he had to do after that was listen.

Back in his car, he put on the earbuds that were attached to the phone-like device that carried the app that was linked to the bug that lay in the house that Jack built!

What an amazing world we live in!

He heard Pilford and the old guy—turned out his name was Weaver—talking about a lot of things, but the one really important thing he heard was their destination.

Cape Cod.

Big place to search, but then he heard Weaver repeat the address. North Shore Boulevard in East Sandwich.

Bingo.

He filled the tank up with gas and was on his way to Massachusetts before Pilford. That gave him time to check in with one of the local rental agencies and find himself a place to stay. A super-cheap cabin, about twenty by twenty feet, a quarter of a mile down the road from where Pilford and Weaver were staying. There was no water view—it was on the other side of the road from the beach houses. That was okay. He wasn't here to sightsee.

It was a neat little place. One room, basically, with a bathroom notched out of the corner. An aged, hulking refrigerator with sides thicker than a steel vault, a counter with a big porcelain sink, no cabinets under it, but a wooden shelf that held a few pots and pans. In one corner, an actual old woodstove with a pipe that led up through the roof. The folks who rented it out had left a small stack of wood alongside it, plus a wrought-iron stand that held a small shovel, tongs, a poker, and tiny broom.

Quaint.

But Cory didn't think it was cold enough to bother lighting a fire. As a backup, there was a small electric fan on the shelf he could plug in if he needed it.

Before he went to check out Cape Cod Bay, he parked his van behind the cottage. The back end was slightly visible to anyone driving by, but they'd really have to be looking for it.

Strolling along the beach, standing there with his toes in the sand, feeling the water rush in around his ankles, filling his lungs with the cool sea air was pretty damn nice.

And you met the most interesting people.

Now, back in the cabin, he had to think about how he was going to do this. There was a time when he believed that his subjects should live with their punishment, but his position on that was evolving.

He took a seat at the small table in the kitchen nook of the cabin and took out his cell phone. He'd powered it off hours ago. He didn't want to run the risk of using it to track Pilford, in case they were on to him, which he now understood was a real possibility.

Maybe just for a few seconds.

He turned on the phone and saw that he had a message. He put it to his ear and listened.

"Cory, it's your father. Call home immediately."

"Yeah, I don't think I'm going to do that," he said aloud. He deleted the message and powered the phone off once again.

"What do to, what to do, what to do," he said. "I don't suppose you have any bright ideas?"

Carol Beakman, unconscious and tied to one of the two single beds in the small room, did not.

FORTY-THREE

CAL

Back at the beach house, Jeremy and I resettled ourselves on the deck. Soon, we would have to start thinking about dinner, but there was still time to chill out. The only problem with that was that Jeremy was more than a little preoccupied by the discussion we'd had while walking along the beach.

"That was quick thinking, saying your name was Alan," I told him, looking out over the bay from my chair.

"Well, I'm not an idiot," he said.

I gave him a smile, but the young man did not return it.

"I've been giving what you said some thought," he said. "You know, about how I drove the car."

"Okay," I said.

"Maybe it's *because* I was drunk that I was able to drive it," he said.

"I'm not following."

"Like, okay, don't they say that if you fall down or something while you're sober, your muscles tense up, and you might actually break some bones. But if you're drunk, you're all kind of rubbery and you don't tense up, so you don't get hurt as bad."

"That sounds like a study funded by teenage boys," I said. "But carry on."

"So maybe I've always known in my head how to drive a stick shift, but when I tried it in your car I was so tense I did a really bad job of it, but because I was drunk, I was relaxed and did it just fine."

"That's quite a theory," I said.

"What do you think?" he asked.

"I don't know what to think."

"If you don't know what to think, why'd you have to bring it all up in the first place?"

I sighed. "It's kind of what I do."

"That's what bodyguards do? Mess with people's heads?"

"I'm not a bodyguard, Jeremy. I'm a detective."

"Well, you haven't really been doing any detecting. You've just been looking out for me and driving me all over the place. It's kind of like you're taking me on a vacation, is all."

"Thank you," I said. "I hope you'll give me a good review on TripAdvisor. I'm trying to up my five-star ratings."

"I'm just sayin', you're messing with my head with all these crazy questions, but you don't have any answers."

"I'm hoping maybe you do."

"Well I don't, okay?" Jeremy shook his head with disgust and frustration. I certainly felt the latter. The feeling was disrupted by the ringing of my cell phone, which I had left on the small table next to me. I snatched it up, looked at the caller.

"I'm gonna take this inside." I got out of the chair, slid open the sliding glass door, and took a seat on the couch. I put the phone to my ear. "Weaver."

"It's Bob."

Bob Butler.

"Hi, Bob."

"Glad I was able to catch you. I know you must be on the road somewhere."

"Yeah," I said. If he didn't know where I was, then Madeline Plimpton clearly had not told him. And I was even more certain that she had not told Jeremy's mother, Gloria.

"How's Jeremy?" Bob asked.

"He's good," I said. I thought back to when he was pounding his fist into his leg, how I'd wondered whether the kid needed some kind of help, but decided this was not the time to get into that. "How are things at your end? How's Gloria?"

"Well, she's Gloria. But she's okay."

"You're still at Madeline's, right?"

"That's right."

"What can I do for you, Bob?"

He hesitated a moment, then said, "I had the strangest call from Grant Finch."

"Okay."

"He said you called him speculating that maybe Jeremy wasn't driving the car that night."

"That's right," I said evenly.

"Like, tell me about that."

I told him, briefly, about our experiences in my Honda earlier that day.

"Jesus," Bob said. "I mean, I don't know what the hell to make of that."

"Grant was rather dismissive," I said. "But he clearly thought it was important enough to call and tell you."

"Well, yeah. And he was still a bit dismissive about it, but he thought we needed to know you'd raised the point. The thing is . . ." His voice trailed off.

"The thing is what?" I asked.

"I'm not as inclined to discount it the way Grant did."

"Okay."

"I mean, what do *you* make of it?"

"At the very least, I think it should have been mentioned at the trial. Would have raised some reasonable doubt."

"Reasonable doubt of what?"

Now it was my turn to hesitate. "Reasonable doubt about whether Jeremy was in the car to begin with."

"That's what I thought," Bob said. "But we were there, we saw him get out."

"But I haven't heard of anyone who saw him get in."

"God, Weaver, what are you saying?" When I didn't answer right away, he said, "Are you thinking someone could have put him in the car? That someone else took the car, hit that girl, and then put Jeremy behind the wheel?"

"It's one theory," I said evenly.

"Do you have another one?"

"Yes."

"What?"

"What do you know about Charlene Wilson?"

"Jeremy's friend?"

"That's right. She's made a point, twice, of seeing Jeremy in the last two days. I'm guessing she's kept in touch with him before that."

"Sure, yeah. They're pretty close friends."

"How close?"

"Uh, what are you asking?"

"Does Jeremy love her?"

"Love her?" Bob asked. "I mean, who knows what kinds of thoughts are swirling around in a boy's head?

I know he likes her. They've known each other a long time."

"Do you think he loves her enough to take the blame for something she did?"

"Christ, Weaver, what are you getting at?"

"Look, this is just a theory at the moment. Maybe Charlene wasn't driving that Porsche, but I'm as sure as I can be that Jeremy wasn't."

"This is . . . this is making my head spin."

"You were at the party. Do you remember seeing Charlene? Was she drinking, too?"

"I just . . . I just don't remember. I remember Alicia—that's her mother—being there, and her husband, too."

"The thing is, if Galen was dumb enough to leave that key in the car, even after the first time Jeremy tried to start it up, then anyone could have taken it. And whoever that was probably knows how Jeremy ended up behind the wheel."

"Honestly, I don't know what to do with this speculation. I don't know whether to tell Gloria. I think it would send her into a tailspin or something. But do you think, I mean, do you think there might be grounds for an appeal? That we could get this whole thing opened up again?"

"Did you ask Finch that question?"

"In a manner of speaking. But he said we as much as acknowledged Jeremy did it when we went with the defense that he didn't understand the consequences of his actions. So we wouldn't have much chance taking another run at it."

"He's the lawyer," I said. "He knows this stuff better than I do." I didn't know if it was my place to say what I was going to say next, but what the hell. "I'm not sure

Finch is acting in Jeremy's best interests. Maybe you need to find him a different lawyer."

Nothing at the other end of the call.

"Bob?" I said.

"Yeah, yeah, I'm here. God, what a fucking mess. Look, I want to talk to you more about this, at least before taking it to Gloria. Where are you?"

"Like you said, we're on the road." For all I knew, someone might be listening in to Bob's call, and I didn't want to give our location away. "But we might be back soon. Why don't we give it another day? Maybe we'll be back in Promise Falls by then."

"Okay, sure, that . . . that sounds good," Bob said. "What's Jeremy say about all this?"

"He's either entirely baffled or doing a good job pretending to be. But Bob, something is not right about this."

"I agree," he said. "Well . . . keep in touch."

"Sure thing."

Bob ended the call.

When I went back out to the deck, Jeremy asked, "Who was that?"

"Bob."

"You tell him your nutso theory?"

"What's to tell? Like you said, you must be the first person in history who mastered the art of shifting while impaired."

Jeremy nodded. "It's the only thing that makes sense."

FORTY-FOUR

Albert quickly wheeled his car into the driveway, bringing the nose to within an inch of the garage. It was a separate building at the back of the lot, large enough to hold two cars, with two doors.

He leapt from the car, engine running, and twisted the handle in the center of the right door. He hoisted it up, pushed it into the ceiling, then got back in behind the wheel and hit the gas. The car jumped so abruptly that he didn't have a chance to fully close his door before it hit the frame of the garage opening.

He slammed on the brakes, killed the engine, jumped out and brought the garage door back down. Then he leaned forward and placed his hands atop his knees, struggling to catch his breath.

From inside the car, he heard, "Uhhh."

Albert allowed himself three more deep breaths, then stood and opened the back door of the car. The backseat and floor were drenched in blood. Ron Frommer was on his stomach, his torso on the seat, left arm and leg dangling over the side. Although he was making some soft, guttural noises, he was not moving.

"What's going on?"

Albert whirled around. The side door to the garage had been opened and Constance was standing there.

"You drove in here like a madman," she said. "I was watching from the window. What the hell has gotten—"

"Shut up!" he screamed at her. "Shut the fuck up!"

Constance Gaffney shut up. In thirty-two years of marriage, she had never been spoken to that way by her husband. The words nearly knocked her off her feet.

"Close the goddamn door!" he bellowed.

"What . . . what have—"

"The door!" He was pointing.

She turned and shut the door. Then she took in the scene before her. The car with blood down the side. Her husband, covered in more of it.

And then the man in the backseat of Albert's car.

She opened her mouth as if to scream, but Albert closed the distance between them and clamped a hand over her mouth. He put an arm around her, allowing him enough leverage to hold his hand there and keep her quiet.

"Listen to me," he whispered. "You are not going to scream. You are not going to make a sound. Do you understand?"

Constance Gaffney's eyes looked as though they might pop out of her head and shoot across the room.

"Do you?" Albert asked again.

She managed to move her head up and down. Albert took his hand from her mouth and released his grip on her.

"Albert," she said softly, her lip quivering. "Albert, what's going on here?"

"He's the one!" he said, pointing at Frommer. "He's the one who beat up Brian. The son-of-a-bitch mother-fucking bastard. Him!" Starting to shake himself, he added, "And I bet he's the one who kidnapped Brian. He's the one who marked him up."

Albert put a shaky hand to his mouth, ran it over his chin.

"Has to be," he said. "He just . . . *has* to be."

Constance took a hesitant step forward, but she remained a good six feet from the car. She leaned her head to one side, trying to sneak a better look at the injured man.

"Uhhh," Frommer said.

"Who is he?" she asked.

"Frommer," Albert said. "Ron Frommer. He . . . he came at me. I think, I think he would have killed me. I did what I had to."

"For God's sake, he needs to get to the hospital," Constance said. "He looks like he might . . . Albert, he looks like he might—"

He turned on her, his eyes fierce. "I thought he was dead. I thought I'd killed him. But then . . . he made a noise . . ." He looked around the garage, first at the floor, which had a drain in the center of it, then over to the wall, at a coiled garden hose. He walked to the rear of the building, to a small workbench that sat next to a plastic utility sink. Below the bench were drawers and cupboards. Above, on a pegboard, various tools hung.

He began looking through the drawers.

"I might need bags," he said. "Thick ones."

Then he looked up at the pegboard. His eyes settled on a hacksaw. He grabbed it.

Constance said, "You're scaring me."

He shot her a look. "Really. Isn't that something." He changed his focus from the workbench back to the car. "I'll have to clean it down. The inside . . . that's going to be hard. The outside, that'll be easy. Your steam cleaner."

"What?"

"Listen to me, you fucking cow. *Listen to me.* I'm going to need your steam cleaner."

Constance took a step backward, toward the side door.

"And get me some clothes," Albert said.

"Clothes?"

He gestured to himself. "Look at me. I have to get out of these. I can't be seen like this. Shoes, too."

Constance stood there, dumbstruck.

"Now!" he shouted.

She fled the garage. In her haste, she did not close the side door. Albert went over and shut it, then turned back to look at the car.

He stood there for the better part of a minute, steeling himself. Finally, he walked over to the trunk and opened it. Picked up the crowbar he'd taken from Ron Frommer's truck. Felt its heft in his hand. Then he went around to the other side of the car and opened the back door.

Ron Frommer's head was directly in front of him.

Albert raised the crowbar over his head and brought it down.

Whack.

Again.

Whack.

Ron Frommer made no further sounds.

Albert staggered two steps back and rested his back against the garage wall.

"You hurt my boy," he said. "You did it. I know you did it. I *know* it was you."

He dropped the crowbar. It hit the cement floor with a loud, dead clang. Slowly, he regained control of his breathing, felt his heart rate getting back to something approaching normal. He felt oddly calm.

For the first time in perhaps his entire life, Albert Gaffney felt empowered.

He looked at the dead body of Ron Frommer and thought, *I did that. I actually did that.*

The door opened again. Constance entered carrying a bundle of clothing and a pair of running shoes. Slowly, he turned his head to look at her.

"Albert," she said softly. "Albert, you're smiling."

He said, "It's done."

She said nothing. She set the clothes and shoes on the workbench. "I got you some fresh boxers, too. I didn't . . . I didn't know if it had sunk through your pants."

Albert went back to the other side of the car, grabbed Frommer by the legs and dragged him out of the vehicle. Frommer's body slithered out, his arms stretched above him. When Albert let him fall to the concrete floor, Constance let out a small gasp.

Her husband took another moment to catch his breath. He looked down at the body for the better part of a minute, pondering how he was going to go about this.

"I heard something," Constance said.

Albert, who seemed to have drifted into some sort of trance, looked up. "What?"

Constance had walked to the garage door. There were two small, grime-covered windows at shoulder height in each of the two doors.

"Someone's here," she said. "There's a car stopped on the street."

Albert tried to swallow, but his throat was too dry. "Who? Is it Monica? Tell her to go somewhere, anywhere, just—"

"Not Monica," she said. "It's the policeman. The one with the funny name. Duckworth."

FORTY-FIVE

About half an hour earlier, Barry Duckworth had put
the jar containing what he presumed were Craig Pierce's
body parts into an evidence container, then gone out to
his car and placed it gingerly into the trunk. Then he
went back into the house.

Alastair Calder had been standing inside the front
door. When Duckworth returned, Alastair said, "My boy
is some kind of monster, isn't he?"

"I need a picture of him," Duckworth said.

"How could he have something like that under this
bed? How could he be doing whatever it is he's been
doing and I didn't know anything about it? Maybe . . .
maybe what's in that jar isn't what it looks like. It might
be from an animal or something."

"I need to find Cory as soon as possible," Duckworth
said. "Not just before he hurts anyone else, but before
anything happens to him. I think he's playing a very dangerous game right now."

"Dear God, this is beyond imagining."

"I know."

"I . . . I think maybe he needs help."

"That might be true. But right now, I need a picture
of your son."

"Um, let me see what I can find."

Alastair went into a room off the kitchen that featured
a large television, tucked into an entertainment unit, a
long, cushy couch and two reclining chairs. He opened

a door on the unit and brought out a large photo album.

"I have some in here," he said. He sat on the couch and placed the album on the coffee table, then opened the binder and pointed to a shot of a woman and three children sitting on the floor in front of a Christmas tree.

"This is from the early nineties, I think," he said. "This was my wife, and this is Cory, and this is his brother and his sister."

"He looks about nine or ten years old there," Duck-worth said.

"Yes, I believe so."

Duckworth said gently, "I need something more recent."

"Oh, of course, what was I thinking?" But Alastair had become fixated on the photo. He could not stop looking at it.

"Mr. Calder," Duckworth said.

Alastair turned and looked at him. "You never know what's coming. You see them when they're just children, and the world seems so open to them, so full of promise. Those are the days when you are allowed to dream." He grimaced. "And then as they get older, you see the potential they have. At times, it just seems limitless, that they can do anything. A little older yet and reality begins to set in. You see, instead of limitless potential, the limi-tations. That maybe they won't make of their lives what you might have hoped. I was lucky, I think. Two out of three isn't bad, right? But even with Cory, with a child that won't be reaching for the top rung of the ladder, you hope that while he might not make the world a better place, he won't make it worse."

"It's all a crap shoot," Duckworth said.

"We think we have this ability to control things,"

Alastair went on. "It's when we try to direct our children's lives that we realize how powerless we really are."

"A picture?" Duckworth reminded him.

Alastair sighed. "Let me see if I have anything on my phone. I can't remember the last time I printed out a picture or had one developed."

Duckworth followed him to the kitchen, where Alastair found his cell sitting next to the landline. He picked it up. "Give me a second."

He opened up the photo app and thumbed through some shots. "Here's one," he said. "I took Cory out for his birthday. We went to the Clover, the steak house. Cory likes beef. There he is."

He handed the phone to Duckworth. The picture showed Cory sitting, presumably across from his father, smiling at the camera, a waiter lingering in the background. But there was something odd about the shot. The smile seemed somehow empty, as though the facial muscles needed to make it were operating independently of any messages from the brain, or the heart. But it was a good enough picture for identification purposes.

"I'm going to email this to myself," Duckworth said.

Alastair nodded wearily. "I'll keep trying to reach him," he said.

"I can't expect you to do what I'm going to ask, but I'd rather you didn't tell him the police are looking for him. Just ask him to come home. And let me know if he does. I'd like the opportunity to speak with him before things get out of hand."

"I feel . . . as though I'm betraying him. But," and the man appeared to be struggling for the right words, "I feel he's betrayed all the love and commitment my wife and I showed him over the years."

"A couple of final things," Duckworth said.

Alastair gave him a look that suggested he wasn't sure he could take anything else.

"Yes?"

"What's Cory driving?"

"He has a van. A Sienna. It's black."

"Registered in your name or his?"

"Mine. It . . . it makes the insurance cheaper if it's under my name. Part of the family fleet, if you will."

"I can have it looked up, but do you know the license plate off hand?"

Alastair nodded and told him. Duckworth wrote it down in his notebook.

"Last thing, sir," Duckworth said. "Does Cory possess any firearms?"

"What? No, I'm not aware that he does."

"How about yourself?"

"I'm not a collector or anything like that. I don't care much for this country's obsession with guns. It's nothing short of madness."

Duckworth noted that the man had not said he didn't have one. "But?" he prompted.

Alastair sighed. "A few years ago, when my wife and I were advocating on behalf of an abortion clinic, we received some death threats. The police didn't believe they would be acted on, but they took them seriously just the same. It was a woman from the Promise Falls police. I think her name was Rhonda."

"Rhonda Finderman," Duckworth said. "She's the chief now."

"That's right. I saw her on TV—you, too—last year when all those people got poisoned. Thank God Cory and I were out of town at the time."

"What did Rhonda tell you?"

"She suggested I might want to get myself some protection."

"A gun."

He nodded solemnly. "I was reluctant at first, but one night there was a phone call, from an unknown number, and this man said that when they found me, what they would do to me would be slow and painful. It was very frightening. So I decided to take Rhonda's advice. I bought a gun. A revolver."

"Where do you keep it?"

"Locked up in my bedroom," he said. "At the time of the threats, I kept it next to my bed, by the lamp, so I could get it quickly if I needed it. But as time passed, and the threats stopped, I kept it locked up at all times. Still in the bedroom, but not immediately accessible."

"Can you show me?" Duckworth asked.

Alastair nodded and led the detective to the stairs, grabbing a set of keys from a decorative bowl on a table near the door along the way. When they got to the second floor, this time they went left instead of right.

"I hope I'm following rules regarding storage," he said. "I wouldn't want to get in any trouble."

"Don't worry," Duckworth said.

The bedside nightstand had a drawer across the top, and a cabinet door below. Alastair went down on one knee and, using one of the keys, unlocked the door.

"Here we go," he said, and Duckworth could hear the relief in his voice. He brought out a small case made of hard plastic and set it on the bed.

"This needs a key, too," he said. The key for the gun case was not on his chain, but tucked under some papers in the nightstand drawer. He lifted the case up onto its side, inserted the second key, and opened it.

The inside of the case was lined with soft gray foam. There was the slight impression of a gun in the foam, but no actual weapon.

"Oh no," Alastair said.

FORTY-SIX

Cory Calder looked at Carol Beakman, sleeping so peacefully—well, okay, drugged to the eyeballs was more accurate, but no need to nitpick—and wondered whether bringing her along was such a brilliant plan.

It had seemed like a good idea at the time.

It wasn't that he'd spared her life because she'd somehow touched his heart. It wasn't because she didn't deserve to die, although she certainly didn't.

Cory had seen her as insurance. And insurance was very much what he was going to need.

Thing were starting to fall apart, and fall apart very quickly. Cory saw Carol Beakman as leverage. A future ace in the hole, as it were. Something to trade if things went south. Well, not so much *if* they went south, as *when*.

Cory knew the clock was probably running out on him.

But despite that, he hadn't lost sight of his goal. That was what this had all been about from the very beginning. Making a difference. And he was goddamn well going to do that.

He had a feeling Jeremy Pilford would be his last stand. He'd made a great debut with Craig Pierce, and Pilford would be the closing number. A short but memorable career. Not that he wouldn't have liked it to be much longer, but once he was done with the Big Baby, it was a safe bet that everyone would know who he was. No more anonymity. No more solitary celebrations.

No longer would it just be his work that was famous. It would be *him*. Cory had no doubt of that. His exploits would spread far beyond websites like Just Deserts. He'd make the evening news. He'd be on CNN.

The world would know his name.

Did the world know his sister's name? Did the world know his brother's name? Fuck, no. They'd gone and devoted their lives to such *noble* causes, and what did they have to show for it, really?

Losers.

Even his parents, with all their advocacy work over the years, never achieved the kind of fame he was undoubtedly going to earn.

He just wanted to be able to enjoy it. And to enjoy it, he had to stay alive.

That was where Carol Beakman came in.

Cory could imagine any number of scenarios where he might need her. At some point, the police might corner him. Storm a building. Come in with guns blazing. That was how they operated. Shoot first, ask questions later. But they wouldn't want to do that if he had the woman with him. They'd have to be more careful.

She'd be his lifesaver when the going got tough. And what the hell, if it turned out he didn't need her, he'd dispose of her.

Like he did with Dolores.

But man, that did hurt. Cory had *loved* Dolores. Really, *really* loved her. She was his first real girlfriend, which was saying something for a guy in his thirties. Cory was not exactly the most popular student in high school. (Again, not like his siblings, who were getting laid practically out of kindergarten.) But Dolly and him, they'd really connected. How many girls were willing to come along to watch a dog make Alpo out of somebody? Plus, she was way more than a bystander. She was the one who got Pierce's attention out back of the pizza place where he worked, which allowed Cory to come up from behind, put the chloroform-soaked rag over his mouth. Dude powered down like a twenty-year-old laptop.

She'd helped him with Pierce, and she'd helped him with the other guy—only problem there was that it was the *wrong* guy. Dolly'd been idly going through Gaffney's wallet, and had pulled out his driver's license. Said: "Uh oh."

Cory'd never forget that *Uh oh*.

Well, he felt bad about it, too. The poor bastard didn't deserve what had happened to him. But it had happened in good faith. Cory honestly believed it was Jeremy Pilford they were marking up. His intentions were honorable. Sometimes there was collateral damage. Get over it. Move on.

Maybe that was the turning point for Dolly. Although, he had to admit, there were warning signs even before that.

Like that time Dolly asked whether they were just as bad as those they targeted. "Maybe someone else," she once said, "will come after us the way we went after the first guy."

She could never say a target's name out loud. Not Pierce's, not Gaffney's. Pilford, she could say his name, because they hadn't done him yet. But if they'd gotten him, she'd have had amnesia when it came to the guy's name. It was her way of distancing herself, tricking her mind into believing she wasn't involved. Cory, on the other hand, couldn't say Pierce's name enough, at least so long as no one other than Dolly was listening.

One time, she started talking about what the police would do to them if they got caught. What was it she'd said?

"You're the one they're really going to go after, once they know it was all your idea."

Yeah, that was it. What the fuck did that mean? Cory had a pretty good idea. Dolly was already thinking ahead. If they got picked up, she'd sell him out. Say she was coerced. Say she was scared to do anything but go along with what he wanted.

He loved her so much. Funny how one's feelings for someone could turn on a dime.

He'd started watching her more closely since the Gaffney fuckup. Tried to read between the lines of everything she said and did. There was definitely something wrong.

And then Carol Beakman showed up. At the door, for Christ's sake.

Maybe if she'd phoned Dolly on her cell, everything would have turned out differently. But Carol didn't have Dolly's cell phone number, and when she tried to call her on the landline at her parents' house, she'd found it disconnected.

So she drove to the house, came to the door, and that was really when everything started to go to shit.

He and Dolly had been sitting in the kitchen. She'd fried him up a couple of sausages on top of the stove, was about to put them into buns, when there was a rapping at the front door. Cory could see the instant panic in her eyes. *This was it!* They'd come for them. She'd put the pan back on the burner, didn't even think to turn off the gas before she went to see who it was. Cory turned off the stove, and by the time he'd joined Dolly, the door was open, and he could see that it was not the fucking FBI or Starsky and Hutch or even Dudley Do-Right of the Mounties.

It was that woman Dolly had talked to just as they were nabbing Brian Gaffney, who was supposed to be Jeremy Pilford, but you couldn't dwell on these things forever.

Anyway, now here she was again.

She was so sorry to bother them, she said. But there was this situation that had come up, something about her boyfriend and the fact that his father was a cop, and the way she rambled on, it was hard to make any sense of what she was saying.

But then she said something that really caught Cory's attention.

Right about the time that they ran into each other outside Knight's, a man had been kidnapped and held captive and his body tattooed. Just a horrible thing. Carol and her boyfriend had been seen on the bar's video, which led the police to them. Carol hadn't given the police Dolly's name, but the more she considered it, the more she thought she should get in touch with Dolly in case she had any information that might help the cops.

"It was just unbelievable," Carol said. "I saw a picture. What was done to this guy, it was horrific."

Cory thought it could have been handled so well. All Dolly had to say was, *Gee, thanks for telling us, but we didn't see a thing, did we, Cory?*

But *no*.

She looked at Cory, her lip all quivery. Said something like *Oh my God oh my God oh my God*.

Or words to that effect. She totally lost it.

"We're fucked!" she said. "They're going to find us!"

Cory had tried to laugh it off. Told this Carol Beak-man that Dolly was just messin' with her. But Dolly wouldn't calm down, and Cory could see Carol had to be thinking, holy shit, what did I just walk into here?

So she started to leave.

Which didn't strike Cory as a very good idea. Hold on, he said to her. There's been a misunderstanding. Let's try to sort this all out.

But Carol was already heading to her car. Cory was about to shoot out the door after her, but not before telling Dolly to get a grip, look what she'd done.

Dolly'd screamed, "It's over! I can't do this shit any more. I can't, I can't! You're crazy, that's what you are! You're a fucking psycho!"

Cory found his hands around her neck. He pushed her up against the wall and squeezed with everything he had. She put up a good fight, he had to give her that. Kicked and flailed about, but he didn't let go, didn't stop squeezing. Not until she slid down the wall and crumpled into a heap on the floor.

But that still left Carol Beakman.

He charged out the door. Incredibly, she was still there. In her rush to escape, she'd fumbled with her purse and dropped it next to her car. She was on her knees, scrabbling through the contents that had spilled out, searching frantically for her keys.

Cory kicked her in the head.

That was all it took. Carol's head bounced up against the fender of the Toyota, and then she slid to the ground. Cory picked her up and carried her into the barn. Secured her to the metal cot where he had performed his artistry on Brian Gaffney.

He had mixed feelings, at first, at discovering she

376

was still alive. But he soon saw the advantages of keeping her that way. He actually thought maybe Dolly had been right, that the police could be getting close, and if that was the case, Carol Beakman might be useful.

Now, sitting in this tiny cabin in Cape Cod, he realized he should have taken more time to think through all the other aspects of his predicament.

His first thought had been to get rid of Dolly, and Carol Beakman's car. He put Dolly into the trunk of the Toyota, then drove his van to within a mile of the industrial park where he intended to leave the car. After hoofing it back to the nearest bus line to downtown Promise Falls, he got a cab to drop him half a mile from Dolly's place. More hoofing. Then he drove Carol's car to the tile place, hours before they opened, and left the vehicle out back by a Dumpster.

He walked back to his own vehicle from there and, after doing some online research to check on the latest Pilford sightings, headed for Kingston.

And from there, the Cape.

But not before loading a thoroughly drugged Carol Beakman into the back of the van.

One did not abandon the mission because of a few setbacks.

So now here he was, in East Sandwich, only a few beach houses away from Jeremy and that bodyguard of his.

It was time to get this done.

Cory's regret was that this time there would be less artistry. Craig Pierce's fate had had a certain sense of style to it. And the work he'd mistakenly done on Brian Gaffney was to have been Jeremy Pilford's fate. If they hadn't fucked things up, it would have been a fitting punishment.

But Cory wasn't going to leave that kind of mark on Jeremy now. First of all, it wasn't feasible in these new circumstances. Not here, not with that old guy hanging around him. Besides, the whole tattoo thing seemed old hat now.

This time, he had to be pragmatic. Do what had to be done. Which was exactly why he'd brought along his father's Smith & Wesson. That dandy little revolver he kept locked away next to his bed.

The funny thing was, it wasn't as though Cory had taken it today. He'd used his father's key to unlock the cabinet, then used the second key from the drawer to unlock the case, months ago.

He had just never needed it until now.

He could have done it on the beach when he ran into Pilford and his friend. He'd had the gun on him at the time. Could have whipped it out. *Bam. Bam.* All done. But right in the open, in broad daylight, it felt too risky. There was that older couple way up the beach. They might have heard the shots, despite the sound of the waves crashing into shore.

But now it was nearly dark.

The conditions were right.

FORTY-SEVEN

Duckworth gave Alastair Calder his card and returned to his car. He keyed the engine, but before driving away he called the station to confirm that they had the emailed photo of Cory Calder. Once that was done, he gave instructions that the entire state, not just Promise Falls, needed to be on the lookout for him. He provided a description of the van, and added a warning.

"Calder is wanted in connection with a homicide investigation. He should be approached with extreme caution. He may be armed."

Then he raised another matter he had not forgotten about. "Calder's also wanted for questioning in the disappearance of Carol Beakman."

He put the phone away and put the car in drive. Next stop: Madeline Plimpton's house.

He was confident in his assumption that Brian Gaffney had been mistaken for Jeremy Pilford, that the message inscribed on his back was meant for the so-called Big Baby. "Sean," Duckworth believed, was supposed to be "Sian."

Once he'd learned Pilford was staying at the Plimpton house in Promise Falls—that there had been a protest there since his arrival—he knew he was on to something. He could feel it. Not only was the young man at risk, so was everyone else in the Plimpton house.

And maybe not just from Cory Calder.

He did a quick check to confirm the address, and

ten minutes later was pulling into the driveway. He'd been past this house many times, and he certainly knew Madeline Plimpton. He had met her frequently in the past twenty years, when she was still publisher of the now dead *Promise Falls Standard*, and her profile in the community was much higher than it was now. Duckworth wondered how one dealt with having presided over a mini-empire for decades, only to see it wither and die.

As he rang the bell, he noticed the plywood nailed over one of the two windows that flanked the door. He spotted part of a gray-haired head through the undamaged pane, and then the door opened.

Madeline Plimpton said, "Yes?" And then, "Oh."

"Ms. Plimpton," Duckworth said. "I don't know if you remember me, but I'm Detective Barry—"

"I know exactly who you are," she said, and reached out and took his hand in hers. "What a pleasure to see you, Detective Duckworth. What can I do for you?"

"It's more like what I can do for you," he said, and nodded at the boarded-up window. "You've had some trouble here."

The woman smiled wryly. "Yes, we have. But surely they don't have you on broken window duty."

It was his turn to smile. "No. I understand you have a guest. Jeremy Pilford."

She sighed. "I'm afraid my grand-nephew is not here right now." A weariness infused her voice. "But come in and meet his mother, and her partner."

He followed her into the house, through the kitchen, and out to the screened-in porch at the back of the house that was filled with generously cushioned wicker furniture. Madeline appeared surprised to find no one there.

"Oh," she said. "Where have they gone?" She gazed

out into the backyard, where a man and a woman were standing face to face, talking heatedly. "Oh, of course, they're arguing."

They went outside, crossed the yard. The couple cut their discussion short and turned to take in Madeline and this new visitor.

"Gloria, Bob, this is Detective Duckworth, with the Promise Falls Police."

He offered a hand and they each took it, hesitantly.

"Have you caught the asshole who broke Madeline's window?" Bob asked sharply.

Duckworth shook his head. "That was from the protest last night?"

"No," Madeline said. "Someone threw a rock through the window earlier in the day. The protest was later. At least the police were here for that. No one got close to the house."

"You can't believe what we've been through," Gloria said.

"Why are you here?" Bob asked.

"I came to speak to your son," Duckworth said to Gloria. "About his safety."

"He's not here," Gloria said.

"I told him that," Madeline said.

Gloria continued, "We all know about his safety concerns. The whole Internet wants to hurt him."

"I'm here about a very specific threat," the detective said.

Everyone's eyebrows went up a notch.

"Does the name Cory Calder mean anything to anyone here?"

They exchanged looks, shook their heads. "It doesn't ring a bell," Gloria said.

"So you haven't noticed a comment online, for example, from someone with that name? No emails from someone like that?"

Bob said, "There have been so many hateful comments online, yeah, he might be there, but you're talking hundreds, God, thousands, of people who've put in their two cents' worth about Jeremy's trial. It's the proverbial needle in a haystack."

Duckworth nodded. "Sure, I get that."

"What kind of threat is this?" Madeline asked.

"There was an incident. Someone got hurt. It was mistaken identity. I think Jeremy was the intended target."

"What?" Gloria asked. "What happened?"

Duckworth said, "What's important right now is your son's safety. Where is he? When's he coming back?"

"I don't know," Gloria said.

Duckworth was unable to conceal his sense of alarm. "What? You don't know where he is?"

"It's not like that," Bob said. "He's being protected."

"Protected how?"

Madeline said, "We hired someone. It wasn't safe for Jeremy here. We're quite confident that he's in good hands."

"Where? With whom?"

Bob said, "We don't know where. That was the whole idea. That his location be kept secret. Even we're in the dark."

"I hate it," Gloria said. "Not knowing where my boy is. I can't help thinking that letting him go with Mr. Weaver was a bad idea."

"Wait," Duckworth said. "Weaver? Cal Weaver?"

"That's right," Madeline Plimpton said. "Don't tell me we've made a terrible mistake."

He shook his head. "No, not at all. Cal's a good man. I know him. If Jeremy's with him, I'm sure he's being well looked after."

There was a collective sigh. "Well, thank God for that," Madeline said.

"But I'd still like to know where they are. I need to tell Mr. Weaver what I've learned."

Bob and Gloria shrugged. But Madeline's lips went in and out, as though she were debating whether to reveal something.

"What is it?" Duckworth asked.

"I know where they are," she said.

Bob's eyes widened. Gloria said, "You knew and didn't tell us?"

"For God's sake, Gloria, the last person I wanted to tell was you," Madeline said.

"Go to hell," her niece snapped back.

Bob said, "Madeline, whatever you've been keeping from us, it's got to be safe to tell the detective here. And I'll make sure Gloria keeps a lid on things."

"You talk about me like I'm a child," Gloria said. She said to Duckworth, "They took away my phone."

"And then you stole it back," Bob said, "and gave it to Jeremy. Look how that turned out."

Duckworth looked at Madeline. "Should we go someplace and talk?"

"No, it's fine. They're at my place."

"Your place?" Duckworth said.

"Oh for God's sake, they're in the Cape," Gloria said. "Why didn't I think of that? I'd forgotten you even had that house. It's not like we've been invited there in years."

"Cape Cod?" Duckworth asked.

Madeline nodded. "A beach house. I haven't been there in a long time. A property management company looks after it for me."

Duckworth got out his notepad. "Address?"

Madeline gave it to him.

"Is there a phone there?"

"No, but I have a cell phone number for Mr. Weaver."

"Okay, good." Duckworth looked at Gloria. "I trust you'll have no problem with my speaking to your son?"

"No, of course not," Gloria said. "Just don't upset him."

Duckworth smiled. "If he's with Cal Weaver, I don't imagine there's all that much to worry about. And as you say, no one knows they're there."

FORTY-EIGHT

CAL

"Give me some names," I said to Jeremy.

"What names?"

We were sitting in the upstairs living room, gazing out over the bay as the sun started going down. The clouds were streaked with orange and yellow. Another tanker ship could be seen near the horizon.

"People at the party," I said. "The night it happened."

"I don't know. Lots of people."

"Think."

"Why do you want to know?"

"I might want to talk to some of them."

"What for?" he asked.

I sighed. "I have some questions."

"You're going to stir things up," he said.

"What do you mean?"

Jeremy frowned. "I don't know. You're going to cause all kinds of trouble if you start asking people things."

"Don't you want to know what happened?"

"I know what happened. I ran over Sian McFadden and killed her. I don't know how I did it. But I did. You're making me crazy."

"Sorry," I said.

He shook his head. "We should watch some TV or something. Or go somewhere. Go to a movie maybe. This place is pretty and all but it gets boring real fast.

There's sand, and there's water, and that's about it."

I pointed to the remote on the coffee table. "See what's on."

He snatched it up and pointed it at the TV. I hadn't seen a non–flat screen in some time. This one was about a thirty-six-incher, which made it nearly two feet deep.

"That thing must weigh five thousand pounds," Jeremy said. "It's not HD or anything." He paused. "Do you think they'd have had TV in prison?"

"In your own cell?"

"Yeah."

"I don't know. Was that the thing that scared you most about going to jail?"

"God, no," he said. "I figured I'd get killed there. Or worse."

"Something worse than being killed?"

"I've seen movies and stuff. About guys being raped and everything. There were nights, during the trial, I couldn't sleep at all. I couldn't stop thinking what they'd do to a kid like me."

"It can be bad," I said.

"That's why I don't want you messing around with this. If you start stirring up shit, they might reopen the whole case, and this time they'll send me away for real."

I saw that fear again in his eyes. I decided maybe I should lay off this for a while. I pointed at the TV. "See what's on."

All that came up on the TV was static.

"Aw, man," Jeremy said. He started flipping through channels, but they were all the same.

"I guess Madeline didn't pay the cable bill," I said. "Maybe she doesn't hook it up until the busy season."

"Can we go out or something? What if we drove into

town and got some ice cream? I saw a place when we went for groceries."

I thought about it. As pretty as this place was, I did feel like a change of scenery. "What the hell, let's do that. I wouldn't mind hitting a bakery, if there's one open. They've got these things called whoopie pies."

"Whoopie pies?"

"They kind of look like a hamburger, but the bun part's chocolate cake, with whipped cream in the middle."

"I want ice cream," Jeremy said.

I nodded. "Meet me at the car in three minutes."

I hit the bathroom, grabbed my jacket, made sure I had some cash and my car keys—I thought of something my late father used to say when he was heading out: "Spectacles, testicles, wallet and keys"—and went outside, where I found Jeremy standing next to the Honda. I locked up the beach house, got in behind the wheel and said, "Shit, I forgot my phone."

"Oh yeah, so I'm not even allowed to have one, but you can't go five minutes without yours." Jeremy pointed a finger at me. "You've got a problem. You know that? You can't deal with your problem until you admit you've got one."

I grinned. "Shut up."

"You're just mad 'cause I'm right."

"Fine," I said. "I can quit any time I want."

"Oh yeah, I've heard that one. That's what my mom says about booze."

It was meant to be funny, but he suddenly went very quiet.

"The hell with the phone," I said. "How long does it take to get ice cream? Someone wants to reach me, they can leave a message."

"That came out wrong," he said as I backed the car down the narrow driveway. "About my mom."

"It's okay," I said.

"I mean, she's kind of messed up, but I love her," he said.

"Sure," I said. "Everyone loves their mom."

FORTY-NINE

Once Barry Duckworth was behind the wheel, he got out his phone. Cal Weaver was already in his list of contacts. He brought up the number and tapped it. The phone rang eight times before going to voicemail.

"Cal, it's Barry," Duckworth said. "I've just been at the Plimpton house and know Jeremy Pilford is in your care, which is a good thing, but there's something you need to know. Despite all the various threats made against the kid, I think there's one very credible one. A guy named Cory Calder. He could be armed. The guy's a whackjob, Cal, and you need to take this one seriously. I don't have any reason to believe he knows where you are—Ms. Plimpton filled me in, by the way—but you need to be on guard just the same. Call when you get this, and in the meantime, I'll send you a picture of this guy in case you should happen to run into him. Take it easy."

As he drove away from the Plimpton house, Duckworth realized he was only a mile from Brian Gaffney's parents' place. He wanted to see how Brian was doing. The young man might have been released from hospital and gone to stay with his family for a while, which would give Duckworth a chance to ask him whether the name Cory Calder was familiar to him. He had his doubts that it would, but it was still worth posing the question.

As he pulled up in front of the Gaffneys' house, his gaze went to the opposite side of the street. A rental cube van was backed up to the open garage of Eleanor Beecham's place. The front door was propped open with a stick.

A short, heavyset guy with curly hair who Duckworth did not recognize came out holding a chair from a kitchen dinette set. He put it in the back of the van, and as he re-emerged, Harvey Spratt, the man Duckworth had spoken to the previous day, exchanged a few words with him.

Maybe there was time for another quick chat with the folks looking after Mrs. Beecham. Norma, in particular. Duckworth had what he would call a lot of balls in the air right now—a tattooed man, a murder, a missing woman, an Internet target—so he didn't really have time for this, but since he was here, he decided to follow up on what had been bothering him since his first visit.

He got out of the car and approached the house. Harvey spotted him and said, "Back again?"

Duckworth nodded amiably. "That I am."

"We're kind of busy at the moment," Harvey said as the man helping him stopped to see who he was talking to.

"Just like to talk to Norma a minute," Duckworth said.

"Well, she's pretty busy too."

Duckworth stood there. "I'll wait while you get her."

Harvey mumbled something under his breath, then poked his head into the house. "Norma!"

From inside, "What?"

"Get out here!"

"What is it?"

"That policeman's here again."

Silence.

Then Duckworth heard someone stomping through the house, and seconds later, Norma was at the door.

"What's going on?" she asked.

"Good day, Ms. Lastman," he said. "Do I have that right?"

Norma's right cheek twitched. "You can call me Norma."

"But your last name is Lastman? That's what you told me the first time I was here. That's what Eleanor—Mrs. Beecham—said your name was, too."

"Yup, that's right," she said, stepping out of the house and onto the lawn.

"She was telling me," Duckworth said, "that after you'd been working here a while, you discovered that the two of you are actually related to each other. That she's your aunt."

Norma nodded slowly. "She said that?"

"Yes, she did."

"Well, yeah, we did find out there was a connection." She smiled nervously.

"She said your father was her brother. What was his name?"

Norma didn't answer immediately. Duckworth could almost see the wheels turning. "It was Sean," she said. "Sean Lastman. But I never really knew him."

"That's quite something," Duckworth mused. "Must have brought you closer together. I mean, you weren't just employee and employer any more. You were niece and aunt."

"You could say that," Norma agreed.

Duckworth asked, "You ever been married, Norma?"

"Sorry?"

"I said, have you ever been married?"

"No. Me and Harvey, we're probably going to get married."

Harvey, coming out of the house carrying a couch with the other man's help, smiled in their direction.

"Soon!" he said.

"Harvey doesn't like to rush into anything," Norma said, laughing and shaking her head.

"Yeah, some men are like that," Duckworth said. He tipped his head toward the van parked in the driveway. "That's yours, right?"

"Hmm?"

"Not the big rental, the regular van. Harvey said yesterday that it's yours."

She nodded. "Yeah, it's mine."

"What's funny," Duckworth said, "is that I ran the plate to see who it was registered to, and you know what name came up?"

Norma said nothing.

"Norma Howton. So what I'm wondering is, if you were born Norma Lastman, and you've never been married, why's your van registered in the name Norma Howton?"

Norma struggled with a response. "Um, maybe you called it in wrong. There could be a mistake."

"I don't think so."

Harvey emerged from the big cube van. "What was that?"

"Just asking your girlfriend if her last name is Lastman or Howton," Duckworth said.

Harvey and Norma exchanged a nervous look.

"Tell you what," Duckworth said. "Why don't you see if you can come up with an answer while I go across the street and talk to those folks? When I come back, we'll see what you've thought up. And then we can also talk about what appears to be going on here."

"What would that be?" Harvey asked.

"Charming an old lady out of her money and possessions," Duckworth said. "Maybe you can work on that story, too." He smiled. "Be back in a bit."

He headed back across the street. As he started up the driveway to the Gaffney house, Constance Gaffney emerged, grim-faced, from a side door of the garage behind the house.

"Hello, Detective," she said, trying to break into a welcoming smile.

He tipped his head. "Mrs. Gaffney."

"Brian's not here," she said quickly. "My husband's not here, either. Sorry. Do you want to come back later?"

"Where's Brian?" he asked.

"He's back in the hospital," she said.

"Back?" Duckworth asked. "You mean he was discharged, but he was readmitted?"

She blinked. "Um, he left yesterday. Like, on his own. He just walked out. He shouldn't have, but he did. And then he got hurt, so—"

"Brian got hurt?"

Constance Gaffney opened her mouth as if to say something, but nothing came out.

"Mrs. Gaffney? You said Brian got hurt."

"It was nothing. I just meant, his back hurts. You know, from all the needles or whatever went into it."

"It sounded like you were going to say he got hurt when he left the hospital."

"No," she said, shaking her head furiously. "No, no. I meant he was hurting himself by leaving the hospital."

Duckworth nodded slowly. He was thinking he didn't

need to have been a cop for as long as he had to spot when someone was lying. A patrolman his first day on the job could see that Constance Gaffney wasn't telling the truth.

"I guess I'll drop by the hospital, then," he said.

"Okay," she said.

"Though I might as well ask you what I was going to ask him," he added.

"I'm sure I won't know," Constance said.

"You might want to wait until I've asked the question."

"Well, yes, okay. What is it?"

"You ever heard the name Cory Calder?"

"Cory who?"

"Calder."

"Who's that?"

"Do you recognize the name?"

She shook her head slowly. "No, I don't. Should I?"

"Not necessarily," he said.

"Who is he?"

"I'd really like to ask your husband if he's heard of him."

"Well, if I haven't heard of him, I'm sure my husband hasn't."

That prompted a grin from Duckworth. "You're sort of mentally connected, are you?"

She laughed nervously. "No, but I'm pretty sure he wouldn't know who he is."

"Mrs. Gaffney, are you okay?"

"Am I okay?"

Duckworth nodded.

"Of course I'm not okay," she said, suddenly indignant. "How could I be okay when Brian is in the hospital, when someone has done something so horrible to him? How could anyone be okay at a time like this? And how are we going to get that mess off his back? I've heard they can remove those things, but it must be awfully painful. They use lasers or something. I was looking it up on the Internet. It's horrible, just horrible."

She stopped abruptly, as though something had just occurred to her.

"What was the name again?"

"Cory Calder."

"Do you—are you thinking he's the man who did it?"

"We want to talk to him," Duckworth said.

"What does that mean? Does that mean you suspect him? Is that what that means?"

"He's what we would call a person of interest."

Constance's hands were shaking. She linked them together to make them stop. "Are you sure there wasn't another name? Another person of interest?"

"That's the only name I have at the moment. Why? Were you expecting me to mention someone else?"

"No!" she said. "Why would I? It's just, this person of interest, as you call him, he might not have acted alone. He might have had help."

"That's possible. As I said, I'd like to bounce that name off your husband, too," Duckworth said.

"I told you, he's not here."

"Does he carry a phone?"

"Why don't I ask him about this Cal Colby when he gets home, and if he recognizes the name, I'll have him call you."

"Cory Calder," Duckworth said. "Not Cal Colby."

A nervous titter escaped her lips. "Right." She was looking over Duckworth's shoulder at the house opposite.

"I guess Mrs. Beecham's moving out," she said. "Maybe she's going into a nursing home."

"I wonder," Duckworth said. He was about to turn and look across the street when something else caught his eye.

"Mrs. Gaffney, are you sure your husband isn't home?"

"Hmm?"

"I thought I saw someone in that window." He pointed to one of the small, square windows set into the garage door.

"I don't think so," she said. "I was just in there. I took out the trash." She forced a laugh. "I think if he'd been in there I would have seen him. Soon as I go into the house, I'll call him, find out where he is, and have him call you. Would that be okay?"

Duckworth said slowly, "I guess that would be fine, Mrs. Gaffney. I appreciate your—"

That was when they both heard the shrieking. Not from the garage, but from across the street. Eleanor Beecham, struggling to support herself in the doorway of her home, was crying, "No! No! What are you doing? Stop it! Stop it!"

Harvey Spratt and the other man emerged from the back of the van, heading back to the house. Mrs. Beecham had both hands on one side of the doorframe, but it wasn't enough to keep her from sliding down. Norma appeared behind her.

Duckworth said, "Shit." He glanced both ways before running across the street, reaching into his jacket for his phone along the way.

When Harvey saw the detective, he went slack-jawed. He said something to the other man that Duckworth couldn't hear. Norma was struggling to get the woman to her feet, saying, "For God's sake, Mrs. Beecham, didn't I tell you to stay downstairs?"

Duckworth, panting, said into his phone, "It's Detective Duckworth, Promise Falls Police. I need an ambulance." He barked out the address, resisted any further questions, and was slipping the phone back into his pocket as he reached the front door.

"Mrs. Beecham," he said.

"She's fine!" Norma said, pulling the elderly woman to her feet, holding her under the arms. "There's nothing going on here!"

"Who's that?" the old woman asked, pointing a leathery finger at the man who'd been helping Harvey load furniture.

The man said, "Hey, I'm just buyin' some stuff."

Duckworth said to Mrs. Beecham, "Did you give these people permission to sell your things?"

"No! I heard all this racket and I climbed up the stairs and everything's gone!"

"She doesn't understand," Norma said.

"Why don't you explain it to me?" Duckworth asked her.

"We're helping her," the woman insisted. "We're getting her ready."

"Ready for what?"

Norma ran her tongue over her lip. "To go to the facility."

"What facility?" the old woman asked.

"Yeah, what facility?" Duckworth echoed.

"It's in Albany," Norma said. "Pine Acres."

"Show me the paperwork."

"Paperwork?"

"Give me a name," Duckworth said. "Whoever does

the admissions." When Norma hesitated, he said, "Okay, I see what's going on here."

"Can I load this stuff or what?" the man asked.

Duckworth said to him, "What'd you pay for all these things you're taking?"

"Two grand," he said.

Duckworth said to Harvey, "Give him his money back."

"No way," Harvey said. "You got no business interfering in a private transaction."

"Show me something," Duckworth said. "Emails, paperwork, anything that proves that Mrs. Beecham is moving to a seniors' residence, and that someone here has been given legal permission to act on her behalf. Do you have a power of attorney for her?"

Norma and Harvey exchanged looks. Norma said, "I'm sure we have that somewhere. Tell the man, Mrs. Beecham. Tell them we're helping you. But first, let's get you off your feet."

She helped the old woman back into the house, but once inside, there was no place to sit. The living room had been cleared of furniture, marks on the faded carpet indicating where the couch and chairs and coffee table had once been. Norma led Mrs. Beecham to the stairs that climbed to the upper level and got her settled on the second step.

In the distance, a siren wailed.

"I don't understand," Mrs. Beecham said. From her perch on the stairs, she looked into the living room. "Where's the sofa?"

"We can get those documents you want," Harvey said to Duckworth. "It just might take a day or two. Give me a card and we'll be in touch."

Duckworth said, "Mrs. Beecham, I have some people coming to check you out. That's the first thing we want to do, is make sure you're okay. Then we want to sort out what's going on here."

"Did you hear what I said?" Harvey asked. He was standing right next to Duckworth now, crowding him as he spoke with Eleanor Beecham.

"Stand over there, sir," Duckworth said.

"I'm asking, did you hear me?"

"And I said, stand over there."

"You give us a couple days to get the paperwork you want."

Duckworth viewed him with undisguised annoyance. "Why don't we just phone Pine Acres right now and confirm what you're saying? How about that?"

Norma and Harvey exchanged looks once again, but this time there was a higher level of concern.

"I don't know if there's anyone there today," Norma said.

"Why? It's not a weekend."

The siren grew louder.

When Duckworth returned his attention to the old woman, Harvey reached out and grabbed him by the elbow. Duckworth turned suddenly, shook off Harvey's hand, and pointed a finger in the man's face.

"Sir! Do not touch me. I'm warning you, if you touch me again, I'll place you under arrest."

"This is bullshit," said Norma, who was behind Duckworth. Without warning, she extended her arms, placed her palms on the detective, and gave him a forceful shove. He stumbled forward into Harvey, who shoved him back in the other direction. Duckworth feared he was going to fall right onto Eleanor Beecham and injure her—he might have lost *some* weight, but he was still a pretty heavy guy—so he tried to pivot in mid-fall. He landed hard on the step next to her.

Harvey's face flushed red. He brought back a leg to kick the detective, but Duckworth shifted quickly and Harvey's shoe connected with the stairs.

"Stop it!" Mrs. Beecham screamed.

Harvey decided another kick was not the way to go. He formed a fist and swung at Duckworth, connecting with his chest as the detective attempted to get back up. He was thrown back onto the stairs again.

Duckworth pulled back his jacket and reached for the gun holstered at his side. The last thing he wanted to do was discharge his weapon in the close quarters of this house. Harvey was causing him a lot of grief, but he was not armed. But Duckworth believed he needed the persuasion that his gun would provide to get things under control.

As he was about to draw his weapon, however, the odds got a little more even.

Albert Gaffney, dressed casually in a pair of sweatpants and a T-shirt, had run into the house. He charged Harvey from behind and threw him into a wall, hard enough that the man's head dented the drywall.

Harvey went down like a rag doll.

He put a hand to his head. "Son of a bitch!"

Albert looked at a somewhat stunned Duckworth and extended a hand to help him to his feet.

"Constance said you had something you wanted to ask me," he said.

FIFTY

CAL

If I'd known we were going to end up at the movies, I'd have gone back into the beach house for my cell. It was a long time to be without a phone.

After heading into Sandwich for some ice cream, Jeremy continued to complain about the cable not working at Madeline's place. I grabbed a discarded newspaper on a nearby table and found an ad for a Cape Cod movie complex. The seven o'clock shows were already under way, but we could hit one that started after nine. I handed the paper to Jeremy—he was working on a banana split with enough whipped cream to bury a Volkswagen—and asked him if any of the shows interested him.

He pointed. "That one."

It was some superhero thing. When I was a kid, the only costumed crime-fighters on my radar were Batman, Superman and Spider-Man. I knew there were more, but they were the only ones I cared about. These days, though, there were so many, it was a wonder there was enough evil in the world to keep them all occupied.

"Yeah, sure," I said.

"What if someone recognizes me?" he asked. "Like at the hotel?"

When we got back to the car, I gave him the Blue Jays baseball cap he'd worn in the grocery store and told him to keep it pulled down hard until we found our seats and they killed the lights. That seemed to do the trick. No one gave us a second look.

On the way to the theater, Jeremy said, "I could probably come up with a list."

"Huh?"

"Of people at the party. People you could talk to."

"Okay," I said.

"But I don't know what the point is."

"Let me worry about that."

"I mean, it's not really your job, anyway."

"I'm an investigator. I investigate."

"It's not what you were hired to do. Don't expect my mom or Bob or anyone to pay you for doing something extra. Especially Bob. He's all business. Everything done by the book. They'll say you're trying to pad the bill."

"I'm not charging them anything extra," I said.

"I'm giving you a heads-up. They'll be pissed."

Maybe he was right. Maybe this wasn't my concern. I'd been hired to look after him, plain and simple. I hadn't been hired by the defense.

But I couldn't help but feel bad for the kid. Outside of his family and Bob, I thought I might be the only one on the planet who felt that way. His father sure didn't seem to have much time for him.

"We'll talk in the morning," I said. "Maybe you can give me some names then."

He shrugged.

We got our tickets, a bucket of popcorn big enough that it could have served as roofing insulation for a medium-sized house, and some Cokes. Jeremy and the rest of the audience were pretty taken with the movie, cheering at the end, especially when there was a teaser about the next instalment in the series. I knew I'd only be attending under threat of death. All these flicks were the same. Regular guy somehow gets super-powers. Comes up against villain with even greater super-powers. Big fight at the end where hero prevails, but not before the two of them have engaged in an epic, never-ending fight that pretty much levels a city. But it doesn't matter if thousands of innocent people are killed in the crossfire, because the superhero's girlfriend is okay.

It was nearly midnight when we got back to the beach house. I wished I'd left some lights on. I kept the head-lights shining on the back door long enough for me to get the key in. As soon as I had it open, I flicked on the inside and outside lights and gave the high sign to Jeremy, still in the car, to kill the headlights.

There was a smell in the air I didn't like. I thought it might be gas, or something chemical. I wondered if it was blowing in off the water, or coming from one of the nearby cottages. While the houses close to us didn't appear occupied, they all had boats of varying sizes sitting on trailers in their yards. I wondered if someone had spilled some fuel getting a boat ready for an outing. Or, worse, someone had tried to steal some gas by siphoning it out of a tank.

Once in the house, Jeremy went straight to the fridge, looking for a snack. I'd had so much popcorn that not only did I not want anything else to eat, I was in need of some Pepto-Bismol. I'd brought none, so I settled for a few antacid chewables instead.

I hit the lights upstairs and found my phone on the bed. I fired it up. I'd missed a call, plus there was a voice-mail. And an email. I checked the voicemail first. It was from Barry Duckworth, my friend on the Promise Falls

Police. I listened closely, saved the message when it was finished.

Then I opened the email Duckworth had said he would send me. It was a photo of this Cory Calder he'd warned me about.

"Shit," I said, looking at the shot of the guy who'd talked to us on the beach.

I looked out through the sliding glass doors to the blackness of the night and felt, suddenly, very vulnerable. I went over to the wall switch and flicked it down, killing the lights.

"Jeremy," I said, just loud enough that he would hear me downstairs.

"Hmph?" He had a mouthful of something.

I went to the top of the circular metal staircase. Evenly and calmly, I said, "We're leaving."

"Hmm?"

"Pack. And turn off any lights downstairs. Now. Work the best you can in the dark. Get your stuff. Quick as you can."

"What's going on?" he asked, his mouth now clear of food.

"Do it."

Three seconds later, the lights downstairs died. The staircase was only wide enough for one, so Jeremy waited at the bottom while I came down. His bedroom was up, mine below. We went into our respective rooms to throw our things together. I had my suitcase on the bed and my stuff dumped into it in under a minute. One thing I held onto was my gun.

I became aware that a light had come back on. Softly, I called upstairs to Jeremy. "I told you, lights out."

"I didn't do it," he said. "I thought that was you."

It was then I realized that the light wasn't inside the house. It was coming in through the windows. I turned my head quickly to look through the pane of glass in the back door, thinking maybe someone was shining their headlights up against the house.

It wasn't headlights. It was fire. And it wasn't coming from just that side of the house, either. Within seconds I could see flames leaping up past the windows on all four sides.

Someone was torching the beach house.

FIFTY-ONE

Maureen Duckworth, dressed in a robe that she had cinched at the waist, found her husband sitting at the kitchen table, still in his suit, tie askew, a few minutes before midnight. A half-full bottle of beer sat in front of him, as well as his phone and a bottle of Tylenol.

"Aren't you coming to bed?" she asked.

"Yeah," he said. "I need a minute, that's all."

She sat down across from him. "Trevor and I were in touch all day."

Duckworth nodded solemnly. "Me too. I didn't see his car out front."

"He's still sitting in the parking lot at Carol's apartment."

"My God, it's been like seventeen hours."

"He's still hoping she'll come home."

Duckworth's head went slowly up and down. "Yeah," he said.

"*Is* she coming home?" his wife asked.

"I don't honestly know. Maybe I should go see him. Wait with him."

She placed a hand over his. "You can't go out again. You look like you can barely keep your eyes open."

He put the bottle to his lips, tipped it back. "He showed me his tattoo."

"He told me."

Duckworth's eyes started to mist. He had to look away

from Maureen. He stared at the window and the darkness that lay beyond. "I had no idea."

"He loves you. He respects you."

Duckworth shrugged.

"Stop it," Maureen said. "You two may butt heads now and then, but you're his hero."

"Yeah, well, I don't know." He paused. "There are a lot of things I don't know. Like where Carol is. She's out there somewhere. She may be with this Calder character. But is she alive?" He shook his head slowly. "I don't know. I'd say the odds aren't good."

"You haven't told Trevor that?"

"No, I haven't."

They were both quiet for several moments. Finally Maureen said, "What's with the Tylenol?"

"I hurt."

He told her about what had happened at Eleanor Beecham's house. Getting shoved about by Norma and Harvey. Punched in the chest.

"They were both arrested and charged with assaulting an officer," he said. "Social services swooped in to deal with Mrs. Beecham. That guy whose back got tattooed? His father showed up just in time. Saved my ass."

"Well. Lucky he was there."

"Yeah."

"Where does it hurt?"

"Kind of all over."

"Point."

Duckworth thought a moment, then raised his hand into the air, pointed down toward his head, and twirled his finger around. "That general area."

She smiled. "You look exhausted."

"It's been a long day."

"I mean, all the time. Ever since what happened a year ago."

"Yeah," he said. "I think about it a lot. Randy phoned me, begged me to come to the memorial. Wants to give me a stupid plaque."

Maureen nodded. "I think you should go."

"I don't want to."

"But you should. People are grateful for what you did. Let them show you." She hesitated. "He called me, too."

"Finley called you?"

"He asked me to talk you into it."

Duckworth grinned. "The bastard. He told me a memorial without me present would be like a massage without a happy ending."

"He phrased it a little differently with me," Maureen said.

"What did you tell him?"

"I told him it was up to you. It's all up to you."

He studied her face. "What if I wanted to quit? Take early retirement. Do something else."

"That'd be up to you too."

"You'd like me to, wouldn't you?"

"I've never said that. You're doing what you love. I couldn't ask you to give that up."

He flipped his hand over and squeezed hers. "I think about it once in a while."

"About quitting?"

He nodded very slowly. "It's a young man's game." He gave a wry smile. "It's a thinner man's game, too."

She got out of her chair, came around the table, sat on the one next to him. She leaned her body into his, rested her head on his shoulder. "I'll go along with whatever you decide, but it has to be what you want. I don't want you doing it for me."

"Why would that be so bad?"

Maureen shifted in her chair, her knees touching his thigh. She leaned in and planted a soft kiss on his cheek.

"Someone needs to shave," she said.

"I'm going for the *Miami Vice* look."

"My God, how long ago was that?"

She gave him another kiss, then cupped his chin with her hand and turned his head to her. She touched her lips to his and held them there for several seconds. Duck-worth raised a hand and rested it on her cheek.

"I love you, you know," she said.

"For the life of me I don't know why," he said.

"Oh shut up."

"You'd been out with some hot guys but settled on me."

"I never settle."

"I didn't mean it that way. But you could have done better."

"And you could have done a lot worse," she said, and gave him another quick kiss. "I picked you." She grinned. "No one else came close."

He held his wife in his arms as he said, "I had to call Cal Weaver today. You remember him?"

"Of course."

"Left him a message." He reached for his phone, flipped it over, brought it to life for a second. "I wish he'd call me back. Anyway, I was thinking about what he does."

"Working privately, you mean?" She linked her fingers at the back of his neck.

"Yeah. Getting to pick and choose what you do,

instead of having to deal with everything that drops into your lap."

"You want to be peeping into people's bedrooms, gathering evidence for divorce cases? That's beneath you. I can't see you being happy doing that."

"I don't think Cal does a lot of that kind of work."

"If he gets hungry enough, I bet he does."

Duckworth shrugged. "Maybe. But you know, if I quit, I'd qualify for a pension already. Not a huge one. But I could supplement it with private work. I'd still get to do what I'm good at, but with less risk."

"Cal doesn't face risks?"

"Maybe sometimes. But nothing all that serious."

FIFTY-TWO

Albert Gaffney was slumped on the couch watching *NCIS* on the TV when his wife came in and sat down on the recliner.

"It's late," Constance said.

"How is he?" Gaffney said, not taking his eyes off the screen.

"He ate most of the soup. And a tuna sandwich."

"Well, that's something," he said.

"Isn't this a repeat?" she asked, glancing at the set.

"I think so, but I'm not really concentrating on it. Where's Monica?"

"She's in her room, listening to music."

"Hmm."

"Albert," she said.

He couldn't take his eyes off the screen, as though mesmerized by it.

"Albert, turn that off," she said gently.

Slowly, he turned his head to look at her. He seemed to be weighing her request. Finally, he picked up the remote and clicked it off.

"What?"

"We . . . we need to talk about things."

"There's nothing to talk about. Everything's done. The car's clean. The garage has been hosed down. It's all been taken care off. All you have to do, Maureen, is keep your mouth shut. If you keep your mouth shut, we'll be fine."

"It wasn't . . . He wasn't the one."

Albert stared at her.

"They're looking for that Calder man."

"I know. I talked to Duckworth."

"So . . . that means it probably wasn't the man who
. . . That man. He's not the one."

"He's the one," Albert said. His jaw tightened. "And
even if he wasn't the one who put those words on Brian's
back, he still hurt him. So . . . there's that."

He hit the button to turn the TV back on.

"Albert."

He sighed, killed the TV again. "What now?"

"The police will be asking questions. They'll be
coming back."

"No one saw me. No one saw me at the dump, either.
No one saw anything."

"There's Brian," she said.

"What do you mean? He's home now. He's going to
be okay." He gave her half a sneer. "You got what you
wanted. He's back with us."

Constance looked at him, wondered what Albert had
become. She'd never feared him before, but she did
now.

"The police will be coming to talk to Brian," she said.
"When Frommer's wife reports him missing, if she hasn't
already, she'll probably tell them about the fight he had
with Brian. They'll want to question him."

Albert shook his head slowly. "It'll be okay. Brian was
in the hospital all through the time that Frommer was
missing. He has witnesses. It will be okay." He paused.
Worry crept across his face. "Unless . . ."

"Unless what?"

Albert rose and left the room without saying anything

else. He went upstairs and lightly rapped on the door to his son's room.

"Yes?"

He pushed the door open. Brian was in bed, his head on the pillow. He had his bedside lamp on and was reading a Sin City graphic novel.

"Got a sec?" Albert asked.

Brian put his book face down on the covers. "Sure."

Albert came in and sat on the edge of the bed. "It's good to have you home."

"It's good to be here. I think I might give up my apartment."

"Well, get yourself well and then you can think about that. It might be the right thing to do."

"The hospital gave me some pills. They're kind of helping with the pain."

"Good. That's good. Look, there's something we need to discuss."

"Okay."

"When I was driving around and found you, you told me about Ron Frommer, what he did to you."

Brian nodded.

"Who else did you tell?"

"I didn't tell anyone. Remember, I was afraid of getting him in trouble, in case he took it out on Jessica."

"That's right. So you didn't tell them at the hospital?"

"No."

"You didn't tell the police?"

"No."

Albert nodded. "Okay. It's possible, there's a chance, that the police might want to talk to you about him."

"Did you tell them? Dad, I told you not to."

"No, no, I didn't do that. But if Jessica were to tell

413

them about the two of you, then the police might come talk to you."

"Oh, yeah, I guess. But only if she told them. Why would she do that? She's not going to want to get him into trouble."

"Well, she might," Albert said. "You see, if anything were to happen to Ron, they'd want to talk to anyone who'd gotten into an argument with him in the last few days."

Brian looked puzzled. "I don't understand. Am I in trouble?"

"No. How could you be? You were in the hospital. If something happened to Ron, well, you couldn't have had anything to do with it." He paused. "But there's one thing I need you to remember, in case anyone ever asks you any questions about him."

"What's that?"

"You never, ever told me his name. You never, ever told me where he lived."

Brian's look of puzzlement grew. "But I did."

"No," his father said firmly. "You did not."

Brian let this sink in for a few moments. "Okay," he said, finally. "I never did."

Albert smiled. "That's good. And no matter how many times someone might ask you the question, it's always no. You never told me."

Brian's head slowly went up and down. "Right."

Albert patted his son's blanket-covered thigh. "That's good, son. That's good. Now, you get better, okay?"

"Okay."

"And when you're better, we're going to see what we can do about your back. Right?"

Brian nodded.

Albert stood and walked to the door. As he was slipping into the hall, about to close the door, Brian said, "Dad?"

"Yes, son?"

"I love you."

"I love you too, Brian."

FIFTY-THREE

Carol Beakman was awake.

Barely.

She could hear the man moving about, wherever it was they were. She'd been drifting in and out of consciousness. Whatever he'd done to keep her groggy was wearing off, and while she wanted to work at freeing herself—she was secured to some kind of bed—she didn't want to draw any attention to herself.

The first thing she had to do was let her head clear some, and figure out just what kind of fix she was in.

Things were coming back to her.

Going to Dolly Guntner's place. Telling her that the police were looking into what had happened outside of Knight's bar. Dolly freaking out, and her boyfriend Cory—*yeah, that's his name, that's who grabbed me when I tried to get into my car*—freaking out because *she* was freaking out. Which made Carol think that not only did Dolly and this Cory know about what had happened at Knight's, they'd had something to do with it.

And then she'd dropped her damn purse. *God, just like some dumb broad in a horror movie.* Everything scattered, keys obscured in the mess. She'd lost the seconds she'd needed to get into the car, lock the door, get the hell out of there and call Trevor. Tell him to call his father.

Things went dark for a long time after that.

She'd had the sensation of moving. She was lying on her side, arms tied behind her back, ankles lashed together. She was in a truck or a van.

She'd blank out for a while, wake up again. Groggy most of the time.

Cory liked to talk, but she was pretty sure it was more like he was talking to himself and not to her. She didn't believe he thought she could hear him. He'd be sitting behind the wheel, saying things like "Did you bring your bathing suit? Because we're going to the beach! You ever been to Cape Cod? Yeah, well, me neither, but I bet it's nice."

Other times, it was as though he were trying to persuade her he wasn't a bad person.

"What happened with Dolly," he said, "was not the way I wanted things to go. But she was freaking out. I think she was going to go to the police, tell them everything. What was I supposed to do? Right? She'd lost sight of how important it was, what we've been doing."

He'd glance back sometimes into the cargo area, say, "I'm going to be famous. People are going to talk about me. I'm making a difference. You know what I am? I'm an instrument. An instrument of justice. Of revenge."

He kept asking her what he should do next.

"It can't be like the others," he said. "Not like Pierce, not even like the one we fucked up. This time, it's just a matter of getting the job done. Brought a little something of my dad's to help me out."

Total fucking whackjob.

For a while, she wondered, when she was in her more delirious state, whether he was with MetLife or something. Kept talking about her getting insurance. Then she realized *she* was the insurance. Yeah, that was what he was saying. Like she was a kind of hostage or something.

His ace in the hole. When things went south, she was his ticket to safety.

Maybe that was a good thing. Maybe that meant he would keep her alive. But it didn't mean that Carol Beakman wasn't very, very frightened.

She wondered what services he might be expecting her to provide beyond hostage. So far, there was nothing to suggest that sexual predator was part of his profile. Not that that was any great comfort.

Stop thinking about that. Think about getting away. Think think think think.

When they'd reached their destination, she'd had the sense of being moved from the van into a building. Being carried over Cory's shoulder, then being placed on a bed, a cot. Like one of those rollaway beds made of springs, with tubular metal framing. He put her face-down, tied her wrists to the top frame, ankles to the bottom.

Got her a blanket.

"I don't think it's worth making a fire," he said. "And smoke coming out the chimney's going to attract attention, maybe, you know?"

He gave her a nudge. "You waking up? You've been out a long time."

She said nothing.

"You should be good for a while," he said.

Again she said nothing. She'd been keeping her eyes closed as she regained consciousness, opening them only to slits to take in her surroundings. Then, if she heard the door open and close, and didn't hear his breathing, she'd open her eyes wide.

She was in a shack. Some tiny cottage. She believed she was near water. She could smell ocean in the air, hear the squawking of gulls. And Cory had said they were going to Cape Cod. He'd followed someone here, that much she'd figured out. At one point she opened her eyes a millimeter and saw him holding something. But then he turned his back to her, and she lost sight of it.

It had looked like a gun.

Her fear went up a notch.

It was getting darker, and Cory did not want to turn on any lights in the cabin. He had pulled a wooden chair to the window on the far wall. He sat down and stared outside.

"They're going out," he said. "Shit. Where the hell are they going?"

In the dim light, Carol slowly began to twist her wrists against the rope that bound them to the top frame. Her fingers had been going numb, and when Cory had been looking the other way, she'd been wiggling them, trying to keep the circulation going. The rope around her ankles was not secured as tautly to the bottom frame, allowing her to inch her body further up the cot. When she had the opportunity, she'd be in position to get her teeth on the rope.

After a period of time—Carol was having trouble tracking the hours, but it was fully dark now—Cory got up from the chair and began to pace the room. "They've been gone for fucking ever! Where the hell are they? What if they've gone back and I'm sitting here?" He shook his head angrily. "Time to listen in again."

He went outside. Carol thought she heard the sliding door of a van. Some time later—ten minutes, twenty?—he returned. She heard him muttering, "Nothing, nothing."

And then he left.

Carol picked away at the ropes with her teeth, but she wasn't making any headway.

A short while later, the door burst open again. Cory went back to his post by the window.

"Okay, okay," he said. "Here we go."

Carol heard a car drive past the cabin.

"I bet they went to a movie," she heard him say. "What else could keep them out that long?"

A pause, then, "Okay, good, good. They're heading in."

He stood quickly, took a couple of deep breaths. "This is it," he said under his breath, before going out of the door and closing it behind him.

Carol didn't know what "it" was, but she had a pretty good idea it wasn't going to be anything good.

She inched forward again and resumed working at the rope with her teeth.

FIFTY-FOUR

CAL

As best I could tell, the entire beach house was surrounded by fire. Something flammable—maybe gas, maybe something else that didn't smell quite as strong—had been poured around the perimeter of the building. Flames licked above the first-floor window ledges.

"Cal!" Jeremy shouted from upstairs.

"Hang on!"

"Fire!" he said. "There's a fire!"

I ran into the kitchen area and started throwing open cupboards. Even without any lights on, the glow from the flames was bright enough to make out shapes. I remembered seeing a fire extinguisher somewhere when we were opening cabinets and closets to see how well equipped the place was.

I found one under the sink. Not a huge one, but something that would do the trick to put out a small kitchen fire. The canister was no thicker than a soup can, and about a foot and a half tall. Maybe it would be enough to get us out the door. I grabbed it and pulled the pin that would allow foam to be propelled from it once I squeezed the trigger.

Then it occurred to me that there might be another way out.

Taking the extinguisher with me, I went up to the

second floor, where I found Jeremy with his backpack slung over his shoulder.

"This way!" he said, heading toward the sliding glass doors that led to the elevated deck.

That was what I'd been thinking. The fire was at ground level, but the deck was attached to the second floor. We could escape through the glass doors, take the stairs down the side of the house and jump over the flames. If they were too high to do that, we could leap off the deck into the sand. I was confident it would break our fall.

Jeremy was heading for the doors when suddenly I reached for his arm and said, "No."

"What?"

"That's the way he wants us to go. It's the one way out he's left for us."

Jeremy looked at me wide-eyed. "What are you saying?"

"I'm saying he wants us to go out that door."

"Who's *he*?"

The smell of smoke was getting stronger. The flames surrounding the first floor of the house were casting light into the second-floor windows.

"What's gonna happen if we go out that way?" Jeremy asked, pointing to the deck.

We get picked off, I thought.

"It's not safe."

"It's not safe to stay here!"

That was true, too.

If this guy Duckworth had warned me about was outside waiting for us to come onto the deck, where would he be?

The boardwalk. The roughly hundred-foot-long

422

raised walkway that led over the grassy area to the beach. It would be the perfect place for someone to wait, rifle trained on the entry to the deck, and take us out, one after the other. A night scope would do the trick, but even without one, we'd be pretty visible. It was a clear night sky, and the fire was doing wonders to light up the surroundings.

"Back downstairs," I said.

"You knew this was going to happen?" Jeremy asked, trailing me down the steps to the first floor. "That's why you said we had to go?"

"I got a warning," I said. "That guy we met. On the beach."

"What? How did he—"

"Not now."

We were at the back door. I unlocked it. One hand was on the doorknob, the other on the extinguisher.

"Soon as we get out, run like hell, but stay low, try not to be seen, be quiet. Go to the place next door, the house on the east side, hide someplace, anyplace, wait for me to call when the coast is clear."

"What about the car?"

"No time. Takes too long to get in, start it. He'll be on us." I looked at him, placed a hand on his shoulder. "We're going to be okay."

He nodded, but he looked far from convinced. Maybe that was because I didn't look all that convincing.

"You ready?"

Another nod.

I turned the knob, which was hot on this side, and pulled the door open, squeezing the trigger on the extinguisher at the same time, aiming it low at the source. All I had to do was clear us a narrow path. Once we were a foot or two from the building, we wouldn't have to worry about the flames any more.

Only about taking a bullet.

I doused the ground with foam, smothering the flames in our path. "I'll go first," I said.

I stepped out, took a few strides to the Honda and crouched behind the fender. I waved Jeremy forward. He scooted out of the house and joined me by the car. Now we could see just how bad the fire was. The flames were spreading up the walls of the building, some of them licking the eaves of the second floor.

I pointed to the closest neighboring house. "Make yourself scarce."

Jeremy gave my arm a squeeze and slipped away into the darkness. His feet crunched on the gravel—most of the driveways around here were crushed shells rather than stone—but it couldn't be heard over the roar of the fire.

I put down the extinguisher and took out the gun, which had been tucked under my belt. Slowly I moved from one end of the car to the other, which afforded me a better view of the boardwalk that led to the beach. I had to blink a few times to focus and adjust my eyes to the darkness.

As I'd suspected, there was someone there. Little more than a dark figure, barely illuminated by the flames. He had something in his hands, and it was aimed in the direction of the deck.

He had to be wondering why it was taking us so long to come out. It didn't seem likely he'd stay there much longer. After about thirty seconds of watching him, I could sense his impatience. He lowered the weapon, took several steps closer to the beach house. He stopped, cocked his head, studied the place, then took two more steps in my direction.

I grasped my gun in both hands and rested my arms across the top of the trunk to steady my aim. If this were the movies, I'd be able to drop this asshole from here in one shot. But it was dark, my guy was a good seventy feet away, and, standing with his side to me, he presented as a narrow target.

I needed him closer.

He'd gone to a lot of trouble to kill us. I didn't expect him to give up. But things hadn't gone as planned, and now he had to be wondering if he'd fucked up. He continued to move slowly toward my location until he was at the top of the set of steps that led down from the boardwalk to the open area between our beach house and the one to the west.

He was only thirty feet away now.

He came around the corner of the house and saw the gap in the flames where the door was. I thought I saw him mouth an obscenity.

I said, "Freeze!"

Sometimes you go with the phrase everyone knows. Of course, when you shout something like that at someone, they move. Maybe not a lot, but it's a jolt to hear that yelled at you. His body tensed, and he turned in my direction. I could see now that what he'd been carrying was a rifle.

Takes a little longer to raise one of those and aim. It was no six-shooter.

"Don't even think of it!" I said.

But darned if he didn't go and think of it anyway.

He went to bring the weapon up into a firing position. I pulled the trigger.

I must have caught him in his left shoulder. He spun

hard to the right, stumbled back. But he managed to hold onto the rifle even as he went down to the ground.

I stood, but moved to the center of the car, where my body was at least partly shielded up to my chest. I still had the gun in both hands, my arms extended over the roof of the vehicle.

"Stay down!" I shouted.

He'd landed on his side, had rolled over onto his back, and was struggling to get into a sitting position. I figured I had the better part of four seconds to get to him before he could attempt to line me up in his sights again.

I came around the car and charged. Arms pumping at my sides, gun in my right hand.

He saw me coming, and he had to know he didn't have time, but it didn't stop him from trying. He went to swing the rifle in my direction, but before he could, I launched a kick directly at his face.

Got him, too.

His head snapped back and his upper body thudded to the ground. He lost his grip on the rifle. I snatched the weapon, tossed it, and stood over him, my gun aimed squarely at his head. The fire made his sweat-drenched face glow like neon.

It was my first really good look at our would-be assassin. He was about five ten, a hundred and eighty pounds, mid-forties, gray hair cut to within an eighth of an inch of his scalp.

I probably did something approaching a double-take as I asked him, "Where the hell is the other guy?"

By "the other guy," I meant the man Barry Duckworth had emailed me a picture of.

Cory Calder.

This was not that guy.

426

FIFTY-FIVE

Calder watched the Honda pull in behind the beach house. Saw Pilford and the old guy get out, go into the house.

He scurried after the car as it passed his cabin and hid himself behind a hedge that bordered the road. A good spot for keeping an eye on the place.

He'd been thinking about how to do this.

He knew he was going to have to shoot them both. The old dude was there watching out for Pilford, so he would have to take him out, one way or the other. Maybe there was a time when Calder would have felt badly about that. After all, it wasn't this bodyguard who'd run down a girl with a car and got clean away with it. But when you thought about it, wasn't he just as guilty? Weren't all the people connected to Jeremy Pilford guilty to one degree or another? Weren't his lawyers, who'd used that ridiculous defense, guilty? Wasn't his mother guilty for so fucking him up that he didn't know right from wrong?

Sure, Pilford was the *most* guilty. But so many others had played a part. And this man looking out for him was another one for the list.

Cory thought the simplest way to handle it was to knock on the door. Whoever answered first got shot first. Then, when the other person came running to see what had happened, he would shoot him too.

Pretty straightforward.

It made him wonder if maybe he hadn't been

overthinking things with the others. The dog chowing down on Craig Pierce, the whole tattoo number on the other guy.

Just shoot the fuckers.

Kill them.

That was what he would do.

He watched them go inside, turn on the lights. Ground floor first, then the second floor.

Let them get ready for bed, he thought. Let them turn off the lights, then bang on the door. They'd be more disoriented.

But then he thought, what if the old dude's got a gun? If he was hired to protect the Big Baby, he probably had one.

Shit.

He might come to the door with the damn thing in his hand. What then?

Think think think.

Maybe bang on the door, but not stand there like a moron waiting for the old guy to blow his brains out. Bang on the door, then hide. Behind the car, or the trash cans set a few feet to one side. Guy comes out, looks around, looks the other way, then *blam*.

Yeah, that could work.

Cory Calder realized he was very nervous. Far more nervous than he'd been when they'd grabbed Pierce or Gaffney. Those two weren't armed, and once they were knocked out, they didn't present any physical threat.

This time, it was different.

But he'd come this far, and he wasn't about to pack it in. He was going to do this, he was going to shoot those two bastards and maybe even stay long enough to get a picture of a *dead* Big Baby that he could upload to the Just Deserts site, and then everyone in the world would know—

What the hell?

A bright flickering appeared at the perimeter of the beach house. It had started in one spot, then quickly spread around the building.

It was a fire.

Cory squinted. He made out a shadowy figure, carrying something long, running from the corner of the building to the boardwalk. The man—Cory was pretty sure it was a man—went up the boardwalk steps two at a time, then took a position at the midpoint.

What was happening? What was going on?

He very quickly figured that out. Someone else was out to steal the glory from him.

Someone else was going to get Pilford.

"It's not fair!" he whispered to himself. "It's not fair!"

He stepped out from behind the hedge at the end of the gravel driveway that led up to the beach house. Frustration coursed through him like an electric charge. What should he do?

With the house on fire, Pilford and the old man were likely to come charging out at any moment. But from which door? There was already fire trailing across the one they'd used to go inside. The glass doors that led to the deck were on the bay side, and it looked as though this other guy, who appeared to be carrying a rifle, was waiting for Pilford to come out that way.

So *he* could shoot him.

"No!" Cory said aloud. "It's not right."

But what was he to do? If he wanted to shoot Pilford himself, he was going to have to shoot this—this *interloper*—first. Which meant that now he would have to shoot three people instead of two.

He began to hyperventilate.

How dare this person steal his thunder? How dare he go after the glory that Cory had worked so hard to achieve?

The fire was spreading quickly. Lights that had been on in the beach house now were off. Cory could see the man on the boardwalk aiming the rifle at the building. Pilford and the old dude were probably making their escape onto the deck now.

But the man did not shoot.

Suddenly, the back door opened. Cory could make out the man and the kid. The man had something in his hand—a fire extinguisher!—and he put out enough of the flames to allow them to exit the house.

Maybe this was his chance.

But then Pilford disappeared from view, and his babysitter was seeking cover behind the Honda. The man on the boardwalk was heading this way, and—

Shots!

What the hell was going on?

Cory moved deeper into the bushes on the other side of North Shore Boulevard. He could not believe what he was seeing. The man who'd been on the boardwalk going down, the older guy getting the drop on him.

Where was Jeremy? Where had he gone?

He hadn't come this way. He must have run to one of the neighboring beach houses to hide.

Should he go look for him? Cory wondered. Or was he taking a risk even being here? What with that fire starting to consume the beach house, and now gunfire, it was only a matter of time before emergency vehicles started descending on this scene like flies on shit.

Cory didn't just have to get away from this beach house, he had to get out of here completely. And that meant hightailing it back to his cabin, getting in his van and getting the fuck out of here.

Just one small problem there.

Dolly's friend.

He couldn't leave her in the cabin. He might still need her for leverage. Even if he got away from Cape Cod without attracting attention, they were still going to be looking for him in connection with everything else.

So he was going to have to move her from the bed to the car without anyone seeing him. Luckily, his cabin was far enough down the road that he thought he could manage that without being seen.

Yeah, except everything *else* had gone to shit so far. Why not that?

As he ran back to the cabin, he felt his eyes misting up with tears.

"Everything is against me," he muttered to himself. "God hates me! Everyone hates me!"

As he ran, he wiped tears from his eyes. The cool night wind coming off Cape Cod Bay chilled his dampened cheeks.

"Not fair," he said again. "Not fair!"

While he still wanted to kill the Big Baby, he wanted to do something even worse, if that were possible, to that asshole with the rifle who had ruined everything.

He stopped to dig a tissue from his pocket and dab the tears that continued to puddle from his eyes.

All he'd ever wanted was to be somebody.

No, not just somebody. He wanted to be somebody *better*. Somebody better than his brother and his sister.

431

Somebody better than his judgmental father. Somebody who made a difference, somebody who would be talked about for years to come.

He'd come so close to that.

He felt an aching sadness wash over him. What he wished, right now, was that he was home. That he was curled up on the couch in the basement under a blanket, knees pulled up to his chest, in front of the TV.

He could cry all he wanted then.

But he couldn't do that now. He had to keep moving.

A thought occurred to him.

Maybe they wouldn't catch him for the things he'd already done. He'd harbored a sense of inevitability up to now, figuring that sooner or later the police would close in on him. It was the whole reason he'd brought Carol Beakman with him. A hostage had seemed like a good idea at the time.

But if he got in that van right now and drove through the night, he could be hundreds of miles from here by tomorrow. He could ditch the van, steal a car, and keep on going. Two or three days from now, he could be on the other side of the country. He could find a place to hide out while he figured out his next step. Figure out a way to change his identity. Alter his looks. Get some kind of job where you got paid in cash. It would be tough at first, but it sure beat the alternative of spending the rest of his life in prison.

Yeah, that was a plan.

But it raised another question.

What was he to do with the Beakman woman? Let her go? Leave her tied up in the cabin to be found by someone in a few days?

Suppose the police did eventually catch him? Charged

him with various offences? They'd need witnesses to convict.

Craig Pierce hadn't seen him. Pierce had been masked.

Brian Gaffney hadn't seen him. Gaffney had been drugged and blindfolded.

Dolly Guntner certainly wasn't in a position to say anything bad about him.

Which left Carol Beakman. Carol had seen him. And while she didn't actually see him kill Dolly, if the police ever spoke with her, she'd be able to tell them it couldn't have been anyone else but him.

As far as Cory could figure, the only living witness to his crimes was Carol Beakman.

He was nearly back to the cabin.

It seemed clear what he had to do.

And he'd have to do it fast.

FIFTY-SIX

CAL

"Where's the other one?" I asked the man I'd shot. "Where's Calder?"

"Jesus!" the man said, putting his hand to his right cheek, where my foot had connected. There was blood seeping through the shoulder of his jacket.

"Where is he?" I yelled, again, wanting to be sure I was heard over the roar of the fire. The heat was getting intense—it felt like a hot pan pressed up against my right cheek—and if I was going to continue asking this son of a bitch questions, I was going to have to drag him away from the blaze.

"Who?" he said.

"Calder," I said. Although Barry hadn't said so in his message, it seemed reasonable to assume Calder might have a partner, which would mean we weren't out of the woods yet. He might be watching us right now.

"I don't know any Calder!" he said.

I shook my head wearily. "Wherever he is, you need to call him off."

"I told you, I don't know any—"

I brought my foot down on his knee. Hard. I wasn't sure, what with all the crackling sounds of burning wood, but I thought I heard something snap. My new friend yelped loud enough to suggest I was right.

"Goddamn!" he cried, his eyes squeezed shut in pain.

"ID," I said.

"Fuckin' hell! You broke my fuckin' leg!"

"ID," I repeated. "And your phone. Or I break the other one."

"Motherfucker!" he shouted, and opened his eyes to see the gun still trained on his face.

"Now," I said. "Slowly."

He reached into his jacket and pulled out a phone, which he tossed about five feet from me.

"I don't fetch," I said. "If you make me fetch, I'll get annoyed, and if I get annoyed, I might just shoot you in the head. Wallet."

The man swallowed, took three breaths and said, "Back pocket. Have to move."

"Carefully."

He struggled to raise his butt off the gravel far enough to slide his hand under himself and dig the wallet out of the back of his jeans.

"Hand it to me," I said. "With the tips of your fingers."

He stretched his arm up and I took it from him gingerly, watching for any attempt to grab me. I knew that if I were him, I'd be desperate to try anything at this point. He was looking at a very long stay in prison. Arson, two counts of attempted murder. Being an asshole.

"Who's he?" said a voice behind me.

I glanced over my shoulder for half a second to see Jeremy standing there. "You shouldn't be here."

"I saw you drop him, figured it was okay," he said. "Which was kind of awesome, by the way. But that's not the person we met on the beach."

"I know."

"Who is he?"

I handed him the wallet. "You tell me."

435

I kept my eyes on the man while Jeremy opened up the wallet and started looking through it. "Okay, I've got his driver's license." He tilted it toward the fire to get enough light to read it. "He's Gregor . . . Hang on. Last name is spelled K–I–L–N."

"Kiln," I said, looking down at the man. "Did I say that right? Like the oven for pottery?"

The man grunted.

"I'll take that as a yes." To Jeremy, "What else can you tell us about Mr. Kiln here?'

Jeremy held up more cards to the flames. "He lives in Albany. He was born in, uh, 1973. He's got some Visa cards and shit like that."

"His phone's over there."

Jeremy spotted it, scooped it up off the ground. "What do you want me to do?" he asked.

"Check emails, recent calls."

"Listen," Gregor Kiln said, "maybe we can work some kind of deal."

I thought I heard conversation, looked down to the end of the driveway, where half a dozen people, some in what appeared to be pajamas, had gathered. A man was coming our way.

"I've called the fire department!" he shouted. "Ambulance, too! That man hurt?"

I said, "Please stay back, sir!"

"You need to come away from the—"

"I know! Please go back by the road!"

The man stopped, hesitated, clearly puzzled by my reluctance to accept assistance. But he did as I'd told him and retreated to the road, where he huddled with the others, undoubtedly speculating about what the hell was going on.

For the first time, I started hearing sirens.

"Did you hear me?" Kiln said. "A deal?"

"You're not in what I'd call a good bargaining position," I said.

"I give you a name, you let me go."

"A name?" I said. "What do you mean, a name? Like, the name of a website? A person? What?"

"A website?" Kiln said.

I realized, at that moment, that this was not like the other incidents. This was not the outgrowth of some social-media outrage. This was something very different.

"Give me the name," I said.

"We have a deal?"

"No."

"No name."

Jeremy said, "I found something."

I gave him a quick glance as the wail of the sirens grew louder. "What?"

"No interesting emails, but there's a number here. Some calls around five hours ago. And a text."

"Read it to me."

"Okay, the text is from the same number as the calls. Um, someone says, 'Needs to be done tonight.' And Kiln here says, 'No problem.' And then the other guy—"

"Is there a name for this other guy?"

"No. But the other guy, he says, 'Confirm when done.'"

If it was a guy. My mind was racing, trying to figure out who knew that Jeremy and I were in Cape Cod.

Only one name came to mind.

Madeline Plimpton.

But did that make sense? Not only had this man I'd shot known where we were, but Cory Calder had known we were here, too. Did it make any sense that Jeremy's great-aunt would tell either of them where to find us?

"What else?" I asked Jeremy.

"That's it."

The fact that we had a number to connect to those calls and texts was a start. I got out my own phone, brought up the number I'd used to call Madeline Plimpton.

"Read me the number," I said to Jeremy. He called it out, and I compared it to what I had for Ms. Plimpton.

Not a match.

Not that that really proved anything.

I gave Kiln a wry smile. "With that number on your phone, maybe we don't need you to give us a name."

Kiln said nothing.

A fire engine screamed to a stop at the end of the driveway, and slowly turned in. I asked Jeremy to hand me Kiln's phone, then said, "Help me move this asshole."

We each grabbed an arm and dragged him across the gravel and into the backyard of the neighboring beach house. As we dropped his arms, a fireman ran toward me.

"Paramedics on the way!" he said. Then a look of alarm crossed his face as he saw the gun in my hand. I had it pointed to the ground.

"Police, too?" I asked.

The man nodded. "Why?"

I nodded toward Kiln. "He's our firestarter."

The fireman shook his head. "He torched the place?"

I nodded. "That, and more. I can't have him heading off in an ambulance. We need the police."

"I'll alert them," he said, and then glanced at the beach house. "It's a goner, but maybe we can stop it from spreading to the other houses."

I nodded and watched him run off. His fellow

438

firefighters were unspooling hoses and dragging them toward the house.

There were two calls I needed to make. The first was to Barry Duckworth. It was late, but I was pretty sure he'd want to hear from me. For the second call, I'd need someplace quieter.

But I didn't want to let Gregor Kiln out of my sight. Even with a bullet in his shoulder, and quite possibly a broken knee, he struck me as someone who'd try to make a run for it if we let down our guard.

Jeremy said, "What do you think happened to the other guy? The one on the beach?"

I gave him a smile. "Jeremy, I have absolutely no idea what's going on." I held up Kiln's phone. "But I think maybe I'm gonna find out. I'd like to let Mr. Kiln's friend know the job is done."

FIFTY-SEVEN

Barry Duckworth was in a deep sleep when the cell phone on his bedside table began to buzz. If Maureen hadn't given him a shove on the shoulder, he might have slept right through it.

"Barry," she said. "Barry!"

He opened his eyes, reached for the phone and knocked it to the floor. "Shit," he said. He leaned down, his hand hunting in the dark for the device as it continued to buzz. He found it, hit the button to accept the call and put the phone to his ear without seeing who it was.

"Duckworth," he said as Maureen switched on the lamp on her side of the bed.

"Barry, it's Cal Weaver."

"Jesus, Cal." Duckworth threw back the covers and planted his feet on the floor. "What's happening?"

"A lot. Your guy Calder was here. We met him on the beach today."

"Tell me everything."

Weaver brought him up to speed, ending with the fire at Madeline Plimpton's beach house, how it was designed to force them out of the house so they could be shot.

"I knew you were there," Duckworth said. "I knew Jeremy Pilford had been staying with her. Went there today, met her and the boy's mother and her boyfriend. Warned them about Calder. He torched the beach house?"

440

Weaver said no, that he'd caught a man named Gregor Kiln.

"I'll check into him," Duckworth said.

"I don't think this is related to the social-media outrage surrounding Jeremy," Weaver said. "This Kiln has the ring of a professional about him."

"I'm on it."

"And I need another favor. A number I want you to check. It's probably a burner, not traceable."

Duckworth reached for the pad and pen he always kept by the bed, tucked the phone between head and shoulder, and said, "Fire away."

Cal gave him the number.

"Okay, I'll get right on it."

"And assuming it is a burner, and we can't attach a name to the phone, I've got something I want to try."

Cal told Duckworth what he wanted to do, and what he thought he might need from Duckworth to make it happen.

"And I need you to talk to the locals here," he added, "and have them keep a lid on things. At least for twelve hours."

"I'll do my best."

"Nothing gets out about what happened here beyond the fire."

"I said I'd do my best," Duckworth said. "And I've got a favor to ask you."

"Go ahead."

"We've got a missing-woman case. Carol Beakman. I think her disappearance is linked to this Calder character."

Maureen suddenly sat up in bed.

"What do you think's happened to her?" Weaver asked.

"I'm fearing the worst."

"Shoot me a picture. I'll keep my eyes open."

"Will do."

"Local cops are here," Weaver said. "Gotta go. I'll get the name of whoever's in charge and text it to you."

"Good. How's the kid?"

"Jeremy?"

"Yeah."

"He's okay," Weaver said. "Can't get into it now, but there's something not right there."

"What do you mean?"

"Later."

"Okay. And when the dust settles, there's something I want to talk to you about."

"What?"

"Later," Duckworth said. He ended the call, set the phone down and stood up out of bed.

"Carol?" Maureen said.

"Nothing," he said. "But Cal encountered Calder in Cape Cod. We know he's been there, and still might be. I need to get on to the Mass state police."

Duckworth reached for his pants, pulled them on, then went to the closet for a fresh shirt.

"What's the thing you want to talk to him about?" Maureen asked.

Duckworth found a white shirt that still had a cleaning tag attached and removed it from the hanger. "Career advice," he said.

FIFTY-EIGHT

As Cory inserted the key into the cabin door, he considered ways to get rid of the body.

He hadn't thought things through very well when it came to his girlfriend. Carol's car with Dolly's body had to have been found by now. He should have taken more care, thought of a way that neither of those things would have been discovered for some time, if ever. He had to admit it. He'd panicked. Had he had more time to think things through, he could have run them off a bridge, for example. Left them at the bottom of a river.

He needed to do something like that with Carol's body.

Once she was dead, he'd put her in the van and look for a suitable spot to dispose of her. Deep in a forest, say. Maybe he'd get lucky and find a shovel in the cabin somewhere that he could take with him. He'd dig a deep hole, toss her in, cover her up. Someone might find her some day, but it could be weeks, even years.

At least now he had more time to do things properly. When he was getting rid of Dolly and Carol's car, he was working to a deadline. He was on the trail of Jeremy Pilford and didn't want to lose him.

Well, so much for that project now.

Cory's priority was saving his own ass.

He got the door open but did not run his hand along the wall searching for the light switch. He couldn't have anyone looking in, certainly not as the road began to fill up with gawkers and emergency equipment. Even with the flimsy curtains pulled across the windows, the silhouette of a man moving a woman's body was very likely to attract attention.

He would kill Beakman—smothering her seemed the best way to go—then move her body out and wipe down the cabin. Doorknobs, toilet handle, anything he could think of he might have touched. Leave no personal traces behind. Get behind the wheel and slowly drive away.

Cory knew he could never go home again, that he had seen his father for the last time. He was simultaneously depressed and delighted. He loved the man, at some level, but despised him, too.

The relentless belittling with a dollop of tenderness. "*You should try harder to make something of yourself, but maybe you are what you are.*" Followed by a look of resignation and disappointment.

He slipped into the cabin and closed the door silently behind him. Even though it had been dark outside, his eyes needed to adjust further to the gloom of the cabin. But he was able to make out the basic shapes of its contents. The wooden table and four mismatched antique chairs in the center of the room. The sink and counter along one wall. The wood-burning heater on the opposite side of the room, the chimney pipe leading straight up and through the ceiling.

And, finally, the two beds along the left wall. One empty, one not.

Yes, suffocation seemed the simplest way to go. Clamp a hand over her mouth, squeeze her nostrils shut, and wait until the life was snuffed out of her.

You did what you had to do.

He worked his way carefully across the darkened room and stood beside the bed.

"Everything's gone wrong," he said. "It's all gone to shit. Someone else tried to do it, and he fucked it up. I've lost my chance. I have to leave." He paused. "I can't take you with me. At least, not . . . Well, I can't. I'm sorry it had to be this way."

He sat on the edge of the bed and put a hand out to rest it on her back. He felt a strange need to comfort her before he did what he had to do.

But his hand found nothing. It went all the way down to the surface of the bed. Frantically, he patted the bed from head to foot.

"Where are you?" he shouted, turning sharply to look into the dark room.

His first thought was that if she'd managed to get loose, she wouldn't have stayed around to await his return. She must be gone.

But then he thought he heard breathing.

Someone else was in the room.

"Where are you?" he said again, rising off the bed and whirling around, just in time to see a shadowy figure swinging something his way.

The steel poker from the wood-burning stove caught him across the side of the head and he staggered across the room. Feebly he raised his arm to ward off a second blow, but the poker hit him so hard he was sure he felt the bone in his forearm snap.

He dropped to his knees as the poker came around for a third time, this time catching him across the neck.

He hit the floor, writhing and gagging. He rolled onto his back, and as he looked up, a sliver of moonlight coming through one of the windows briefly lit up the face of his attacker.

What Cory saw was so unimaginably horrible he managed to utter a gasp between choking noises.

"Nice to see you again," said Craig Pierce.

FIFTY-NINE

CAL

Barry Duckworth called me back more quickly than I had expected.

"Nothing on that phone," he said. "It's a burner. I can't connect a name to it."

"Okay," I said. "I'll get back to you."

I had been talking with an officer named Higgins from the Town of Sandwich Police Department, filling him in on what Gregor Kiln had tried to accomplish. I wouldn't let Kiln out of my sight, even as the paramedics examined him. I wouldn't do that until someone had cuffed his wrists and shoved him into the back of a cruiser. If he left here in an ambulance, I was going to insist that a cop go with him.

"So this kid," Higgins said, nodding his head toward Jeremy Pilford, who was standing a few feet away watching the fire department douse the flames that had engulfed Madeline Plimpton's place, "is the one that was all over the news?"

"Yes," I said.

Higgins pointed at Kiln. "So you shot that guy?"

"I did."

"And broke his knee?"

"Possibly."

"Maybe I should be arresting you."

"I explained to you what he was trying to do."

447

"Yeah, but you might be givin' me a story."

"See if he wants to file charges," I said. "My guess is he's got bigger things to worry about."

Higgins pinched the top of his nose, as though trying to ward off a headache. "Look, I think I'm gonna have to bring the chief in on this. Arson, attempted murder, the Big Baby case? You shootin' this guy. If the chief doesn't hear about it till morning, my ass is gonna be in a sling."

"Good idea," I said. I asked for the chief's name—it was Bertram—and contact info so that I could forward it on to Barry. While I'd been fairly forthcoming with Higgins, I'd not mentioned that Kiln's cell phone was in my pocket.

Higgins excused himself to call his boss. I sent a message to Barry with the info about the chief. Jeremy wandered over and said, "Madeline's not gonna be very happy. Have you called her and told her what's happened to her place?"

I shook my head. "No, and I'm not going to."

For all I knew right now, Madeline was the one who'd sent this guy, although I still couldn't fathom why she would do that.

"And if you've magically managed to pull another cell phone out of your ass," I said to Jeremy, "I don't want you doing it either. We're on radio silence for a while."

"On what?"

"We're not calling or talking to anybody. Don't call your mother or Bob or your girlfriend Charlene or anyone."

"Why?"

"Just go along with this, okay?"

Jeremy shrugged. "I guess."

"No, no guess. Promise me."

"Fine, I promise. What are we gonna do now? We've got no place to stay."

"I think we'll be heading home very soon. At least as soon as they'll let us."

Two more police cars had arrived, and four officers—two men and two women—got out. Higgins, a cell phone to his ear, waved over one of the women and started a conversation with her. He pointed to Kiln, and the woman nodded several times. As she walked over to where the paramedics were treating our shooter, Higgins resumed his phone conversation.

Then he called me over.

"Chief wants to talk to you," he said.

I took the phone. "Hello?"

"Weaver?"

"That's right. Chief Bertram?"

"Yeah. You're private?"

He sounded very deeply pissed, and I didn't think it just had to do with the fact that Officer Higgins had woken him up.

"Yes," I said. "Look, I know you have a lot of questions, but before you begin, I'd like to offer my apologies."

"Huh?"

"I just brought a shit storm of trouble your way. That wasn't my intention. I came here with the Pilford boy because I thought he'd be safe here. He's been the subject of countless death threats. It didn't work out. I'm sorry."

I wasn't, actually, but I didn't see the point in getting on the wrong side of this man from the get-go.

"Well," he said, his voice sounding slightly softer than a moment earlier, "you sure got that right. I'm comin' out there shortly, but in the meantime, I need you to bring me up to speed."

I told him the same story I'd told Higgins. "You're going to be hearing, any moment, I think, from Detective Barry Duckworth of the Promise Falls Police."

"Where the hell is that?" Bertram asked.

"New York state. North of Albany. He's going to ask you something on my behalf."

"What might that be?"

"Nothing to the press for about twelve hours. Except that there was a fire."

"Not likely to be any questions for that long anyway," Bertram said. "This isn't exactly Manhattan. We don't have CNN watching our every move. But let me ask you why."

"I'd like whoever sent this Kiln guy to kill us to think the job got done."

There was a long pause at Bertram's end. Then, "I'll talk to your Duckworth guy. See if you're on the level. My phone's beeping now."

"Take the call," I said, and handed the phone back to Higgins.

Kiln was being loaded into the ambulance. The officer Higgins had spoken to climbed in with him. I ran over before they closed the doors.

"Where you taking him?" I asked.

"Hyannis," said the paramedic.

I fixed my gaze on the officer. "Don't take your eyes off him."

She looked at me skeptically. "And who are you?"

"Just don't," I said, and closed the doors.

The ambulance rolled down the drive, red light flashing but siren off, and sped off once it had reached the road. I'd strolled down the driveway after it and watched it disappear into the distance.

Here, a hundred feet or so away from the charred beach house, things were slightly calmer, and quieter. I got out Kiln's phone, brought up the number he'd most recently been in touch with, and dialed it.

It rang five times.

"Yeah." A man's voice.

Definitely not Madeline.

It was low, almost a whisper, as though someone else was in the room he did not want to wake. One word certainly wasn't enough for me to recognize the voice, and there was no reason to believe this was someone I'd ever spoken to before, anyway.

I didn't have the skills to do an impersonation of Gregor Kiln, but maybe it wouldn't be necessary. I was going to be whispering, too.

"It's done," I said.

"Okay."

"Both of them."

"Fine. Next week."

Next week what? Payment? I didn't want to ask.

"Need a meet sooner," I said.

"Next week."

"No," I pressed. "There was a complication."

A pause. "What kind of complication."

I dropped my voice even lower. "Can't discuss now. In person."

"Shit." Another pause. "Ten. Usual place."

And where was that?

"Ten's good," I said. "But not the usual place. Think it's being watched."

"What?" His voice went up. "Why? What's going on?"

"Told you, can't now. Tomorrow, ten, take a booth at the back of Kelly's."

"What the hell is Kelly's?"

"Diner, Promise Falls."

"Why the hell do I have to go up there?"

"Just be there. End booth, by the door to the kitchen."

There was another pause. Had he figured it out? Did he know I wasn't Kiln? I could feel blood pulsing in my temple.

"You there?" I asked.

Another three seconds passed before he answered. "Fine, I'll be there."

He ended the call. I closed my eyes, kept playing his voice back in my head, wondering if I'd heard it before.

Maybe. Then again, maybe not.

When I opened my eyes, I saw a woman running up the road toward me. She was waving her arms frantically. She had what looked like short lengths of rope trailing from her wrists.

She screamed: "Help me! Help me!"

As I ran toward her, I thought that Cape Cod was perhaps not the idyllic vacation spot I'd been hearing about all these years.

SIXTY

Gloria Pilford rolled over in bed and saw Bob sitting there, hunched over, his back to her. A sliver of light sneaking from the hallway of Madeline Plimpton's house through the slightly opened doorway was enough to cast shadows.

Bob extended an arm and put his cell phone on the bedside table.

"What's going on?" Gloria asked. "Is something going on?"

"No," Bob said. "Go back to sleep."

"What time is it?"

"Around one," he said.

"I think I only just got to sleep," she said. "I was awake for the longest time." She sat up. "Who were you talking to?"

"Nobody."

"You were on the phone. I heard you whispering. Were you on the phone?"

Bob turned and looked at her sharply. "For Christ's sake, just go back to sleep."

Gloria shifted her body toward the headboard so she could prop herself up against it. "I want to know what's going on."

"Nothing!"

Bob stood and walked across the room to the door and disappeared into the hallway. Gloria threw back the covers, grabbed a housecoat that had been draped over a chair, threw it around herself and went in pursuit.

She spotted Bob descending the stairs. When he reached the bottom, he turned in the direction of the kitchen.

"Wait," she said, scurrying down the steps in her bare feet. "Talk to me."

Bob kept walking. Once in the kitchen, he went straight to the cupboard where Madeline kept various kinds of liquor. He put his hand around a bottle of Scotch, grabbed a glass, poured himself two fingers' worth, and knocked it back. He poured more Scotch into the glass and was about to drink it when Gloria reached up and grabbed his arm.

"Careful, goddamn it," he said. "You'll spill it."

"I thought I was supposed to be the one with the drinking problem," she said.

"I need a little something, is all. Is that a crime?"

"Tell me who that was on the phone."

"It doesn't matter," he said. He'd freed his arm from Gloria's grasp and downed the second drink. Before he could reach for the bottle again, Gloria grabbed it, then upended it in the sink.

"Oh for God's sake," Bob said wearily. "You think that's the only thing to drink around here?"

She left the empty bottle in the sink, stood with her back up against the counter and folded her arms across her breasts. "I want to know what's going on."

"It's just work," he said to her. "It's nothing for you to worry about."

"You're up in the middle of the night, trying to drink yourself blind, and you tell me it's nothing to worry about. Jesus, Bob, you think I'm not used to worrying about things?" Her face grew suddenly alarmed. "It's not about Jeremy, is it? Is he okay? Was it him?"

He looked her straight in the eye. "It wasn't Jeremy."

"Was it Weaver? Did he call you?"

"No. He didn't."

"Then who was it?"

Bob gripped Gloria by the shoulders. "Believe me, it's
. . . it's nothing. Just sorting some things out with work."

"You get work calls at one in the morning?"

He gripped her harder, squeezed. "Let. It. Go."

Gloria struggled to shake him off. "Get your hands off
me, you son of a—"

"What the hell is going on?"

It was Madeline. Also wrapped in a robe, she walked
bleary-eyed into the kitchen, blinked several times, then
looked fiercely at Gloria and Bob.

"Nothing," Bob said.

"That's what he keeps telling me," Gloria said. "But
it's definitely something."

"For the love of God, it's *always* something with
you two," Madeline said. "Is it Jeremy? Has something
happened?"

"No," Bob said quietly.

"I'll call him," Madeline said.

"He doesn't have a phone," Gloria said. "Not any
more."

"The detective. Weaver. I'll call him and see if
everything's okay."

Bob raised a hand. "Madeline, it's one in the morning.
Let the man—let Jeremy—have some sleep. We can't
go calling them every five seconds to see if they're okay.
You know where they are, you know they're safe."

Madeline appeared unconvinced, as did Gloria.

"So what if we wake them up," Gloria said. "They

455

can go back to sleep after. I need to know that my son is okay." She stepped away from the counter and approached Madeline. "You're the only one who has a number for the man. Call him."

Madeline nodded. "My cell's up by my bed. I'll be right back."

Bob was shaking his head. "I don't think it's a good idea."

Madeline ignored him and kept on walking. Bob turned to make his case to Gloria. "You have to trust the man to do his job.'

It was Gloria's turn to have a drink. She'd opened the refrigerator and pulled out a bottle of white wine. She filled a glass nearly to the top and took a sip as Bob watched disapprovingly.

"Look what's happening to us," he said.

She eyed him with wonder. "Are you surprised? After what we've been through? After what *I've* been through? Letting the lot of you humiliate me on a world stage?"

She took a large swallow. Her eyes misted over and her lower lip trembled. "I'm so ashamed. I'm just so, so ashamed."

"Gloria," Bob said tiredly. "Go back to bed. Take your drink with you if you want."

Madeline returned to the kitchen, cell phone in hand.

"Did you get him?" Gloria asked.

"I'm just trying now," she said. She studied the screen, tapped it with her thumb, put the phone to her ear. "It's ringing."

Gloria and Bob went silent, stared at Madeline.

"Still ringing," she said. "Maybe he's got the phone muted."

"Yes," Bob said. "That makes sense."

"No," Gloria said. "That doesn't make any sense. Not under the circumstances. Like, if the police had to call him, like the detective who was here. Mr. Weaver'd have to leave his phone on in case there was an emergency."

"Then—that's six rings—maybe they're just sleeping through it," Madeline said.

"I'm sure it's been a very long day for them," Bob said. "I'm sure it's nothing."

"That's eight rings," Madeline said. "Now it's going to—Hello, Mr. Weaver? It's Madeline Plimpton. Please call me the moment you get this. We're desperately worried about Jeremy. Please call."

She brought the phone down where she could see it, ended the call, and gazed hopelessly at Gloria and Bob.

Gloria put down her glass and placed both hands over her mouth. "Oh God," she said.

Bob said nothing.

SIXTY-ONE

Cory Calder, on the floor, blinking blood out of his eyes, looked up at Craig Pierce and said, "Where's the girl?"

"What girl?" Pierce said.

Cory put a hand to his temple, felt blood, then moved it to his neck. The pain was excruciating.

"You were too clever by half," Pierce said.

"I don't . . . I don't know what you're talking about."

"Don't you want to know how I found you?" Pierce offered him half a smile with his grotesque, partially eaten face. "It was actually so fucking easy."

"I . . . I . . ."

"It was revenge. Revenge with a J. Your clever little signature on the Just Deserts posting. I mean, you can't spell worth a shit, but that was deliberate, right? Thing is, if the only place you'd ever used it was on that site, you'd have been fine. But I did a search, found you'd used it on other sites. With your real name attached. Looked you up, found you lived right in my own backyard."

"Please, you've made a mistake."

"Drove by your house, kept watch on you, stuck a little tracker to your van. You've been hunting that Pilford kid, haven't you? He was next on your list."

"I need a doctor," Cory said, starting to cry. "Please, please get me some help."

Craig clucked his tongue sympathetically. "Is it all hurty?"

"Everything . . . It all went wrong," Cory said, a

bloody tear running down his cheek. "It's not fair. It's not fair."

"Ahh, who's the big baby now?" Pierce asked, wrapping both hands around the poker and driving it straight down, like a spear, through Cory Calder's heart.

SIXTY-TWO

CAL

I let Jeremy sleep on the way back.

He nodded off next to me a couple of miles out of Sandwich, even before we went over the Sagamore Bridge. There was a McDonald's on the other side. I did the drive-through and grabbed coffee and a couple of breakfast sandwiches. Jeremy woke up long enough to wolf one down, then went back to sleep. We'd never gotten to bed the night before, and what with all the commotion that followed, there'd been no opportunity to nod off.

I hadn't had a chance yet, but I was far from sleepy.

I was anxious to get going. I had an appointment to keep with the man who'd answered Kiln's phone, and I was going to have to drive flat out to get back to Promise Falls in time to keep it.

A lot had happened since the phone call.

First, there'd been that woman running up the road, who turned out to be Carol Beakman. As soon as she told me her name, I recognized it from my chat with Barry Duckworth. She told me she had been kidnapped by Cory Calder but had managed to free herself while he was out of the cabin. She'd wandered up North Shore in the other direction, banging on doors, failing to find anyone home. Then, when she saw all the commotion at the other end of the road—fire trucks and ambulances and police cars—she started running that way.

I identified myself, told her I had just recently been speaking with Barry Duckworth, that he'd been trying to find her. She burst into tears at that point and said she had to let his son Trevor know she was okay.

Before I offered her my cell phone to call him, I had to assess whether Calder remained a threat.

"I don't know," Carol said. "I don't know where he is." She glanced back down the road and said, fearfully, "Unless he's gone back to the cabin."

I hailed Higgins, told him in as few words as possible that Carol Beakman had been abducted and that her kidnapper, a man named Cory Calder, might be found a short distance down the road.

He rounded up another officer and together they booted it down the road and stormed the cabin while Carol and I watched from afar. A few seconds later, lights came on, and a few seconds after that, Higgins emerged and shouted at the top of his lungs: "Weaver!"

I left Carol in the care of another officer and ran.

"Have a look and see if that's your Calder character," he said, pointing his thumb inside.

I took three steps into the cabin and looked at the bloody, beaten body on the floor in front of me. A poker was sticking straight up from his chest. It was hard to be one hundred percent certain, given that much of his face had been turned to pulp, but this looked like the man Jeremy and I had met on the beach.

I came back out. "I think so," I said.

"This is turning into one clusterfuck of a night," Higgins said.

I went back to see how Carol Beakman was doing. Another team of paramedics had arrived and were checking her out. At that point, I gave her my phone so that she could call Trevor Duckworth.

There was a lot of crying.

Not long after she'd handed the phone back to me, it rang.

Barry.

"Name a favor," he said. "Whatever it is, it's yours."

Once we were done, the phone rang yet again, and I saw that it was Madeline Plimpton. I nearly answered, then decided against it. Maybe I was being paranoid. But she'd just have to worry until later.

Police Chief Bertram arrived moments later, and appeared dismayed that between the time of our conversation and his arrival, a mere shit show had turned into a disaster movie.

There were so many questions to be answered, and statements to be made, that I was worried we wouldn't get away in time for my meeting in Promise Falls. But around five thirty in the morning, Jeremy and I were allowed to leave.

We didn't have to pack. His backpack and my suitcase were still in the beach house, burned by now to a crisp.

Jeremy woke up somewhere around the exit to Lee, almost to the Massachusetts–New York line.

"What do you think happened to that Calder guy?" he asked. "Who killed him?"

"I don't know."

"Maybe it was that woman he'd kidnapped."

"I don't think so," I said.

"Maybe Kiln?"

"Possibly," I said. "Right now, I'm happy to let the East Sandwich police figure it out."

About a mile later, he said, "I'm kinda glad to be going home."

"I can't take you straight there," I told him.

"What are you talking about?"

"It's like I told you last night, we're going to fly under the radar for a few more hours."

"Radio silence, under the radar. Where do you get these phrases?"

"I watch a lot of movies," I said. "Let me put it another way. We keep our mouths shut. I don't want anyone to know we're back in town, that we're alive."

"What, like, including my mom?"

"Everyone," I said.

"Yeah, right, my mom sent someone to kill us. That's what you think?"

"No. But your mother has a history of being a bit careless with information. That's why we're not telling anyone we're back. Not for a few more hours."

"I don't get why," he said.

We passed the sign that welcomed us to New York state, and were delivered from the Mass Pike to the New York Thruway system. "I don't think what happened last night had anything do with Just Deserts or any other social-media outrage."

"Then what?"

"If and when I have something confirmed, I'll lay it all out for you. And your mom."

"Is it the stick-shift shit?"

"You're gonna have to wait. I'm going to drop you at my sister's."

Jeremy shook his head. "No way."

I gave him as stern a look as I could muster. "It's not up for debate."

★

I called ahead to my sister's house and got her husband Dwayne. I said I had a favor to ask of them, and Dwayne, being somewhat in my debt from a previous incident, told me to name it.

I dropped Jeremy off and then made one last phone call to see if things were good to go.

They were.

It was five minutes to ten when I parked half a block down from Kelly's Diner. As I reached the door, I did a scan of the street in both directions.

Nothing out of the ordinary caught my eye.

I pushed open the door and went inside. The morning rush was over. Only about half the tables were busy. There was a line of booths down the right wall, and the high-backed seats made it difficult to see who was occupying them.

But at the last booth, right ahead of the door to the kitchen, I could make out half a body. A leg, part of a shoulder, an arm on the table.

I walked past the other booths, and when I got to the last one, I offered up a smile.

"You still thinking of selling that Porsche?" I asked.

Galen Broadhurst looked too stunned to answer.

464

SIXTY-THREE

CAL

Galen Broadhurst's body language told me he was seriously considering slipping out of the booth and making a run for it.

"Don't even think about it," I said, sliding in across from him. "You might be able to outrun me in your Porsche, but on foot, you haven't got a chance."

Broadhurst resignedly shifted his butt back to the center of the bench. The table between us was bare.

"You didn't order anything?" I said. "The coffee's very good here." I gave a wave to the waitress, who shuffled down our way. "Hey, Sylvie, how's it going?"

"Good, Cal," she said. "You?"

"Just great. Two coffees, I guess." I glanced at Broadhurst. "Or are you a tea man?"

"Coffee," he said quietly.

"Anything to eat?" Sylvie asked.

I pursed my lips. "I think we'll just start with coffee and see where it goes from there."

Sylvie nodded and slid away.

I turned to look at Broadhurst. "In the movies, this is where you'd say you thought I was dead."

"I'm not saying a fucking thing," he said. "You're probably wired for sound anyway."

"Would you like to check?" I asked, and held out my arms, inviting him to pat me down.

"Open your shirt," he said.

I smiled and as I undid the buttons said, "A little musical accompaniment would be nice."

I opened my shirt wide to reveal my chest and stomach. No wire, no eavesdropping devices.

"Satisfied?" I said.

Broadhurst made a grunting noise. I did up my buttons quickly. Didn't want to give Sylvie heart palpitations.

"You know who I thought you were going to be?" I said.

Broadhurst waited.

"Grant Finch. Your lawyer friend, who did such a standup job defending Jeremy. Because it was him I raised my concerns with. So I guess then he talked to you to discuss our phone call. And you got very, very scared. Sound about right?"

Broadhurst remained silent.

"You want to know what tipped me first that something just didn't fit right? And this was even before I found out Jeremy couldn't drive a stick to save his life. That bullshit story that you left the keys in the car. Even *after* you found a drunk Jeremy and Sian McFadden sitting in it, trying to start it. That, as they say, beggared belief. You initially left your keys in the ashtray. Okay, I can buy that, since the car was right out front of your house, and the house is set way back from the road, so the risk of theft is minimal. But then Jeremy finds the key, tries to start the beast. You intercede. Then we're supposed to believe you *still* left the keys in the car. And you love that car. Who wouldn't?"

I lowered my voice conspiratorially, leaned in. "I have to be honest here. When I called about the car, like I was interested in buying it? I'm not. I'm sorry if I got your hopes up."

I sat back up. "Anyway, I believe you held onto the keys. So, if you had 'em, stands to reason that when that car started up, you were behind the wheel." I studied his face, looking for a reaction. "Am I boring you?" I asked.

Sylvie showed up with two china mugs of coffee.

"Oh, this is great," I said. "I don't know when I've needed a coffee more. There you go, Galen."

We each had our mugs in front of us.

"Cream and sugar's right there," Sylvie said, pointing to the far end of the table to the chrome holder that also contained ketchup and mustard, salt and pepper.

"Allow me," I said, reaching for the glass jar of sugar and a small metal jug of cream.

"Not really thirsty," Broadhurst said.

"Suit yourself." I took a sip of coffee and smiled. "Thanks, Sylvie. It's just what the doctor ordered."

"You're so full of it," she said. "If you boys get hungry, let me know. We got a pancake special."

"Ooohh, let me think about that," I said.

Sylvie understood that she was being dismissed, and left.

"So, where were we?" I said to Broadhurst. "You got in the car. You drove it. You ran down Sian McFadden. But I guess I'm getting ahead of myself. How'm I doing so far?"

"What do you want?" he asked.

"Ah, he speaks," I said. "I've come to do you a favor. I've already done you a solid."

"What's that?"

"Your friend Gregor Kiln."

Broadhurst blinked. "I don't know—"

I held up a hand. "Please. Don't embarrass yourself. And you didn't let me finish. I've got good news."

Broadhurst eyed me like a mouse waiting to hear the cat's deal. "What?"

"Kiln's dead. I killed him."

Broadhurst swallowed.

"So he's not going to be telling anyone about you hiring him. But I have to say, he wasn't very good."

Hesitantly, Broadhurst asked, "What about the kid?"

"Jeremy?" I smiled and shook my head. "He's alive, but he's not going to be a problem for you."

"How do you mean?"

I leaned forward again. "This whole stick-shift thing I raised with Finch? I never brought it up with Jeremy. Far as he knows, he still drove that car. He doesn't even know it's *got* a manual transmission. I don't know if you and Grant gave that a thought. I guess it never even came up. So, anyway, that problem is no longer on the table. The kid thinks he did it."

"Okay," he said slowly.

"And he doesn't know about Kiln. I caught the son of a bitch setting fire to the beach house. Took him out fast. Bundled him up, weighted him down, took him out into Cape Cod Bay. He's not going to be coming back up." I smiled. "I know how to do these things."

"But . . . the fire . . ."

I shrugged. "Arson. Told the cops that all sorts of Internet whackjobs have been trying to get Jeremy. Could have been any one of a thousand nuts. That was the plan, right? That the cops would think it was one of them, not a targeted hit because of what I'd figured out."

Broadhurst wrapped his hands around the warm mug of coffee.

"So here's the thing," I said. "You're pretty much in the clear. Only one who really knows the score who shouldn't is me."

His eyes narrowed. "Let me guess."

I smiled. "I bet you're going to get this right."

"How much?"

"Well, I've been thinking about that," I said. "But before we talk money, I just want to know what happened after you ran down the girl? Did you even try to save her?"

A long pause. "Yes," he said. "I mean, I would have tried, if she'd been alive. I would have done the right thing."

"Of course you would."

"I . . . I had an argument with one of the party guests. This woman I'd been seeing. Stupid bitch said I'd been fooling around on her."

I grinned. "Was she right?"

Broadhurst grimaced. "Kinda. Anyway, I'd had a little too much to drink, and said some things, and I needed to blow off some steam. I slipped out the back door of the house, came around to the front and got in the car. Took off up the road and . . . You have to understand, I wasn't drunk. Even though I'd had a few drinks. I wasn't weaving around or anything."

He let go of the mug, made two fists and pushed them into his eyes. "It was a total accident. It was the *girl's* fault."

"Shit happens," I said offhandedly.

"She . . . she just came out of nowhere. Ran across the road, right in front of me. I tried to swerve, to miss her, but I still caught her . . . and then I ran into the tree. I got out, I ran over . . . Oh Jesus."

He was struggling to hold it together.

"Hey, look," I said. "Kids do dumb stuff."

"Yes," he said. "It wasn't my fault. But . . . but if they'd tested me, I'd probably have been over the limit. Maybe . . . way over."

"I drive over the limit all the time," I said. "Still drive fine."

Broadhurst nodded.

"So," I said, "how'd you get the kid into the car?"

"It wasn't . . . the first thing I did. I was thinking about the girl."

"Of course."

"I . . . I went over to see how bad it was. And . . . she was gone. I felt for a pulse, checked for any signs that she was alive, and . . ."

I nodded. "Right, she'd bought it. I'm guessing Jeremy was nearby."

"Yes."

"Passed out?"

He nodded.

"On a bench. I went over . . . I don't know when I got the idea exactly. It just . . . came to me. I saw a way to get out of this. He'd . . . he'd already tried to take the car once. I figured, if I put him behind the wheel . . ."

"Quick thinking," I said, with just a hint of admiration.

"I got my arms under him, but he was hard to move. He's . . . heavy, and I'm not as young as I used to be."

"Then . . ."

"I guess when the car hit the tree, it was loud enough to be heard. I mean, at least by one person," Broadhurst said. "I looked, saw someone running. I thought . . . I thought, I can't do it. I can't pull it off. But then . . ."

"But then you saw who it was," I said. I had a pretty

good idea who it would turn out to be.

Broadhurst nodded. "I kind of blackmailed Bob into helping me. Said if I went to jail, our multimillion-dollar deal would fall through. He'd lose a fortune. On top of that, the McFadden girl, her father was one of the major investors. You think he'd buy into the project of a guy who ran down his daughter? Bad enough it was my car. Anyway, Bob didn't take a lot of convincing, He helped me get Jeremy into the Porsche." He took in a long breath. "Bob was the one who slammed Jeremy's head into the steering wheel, so there'd be blood for a DNA match, if it came to that."

"And then, when other partygoers showed up, you and Bob acted like you'd just got there." I thought a moment. "Did Finch know?"

Broadhurst shook his head. "No. After you called him, he called me, said he was going to have to talk to Gloria, see if maybe there really were grounds for an appeal. I told him no, Jeremy had to have done it. And I think I convinced him. We've been friends a long time and he trusts me. And come on, let's give Grant some credit. He got that kid off. That Big Baby defense was a stroke of genius. A long shot, but it worked. Everybody wins."

Yeah, I thought. Everybody wins. I thought about Jeremy in my car, pounding his fists into his thighs.

"It was Bob who told you we were in Cape Cod," I speculated. "You knew where to send Kiln because Bob was there when Madeline told Detective Duckworth."

"It was his idea," Broadhurst said.

That threw me.

"But I thought it was your idea, to put Jeremy behind the wheel."

"Not that," he said. "To have you and Jeremy killed.

Bob said that was the only way out of this. But I know people, or people who know people, who can get that sort of thing done."

And now, for the first time, he smiled.

"Which is why, if you think you're going to shake me down, you're mistaken."

"Hey, come on," I said.

"If I could find one Kiln, I can find another," he said.

"Well . . ." I let uncertainty creep into my voice, "maybe I'll go to the cops."

Broadhurst's smile turned into a grin. "And tell them what you did to Kiln? Killing a man in self-defense, that might fly, but burying him at sea? That kinda suggests something else, don't you think?"

I licked my lips nervously. "Look, I wasn't going to ask for that much. Fifty grand. That's peanuts for a guy like you."

He shook his head. "You're an amateur, Weaver. A fool. You stuck your nose in where it didn't—"

His eye caught something that made him stop. He was looking at the door. I turned, pushed myself up an inch to see over the top of the booth.

Barry Duckworth and two uniformed officers were approaching.

I settled back down in my seat, reached over to the small chrome rack from which I'd grabbed the sugar, and turned it around to reveal the wireless transmitter.

I said to Broadhurst, "Next time, strip-search the condiments."

SIXTY-FOUR

Brian Gaffney was cutting the lawn at his parents' house when Jessica Frommer's car stopped at the curb.

Albert had gone back to work today, but he had taken Constance's car. He'd said something about his car being overdue for a service, that he didn't want to run up any more miles on it until he'd taken it in to his mechanic.

Constance was at the grocery store picking up a few things, but she had borrowed Monica's Volkswagen Beetle. Monica said she didn't need her car today. Before Constance had left, Brian had told her at breakfast that he wanted to cut the grass. He needed something to do, he'd told her, but she had objected strenuously. He had to rest after all he'd been through, she said. He shouldn't be doing anything physical.

Okay, Brian said. But as soon as his mother left in the Bug, he decided he was going to cut the grass anyway.

It would get his mind off things. It would get his mind off all the terrible things that had happened to him. It would also get his mind off whatever was going on between his parents. His mother hadn't been taking her usual shots at his father. They were both very, very quiet.

Something was going on.

Brian wasn't even sure he wanted to know what it was.

So he went out to the garage and swung open the door on the left.

There was his father's car, looking, Brian thought, cleaner than he had ever seen it.

That was strange.

Considering that Brian worked at a place that cleaned cars, and *also* considering that he was able to give members of his family a discount—like, *free*—and considering even *further* the fact that he had seen this car go through the wash a couple of days before he went missing, why had his father gone to the trouble to wash it himself in the last day or so? Brian remembered that when his father found him, after Brian had walked out of the hospital, this was the car he'd been driving.

And it wasn't this clean then.

Not only that, but even the floor of the garage was cleaner than Brian could ever remember seeing it. It was actually damp in a few places.

Weird.

He found the lawnmower at the back of the garage, checked that it had gas in it, and wheeled it out to the front yard. He did feel it in his ribs when he pulled the cord to start the machine up, but pushing it back and forth across the yard didn't hurt at all.

He had about half of it done when Jessica's car pulled up to the curb.

Brian killed the mower.

"Hey," she said, getting out of the car. She'd left all the windows down, and Brian noticed that her kid was in the back seat.

"Hey," Brian said.

"I went to the hospital to see you and they said you'd been discharged. When I didn't find you at your apartment, I figured you might be here. I looked in the book and this was the only other Gaffney in Promise Falls."

"Yeah, they let me out."

"I'm sorry about everything," she said. "I should have told you. I was going to tell you eventually, you know, that I was married. There just never seemed a good time."

"Yeah, well."

"Anyway, I wanted to say that."

"Okay, then." Brian shrugged. "I guess I should get back to it. I'm moving back in with my parents, so I want to help out and stuff."

"There's something else," she said.

Brian waited. Jessica took a few steps closer, and when she was six feet away from him he could see that she had been crying. "What's wrong?"

"It's about Ron," she said.

"What about him?"

"He's missing."

Brian took several seconds before saying, "Oh."

"He was doing this job? This house outside of town. His truck's there but he's not around. He's been gone over twenty-four hours."

"Jesus," Brian said.

"At first I thought, maybe he left me. Which, you know, might not be such a bad thing. But if he left me, he sure as hell would have taken his truck. He loves that truck more than he loves me. He's not answering his cell phone or anything."

"I don't know what to say. Have you called the police?"

Jessica Frommer nodded. "Yeah. They're looking into it."

"What do they think happened?"

Jessica shook her head. "They don't know. They said they found blood."

"Blood?"

"Like, on the ground."

"That," Brian said slowly, "sounds bad."

"That'd mean maybe someone hurt him," she said. "At first I thought, and don't be mad when I say this, but at first I wondered, maybe you had something to do with it."

"Me?"

"Because of Ron beating you up and all. You'd have plenty of reason to want to get back at him."

"Jess, I've been in the hospital."

She nodded. "Yeah, I know. That's what I wanted to check first, before I told the police anything about you."

"What?"

"The police asked if there might be anyone who's got it in for Ron. And I thought of you, but I didn't give them your name because I didn't want to get you in trouble. I wanted to find out if you were in the hospital, and you were, so now I'm not going to give them your name."

"Jeez, Jess, thanks for that."

"But then I thought, did you tell anyone?"

Brian wondered if it was getting hotter out. He could feel beads of sweat forming on his forehead.

"Did I what?" he asked.

"Did you tell anyone about Ron beating you up?"

Brian thought about what his father had said to him. "*You never, ever told me his name. You never, ever told me where he lived. And no matter how many times someone might ask you the question, it's always no. You never told me.*"

Brian said, "I never told anyone his name. I never told anyone where you live. Not ever."

Jessica sniffed.

"Mommy!" the little girl in the car cried out.

"Just a second, sweetheart!" Jessica shouted over her shoulder.

"Never," Brian added.

Jessica nodded. "Okay. The thing is, Ron wasn't all that nice a guy. He probably pissed off a lot of other people. Could be anybody, when you think about it." Another sniff. Brian dug into his pocket, pulled out a shredded tissue and offered it to her.

"That's okay," she said, wiping her cheeks on her sleeve. "Anyway, I should go."

"Okay."

She gave him an awkward half-second hug, then got back into her car. Brian stood there and watched as she put on her seat belt. The little girl in the backseat looked at him and pointed. "You're the man my daddy beat up!" she said.

As the car drove off, Brian wondered if there was any chance the police would be questioning *her*.

SIXTY-FIVE

CAL

Once Galen Broadhurst had been put into the back of a Promise Falls cruiser, Duckworth came over to me and said, "Well done. Now we just have to pick up Bob Butler."

"Broadhurst and Butler sacrificed that poor kid to save their own asses and line their pockets." I shook my head. "The bastards."

Duckworth gave me a look that said he'd seen enough things in life not to be surprised any more.

"I'm going to pick up Jeremy," I said, "then head out to Madeline Plimpton's house. He wants to talk to his mother, let her know he's okay."

"We should go together."

I looked at my watch. "Thirty minutes?"

He nodded. As he turned to leave, I said, "What was it you wanted to ask me? On the phone last night."

Barry poked his tongue around the inside of his cheek. "You know what? Don't worry about it. Whatever I was going to ask, I think I've changed my mind."

I pointed my Honda back in the direction of my sister and brother-in-law's house. I found Jeremy sitting on the front step talking to Celeste. He was on his feet when he saw my car, and ran to the street to meet me.

"What's going on?" he asked as I powered down the window.

I gave Celeste a wave. "Thanks!"

"Nice kid!" she shouted, getting up and going back into the house.

Jeremy craned his neck around to respond, a slightly stunned look on his face. "Thank you," he said.

I was willing to bet it was the nicest thing anyone had said to him in months.

He got in the car next to me. "Well?"

"Taking you home," I said.

"What happened?"

I was going to tell him on the way, but thought better of it. This was something I had to tell him eye to eye. I shifted in my seat to look at him.

"You didn't do it. You didn't drive the car. You didn't run down Sian."

His chin began to tremble. "What . . ."

"Galen Broadhurst was driving the car."

"How do you know?"

"He told me."

Now his hands were shaking. "Oh my God. Oh my God."

"There's more," I said gently. "Bob Butler helped him."

I gave him the details, briefly and slowly, including the news that it had been Bob's idea to have us killed. I couldn't imagine how much it was to take in. Elation matched by betrayal.

He burst into tears. He started sobbing. I reached out with both arms and pulled him close to me, patted his back.

"The nightmare's over," I said, although I knew it was going to take a while for all of this to sink in. And there was going to be fallout. A lot of it.

The boy could not stop shaking. "Bob—he paid my legal bills."

"Yeah, well, I guess he was feeling pretty guilty. It was the least he could do. Getting you off, so long as the blame didn't shift elsewhere, was a pretty safe game for him to play."

"My mom," he said. "I have to tell my mom. I have to tell her what a bastard he is."

"We're gonna do that," I assured him. "We're gonna go over there now."

Jeremy struggled to pull himself together. I found tissues in the glove box and dug out a handful for him.

"Thank you so much," he said.

"They're just tissues."

"I mean, for everything. For figuring out that this whole thing was fucked up. For giving me my life back."

I gave him a moment to get settled back into his seat, facing forward, before I keyed the ignition. "Let's go," I said.

I'd told Duckworth thirty minutes, but only twenty-five had passed when we pulled into the driveway of Madeline Plimpton's house. Tires crunching on gravel was not enough to bring anyone running outside to greet us, but I could hear movement in the house when I rang the bell.

"Can't we just walk in?" Jeremy asked.

"Not our house," I said. "Manners."

The door opened. Ms. Plimpton's dour expression turned into one of joy when she saw us there.

"I tried all night to reach you!" she said, throwing her arms around the boy. "You had us worried sick."

A second later, Gloria emerged from the kitchen area

and shrieked. She had to pry Ms. Plimpton off Jeremy so she could hug him herself.

"I'm so glad you're home!" she said. "It was a huge mistake, sending you away!" He tried to move her away as she planted kisses on his cheeks, then gave up and let her continue.

I said to Ms. Plimpton, "Where's Bob?"

"He's in the kitchen," she said, and as she turned herself in that direction, Bob appeared.

Briefly.

It took him half a second to see who'd arrived, and another half a second to realize he was in deep shit.

He turned and ran.

I bolted after him.

Ms. Plimpton said, "What on earth?"

"He did it!" I heard Jeremy say. "He sent that guy to kill us!"

"What?" Gloria said.

Bob was on the far side of the kitchen, attempting to open the sliding glass door. But a wooden stick down in the track, designed to keep out burglars, had thwarted him. I caught up, grabbed him by the back of his jacket, and flung him across the room. He stumbled over two kitchen chairs, scattering them, and landed on his side. There was the look of a trapped animal in his eyes.

"Don't get up," I told him. "If you try, I'll fucking kill you."

He seemed convinced.

"You look as surprised to see me as Galen did. They just arrested him. They're coming for you next."

Jeremy, Gloria and Ms. Plimpton had joined us in the kitchen. The two women were open-mouthed at the scene.

"Is it true?" Gloria asked Bob. "You sent someone to *kill* them?"

"It's bullshit!" Bob said. "Whatever they're saying, it's bullshit."

"You haven't heard half of what he did!" Jeremy shouted. He was trembling again. I was feeling immensely worried for him. He was totally on the edge.

Pointing at Bob, he said, "He helped that shitbag Broadhurst! The two of them put me in the car!"

Ms. Plimpton looked like she'd just seen a pig fly through the kitchen. "What?"

Jeremy said, "They framed me! They made me think I'd done it! They made the *world* think I'd done it!"

Ms. Plimpton glared at Bob. "My God, is this true?"

What struck me, at that moment, was that Gloria didn't ask that question, or anything close to it. My eyes were darting back and forth between her aunt and Bob. Maybe she was just in shock.

"I told you, don't listen to them," Bob said. "This is crazy."

"No, it's not crazy," I said. "I got it all from Galen. We know what happened."

Jeremy turned to his mother. "You hear what I'm saying? You hear what this son of a bitch did?"

Gloria, her voice softer than I was used to, said, "I'm sure there's some explanation."

"What's that mean?" Jeremy asked. "Don't you believe us?"

I said, "I think she does, Jeremy."

Gloria turned my way.

"You don't look like this part is new to you," I said to her.

"Gloria?" Ms. Plimpton said. "What's he talking about?"

"The part about Bob sending a hit man after us, you looked surprised at that," I said. "But not the other part."

The room suddenly fell very silent, all eyes, even Bob's, on Gloria.

"Mom?" Jeremy said. He was full-out shaking now.

"I didn't know," she whispered. "I didn't know . . . at first."

"When *did* you know?" I asked.

She looked at her son, reached a hand up and touched his cheek. Jeremy was too stunned to pull back.

"I heard them talking," she said. "Bob and Galen. Soon after the accident. I . . . I confronted them. I . . . I was going to do something, but . . . everything was too far along."

Jeremy whispered, "How . . . how could . . ."

"I think I know how," I said. "What did they tell you, Gloria? That if you came forward at that point, they'd go to jail. Galen *and* Bob. That deal worth millions would die. You'd be worthless. They told you they had a strategy to get Jeremy off, or at least make it so he served very little time in prison. Was it something like that?"

Tears were running down her cheeks. There was a nod. "If it hadn't worked," she said weakly, "I told them, that if they sent Jeremy to jail, then I'd have to say . . . I'd have to say something . . ."

"You let them do this to me," Jeremy said.

"But I let them humiliate *me*," she told him. "I let them make a laughing stock of me, because I *love* you. I was willing to do anything to save you. I didn't care. I did it for you."

"You were willing to do anything but tell the truth," he said, his voice weak, crumbling.

"Jeremy," I said. "We should get you out of here."

"Bob was your ticket," Jeremy whispered. "A ticket to a better life. More money, all the things you wanted."

"I . . . I just need to explain it to you better," Gloria said. "I told you, things were so far along. It was . . . it was a case of the lesser evil."

We seemed to have an abundant supply of that at the moment.

A shout from the front of the house. "Weaver!"

It was Duckworth.

"Back here!" I called.

He was in the kitchen in three seconds, one uniformed officer trailing him. He saw Bob on the floor and looked angrily at me. "You were supposed to wait."

I didn't know what to say.

Duckworth pushed me aside, straddled Bob and told him to lie face down and put his hands behind his back. "I'm placing you under arrest, Mr. Butler," he said. He cinched some plastic cuffs onto the man's wrists and told him to get up. Awkwardly, Bob got to his knees first, then stood.

He allowed himself to be walked out of the kitchen. He kept his head bowed, avoiding eye contact with any of us on the way out.

The kitchen was very silent again.

"You have to understand," Gloria said pleadingly. She reached out to touch Jeremy's arm, and he recoiled as though she were a poisonous snake.

"I don't believe it," he said, more to himself than any of us.

"Oh Gloria," Ms. Plimpton said. "How could you?"

From the front door, Duckworth shouted my name again.

I approached Jeremy. "I'll be back in a minute, okay? We're going to work this out. You can stay with me. We'll get you out of this house."

He seemed close to catatonic.

"Just give me a minute," I repeated.

I walked briskly out of the kitchen. Ms. Plimpton followed me.

"Tell me this isn't true," she said.

Duckworth was standing just outside the door, pointing a finger at me as the officer put Bob into the back seat of what looked like the same cruiser that had taken Galen Broadhurst away.

"You screwed this up," he said. "You should have waited."

"Things happened quickly," I said. It was a weak defense, I knew. "But we've got them. We've got the lot of them."

"Someone please tell me exactly what's going on," Ms. Plimpton said.

Duckworth was shaking his head angrily.

That was when I remembered something Jeremy had told me the day before. About what was in one of the kitchen drawers.

I said to Duckworth, "I don't want to leave Jeremy. He needs to see somebody. The kid's falling—"

And then we heard the shot.

Ms. Plimpton screamed.

Duckworth bolted into the house. We both started heading for the kitchen, but stopped short of it. We didn't know what we would be running into.

"Ms. Pilford!" Duckworth shouted. "Are you okay?"

"Jeremy!" I said. "What's happened?"

There was nothing for several seconds. Then Jeremy's voice.

"I'm going to come out," he said. "I've put the gun down."

Duckworth and I exchanged fearful looks.

Jeremy walked calmly out of the kitchen, stopped, looked at me, and managed to make his quivering lips smile ever so slightly.

"I did it," he said. "I take full responsibility." He paused. "I own this."

I took him into my arms, while Duckworth ran into the kitchen to see how bad it was.

PROMISE FALLS TRILOGY

'You should treat yourself to the whole Promise Falls trilogy' Stephen King

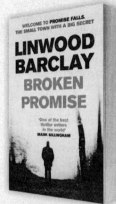

#1 BROKEN PROMISE

When David Harwood is asked to look in on his cousin Marla, who is still traumatised after losing her baby, he thinks it will be some temporary relief from his dead-end life. But when he arrives, he's disturbed to find blood on Marla's front door. He's even more disturbed to find Marla looking after a baby – a baby she claims was delivered to her 'by an angel'.

Soon after, a woman's body is discovered, stabbed to death, with her own baby missing. It looks as if Marla has done something truly terrible. It's up to David to find out what really happened, but he soon discovers that the truth could be worse than he ever imagined . . .

'Nothing is more satisfying than tucking into a new Linwood Barclay novel, and this is one we've all been waiting for' Shari Lapena, author of *The Couple Next Door*

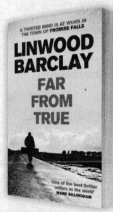

#2 FAR FROM TRUE

A freak accident has killed Lucy Brighton's father. And when she goes to his house, she's convinced that someone has broken in. She asks private investigator Cal Weaver to look into it – but isn't prepared for what he'll find.

Cal discovers a secret 'playroom' in the basement, complete with video equipment, and it looks as though there's a missing recording. As Cal investigates further, and more people start dying in suspicious circumstances, it's clear that someone is targeting Promise Falls. But who – and how far will they go?

> **'Barclay's great talent is to infuse the most everyday things with extraordinary menace'**
> *Daily Mail*

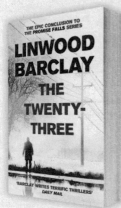

#3 THE TWENTY-THREE

The day begins like any other Saturday – a shower, coffee, breakfast. But suddenly, all hell breaks loose in the town of Promise Falls. People are dying in the street – the hospital and emergency services are overwhelmed by sheer numbers. Is it mass food poisoning, a virus, or something more sinister? Has some*one*, rather than some*thing*, caused this?

Detective Barry Duckworth is already investigating two murders and an explosion at the town's drive-in. He starts to wonder if these crimes and the new attacks are connected to the mysterious incidents in Promise Falls. But who is sending these deadly messages, and how can they be stopped?

Find out more at
www.linwoodbarclay.com

Sign up to his Facebook page
https://www.facebook.com/linwoodbarclay

Or follow him on Twitter
@linwood_barclay